HILLDIGGERS

Neal Asher was born in Billericay, Essex, and still lives nearby. He started writing SF and fantasy at the age of sixteen, and has since had many stories published. His full-length novels include *Gridlinked*, *The Skinner*, *The Line of Polity*, *Cowl*, *Brass Man*, *The Voyage of the Sable Keech*, *Polity Agent*, *Prador Moon* and *Line War*.

NEAL
ASHER

HILLDIGGERS

TOR

First published 2007 by Tor

First published in paperback 2008 by Tor
an imprint of Pan Macmillan Ltd
Pan Macmillan, 20 New Wharf Road, London N1 9RR
Basingstoke and Oxford
Associated companies throughout the world
www.panmacmillan.com

ISBN 978-0-330-44153-7

5 7 9 8 6

A CIP catalogue record for this book is available from
the British Library.

Typeset by Intype Libra Ltd
Printed and bound in the UK by
CPI Mackays, Chatham ME5 8TD

Acknowledgements

Again thanks to everyone involved in bringing this book to the shelves, including as always my wife Caroline and my parents Bill and Hazel. Special thanks to Keith Starkey for his 'overview' rather than critique of the specific and to Peter Lavery for never letting up despite a million of my words passing under his pencil! Also included must be those others working at Macmillan and elsewhere: Rebecca Saunders, Emma Giacon, Steve Rawlings, Liz Cowen, Jon Mitchell, Liz Johnson, Chantal Noel, Neil Lang, Stephen Dumughn, and many others besides.

1

Brumal and Sudoria only come into conjunction every three Sudorian years, so during the War the time between conjunctions was used by both sides to rebuild their destroyed infrastructures: to stock up on food and medical supplies; to manufacture new ships, weapons and munitions; and to train new recruits. The cyclic nature of the War was thus sustained for a hundred years and it could be argued that, without the arrival of the Worm, the fighting might have continued for centuries more – and there are those who say it could have continued until the sun went out. Fleet claim that they were beginning to make some headway against the Brumallians, but such claims had been made before and come to nothing. The prospect of what could have happened appals me. The symbolism of a space-borne Worm bringing a war to an end, breaking the cycle, breaking the ring that was our own self-inflicted Ouroboros – a worm eating its own tail forever – brings me as close to superstitious awe as I have ever ventured. However, styling myself a rational being, I step back from that simply because I know that stranger coincidences do occur.
*   – Uskaron*

– RETROACT 1 –

Tigger – *during the War*

Orbital mechanics had made the war in the Sudorian system almost a seasonal thing, and now the conflict was stuttering to its usual halt as the two contending worlds drew further apart. Since neither side possessed under-space drives or adequate concealment technology, the logistics of sustained conflict over the growing distances involved became increasingly difficult. Tigger – a four-ton drone fashioned in the shape of a chrome tiger embracing a large sphere, like some baroque bonnet ornament from an ancient ground car – observed the attempts to pro-long the fighting by the deployment of supply stations and the launching of swarms of rail-gun accelerated missiles. But these last attempts were doomed to failure, hence the reason this war had dragged on for so long. The drone turned away, still easily managing to remain unnoticed through the use of advanced chameleonware. As he headed towards the planet Sudoria, he observed vicious space battles between Sudorian hilldiggers and teardrop-shaped Brumallian ships – the latter the pro-duct of biotechnology – and registered how once again these contests were reaching a stalemate.

But maybe things were due to change. And finally receiving permission to take a look at the possible reason why, Tigger headed towards Corisanthe Main.

This station lay isolated in space unlike any of the other Sudorian stations, and was heavily defended under an energy-shield umbrella. The Polity – the vast AI-run dominion spreading out from Earth and which put the likes of Tigger at the forefront of that expansion –

possessed similar energy shields. But they were an off-shoot of the U-space tech, which the Sudorians did not possess, so for the Tigger it had been frustrating and annoying that his boss had been so uninterested in investigating this anomalous technology.

Closing on his target, with chameleonware conceal-ing him from prying eyes or inferior scanners, Tigger soon observed the station revealed in all its glory: a vast complex like a floating city, the four Ozark Cylinders projecting at each quadrant, so viewed either from above or below it bore the shape of a cross. Sitting in orbit above the mighty station, Tigger studied it visually – wary of putting himself in the way of any of the rare coded laser transmissions from that place – but over the last year of such 'observation only' his patience had been wearing thin.

'Hey, Geronimo – nothing happening here,' he sent via U-space. 'But if I try anything more active they might detect me. Security is a bit tight here.'

'Call me that again and I'll see about having you recycled as hull plating,' the AI Geronamid replied.

'Sorry, chief, I have terrible trouble remembering names.'

Obviously not amused by this, the AI continued, 'Your present remit is to obtain further information about that particular station—'

'At last,' Tigger muttered.

'Yes.'

'Can't learn much more here just in the visual band.' Tigger really wanted permission to do something a bit more *active*, but he didn't hold out much hope of that.

'Then learn about the station *elsewhere*, and do not

communicate with me again until you have something worthwhile to report.'

After briefly considering his options, Tigger planed down to a remote area of the planet Sudoria, using fusion burners sparingly to prevent him causing ionization that his chameleonware could not conceal, and ultimately to prevent himself causing a crater when he hit the surface. Then he grav-planed over desert to the nearest population centre and, still keeping concealed, accessed information sources there. He began with a library containing books, films, holoflicks, games and interactives all stored on a primitive disk medium. The keepers of that place were subsequently shocked to one day find a hole in the roof and the entire contents of the library gone. Shock did not sufficiently describe their reaction upon finding the entire contents of the library returned, only a few days later. After that Tigger listened to all the broadcast channels of the media; personal, military and government coms; he created search engines, catchers and diverters to locate any mention of Corisanthe Main. It did not take him long to realize he would soon be speaking to Geronamid again.

'No one knows precisely what they're doing in there,' Tigger informed the sector AI. 'But everyone knows what they've got inside there . . . within limits.'

'Within limits,' Geronamid grumbled. 'Just like my patience.'

'Okey-dokey . . . The station remains open to visual inspection by a hilldigger matching its orbit, ready to destroy the entire station should the necessity arise. This is their most important project, and their most dangerous one. As you know, exterior transmission occurs every ten hours, by laser, and only select Fleet scientists and officers are allowed to view the contents of that transmission. From a secondary source I've managed to intercept and decode some of it.'

'Send it to me,' Geronamid interrupted.

'Hold fire – you're gonna have to let me have my moment of glory.'

'Oh get on with it, Tigger.'

'Each of the four Ozark Cylinders holds a combined magnetic and electrostatic containment canister – apparently invented by some dude called Al-amarad Ozark, believe it or not.' Geronamid made a dismissive harrumphing sound, so Tigger continued hurriedly, 'Each of those canisters in turn contains a twenty-foot-long segment of what has come to be known simply as "the Worm". It appeared just a few years before I arrived, threading across the Sudorian system: a thin glowing . . . well, worm-like object fifteen miles long. Thinking it an enemy weapon, perhaps a superstring somehow under Brumallian control, Fleet attacked it using high-intensity lasers. They broke it into four pieces which in turn contracted down into those segments, each of them six feet in diameter. Ever since, their scientists have been carefully studying those segments.'

'What is it, then?' Geronamid asked.

Tigger paused, slightly puzzled at the blandness of this query from the big AI, then in reply sent the transmission he had managed to intercept and record. After a pause the AI said, 'Exotic-matter nanotechnologies.'

'So it would seem. They've been systematically peeling away at it every day and so far have barely grazed the surface layers. But that's where they got the know-how to build their energy shields, and I reckon it's what's going to eventually bring this war to an end. It's just a short step for them now to gravtech, or maybe even underspace technology. It seems the Worm itself is either an alien artefact, or something alive.'

'You yourself, Tigger, are an artefact. You are also alive.'

'Yeah, but you know what I mean.'

'I know a meaningless statement when I hear one.'

'Okay, sorry – been listening to too many of their media channels.'

'Very well, Tigger, keep watching. The time approaches for these people to be made aware of the Polity, but it is not yet. Making contact during a war will only lead to more . . . complications.'

'Oh goody.'

As the communication link closed, Tigger again felt frustrated. Something like this Worm just sitting here all canned up in a space station, and Geronamid was more interested in arguing semantics about the meanings of 'alive' and 'artificial'? The drone rather suspected he still wasn't being told something crucial.

The Worm had been weird enough, but years later Tigger observed strange events. Finally given permission by Geronamid, the drone managed to penetrate military communications and gradually, tick-like, eased himself deeper into the information flow around Corisanthe Main. He observed personnel come and go, the human dramas in the huge isolated population, the exciting discoveries, the boredom and the tragedies. Elsever Strone was a top-flight physicist who had conceived during an information fumarole breach in Ozark One – this was known because she'd had her womb standard-monitored for conception. She had actually been present in Ozark One during conception, which seemed quite odd considering the stringent security around those cylinders. After pregnancy and the early-induced birth of quads, she proclaimed herself to be absolutely elated by the event – before cracking the safeties on an airlock and stepping outside. Tigger watched her die, knowing he would not be able to reach her any quicker than a retrieval squad, and would then be in danger of revealing himself. The squad was still a hundred yards away from her when the bomb she carried strapped against her torso exploded, sending bits of her smoking off through vacuum.

Why had she done that? Stepping outside an airlock was pretty final in itself, so why the need for the explosive too?

Tigger watched the development of the four infants in a crèche aboard Corisanthe Main then still kept an eye on them, literally, when they were dispatched down to the surface. He sent mobile 'ware concealed sensors to watch them, for most certainly something strange had occurred. Cared for by Elsever's mother, Utrain, the four children grew up fast, and were soon displaying an unnerving brilliance. Yishna, Harald, Rhodane and Orduval, they were named, two of who – twenty-five years after their birth and after the War was over – began moving easily into the higher echelons of Sudorian society.

– Retroact 1 Ends –

McCrooger

I tumbled through vacuum clinging inside a ten-foot-wide drop-sphere. The transport had dropped this object, with me inside, fifty astronomical units from Sudoria's sun – at that distance a point of light indistinguishable from the other stars. However, where that sun lay was of little interest to me at that moment for, despite childhood surgical alterations to my temporal bones and inner ear, I was having trouble hanging on to my dinner. I was also spooked. Space had never seemed so dark to me as it did at that moment. Lonely emptiness stretched endlessly in every direction, yet, unfathomably, I kept getting the creepy feeling that someone was nearby, whispering something horrifying just on the edge of audibility, and I kept having to check over my shoulder to make sure no one was there.

Inside the sphere, which was constructed of octagonal chainglass sheets bound together geodesically in a ceramal frame, I wore the low-tech spacesuit Fleet had conceded me – one of their own, and one I had needed to open out at all its expansion points to fit me. The people here were severely paranoid, but then they were only twenty years on the right side of a particularly vicious system war, and the near-genocide that concluded it.

During the ensuing five hours in the sphere, with these mutterings just at the edge of my perception, I began to feel some sympathy with the paranoia of the people I had come to meet. But I fought what I considered to be irrational feelings, concluding that some design flaw in the spacesuit was subjecting me to infrasound, which can cause such effects. Maybe, even, it was a deliberately incorporated flaw.

Towards the end of that time, I began to think that maybe there would be no pick-up. The sphere contained a transponder set in its frame, cued to scramble its own nano-circuitry the moment another vessel took the sphere aboard, thus erasing technology that Fleet had proscribed. If the sphere wasn't picked up within eight hours – one hour inside the limit of my oxygen supply – the transponder would yell for help and the transport would return for me. Thereafter would begin another round of lengthy negotiations over U-space communicator between the Sudorian parliament and Geronamid, who was the artificial intelligence in charge of the sector of the Polity nearest to here. However, just then the halo flash of manoeuvring jets threw an approaching vessel into silhouette. I ramped up my light sensitivity (no Polity technology allowed, but nothing specified about how that same technology could alter the human body) and studied this craft closely.

At first all I could see was something shaped like a pumpkin seed, but as the vessel turned and dipped towards me, its full, disconcerting appearance became more visible. With manipulator arms spread wide, on either side of what appeared to be a cargo door, and a Bridge above with port lights gleaming like spider eyes, it looked insectile and dangerous. It bore down on me fast, then jets fired again to slow it, and the door opened – an iris much like those of Polity manufacture. With the ship's arms moving tentatively on either side of it before finally growing still, the sphere slid into a cavernous hold-space. This seemed to muffle the subliminal muttering I was experiencing, and inside this smaller space I felt less of a need to keep checking over my shoulder. Grav slowly engaged, and I righted myself inside the sphere as it settled to a grated floor. I sat down, legs crossed, and waited. Eventually, bar lights came on down either side of the cylindrical hold. I knocked down the light sensitivity of my eyes and studied my surroundings as if for the first time.

Ball-jointed lasers swivelled in the wall to point towards me. A treaded robot rolled from the rear of the hold and closed saw-tooth arms around the sphere to drag it twenty yards further inside, where a ram descended from the ceiling, clamping it into place, while the robot released its grip and retreated. Pillars now rose from the floor all around, each with metallic protuberances and inset glass lenses that were certainly the business ends of some scanning system. Eventually doors opened to one side of the hold, and six Fleet personnel marched in, five to surround the sphere and the other one remaining to guard the door.

These people wore armoured and powered space-suits that resembled lobster shells, and flat mirrored visors concealed their faces. Each of them carried a short disc-gun carbine from which trailed armoured cables to plug into their suits. This weapon could fire explosive-centred alloy discs at a rate of a thousand a minute, and at four times the speed of sound. That was the top setting. Inside a ship, rate and speed could be tuned down to avoid puncturing the hull, and the non-explosive discs used could also be set to unwind so they entered a human body as a spinning potato peel of metal. Very messy. How did I know all this? Those in charge of Fleet did not want Polity tech to enter the Sudorian system without their approval, and the Polity, but for one exception, adhered to this stricture. The one exception was a drone, which had been here studying this civilization for a quarter of a century and relaying intelligence to the Polity. As a consequence I already knew much about these people and their dirty little secrets.

The political situation here was complicated. Fleet retained power in the system beyond the planet Sudoria by dint of the fact that it controlled the hilldiggers: big-fuck warships that could employ gravtech weapons capable of doing just what their name implied. According to the last report from the survey drone, Admiral Carnasus and his twelve captains ran this fleet, and lieutenants of theirs held twenty-five seats in the Sudorian parliament. A further thirty-nine seats were controlled by the various planetary parties, while another fifteen were controlled by Orbital Combine – the rational scientific political unit holding sway in Sudoria's many space stations which, like the three main Corisanthe space stations, were originally part of the war industry.

When we first contacted them here, subsequent communications made it clear that Fleet did not want any dealings with the Polity, but Combine desperately wanted access to our artificial intelligences and under-space technology, and all but a few of the Sudorian planetary parties wanted trade. Orbital Combine and those parties then agreed to the establishing of a con-sulate on Sudoria. Fleet, being outvoted, cited laws estab-lished during the war here to prevent technological import (though where they had expected it to be imported from back then, I've no idea), but could do nothing, legally, to prevent Polity humans from coming here. I was to be the test case, and it long ago occurred to me that Fleet might now try something drastic to discourage further contact with the Polity.

After a few minutes, three more individuals entered the hold. These wore no armour, and the only visible weaponry they carried were sidearms – probably straight-forward chemical projectile guns. They were clad in the

one-piece foamite suits that were the uniform of Fleet
personnel; garments that closely followed their musculature, though being over a half-inch thick they made
the three of them appear quite bulky. The uniforms were
cut low around the neck and down below terminated in
wide deck boots. Belts and webbing straps held their
sidearms, ammunition clips, an assortment of tools and
the rank patches containing their security scanner bar-
codes. The two to the rear wore around their throats
necklaces consisting of variously coloured bars, perhaps
to visibly indicate their rank to their associates. The one
I assumed to be the boss here, preceding these two, wore
a simple platinum band around his throat. His red
foamite suit stood out in vivid contrast to their dull blue
ones, and he carried fewer tools. But it was the physical
appearance of these three that interested me much more
than their attire, for the people of Sudoria had been
changed by old adaptogenic drugs and technologies to
live on a planet where the temperature did not sink much
below sixty degrees Celsius, and sometimes rose above a
hundred degrees at the equator.

Projecting lower jaws were balanced by the bulbous
rearward projection of the skulls, while their ears were
just shapeless knubs as if seared by the heat of their
world. Their noses ran narrow down the angular jut of
their faces, with nostrils apparently normal but capable of
opening as wide as an average human eye. They retained
their head hair, though some cosmetic genetic tweak
prevented it from growing on their faces or anywhere else
on their bodies. Fleet personnel shaved the front of their
skulls and plaited the rest in a queue in the manner of
the ancient samurai. Their skin was a dark metallic violet
that grew more reflective as the intensity of the sunlight

increased. Though little different in appearance from standard, their eyes possessed nictitating membranes. Webs extended between their fingers, for cooling rather than swimming, but were probably unnecessary here in the ship, with its temperature maintained at a comfortable fifty-five degrees Celsius.

I undogged my suit helmet and placed it to one side. The one in the red suit halted by the sphere and peered inside at me, his nostrils flaring wide and the nictitating membranes momentarily dulling his eyes. I guessed I would eventually learn what such reactions meant, but the twist to his mouth and rest of his expression seemed likely to be a sneer. After a moment he stepped back and gestured for me to step out into the hold. I unfolded myself from the floor, reached over and pulled down the manual locking mechanism, and the door section, consisting of twelve hexagonal chainglass sheets inside a single ceramal frame, thumped up from its seals. I pushed it open and stepped outside.

Hot, damned hot.

I felt a slight shifting of the fibres tangled throughout my body as the two viral forms at war inside me readjusted their positions. Though not myself thermodapted, one of those conflicting viral forms enabled me to easily tolerate this temperature – just within the normal human range – and also other temperatures, both high and low, that would result in those standing before me curling up and expiring. Unfortunately, the second viral form might result in a similar end for me, too. But what would they know; they hadn't seen a 'normal human' in 800 years.

'I am told that you can speak our language,' the boss began.

'Fluently,' I replied. Most people working for ECS loaded languages to their cerebral augs for instant translation, or loaded them via internal gridlinks directly to their minds. Due to certain physiological . . . differences, I couldn't use any form of prosthetic augmentation so had to learn them the old-fashioned way. However, I am, I believe, a competent linguist. It took me a year or so to learn four of the languages spoken here (in one case, sort-of spoken), which brought the total of the languages I was conversant with up to one hundred and twenty, though I suspect I might have since forgotten one or two. 'I presume you are the captain of this ship?'

'I am Captain Inigis,' he replied, 'and knowing your facility with our language you will understand this instruction.' He gestured at me with one webbed hand. 'Strip.'

I shrugged, unsurprised. The dilemma faced by the Orbital Combine and the planetary parties was that those who most objected to my presence here were also the ones necessarily employed to pick me up. So I went through the laborious process of undoing all the catches and stickpads of the suit, stripped it off and kicked it to one side. I stood there for a moment in the absorbent undersuit until the captain gestured again, so I stripped that off too and stood naked before them.

Inigis now walked over to two of the scanning pillars that had earlier risen from the floor and pointed down between them. 'Come and stand here.' I padded over as instructed and noticed the captain quickly stepping back out of the way – touch of xenophobia there. The pillars revolved until their scanning lenses were pointing in towards me. I felt a tingling of my skin and momentary hot flushes as if a blow torch quickly skimmed over it, not held there long enough to burn, but long enough for me to be aware of it. X-ray, terahertz, magnetic resonance, point radar and much else besides. More viral shifting, but no slippage as yet. A faint ringing started in my ears and I suddenly gained the distinct impression that someone else had just entered the hold: a tall man, slightly stooped, features shadowed. I glanced over, wondering how he fitted into this scenario, then felt my stomach sink and my skin prickle. No one there – it had to be an effect of the scanning, since I was receiving the full works without any regard for my health. Someone else would have suffered radiation sickness after this and the cancer-cell hunting nanites in their bodies would have needed to work overtime. In fact I rather suspected Inigis hoped I would die from such heavy inspection. As the scan completed, he seemed rather disappointed I didn't keel over.

Next, Inigis stood over by one of his companions, viewing an unscrolled flimsy screen. I noted how an optic cord joined this screen to the suit of the individual who handed it over, and inspected him more closely. His foamite suit was bulked with additional equipment, earphones covered his ears, a close-viewing screen covered one eye, a microphone was fixed before his mouth, and wires actually penetrated his skull. He seemed to be muttering perpetually, and moving his fingers in a continuous dance while operating the virtual control gloves he wore. *Tacom*, I realized. Fleet communications were run by individuals like this. Returning my attention to Inigis, I could see – even though not quite used to their facial expressions yet – he was at first puzzled, but began to show a growing satisfaction.

'What you're seeing,' I volunteered, 'are the results

of a viral infection I contracted on a world called
Spatterjay. Every native there has it.' I gestured to the
various rings of bluish scar tissue showing on my skin.
'The virus is contracted through the bite of some particularly nasty critters.'

It was a half-truth, really, but I doubted they would
be able to distinguish the dying virus from the one that
was killing it . . . and killing me too. Even so, as I spoke,
a sharp memory returned to me. *I stood upon the deck
of a sailing ship, and oozing along the planking by my feet
was a leech as long as my arm. Blood trickled between my
fingers, my hand clamped against the hole where the thing had
reamed a chunk of flesh from my stomach. A sailor, dressed
only in canvas trousers, his bare skin seeming tattooed with
multiple blue rings, glanced at me unsympathetically and
said, 'Now you're buggered.'*

'I'm supposed to believe this?' Inigis asked, snapping
me back to the present. 'This seems more likely to me to
be some form of organic technology. You were warned
that no such Polity technologies are allowed here.' With
finality he pressed a button that ravelled the flimsy screen
back into its case, and handed this back to his tacom
officer.

'It's not a technology, just viral fibres. Your own
biologists should be able to confirm this.'

'A *normal* Polity human was to be sent,' he insisted
stubbornly.

'I very much doubt Geronamid agreed to that, since
very few "normal humans" exist in the Polity nowadays.
Anyway, any Earth-standard human wouldn't be able
to survive in your environment. He would have to be
thermodapted like yourselves, or kept alive by Polity tech,
which of course you won't allow.' I shrugged. 'One such

as myself seemed the politic choice, since I can survive in your environment and, being so obviously unlike you, I'm less likely to arouse suspicion.' That was all absolute heirodont shit, of course. Geronamid chose me because I could survive in a wide range of environments – including that of the *other* inhabited world of this system – and because I possessed other non-technological advantages.

'It will be necessary to confirm this under question—'

The side door opened and two more people pushed into the hold, past the guard stationed there. One was female – the first I had seen, Fleet being so patriarchal – the other a quite old man, stooped and leaning on a gnarled wooden cane with a gold handle. These two did not wear Fleet uniforms. The woman was clad in a tight-fitting bodysuit, which was black from head to foot and revealed all her curves, and a brightly coloured wrap draped around her hips, its pattern a wormish tangle. The aged man wore baggy trousers and other dress with a decided Arabian air, also a skullcap with cooling veins webbed through it and pipes running down into his clothing. Being old he was unable to keep cool, and this was their solution here. I recognized him from com recordings: Abel Duras, Chairman of the Sudorian Parliament. The woman, whose name I did not know, I rather suspected to be a representative of the Orbital Combine.

'What precisely do you think you are doing, Captain?' she said to Inigis. Then she glanced at me with a slight smile, looked me up and down. 'No concealed weapons, I see.'

I studied her. Lighter-boned than the men, she possessed a pouty soft-faced sexuality emphasized by the kohl round her eyes, lips whitened after the manner of women here, and her black hair long and curly. Despite the adaptation differences she looked like someone I once knew, but when you get to my age most people seem familiar. I wondered if I found her so attractive because her mass of hair de-emphasized the shape of her skull and the jut of her face. She also looked dangerous, probably because of those long canines that protruded over her lower lip even when she closed her mouth.

'Fleet security protocol demands full scanning of the suspect in case he presents a danger to this ship,' said Inigis tightly. 'I have detected organic Polity technology and must secure him until the danger this represents has been assessed and negated.'

'You're overstepping your remit here, Captain . . .' the woman began, anger penetrating her good humour. She desisted when Duras reached out and clamped a hand on her arm.

The old man nodded to himself for a short moment, then raised his head to focus sharp black eyes on the Captain. 'Consul Assessor David McCrooger is not a "suspect", Captain Inigis, but a representative of the Polity – a human dominion on such a scale that boggles the mind, and one that certainly contains war craft quite capable, I rather suspect, of digging their own hills.' He now looked towards me. 'Is that not so, Consul?'

I thought about the cities that were now mass graves on Brumal – the only other inhabited world in this system – and pretended ignorance. 'Digging hills?'

Duras moved rather quickly for such an old man and, before Inigis could object, strode over to stand before me. 'Fleet capital ships are called hilldiggers, because their weapons created mountain ranges on Brumal, but I am sure you've studied the historical files we transmitted and are well aware of this.' He turned and stabbed a finger at one of the Captain's aides. 'You, go find the Consul Assessor some suitable clothing, and confirm that his cabin is prepared.' Duras reached out and grabbed my biceps and, towing me after him, headed for the door.

The snouts of disc-guns wavered in our direction and the Captain seemed about ready to detonate, but I judged him to be overextended and likely in some serious trouble if he pushed this any further. I caught his signal to the guard standing beside the door. The man moved across to block our exit – a delay giving Inigis time to think.

'Yishna,' snapped Duras, 'remove this obstacle.'

The woman moved forward, and the guard, while beginning to turn his weapon towards her, hesitated. She stepped in close, grabbed and flipped him neatly over her hip. He landed with a crash on the floor beside me. Because of the ease with which she did this, I instantly recognized her to be someone to be reckoned with. Combat training had remained obligatory for all Sudorians ever since the War, and the guard, being a member of Fleet and therefore subject to further training, should have been more able than her.

The guard's armour must have absorbed the force of his landing for he still kept hold of his weapon. I saw him swing it, one-handed, up towards Yishna and Duras, pause, then swing it towards me. Was this a standing order, or had Inigis or some other given him instructions over his suit's comlink? Yishna of Orbital Combine attacked one of the guards, at Abel Duras's instigation; the guard's weapon inadvertently fired and blew the head off the Polity Consul Assessor – such an unfortunate incident, but what can you do?

I stooped, quickly grabbed the man's forearms and hauled him to his feet. I could feel the vibration of his suit motors through my hands as he tried to bring the weapon to bear on me fully. It fired a short five-round burst, and shattered metal ricocheted around the hold. Enough – someone could get hurt. I released his left arm, and reached over to take the weapon from his right hand. He punched me with his free hand using the full force of his suit motors. I took that, then I took away his weapon, snapped its power-supply cable and skimmed it away. He tried to bring a knee up into my groin – all reflex now because we'd passed the point where this could have been dismissed as an accident. Tired of this I threw him. His flat trajectory bounced him off the hold wall ten feet away. When he clattered to the ground, he showed no signs of wanting to get up again.

By now the others were closing in, and Inigis began shouting something. Behind me, Duras was cursing. I quickly stepped up beside him, turned the manual wheel on the locked bulkhead door, and pulled it open. Pieces of shattered locking mechanism clattered over the floor. Duras eyed me, glanced at the downed guard . . . and perhaps wondered if Inigis might have the right idea.

'Stay exactly where you are!'

I glanced round. Captain Inigis and his men were ranged around us, every weapon trained. Duras patted me on the arm and stepped out in front of me.

'So, Captain, not only have you insulted the Polity by treating their Consul like a criminal, you have also made two attempts on his life: one by using the kind of scan on him normally confined to inspecting munitions for faults – and now like this.' Duras gestured to the guard who was beginning to make tentative exploratory movements, perhaps wondering how far he could move before things began to hurt.

'I am merely ensuring the safety—'

'Do be quiet, Inigis,' Yishna interrupted. 'You know you've botched this, and if you push it any further there will certainly be repercussions. Probably in Parliament, but definitely in Fleet Command when I describe your incompetence to Harald. My brother and I disagree on many matters, but we have always agreed that idiots should not be allowed to thrive.'

Inigis grew paler as she spoke; I suspected he had just been reminded of a rather unpleasant fact. I studied the woman. Obviously her brother Harald ranked higher in Fleet than Inigis, but knowing Fleet's attitude to any contact with the Polity, wondered if she might be bluffing. How important was her brother? Whatever, it worked for Inigis let us go. While Yishna and Duras conducted me to my cabin, apologizing the while, it seemed some other menacing party accompanied us – whispering grim truths in my ear, yet forever out of sight. An after-effect of the scanning, or so I thought.

– RETROACT 2 –

Harald – *in childhood*

Harald Strone knew where he wanted to be – and had always known. As he walked into Yadis Hall to take the seat at his assigned console, he received some strange looks from the Fleet personnel present and, maintaining a bored expression, removed his control baton from his belt cache.

'What are you doing here, boy?' asked the man who loomed over him.

Harald stared up at him, noted the missing ear and the scarring on one side of the face before turning his attention to the man's ranking necklace: a ship's engineer, retired from service, but looking rather young for that. Harald inspected him further and realized that though his interrogator moved easily and looked intact from a distance, both his legs and his right arm were artificial. Silently, Harald reached back into the belt cache for his identity plaque.

'Harald Strone . . . I see. My apologies, but—'

'Yes, I know,' interrupted Harald. 'I look like I should be out sand boarding and skirl catching. But, as you see, I am eighteen years old and my authorization is in order. I am here to take Fusion Mechanics Grade Alpha.'

The engineer nodded, then moved away, but he did not return Harald's identity plaque. The boy grimaced and quickly slotting his baton into the reader in the console, then began his examination by unscrolling a flimsy screen and pressing his palm against it. As, like a concert pianist, he began rattling away on the ship-clone engineering console, solving the problems thrown up on the screen, he wondered if this time he might get caught. Thus far he had managed to take Grade Alpha in Navigation, Astrophysics, Command Management, Weapons Solutions and Design and Materials Technology. Rather than risk too much exposure, he took the twelve other Fleet examinations at Grade Gamma, had avoided demonstrating the extent of his abilities in combat training, for like his siblings his control of his body was equal to that he exercised over his mind, and had thus far managed to keep his doctorates in Applied Mathematics and Computer Science off the record – mainly because of his facility in the latter discipline. Pursuing their own particular interests, his sister and brother Rhodane and Orduval did get caught and a huge furore ensued, but then they were allowed to continue, though under close supervision. No one, however, had yet caught Yishna, whose computer-science qualifications matched his own, and she was already working as a laboratory technician on the space station Corisanthe III.

The extent of time allowed for this examination was set at four hours. After only one hour, Harald turned off his console and removed his baton, then walked over to the same engineer sitting in the monitoring booth with three other invigilators.

'You realize that by pulling your baton authorization now you'll have to go through the exam again from the beginning?' the man warned.

'Yes, I understand that. May I have my identity plaque back now?'

The man smiled sympathetically. 'Fusion Mechanics can be difficult. I suggest you take one of the applied mathematics courses to begin—'

'Chinzer,' interrupted a female tacom officer sitting beside him, 'before you make too much of an idiot of yourself.' She pointed to one screen on the montage of them before her.

The engineer stared at the information she indicated. 'Well, fuck me.' He looked up at Harald with sudden respect, picked up the ID plaque from the table before him, and handed it over. 'Congratulations, Engineering Candidate Harald Strone.'

'Thank you,' said Harald politely, pocketing his plaque. It was a gratifying response, but he would rather have gone unnoticed. With head ducked, he headed for the exit, and, as he stepped out from the examination room, he realized such circumspection had come too late. The three Fleet security personnel standing outside were obviously waiting specially for him.

'Harald Strone.' The officer in command eyed him almost with bewilderment. 'First, my congratulations on passing yet another Alpha Grade examination – but you must have realized such a level of achievement would not go unnoticed.'

'But I took some with only Gamma Grades too,' Harald protested quietly.

'Yes, you did.' The officer looked towards the others. 'Twelve of them.'

One of the others swore in disbelief.

'And as startling as that is in itself,' the officer continued, 'what we would really like to know is how a twelve-year-old managed to alter his ID to give him an age of eighteen years.'

'I know computers,' muttered Harald. He took out his ID plaque and baton, plugged the plaque into one baton port, and quickly entered the code that would update the plaque, and simultaneously correct the errors he had introduced. Then he held both items out to the Fleet officer.

Puzzled, the officer used Harald's baton to start running up on the plaque's small screen all the information it contained. 'Applied Mathematics and Computer

Science,' he said. Now he was staring at Harald with something more than bemusement.

'I suppose I'm in trouble,' Harald suggested.

The man handed back both plaque and baton, then checked the timepiece on his sleeve. 'No, Harald Strone. In five hours you will be in a hilldigger.'

Harald's expression showed delight, but the machine that was his mind – its oiled and beautifully polished components sliding into position with perfect precision – just ticked off another box and stepped him up another rung.

– Retroact 2 Ends –

McCrooger

I felt edgy, and unable to relax. It seemed I could hear the murmur of voices out in the ship's corridors, yet when I ducked my head through the curtain covering the cabin door to look, I encountered either silence or other sounds bearing no relation to that previous murmur. Within my cabin, shadows seemed to flicker out of synch with whatever was casting them, and occasionally I would catch movement at the corner of my eye as if something had just scuttled out of sight. Clad in loose trousers, a shirt and some kind of embroidered garment that draped over me tabard-like and laced up from under my arms down to my waist, I inspected my cabin more closely – perhaps to assure myself that nothing was hiding there.

It was a small neat cell, similar to those found in the oceanic ships of my homeworld. A mattress rolled out from an alcove set at floor level into the wall, but there were no blankets available – who needed them in this temperature? A spigot operated by a snake-shaped lever shot water into a three-quarter-globe basin, and the toilet was an interesting horn-shaped affair that folded out from the wall and which you applied to the necessary part of you with a sucking *thwock*. When you had finished your business, it then made some very alarming sounds similar to those of a carpet cleaner, as it sprayed and then sucked away water. No towels – moisture on any part of the body being a pleasure as it quickly evaporated. I was inspecting my face in a circular mirror, running fingers through the short grey fuzz on my scalp – hair that never grew any longer and rarely fell out – and trying to figure out the purpose of the various devices slotted into the wall below the mirror, when there came a repetitive *clink-clink-clink* from outside the curtain door.

I jumped in surprise, but luckily controlled the violence of my reaction enough not to break anything.

'Come in,' I called, and turned.

Yishna entered first, then Duras, lowering the stick he had obviously used to tap against the door frame. I noticed how the gold cane grip seemed to be moulded in the form of a beetle of some kind. Yishna studied my spartan accommodation with the same amusement she had shown on first bringing me here. Duras merely grimaced, displaying yellow teeth, then abruptly turned around and headed back through the curtain. Yishna turned as well, with some hand-flip gesture which I presumed meant 'Follow us.' They led me out into a tilted box-section corridor like something out of an Escher nightmare, where it was necessary for me to stoop while walking, and conducted me to another much larger cabin.

This contained a table laden with food and drink, surrounded by four strapwork chairs. These last items I eyed
dubiously.

'Consul Assessor David McCrooger, welcome to the
Sudorian Democratic Union.' Duras turned towards me,
holding out a wooden box.

I accepted it. 'Thank you for the gift. I regret that
I was unable to bring you anything in exchange, but perhaps, should technology proscriptions ever be raised,
I can one day return the favour.' I placed the box down on
a side table, twisted the simple latch and flipped it open.
Inside rested a handgun and a knife. I took out the knife
first, pulled it from its ornate sheath and inspected the
blade. It was similar in shape to a Gurkha knife, though
with a blade fashioned from some translucent ceramic.
I didn't need to touch it to know the edge could probably
shave iron. I carefully replaced it in its sheath, then
picked up the handgun. The grip, fashioned of carved
bone inlaid with gold and what looked like flat polished
emeralds, lay slick in my hand. As I pulled it from the
holster I expected to find myself holding some kind of
ancient muzzle-loader. It was certainly a gun relying on
chemical propellant, but even so was a finely manufactured
automatic weapon. Peering into the box I noticed a row
of ammunition clips underlying the gun compartment.
There was something strange about the cartridge visible
in the top of each clip. I levered out one clip and
inspected it. The cartridge was of some ordinary metal
like brass, but the bullet itself was sharp and fashioned
of some hard black material.

'These gifts are purely ceremonial,' Duras explained,
'but we would feel insulted if you did not wear them at

all times.' He then reached up to undo some catches around the back of his skullcap, before removing it.

So, they felt the need to provide me with the means of defending myself, since it struck me as unlikely that any ceremonial weapons would require armour-piercing bullets. I grinned at him, then abruptly felt a surge of sadness upon noting his cropped white hair and the visible shape of his skull beneath the loose skin of his face. I'd been forgetting that people still actually died of old age here. Their medical science, though advanced, lay some centuries behind that of the Polity, and there were the harsh environmental factors to take into account. Duras was probably at most a hundred years old – a mere junior by the standards of my own world and not really very old by Polity standards. I wondered if I felt sad because death had become for me a very personal preoccupation.

'Orbital Combine also welcomes you to the Sudorian system,' announced Yishna, though the gifts from that political and economic force occupying the many satellite stations orbiting Sudoria were of a rather different nature. In one hand she proffered a palm screen incorporating audio, recording facilities, local netlink and terabyte processing and storage, and also a control baton which plugged into a slot along the bottom of the screen. Both these items had their equivalents in the Polity, but the control baton's construction was rather unique. It was a rod about four inches long and one inch thick, with twist controls and small buttons spaced along it, and a laser emitter at one end which could serve as torch, pointer, measuring and spectroscopic-analysis device. In all other respects this combined unit served as a multiple-function com device: phone, computer access, remote key, bank card – and much else besides. In her other hand Yishna held an old-fashioned paper book I'd already read: a history of the War by someone called Uskaron. I held it up to inspect its plain cover, maybe the safest choice considering its explosive contents.

'So this is the famous book,' I said. 'The one Fleet wanted banned and the one that resulted in a planetwide search for its author.'

'Yes, that's the one,' agreed Duras, but he did not look too happy about this choice of gift.

'I understand he was never found . . . this Uskaron,' I glanced at him, 'but proof of his claims was delivered to Parliament?'

'The veracity of that evidence has yet to be proven,' said Duras tightly.

'But I understand, nevertheless, that Sudorian opinion of both the Brumallians and Fleet has changed greatly in the last few years.'

He merely nodded, so I turned to Yishna. 'I thank Orbital Combine for these gifts. Perhaps, when the time comes, I can conduct you through the intricacies of U-space mechanics, Calabi-Yau space extension matrices, and the like.' I winked at her, and she first looked startled, then realization dawned: maybe I wasn't just a politician, and maybe Polity technology did not have to be something you could physically hold and inspect. Fleet could hardly place import restrictions on what I had brought here between my ears.

'Please be seated.' Duras gestured to one of the chairs. 'I understand that none of our food is likely to be incompatible with your biochemistry?'

'That's so.' I gingerly lowered myself into a chair and, though it creaked loudly and sagged somewhat, it seemed to be holding. The smell of the food started distracting me, but I tried to pay it no attention while we got the social niceties out of the way.

Duras, lowering himself into another of the chairs, commented, 'You're not entirely what we expected.'

Yishna seated herself too and, without any more ado, picked up a bowl with a series of rings on the underside into which she inserted her fingers, and began selecting items from the table and filling it. I decided to do the same, but found the finger holes weren't large enough.

'What did you expect?'

After chomping down something that looked like a deep-fried cockroach, Yishna replied, 'Fleet has been making much of the effete products of a soft civilization run by artificial intelligences. I think Inigis had started believing his own organization's propaganda, so you came as rather a shock to him.' She raised an eyebrow and gestured to the empty chair. 'The Captain, incidentally, will not be joining us.'

I couldn't help but grin, not about the missing Captain's shock but about those supposedly 'effete products'. I was loyal to the Polity but did not actually consider myself a fully paid-up member. Though born and grown to adulthood on Earth, and having spent many years there on later occasions, I still considered a world called Spatterjay to be my home. But I'd met Polity Agents and Earth Central Security personnel who were, quite frankly, frightening. I knew some who could have come out of that drop-sphere naked, gone through Inigis and his soldiers like they weren't there, and assumed total control of this ship in under an hour. Lucky for the Sudorians that the Polity chose to be more diplomatic nowadays, and therefore tended to keep its ECS attack dogs on a tight leash. They sent me instead – the warm and cuddly option.

'You are rather large and, as you demonstrated, uncommonly strong,' noted Duras, while breaking open an object like a razorfish.

After Captain Inigis's lieutenants had finally conducted me to my cabin, they then spent some time trying to locate some clothes that would fit me. Ever since that first leech bite, I had steadily grown in bulk and strength, and density – my body now packed tight with the viral fibres (some of which I could do without it has to be said). I stood nearly six foot six tall in bare feet, and carried the breadth and musculature of a fanatical body-builder, though I weighed about two and a half times as much as he would. I'd got used to it – you did, while the centuries stacked up.

I tried one of the cockroaches and studied the other food on the table. Some of it I recognized as adapted Earth foods: a bowl of miniature lemons like sweets, fried lumps that were probably some form of potato, kebabbed combinations of small vegetables – one looking like a carrot – and blocks of meat, pastries, even canapés – though ones filled with green flies in a clear aspic – and something like jellied eels which I suspected instead to be jellied snake since there wasn't a lot of open water on Sudoria. The cockroach tasted good, rather like glister meat in crunchy batter, and being raised on Spatterjay one tended not to be squeamish about what one ate. It was also rather nice to have it laid out prepared like this and not risk your food taking a bite out of you before you managed to cram it into the cooking pot.

'Just biology,' I explained in reply to Duras's observation.

'Then not some organic technology?' he suggested wryly.

'Certainly not.' I stared at him across the table. 'We have a saying where I come from – "Softly softly catchy boxy" – which very *very* roughly translated means the Polity is not going to come crashing in here stamping on all your traditions and tearing up your social order. The ethos now on the Line – the Polity border with . . . well, everything – is to no longer "subsume with prejudice" any populated worlds or civilizations we encounter. Too much chaos, too much death and destruction results from that, and afterwards, once that civilization has been subsumed it is no longer unique, but just another homogenous addition. So we're playing this by your rules.'

'Which suggests to me that the Polity no longer considers those new worlds it encounters as a threat needing to be controlled.' Duras was undoubtedly sharp. 'Back in the hold I suggested to Inigis that you possess ships capable of digging their own hills. Do you possess hill-diggers?'

I carefully considered my reply. On the one hand I did not want to appear boastful, yet on the other I needed to play this straight with people who, after all, wanted to initiate trade and greater contact. 'You understand that on the whole the Polity is run by artificial intelligences?' Duras nodded. 'Those AIs are everywhere. As far as the ships are concerned, they control them, captain them – for many AIs the ship is actually its own body.'

'But how large and how powerful are those bodies?' Duras pressed, staring at me piercingly. 'I would not want us allying ourselves with a political entity that does not possess the will or capability to . . . perhaps have some bearing on future negotiations.'

Was Duras looking for Polity intervention, should Fleet react badly? It appeared so, for he seemed to be trying to gauge how much help he might expect, and whether we were actually capable of helping. Here it seemed lay a large fault in our policy of not revealing too much, of not wiring up a civilization like this to too much of a culture shock.

I shrugged. 'Quite some time ago the Polity was involved in a war with an alien species called the Prador. Whole worlds were burned down to bedrock and billions died. That war began about two centuries after your colony ship set out from the solar system.'

Yishna whistled past her canines.

'The Polity has moved on since then. Geronamid is an AI sited, mostly, inside one large vessel. That vessel is not allowed to orbit any worlds possessing oceans or crustal instabilities.'

They sat there looking puzzled, then the penny dropped.

'Fuck,' said Yishna. 'Tides?'

'Perhaps now we can turn to my itinerary?' I suggested.

I know that the *Procul Harum* set out just before the Quiet War – that time when the AIs displaced humans as the rulers of humanity and took over in the Solar System, in a conflict surprisingly without resort to massive exterminations. The ship ran on a rather dodgy U-space drive and carried 6,000 passengers in hibernation mode, plus 50,000 frozen embryos and the requisite equipment to start building a civilization. It arrived at the planet

Sudoria a hundred years later, and then the passengers were revived – well, most of them, since hibernation tech-nology wasn't that great back then.

The system they entered consisted of one ubiquitous gas giant, five cold worlds outside of it, two of which orbited each other while spinning round the sun, and one the size of Neptune bearing a large ring system. The inner system consisted of a Mercury clone and two Earth-like planets orbiting within the green belt. The hot world they named Sudoria, and the other one Brumal. Though cold and wet, Brumal seemed more accommo-dating to human life; however, these people were extremely taken with the adaptogenic technologies they'd brought along with them, so many wanted to change themselves to live on the hotter alternative, Sudoria. A schism developed, mutiny and fighting aboard. This could not be allowed to continue, else none of them would manage to reach planetfall, since space being a harsh and unforgiving environment at best, it became even more so when you were trying to kill each other in it.

Eventually the rival sides came to an agreement. Two and a half thousand colonists took their share of supplies and descended in the landing craft to Brumal. Subse-quently the same craft were then supposed to return on automatic to the ship so the other faction could then descend to Sudoria. But the craft were sabotaged on the ground, leaving the prospective Sudoria residents stuck up in space. Eventually they took the only option remain-ing open to them, and did with the *Procul Harum* what it was emphatically not designed to do: *they landed it.* The landing on Sudoria was rough, and surviving thereafter was to be rougher still. They physically adapted to their new environment as best they could. They raised their embryos and began building, but during those harsh times lost U-space tech and much else. It took four and a half centuries for them to get back up into space. And they took their long-term bitterness towards the Brumallians with them.

On Brumal, another living planet like Sudoria, conditions were unexpectedly even more harsh. Orbital surveys, though picking up much life and activity, had failed to detect the acidity of the environment, or, the pioneers having arrived during a calm period, the subsequent out-gassing of chlorine trapped in rocky layers of the crust. The residents first resorted to a basic amphidaption to this watery world, but as conditions changed they were forced to use the adaptation technology again and again. The humans there became exceedingly strange, but their environment toughened them and their almost hive-like social structure and chemically linked mentalities enabled them to quickly rise. They were still at a pre-industrial stage when some Copernicus amongst them first noticed the satellites the Sudorians were putting up. Twenty years later, radio communications were established between the two worlds. Many mis-understandings followed, and public reaction on Sudoria to the first image of a Brumallian was not too brilliant. By the time the first Sudorian ship swung around Brumal there were satellites up in orbit to observe it. Sudorian historians would later insist that one of these satellites fired a missile that destroyed the innocent vessel – though the writer known as Uskaron had rather changed that view of late. A space arms race ensued, then, inevitably, war.

It lasted a hundred years. And the hilldiggers finished it.

2

The lack of intervening oceans on Sudoria allowed our civilization to spread without fragmenting. There were still, however, attempts at forming independent states. The first was initiated by certain Sudorians espousing the ideology of the Blue Orchids – an ideology passed on over five generations by the surviving remnants of that party as it grew into a large secret organization. They attempted to set up a bordered enclave on the coast of the Brak sea to the East of the Komarl but, having learnt the lessons of history, our political predecessors felt they could not allow this. The Sudorian army of the time was immediately dispatched to the area, with instructions to break up the enclave and forcibly relocate the Orchids. There was resistance and there was fighting, but nowhere near the scale of that seen back within the Sol system. We had yet to learn how to get really bloody.

– Uskaron

McCrooger

Crawling mind-numbing terror had turned my mouth dry and my guts rigid as stone. The sky ahead looked like a cataract eye, with the horizon folded up around it.

Baroque old buildings rose to my right and left, leaning
into each other like plotting courtiers. Having seen both
visual effects before, I realized I was standing in a
town within a cylinder world, but was too frightened to
wonder how I'd come to be there. Heading towards the
milky eye of the end-cap I found myself slipping and
stumbling on some uneven hollow-sounding surface
and, peering down, unreasonably knew that the street
was cobbled with skulls, which had been laid over a compacted hogging of human bones. Ahead of me a figure
stepped from a darkened alley and began to drift away
up the street. I hurried to catch up, but just could not
seem to move fast enough. Then I was abruptly right up
behind the same figure and reaching out to grasp one
shoulder. My father turned with his familiar bored *'What
now?'* expression. I glanced away for a moment, trying to
remember what important news I had to give him. I
should have kept my gaze fixed upon him instead, for he
seized the opportunity to transform; rising up above the
buildings to cast me into shadow, growing convoluted
and complex, a tangled living spire of—

Very little transition brought me to wakefulness, but
I lay there paralysed with irrational terror, my eyes still
tightly closed. Something had accompanied me out of
that nightmare into reality and now stood poised above
my sleeping mattress.

This is ridiculous, I thought, and forced my eyes open
while expecting to see nothing. Something dark and
shadowy slid away, muttering, into the walls. I reached
out and hit the light panel set in the wall at the head of
the fold-out mattress and forced myself to sit upright.
The cabin seemed slightly distorted around me, requiring of me some unknowable mental effort to return it to

normality. Eventually I stood up and went to get myself a drink. This had to be an effect of Inigis's scanning, I told myself again, uncomfortably aware that this *weirdness* had started in the drop-sphere, before I even met Inigis.

The next night I visited that cylinder world town again, and fled from my father's doppelgänger. I felt his disappointment in me, and by the third night the nightmare seemed just a desultory attempt to attract my attention, and faded thereafter to feelings of anxiety and moments of panic in the night, though sometimes, while awake, I would catch sight of some figure out of the corner of my eye, turn towards it and find it had disappeared.

I spent most of my time aboard the ship accessing the palm screen and learning how to use the control baton Yishna had given me, reading omnivorously, my mind sponging up as much information as it could process. I reread Uskaron's book all through, then one day left it in the ship's refectory, from where it quickly disappeared – which told me something about attitudes aboard, though I'm not sure what. I ate regularly with Yishna and Duras, and quizzed them as intently as they quizzed me.

On my fourth day aboard, one of Captain Inigis's lieutenants turned up: a thin pointy-nosed man with a ginger queue and a perpetual frown etching his features. Behind him entered a young woman loaded down with a bulky mass of fabric.

'How may I help you?' I asked.

The woman placed her load down on the floor and, utterly ignored by the lieutenant, turned to go.

'Thank you,' I said, smiling at her from where I still

sat cross-legged on my mattress, though I wasn't yet sure what for. She appeared startled by that, then smiled tentatively before ducking through the curtain. The lieutenant just turned his head away from this exchange as if embarrassed to be witnessing it. I knew the Fleet was patriarchal, but his behaviour struck me as plain rude.

'I don't know your name,' I said.

'I am First Lieutenant Drappler,' he stated, then gestured to the stack of fabric. 'We had to have this made for you. It is a shipboard survival suit – should we suffer a hull breach.'

'Oh, very good.' Like I would trust a survival suit received from one of Inigis's men. I would have preferred them to return my spacesuit, which was checked out by a forensic AI before I donned it. He stood there looking uncomfortable. 'Is there anything else?' I asked.

'I am to show you this ship's safety procedures.'

I held my hands out to each side and rose to my feet. 'Please do so.'

Drappler removed a baton from his pocket and pointed it to a row of four squares set high in one wall of my cabin. 'The alarm tone is this.' He pressed a button and a klaxon started wailing. It didn't matter how long they had been away from 'normal' human society, stuff like that didn't change – a loud repetitive noise imparting the meaning 'Panic now.' He shut down the alarm and now the squares lit up. One was yellow with a black band across it, the other three were green. 'This is emergency level one, which indicates you must stay in your cabin. It usually means there might be some shipboard problem, but no hull breach.' Now two of each kind of light. 'Level two: this means hull breach. You must remain in or return to your cabin, and don your survival suit. Bulkhead doors will be closing off the affected area.'

'And if you're caught in that area?' I asked.

'This.' Only one green light left now. 'Now you must proceed to an escape-pod and enter it quickly. The emergency is level three. If it rises to level four, the pod will be ejected.' Now all four lights displayed that black-banded yellow. 'If you see this while in your cabin, you must try to find a pod that has not already been ejected from the ship.' He turned towards the curtain. 'Now the escape-pods.'

'Presumably this is prior to the ship being ejected from existence?' I asked quickly, wanting to delay his departure. A moment ago I had spotted someone lurking beyond the curtain, and I didn't want him to pull it aside only to reveal that there was no one there.

'Just so,' he replied, turning back to me. 'Shall we proceed?'

I glanced up at the four black and yellow lights again. 'Do you have wasps on Sudoria?' I used the English word as there seemed no obvious alternative in their language.

'What . . . what are wasps?'

'Never mind, it's not important.' I let him lead me out.

The pod procedure was simple enough. Once the emergency hit level three, the pod doors, which were scattered throughout the ship, automatically unlocked. Drappler took me through the manual procedure should there be any problems with that. I tried not to break anything. A short access tunnel led through into the pod itself – its own door remaining open until level four was reached, at which point ship systems closed the doors on any occupied pods and ejected them, or else you did both those operations manually.

'How much air?' I asked.

'This is a five-man pod,' Drappler said inside the cramped space. Great. 'If five men occupy it, enough for twenty days. The pod's distress call should get someone to it within that time. The pod will also point itself towards the nearest Fleet beacon, and use three-quarters of its fuel in a concentrated burst. If you are near either Sudoria or Brumal, it will send itself there and effect re-entry using first its engine then a polymer parachute.'

I thought all his estimates and suppositions overly optimistic. Right out here the nearest Fleet ships would be some weeks away, as were the nearest habitable worlds. Back up in the ship's corridor I shook his hand. 'Earth custom,' I told him after his initial startlement. 'I want to thank you. I feel so much safer now.'

His nostrils flared as he muttered something along the lines of, 'Think nothing of it,' then headed quickly away wiping his hand on his foamite suit. When I returned to my cabin I found Yishna waiting inside, seated on my mattress. Maybe she'd been the one lurking outside earlier – rather than that other dark illusory figure.

'They are so solicitous of my safety now, it's heartening,' I told her.

She gave me a louche smile. 'That could be due to the charges ranging from rank incompetence to attempted murder that Duras filed against Captain Inigis.'

'Ah, I see. Is there anything I can help you with?'

Without more ado she said, 'Tell me, if the Polity

were to intercede here, what would be their policy on imprisoned sentients?'

It was such a simple question, but I sensed an underlying tension. For a moment the room distorted around me again, shadows appeared displaced and it seemed some other individual was listening intently. I wondered then if these effects were more to do with the war between the two viral forms occupying my body than with Inigis's rough scanning of me earlier.

'That depends. In the case of corrupt totalitarian regimes a full amnesty to prisoners is granted, though those guilty of capital crimes would be checked for socio- or psychopathic tendencies. Your regime is not such, so cases would be reviewed under Polity law and those found innocent of any crime would be released. But intercession is unlikely.'

She was studying me very closely, her gaze intense as if trying to penetrate behind my eyes. In that moment it occurred to me that she had not said imprisoned 'people' or 'citizens' but 'sentients'. That put a whole new gloss on the reason behind her question, and I shivered. I think she noted that reaction. Glancing aside, she stood up, then faced me again, her gaze no longer so unnerving.

'I will perhaps ask you this again when you visit Corisanthe Main.'

'Interesting place,' I said, gesturing to her gift of the palm screen with attached control baton. 'I would be most interested in seeing this Worm.' I paused for a moment, because this was critical. 'I am sure Polity scientists would be interested in anything you might be prepared to share with them concerning it, just as they would perfectly understand if you decided not to share anything at all.' It was the diplomatic thing to say, yet I was still having trouble getting my head around the idea of Polity AIs taking a none-of-our-business attitude to a seriously weird piece of alien technology.

'Information is best shared,' she said noncommittally. Now she gazed at me with a look I can only describe as prurient, and for the first time in many years I actually felt nervous in the presence of a woman.

'Was there anything else?' I asked.

She stood up from the mattress and ran her hands down from her neck to her thighs. 'No, I think that's it.' The atmosphere almost crackled. She stepped up to me and took hold of the fabric of my shirt, running it through long-nailed fingers. 'Oh,' she said briefly, abruptly turning and heading for the curtain. She shot one final coquettish look at me then departed.

It took me a moment to put my thoughts back into order. I realized I'd just been played, and that this last part of our encounter was the one I was supposed to remember. She was, I realized, not only dangerous physically – this evident from the way she had dealt with the guard in the hold upon my arrival aboard this ship – but clever and manipulative.

– RETROACT 3 –

Yishna – *to Corisanthe Main*

'I knew your mother, you know,' he said.

At twelve years old Yishna had managed to pass herself off as eighteen. Now, purportedly a twenty-year-old, everything she was working towards hung in the balance. Her documentation had been approved, her promotion confirmed, and her luggage was already aboard the interstation shuttle here on Corisanthe III, ready for the journey to Corisanthe Main. Now this: *I knew your mother.*

'Really,' said Yishna, no clever get-out clauses occurring to her. She should have taken this eventuality into consideration. Her all-consuming aim to study the Worm aboard Corisanthe Main was, despite the size of that station and its population being in the tens of thousands, sure to put her in the way of some who had once known Elsever Strone.

'Please, take a seat.' With a short pecking gesture with his forefinger and thumb pressed together, Oberon Gneiss, Director of Corisanthe Main, indicated the seats on the other side of the alcove. Once she did as he asked, he elbowed the wall control to slide out a table surface between them, then picked up a matt-black case and dumped it before him. As he studied her, she noticed how his yellow eyes, with their irises deeply delineated, almost spoked, somehow gave him an almost insentient look.

'A very clever and a very complex woman was Elsever Strone. She too earned her position on Corisanthe Main when quite young.' He cocked his head at her queryingly. 'But not as young as you, it would seem.'

'Elsever Strone?' Yishna pouted thoughtfully. 'I've heard the name, but I don't see the connection. My name is Deela Freeleng – perhaps you have mistaken me for someone else?' She smiled at him brightly.

He shook his head, more of a twitch really, as if to

discourage an irritating insect. 'All three of your siblings have been caught advancing themselves through the Sudorian education system faster than seemed possible. But upon review and retesting it was discovered that though they had altered their ages in their records, they had not cheated in respect of their qualifications. Your brother Harald was caught at the age of twelve, a year after Orduval and Rhodane. You have evaded detection because as well as your age in your record, you changed your name too.'

Yishna sat still and quiet. She could have continued arguing that she was Deela Freeleng, but knew that a few simple tests would find her out. Her combat training would not help in this situation – she and her siblings had excelled at this regimen that had remained obligatory ever since its introduction during the War and it had helped them in many a tight corner. She wondered if using sex might get her out of this, having employed it ruthlessly since puberty, but now felt it somehow wrong to resort to that to attain her final goal. However, that was not the whole of it: there was something distinctly odd about Director Gneiss which made her suspect he would not be easy to manipulate. She could not read him as easily as she did others, which suggested he was either incredibly complex or that his motivations were not something she had encountered before.

'Have you been told how your mother died?' Gneiss asked.

'An accident aboard Corisanthe Main. She went outside without filing her plan and somehow put herself in the way of a com laser.'

'Yes – her fault.' Gneiss opened the case and took out a touch screen, switched it on and called something up, before sliding it across to her. 'Perhaps you would like to read the real report of the "accident".'

The document was long, but it took Yishna only moments to speed-read and absorb it.

'Suicide?' she queried. 'Why?'

Gneiss shrugged, slid the screen back towards him, and called up something else. 'As you can see by that report all of your mother's actions are well detailed, and the conclusion reached is that she was suffering fast-onset post-natal depression. No one really knows, though.' He paused, elbows on the table and fingers interlaced before his mouth, then continued as if reciting from a script. 'I can provide you with any of the evidence in that report. You can even speak to some of those who were involved and who still work on Cori-santhe Main. I warn you, though, that you'll come to the same conclusions as the investigators, because in the end nobody could ever know what was going on inside your mother's head.'

Yishna carefully considered these words. Super-ficially they gave the impression he had misconstrued her motives in seeking employment on Corisanthe Main, yet she felt they were just a gloss over something else. Decid-ing to react on the surface level she smiled, crossed her legs and leaned forward. 'Director Gneiss, I have no interest in finding out why my mother killed herself. That my mother worked there is merely coincidental to my own interests in that place.'

'I find that a little difficult to believe,' said Gneiss, still from the script.

'Did my siblings advance themselves simply out of curiosity about our mother's death?' Yishna countered. 'No, they did not. From a very young age we all sought and found our vocations in life and pursued them, despite attempts by those in the Sudorian education system to hold us back. Harald wanted to join Fleet, and he has done so. Rhodane's interest has always been biology, and she is conducting much research in that area now. Orduval . . .'

Gneiss leant back, his mouth clamped in a narrow line. He did something strange then, reaching up a hand to press a finger directly below each of his eyes, as if pointing out their weirdness. Because she could not understand this action, it frightened Yishna.

'Yes, I know about your brother Orduval.' Gneiss lowered his hand. 'Unfortunate – but let us return to you. Your own interests span a wide area, covering physics, electronics, computer science and many other subjects. So you claim you are not here just to clarify your family history?'

She stared back, couldn't help putting something lascivious in her expression, and realized that this response was purely due to her fear. 'Knowing my interests and my abilities, where lies the frontier of research for me?'

He smiled tightly and without true emotion. 'Corisanthe Main, obviously.'

'But you are not going to let me go there.' She chose her words carefully so as not to appear arrogant. Reading only the surface of them, the Director's choice of words had telegraphed his intentions. She gave a moue of disappointment and let him get to it in his own time. Let him enjoy his munificence, even if it was only a skin over reality.

'I did not say that,' he replied. 'I just wanted to be sure your aims did not stem from some misguided urge to find out the truth about your mother. I take the same view that Fleet took with your brother Harald, of this being an opportunity we cannot afford to miss. You are undoubtedly brilliant, Yishna, so the alterations you made to your record will be corrected, and you will go to Corisanthe Main. The only proviso is that, once there, you will report regularly to the base psychologist.'

'I'm *going*?' Now she was delighted.

'Yes – but you heard what I said about reporting to the base psychologist?' His reply was toneless, playing the game to its conclusion without any emotional investment.

The rise of practitioners of psychology to positions of power had been increasing apace with the growth of mental illness on Sudoria. Yishna often speculated that their increased numbers had in fact resulted in the growth of mental illness, rather than been merely a response to it.

'Why do I need to do that?' Yishna asked meekly, though knowing precisely why.

'Because, though you are brilliant, your emotional development is still that of a fourteen-year-old girl.' He sat back. 'It is understandable how you got so far. Nutrition has substantially improved since the war years, and girls develop a lot faster now than then. But you are still a *girl* nevertheless.'

He gazed at her steadily and it seemed, almost palpably, that between them some kind of understanding formed. He secretly knew she was no girl and somehow she knew him. This understanding was not open to logical analysis, it was just there, and real.

'I understand,' said Yishna, bowing her head to his ostensible wisdom, and wondering what kind of little-girl persona to adopt for the psychologist. It had been such a relief to stop playing that part when she had finally departed Sudoria. Really, from the age of four she had felt a hundred years old, and necessarily played the child because others never understood the real Yishna, and just became very frightened of her. But to play that role again . . . why not? It might be amusing to probe the depth of the base psychologist's understanding of the human condition. Yes, she would play such games with whoever came to analyse her – but there would be no such games with Gneiss.

He was . . . something else.

– Retroact 3 Ends –

McCrooger

Our journey back into the inner system took two weeks, and towards the end of that time I was suffering fewer of those episodes that struck me as worryingly like the onset of schizophrenia. The length of time taken to travel such a short distance (in Polity terms) made me realize how badly these people needed U-tech, but I was glad of the extended opportunity to come to my senses. I kept busy, perpetually accessing Sudorian histories through my palm screen and taking time out only to get to know the layout of the ship better – wherever Fleet personnel allowed me – and to discuss with Duras the potential siting of the Consulate on Sudoria. But that siting was all somewhat beside the point. Quite simply, Sudoria resembled Earth of a millennium ago, when the politics of nation states were shaped by politicians, the media and public opinion – of the three the media becoming the most powerful. All a very complicated and messy process. By those who wanted greater contact with the Polity I would be employed as a media weapon – my being here already considered a victory. Of course the downside of this was that those – mainly Fleet – who did not want any contact with the Polity, would try to use me negatively in the media too. But I intended to sell the advantages, and they were many, maybe enough to eventually influence Fleet personnel, who also possessed their own voting system and their own little internecine conflicts. Maybe this was why Fleet did not seem in much of a hurry to let me go.

'It has been turned against us,' said Duras.

'If you could explain?' I prompted.

Once again we were sitting around that same central table in Duras's cabin. He eyed me carefully. 'I hoped the charges I filed against Inigis would prevent any further attempts on your life during our journey to Sudoria. But Inigis was last night arrested by his own lieutenants and confined to his cabin.'

'Surely this is a good thing?'

'Not,' said Yishna.

Duras continued, 'Fleet claimed Inigis must be tried by them, and pushed this demand through Parliament.' He explained further, 'The twentieth anniversary of armistice is only a few months away, and there has been much media programming concerning the War, and also, despite Uskaron's book, much nostalgic sympathy aroused. So when Fleet said, "We must try him in full public view to wipe this slur from our integrity" and then put it to the vote, they received the support of most of the planetary delegates.' Duras glanced at Yishna. 'Even some of the Combine delegates voted in favour.'

Yishna said, 'Membership of Combine does not automatically eliminate stupidity.'

'So now either you suspect another attempt on my life, or some attempt to traduce me?'

Duras continued, 'While you are out here, we can't protect you too well. They don't want to move against you overtly, and by now Admiral Carnasus and the rest realize that you are not going to shuffle off your mortal coil with a mere whisper and a sigh. Inigis was a fool, who thought he could raise his position in Fleet Command by getting rid of you. Carnasus, however, will not want you to die aboard a Fleet vessel. After all, Fleet is responsible for you, and will get to look bad if you die wholly in their care, and in such circumstances Combine representatives,' he glanced at Yishna, 'myself and the other members of Parliament would be pushing for Carnasus and his staff to be charged with murder.'

'So, the alien will instead be paraded in court and made to look foolish, dangerous, sly, or any combination of the above?'

'We rather suspect so. It will be an open session aboard the *Ironfist* – all media representatives allowed. However, aboard *Ironfist* the Fleet Admiral, Carnasus, himself wields the power. And that ship is presently in orbit around Brumal.'

Yishna shook her head. 'Fleet will probably draw comparisons between you and the Brumallians. This won't be about Inigis, but about you. Certainly they'll try to find some reason to eject you from the system . . . perhaps because of that "organic technology" Inigis detected inside you.'

'So, how do you think I should deal with this situation?' I asked.

'We will prepare you as best we can,' said Duras. 'There is no system of advocacy in Fleet courts, so you must represent yourself.' He grinned. 'But in the time I have come to know you I feel you to be quite capable of that.'

Our meal time then became a rather morose affair, with further speculations about what Fleet intended. Eventually I changed the subject. I turned to Yishna.

'Tell me about your brother Harald,' I asked.

Her usually seductive expression hardened for a moment, then with a false indifference she said, 'Why must I tell you about him? He is not my only brother.'

'Whatever.'

There were obviously painful memories there she did not want me to probe. Instead she told me about her brother Orduval, but I failed to see how the memories of him could be any less painful.

– RETROACT 4 –

Orduval – *in childhood*

The displays – inside ranks of glass cases stretching into the distance, within the Ruberne Institute's museum – were of more interest to Orduval because of what they *signified*, rather than what they were. Of course Yishna, Harald and Rhodane were utterly absorbed – studying every item intently and whipping through the readout projected up in the glass of each case before moving onto the next. Orduval studied every item no less intently, but his concentration focused primarily on the readouts. Why that choice of words, why this aspect of the exhibit emphasized over that, why phrase the description in quite *that* way? He made comparisons between readouts obviously written before the War, those written during the War prior to this place being closed down and the exhibits being stored away, and those written within the last seven years, after the War had ended and when the exhibits had emerged from long storage. The changing zeitgeist of Sudoria and the political consciousness of the author of each readout became all too evident to him.

Before the War he found the optimism of the times and the societal wealth reflected in the pretentiousness of the writing – in the flowery language and literary flourishes. In the subject matter concerning artefacts from the *Procul Harum*, emphasis was on their archaeological significance only, which contrasted with the Military Intelligence 'Eyes Only' labels fixed on some of these, like the ancient notescreen he presently observed, evidencing how during the ensuing War they had been taken away by wardens of GDS – Groundside Defence and Security – doubtless in an attempt to recover lost technologies. Readouts written during the earlier stages of the War itself were quite often either plain wrong or full of grammatical mistakes – the author obviously being distracted by contemporary events. Some of those written deeper into the War, especially if they concerned *Procul Harum* artefacts, became propagandist, and often a disparaging commentary about the Brumallians crept in, even when the item in question did not require any mention of the enemy at all. Others written a little later seemed devoid of emotion: the exhausted Sudorian now beyond any irrelevancies, merely wise, bitter and tired.

Next, viewing a skirl nest sectioned to show its internal construction, Orduval did note a recent addition to the readout that began to wax a little too lyrical for his taste. Obviously this indicated that wealth and optimism were again on the rise.

Here he paused, noting his sister Rhodane a few paces further along, her face hovering close to a display case, and with her hands pressed against it on either side of her blonde head. She seemed unnaturally still as if frozen in the process of trying to force her way through the glass. Out of curiosity he strolled over to her and peered into the same case.

'Almost certainly it will become politically unaccept-able to have such items on display within the next five years,' observed Orduval. Checking the readout confirmed its authorship during the War, just before all the museum items were stored, and that the Brumallian, grotesquely stuffed and mounted in a threatening pose, had been placed inside the case during that harsh time.

Slowly, Rhodane turned towards him. 'I *know* now,' she announced. 'This is where I fill the gap . . . cancel out the black.'

She had mentioned this before, this gulf in her mind. He always assumed it to be the onset of clinical depression, though he did not entirely understand it himself. At the core of his own mind a white star seemed to burn, around which lust for knowledge spun in ever tighter orbits.

'Perhaps you could explain?' he asked.

'It's my place – my compass.'

Yishna felt this certainty – as did Harald, stronger than any of them. Orduval felt only blurred and frustrat-ing reaches of self-direction. A surge of jealousy filled him, and immediately upon that followed confusion and unease. 'That's nice for you,' he muttered, and with a feeling almost of desperation, headed away.

Moving on through the museum Orduval realized that, continuing at his present rate, he would not see more than a quarter of the artefacts during the day Utrain had allowed them, so he must now manage his time more efficiently. Having strayed into the planetary biology section (where the Brumallian did not really fit) he turned around and began working his way back along another section of *Procul Harum* exhibits. Here he observed family heirlooms on loan to the museum: books, old notescreens, pens, timepieces graded in terran time, clothing and jewellery. One long case even contained pieces of the ship itself – some recovered from old buildings and others dug up from the landing site. Orduval halted by a plaque engraved in some ancient pictographic Earth language, and stared at it for one long confused moment, realizing he simply did not understand it. Desperately searching through the readout he discovered only that the language was Chinese, but not what any of it meant. He would need to research this.

Moving on, he halted before a mannequin representing a pre-landing human and stared at it intently. But the pictographs on the earlier plaque seemed to have come with him, imprinted on his retina and flickering across his vision. Some part of his mind refused to give up trying to understand them, refused to accept that until he learnt more, elsewhere, understanding would be beyond him. He tried to stop the thought process, tried to think of other things, but the spinning in his head just grew faster and faster and the star grew brighter.

Migraine?

He knew the effects, and a blind spot was now developing so that when he looked at the mannequin's face it folded into non-existence. Next the mannequin itself disappeared and something slammed into his face.

I fell over . . .

He was down on all fours when the star flashed bright white light through his mind, and everything went away for a time. It was an experience to which he never grew accustomed.

– Retroact 4 Ends –

McCrooger

Brumal hung there in the blackness like a mouldy apple, a glittering ring encircling it. Red and green predominated on the surface, and cloud masses the colour of iron and cheese mould swirled over this. A greenhouse effect raised the surface temperature here which, were this world like Earth and possessed of a moon to strip atmosphere, would have been cold enough to freeze brine. I studied the planet long and hard, finally discerning the mountain ranges like raised red scars in the green. Many of those were not there just over twenty years ago. In their place once lay cities – nest-like arcologies spreading underground. Those peaks now stood like tombstones over mass graves containing over a hundred million crushed and suffocated dead.

'So what made him decide to open up this?' I gestured down the corridor lying alongside the hull, from whose windows armoured shutters had been raised.

Duras grimaced. 'Despite your request and my

request, First Lieutenant Drappler was not prepared to do anything that lay outside Fleet regulations. He has not taken too well to such a level of responsibility, and is not comfortable giving orders while his captain is still aboard, though confined to his cabin. I rather suspect he contacted Fleet Command for guidance.'

Upon learning of the presence of this viewing gallery aboard, I had immediately tried to gain access to it for, being accustomed to Polity ships with their chainglass screens, panoramic windows and virtual displays providing you on request the illusion that you stood out in vacuum, I was growing claustrophobic.

'There, do you see it,' Duras pointed, 'just coming into silhouette?'

With the raised light sensitivity and magnification of my augmented eyes, I'd noticed it much earlier, but was waiting for Duras to apparently spot it first. This was not because I didn't want to give away too much about my enhanced abilities, but because I did not want to hurt the man's feelings, did not want to make him feel inferior.

'So that is a hilldigger,' I said with due reverence.

From this distance all Duras himself must be seeing was something like a black finger passing across the face of Brumal. I could clearly see its long rectangular body, the big fusion engines to the rear, the weapons blisters spaced evenly down its two-miles length, and the larger Bridge and command area positioned at the nose, and directly behind and below that, the two fins that were the business ends of a gravity-disruptor weapon. Yes, there were Polity ships large enough to store hilldiggers in their holds, but the vessel in front of us seemed no less formidable for that. I just needed to look at those mountain ranges behind it to be reminded.

'Yes,' sighed Duras, with satisfaction.

The Sudorians were proud of their hilldiggers, an attitude especially prevalent amongst Fleet personnel, and present in both Yishna and Duras though their interests conflicted so violently with those of Fleet. But I understood that, because Yishna had told me she was born during the war, and Duras informed me he had once been a Fleet conscript. It is too easy for those standing at a distance to question such pride. As anyone ever involved in a war would say: 'You just had to be there.' The hate may eventually evaporate, but the pride and the grief remain. And, in the end, all Sudorians rightly believed that the hilldiggers ended a conflict that could have dragged on indefinitely exacting a huge Sudorian death toll. I considered parallels to this throughout human history, especially the first use of nuclear weapons on Earth over a millennium ago. Of course those weapons were used against the bad guys – but here that matter had recently become debatable.

'What were the enemy's warships like?' I asked.

'Big, like this,' Duras sketched a teardrop shape in the air, 'and in their space stations they were able to manufacture them faster than we could make ours.' He glanced at me. 'They just kept on getting closer and closer to Sudoria. By the time we manufactured the first hilldigger they'd managed to get eight thermonukes past our planetary defences.'

'Fifteen hilldiggers were constructed?' I observed.

'Eventually.' He paused thoughtfully, then went on, 'They weren't called hilldiggers at first – that nickname came after. We didn't have gravtech weapons until after twelve ships were manufactured.' He closed his fist and cracked it into the palm of his other hand. 'Then we went in and smashed them.'

I knew the details. The big ships had at first comple-mented planetary defences to stop anything getting through. At that time Brumal was lying a full third of its planetary orbit – of about three solstan years – away from Sudoria, whose year is only a thousand hours longer than that of Earth. The first big push came when the two planets drew athwart each other, about a solstan year later, but it proved inconclusive. The next pass, a year later, decided matters.

With their new weapons the hilldiggers clocked up victory after victory. Three of them were destroyed in the conflict, but all the enemy ships were turned to twisted wrecks and the large space stations about Brumal were smashed – hence that glittering ring of debris. Then Fleet moved in to hit the population centres below. The destruction continued because, with the infrastructure of Brumallian society so devastated, methods of communi-cation were knocked out and they themselves so bewildered by what was happening they were unable to negotiate terms of surrender. I rather suspect Fleet would have ignored them anyway during the assault on Brumal itself. Absolute surrender ensued when commu-nications were finally restored.

During the twenty years from then until now, the Sudorians established bases down on Brumal and kept a close watch on the remains of Brumallian society. The hilldiggers were used twice more: once after it became evident the old enemy was building nuclear power plants, and again when a nuclear explosion destroyed one of the Sudorian bases. Subsequent investigation revealed that the explosion was caused by a Sudorian terrorist group who felt sympathy for an old enemy they considered as oppressed as themselves. That was a sure sign of attitudes slowly changing under a regime becoming more liberal after the oppressive restrictions of a century of war. Advanced human societies, go figure.

Our own ship would continue decelerating around Brumal for the next ten hours, before coming in to dock with *Ironfist*. I chatted for a little while longer with Duras, then headed first to the refectory for something to eat – finding myself ignored as usual by the Fleet personnel there – then to my cabin to get some sleep. Later, as we came in to orbit Brumal, I stood again at those windows observing those mountain ranges rucked up along shores where cities once bored deep into the ground, beside the blue-green oceans over which storms now swirled – the environmental fallout from the carnage still evident.

I didn't see the approaching missile, for the armoured shutters slid closed. The impact buckled the floor, flinging me from my feet, and fire sheathed the ceiling before air screaming out of a nearby breach sucked it away.

I didn't need the wasp-lights to tell me we had a problem.

3

So what are Brumallians? If I declare they are utterly alien to us, will that make us feel better about killing millions of them? It is their very alienness that made them less of a threat to us, for as a place to live our world is irrelevant to them, and its resources would be harder for them to obtain than those lying available in extra-planetary asteroids. But despite their strange appearance, they are not really that alien. They still have wives and mothers, fathers and children, bawling babies and sulky teenagers, millions of whom were crushed or suffocated under billions of tons of rock and earth. What did they do wrong to suffer that fate? They communicated with us, but those who ruled us at the time saw only a people that could be portrayed as a threat and used to open the coffers of our society; then they defended themselves when attacked and died fighting to protect their world. And in the end they were martyred by Fleet, and sacrificed to our illusions.

– Uskaron

McCrooger

The lights and the klaxon indicated a level-three emergency in my current location. *Really, you don't say.* I ran along the buckled floor, the breath issuing from my lungs in one continuous exhalation as the pressure dropped. As I rounded the corner, the bulkhead door in the corridor leading inward was just six inches from the floor. I stooped down to catch hold of its lower rim and heaved up. Something thumped behind a nearby wall, and when yellow oily fluid began flooding out of cracks between riveted panels, I realized I'd just burst the hydraulic ram closing the door. After ducking underneath, I then pushed the door all the way down to the floor, where the vacuum developing on its other side sucked it back against its seals. The next bulkhead door was also clos-ing. I treated it in the same way and moved on further into the ship, fortunately approaching my cabin without having to wreck any more hydraulic rams.

'We have been struck by a missile fired from the sur-face of Brumal,' the ship tannoy announced. 'All crew to stations. Don survival suits. Bulkhead doors from Green Five to White Three closing.'

On the other side of those bulkhead doors the emer-gency lights now indicated a level-two emergency, which suited me better. It occurred to me how convenient it would be to Fleet if an attack by the Brumallians resulted in my death. The missile had struck close to me, and I've no doubt the crew had at all times known my precise location within this ship, so I'd felt rather disinclined to use any of the escape-pods in that immediate area. I reached my cabin, took the survival suit provided for me from one of the lockers, inspected it for a moment, then tossed it back inside. Just as I closed the locker door, the ship lurched and sent me staggering backwards. Gravity fluxed, dropping then rising high before stabilizing.

'Reactor breach! Engineering section report. Close

and dump Silo Three. Level-three emergency, non-essential personnel only!'

The announcer was beginning to sound a little rattled, and I glanced up as three wasp lights lit. Experiencing a change of heart, I retrieved the suit and donned it. Maybe Fleet personnel had sabotaged it, but I wouldn't be any better off without it unless they had done something blatant like filling its air supply with poison gas. Another lurch, and then grav went off completely.

'Silo Three—'

Some sort of massive detonation slammed the ship sideways, cannoning me into the cabin wall. The door curtain blew in, smoking in now boiling air. I pulled myself along the wall, dragged open another locker and took out the gifts from Yishna and Duras. I was about to head off and find the pair of them when I saw a light flashing on my little palm screen. I keyed it on and Yishna's face gazed up at me.

'Are you in your cabin?' she immediately asked.

'I am.'

'Get to an escape-pod at once. Duras and I are already aboard one. Maybe there is some plot behind this, but certainly the ship is in serious trouble. One of the conventional warheads detonated inside its silo, space-side. We're going down.'

'Might Fleet be prepared even to lose a ship just to get rid of me?' I suggested.

'Yes, they might.' Her image blinked out.

I threw their gifts into a draw-string bag and pushed myself off towards the door. A crewman was propelling himself along the corridor outside. I recognized the foamite suit worn by ship's cadets. He was young, fat-faced, with an oily queue of black hair and adolescent acne. He glanced at me, panic clear in his features, as I sped past him towards the door leading to an escape-pod. He quickly followed me in and, making no comment, pulled himself down onto one of the acceleration couches, where with shaking hands he strapped himself in. As I did the same, the hatch abruptly closed, and a roar of acceleration forced me down into my couch. Looking up I saw that the emergency lights were still only on level three. The puzzlement mingling with panic in my companion's expression confirmed for me that something was wrong. Only at level four should the hatch close and the pod be ejected.

'My friend,' I told him, 'I think you picked the wrong person to share an escape-pod with.'

He just stared at me while shaking some pills from a tube he had produced and popping them into his mouth. This kind of dependence on drugs seemed quite common here.

After that initial acceleration there came a spell of quiet weightlessness, then began a steady droning which grew into a vibration. I recognized the signs – we were beginning to enter atmosphere. I wondered if someone had fixed for this pod to burn up during re-entry. However, as I began to unstrap myself, the engine started up, decelerating the pod. Evidently not the burn-up then, probably just a parachute failure.

'What did you mean?' asked my companion, after some delay.

I grimaced at him. 'I rather suspect that my surviving to get inside an escape-pod has been factored in to their plans. Tell me, can a pod's internal systems be operated from elsewhere?'

Confusion for a moment, then dawning comprehension, followed by fear. 'Yes, they can – if you possess the command codes.'

I scanned around inside. The five couches were arranged radially, facing in, on a forty-five-degree tilt against the hull. The ceiling was slightly domed above us, and a central column carried various controls as well as storage compartments for food and water. I took the half pace towards the column, deceleration gravity at about two gees. 'Tell me, is it possible to do a manual release of the parachute?'

He nodded, unstrapped himself and laboriously hauled himself up beside me. Keying a palm screen on the column, he called up a schematic of the pod. The pod itself was of pretty simple construction: a sphere with a nose cone on one end, HO motor at the opposite end and with combustion actuated in little more than a dish, and directional thrust from air jets around the pod's equator. The parachute sat underneath the cone, and should be released as explosive bolts blew away the cone itself. My companion appeared ready to cry when, after he input some instructions, the words 'Chute Access Unavailable' then 'Manual Override Unavailable' appeared on the screen, two red diagonal strikes blinking on and off over the nose cone.

'My basic interpretation of that is that we're fucked?' I suggested. He slumped back into his couch, miserable and staring at me accusingly. I turned my attention to the ceiling. Doubtless the chute resided behind that rectangular panel, itself secured in place with about fifty Y-head bolts. The guys who packed the chute probably

used some sort of electric driver to screw those bolts
home, but I doubted there would be one handy in here.
I took out the knife Yishna had given me and inspected
the blade. It was certainly sharp but might also be
brittle, so to try using it to undo the bolts would be a
mistake, and anyway I didn't have the time. Reaching up
I pressed the blade flush against one side of a bolt head,
then pressed, hard. The entire head sheared off and
pinged around inside the pod. My companion looked up,
his mouth falling open.

'How did you . . . do that?'

'It's just a knack,' I replied.

I began working my way round all of the bolt heads,
sending them pinging and clattering all about me. As I
got to the last two, the drive shut off and we were in
freefall. I hauled myself up, clamping my legs around the
control pillar, and managed to shatter the knife blade
while trying to break away the last bolt heads. Two bolts,
damn. I closed a forefinger and thumb around one of
them and tried turning it, but I must have turned it the
wrong way for the head sheared off. Good enough. I did
the same with the remaining bolt. Next, fingers digging
in at the panel edge. Jammed in place. I punched a dent
in the ceiling right beside it, opening a gap, shoved my
fingers in and heaved. The panel tore away from protruding bolt shafts. Peering inside I saw coils of wire packed
in what looked like cellophane wrapping, all attached to
heavy crossmembers, while above these parachute fabric
hung like a padded ceiling. Grabbing one of the crossmembers I pulled myself up until the crown of my head
rested against the covered wires. The exterior of the pod
curved down away from me so, forcing up parachute
fabric, I pushed my arm down that curve and groped

around a bit, eventually closing my hand around a smooth cylinder.

'How many explosive bolts?' I asked.

'Six,' he replied.

This could be rather dangerous. I didn't know how stable the explosive was in the bolts, and if I got this wrong I could get my hand blown off. But then, hitting the earth at a few hundred miles an hour wouldn't do me many favours either. Exploring with my fingers I found that the base of the cylinder terminated in a flat plate welded to the hull, so that was the fixed part. Feeling above this I found a shaft, extending from the cylinder to attach to the nose cone above. I got hold of that, and pulled until it snapped. No explosion. Diametrically opposite this bolt I found another similar, and snapped that off too. Then another bolt, at sixty degrees from a line drawn between the first two, then a fourth opposite that. This one blew just as I snapped the shaft.

'Aaargh! Fuck!'

A sudden roar ensued as one side of the nose cone lifted. Abruptly the pod began tumbling. My friend below, who foolishly had not strapped himself in, yelled in panic as he was flung from his couch. He would have to look after himself however – I needed to get this done quickly, for impact with the ground could be imminent. Pulling out my arm, I inspected the length of steel now punched through my palm and out the back of my hand. No blood of course, for we older hoopers tended not to have much of that stuff circulating in our veins. I extracted the shaft and discarded it, then paused for a moment, overcome by nausea, for while the Spatterjay viral form sealed and began to quickly heal the wound, the other viral form took the opportunity to attack its opposite. But, again, no slippage – no big advantage gained by the killer virus. I reached for another of the explosive bolts.

As the fifth bolt snapped, the cone lifted even further, exposing leaden sky and blasting in the stink of hot metal. The sixth and final bolt obviously could not take the full strain. A loud bang ensued, and a gust of wind threatened to suck me out as the parachute pack disappeared, sideways. The pod jerked hard, wire uncoiled, and cellophane wrapping snowed upward. Another even stronger lurch dropped me down inside the pod beside my companion, who then crawled up onto another couch and hung desperately onto the safety straps. I felt a momentary elation, but that soon disappeared as I saw the tangled mess of parachute squirming above.

'Should slow us a little,' I said – ever the soul of optimism.

'We're going to die!'

'Get yourself strapped in,' I snapped.

But he just clung on. I reached over to lift him up properly into the couch.

Too late.

We hit.

– RETROACT 5 –

Rhodane – *in childhood*

The little girl, Rhodane, sitting on the peak of the sand dune while tying back her long blonde hair, studied the massive gun emplacement, its linear accelerators canted to the sky, like ruined city blocks, from the armoured dome. Five years ago she remembered sitting in this very spot with her fingers in her ears while watching the coil guns send missiles screaming into the sky, and then turning to red streaks high up as air friction heated them. The experience had been exciting, and kept the blackness at bay. The soldiers were now gone, and in their place a big salvage concern had brought in its cranes and treaded machines to take the place apart. A fence now surrounded the gun emplacement itself to keep out the souvenir hunters, and the old barracks buildings nearby had been repainted in the happy colours of a temporary asylum to house the increasing numbers of those suffering mental illness – a fallout from the War, some claimed, while others dismissed it as the result of a society going soft. The place interested her much less now, she realized.

Lowering her attention to a skirl which remained unaware of her silent presence as it rotated its way up towards her, Rhodane returned to her contemplations. The long-legged white beetle would pause every few seconds to run sand through its sieves, spraying out streams of grit on either side of its head, then it would continue its advance while drawing its barbels through the sand in search of its microscopic prey. Rhodane considered what she knew about this creature. She visualized its anatomical structure complete in her mind: its downward-facing blue eyes and sensory tendrils, its ribbed abdomen and sand-scoop wings, the structure of its various internal organs, single lung and single-chambered heart, and the complex spiral gut. In her mind she also now visualized the creature's genome and began relating genes to physical characteristics. She knew this creature in ways that no other human mind on the planet could encompass. She knew many other creatures in the same way, understanding so much more than most other planetary biologists, yet the authorities had taken away her gene sequencers, splicers and construction equipment like they were dangerous toys in the hands of an infant.

Rhodane knew from an early age that she and her three siblings were very different from other Sudorians. All of them could speed-read by the time they were three, read through grandmother Utrain's book collection within a few months, then squabbled over the books and disks their grandmother brought from the local library each week. By the time they reached the age of four, the squabbling decreased as their interests diverged. Rhodane loved biology, Yishna's interests lay towards the physical sciences, Harald focused completely upon Fleet, and Orduval studied history and politics. But their intellects were so broad and inclusive that their areas of interest blurred over into each other's, and so there was still some squabbling. When it came time for them, at this age, to begin their compulsory schooling, Utrain applied for a special dispensation, taking the four of them along to the Ministry of Education so they could demonstrate that already they were beyond anything that First School could teach them – they were even well beyond their contemporaries in physical training, already attending combat classes for those much older than them. Second School, also compulsory, though with the main subjects chosen by the pupils themselves and paid for by their parents or guardians, the four attended only briefly before another special dispensation was made, and they moved on to pursue their own goals with a single-minded purpose possessed by few adults.

Yes, they were different, Rhodane knew, but were her siblings *different* in the same way as herself? Did they feel in their minds that inner hollow, like a hunger that could never be satisfied? Was the acquisition of knowledge to them like an addiction to the opiate extracts derived from strug, the pink rock fern? Did they feel that hollow expanding, and in danger of encompassing their minds in a dank black depression, if they were not constantly in the process of learning something new to feed its hunger every day? Did they fear that adulthood would find them drugged into placid stupidity inside one of those colourfully painted institutions like the one standing just over there?

The skirl drew close to Rhodane's right sandal, so she peered down at it and said, 'Hello, little fellow, how does the sand taste today?'

The skirl froze, so she tapped her fingers against her upper leg, knowing the creature would pick up the vibration through its highly sensitive feet. The skirl raised the central visual section of its head, its two blue eyes revealed at first slitted, then opening wide. It spread its pearly wing cases as it turned, flicked out its sand-scoop wings and they blurred into motion. Emitting the sound after which it was named, it skated off down the dune, spraying Rhodane with sand as it went and causing her to close her nictitating membranes in reflex. Rhodane leapt to her feet and ran after it – trying in her own small way to understand why other children found this game so fascinating. After fifty yards she could feel sweat growing slick on her body. After a hundred yards the creature disappeared from sight.

Rhodane crouched by the hole into which the creature had disappeared and brushed sand away around it, revealing the curve of the underground nest. Calculating from the exposed curve by eye she estimated the spherical nest to be about eight feet in diameter – home then to about a hundred skirls, their own separate segments of the nest filled with their young. Skirls were a strange mix of the social and the independent. When they reached Rhodane's present age, many of the females drew together to weave a communal nest with fibres extruded from their spinnerets. This task took them many years, but once the nest was completed they emitted certain hormones into the air to attract males. Rhodane now mentally reviewed the molecular structure of that same hormone. When the males arrived, a mating frenzy ensued, the males dying in the process. The females then partitioned the nest and laid their own eggs each in their own designated areas. Thereafter began the long process of raising the young, feeding them with a protein soup refined from the skirls' own microscopic diet. Fascinating . . . at least for a little while.

Rhodane stood up and moved away, scanning around for something else to interest her. But she knew this whole area, and its ecology and biology, so very well now. She would therefore return home, study the new disks Utrain had obtained from the library, and thus try to stave off the hollow blackness awaiting in her mind. Utrain had promised to take them to the Ruberne Institute tomorrow, so perhaps something there would help her to feel that all her choices were not yet exhausted.

– Retroact 5 Ends –

Tigger

This endless watching since the end of the War was enough to drive a drone to distraction. Corisanthe Main had developed a strange paranoiac society, as if the Worm were some alien splinter inside the body of humanity here, and all those living aboard the station were the crusty resultant mess of humanity's immune reaction to it. This malaise also seemed to be reflected upon the planet below, with increasing proportions of its population ending up in either asylums or cultist churches. Though maybe the reverse applied, and Corisanthe Main's weird culture merely reflected what was occurring below it. Since the end of the War, the proportion of the population suffering mental illness at some point in their lives had grown to three out of four, and one in four of them ended up permanently committed to an asylum. One manifestation of such illness was the common hallucination of some dark menacing figure who had grown in popular culture into the Shadowman. Since the publication of Uskaron's book, these illnesses had been put down to 'societal guilt' and the Shadowman was described as the Sudorian conscience. It was a worrying phenomenon that Tigger had studied closely, but drawn no conclusions from.

The technologies being constantly developed aboard Corisanthe Main, and quickly applied there, made his scanning difficult, and trying to scan the Worm itself was like trying to shine a torch through a brick. Watching the human dramas played out aboard offered some entertainment, but even with the distinctly odd Director Oberon Gneiss running the station, even that began to pall. So, without asking Geronamid, since he knew what the AI's answer would be, Tigger often went to find entertainment elsewhere, and not necessarily down on Sudoria.

On the surface of Brumal the drone was deep-geoscanning some recent developments in one growing hive city when Consul Assessor David McCrooger arrived. At last things were starting to get interesting.

David McCrooger . . . Tigger pondered that. The new-comer having been a long-time resident of Spatterjay was interesting enough but, damn it, he was also an Old Captain! Admittedly the man had captained a sailing ship there for only a short time, but he was still on a par with legendary names like Captains Ambel, Drum and Ron, who were all now entering the second millennium of their long lives. So, what might one expect from such a character? To begin with he would be unreasonably strong and durable – such men were reputed to possess greater physical strength than Golem androids, and they could easily withstand injuries that would instantly kill other humans. He might also be incredibly knowledge-able and wise. Though that was not a given, even for someone who lived so long, many of them were, and Geronamid would never have employed anyone stupid for such a task.

Moving on, from geoscanning the living Brumallian hive city to the mountains created by the hilldiggers and those mass graves that lay underneath them, Tigger applied only half his mind to the depressing task – the other half perpetually scanning Fleet coms. His other half warned him of activity amidst those ships above, and the news that the Consul Assessor would be coming to Brumal first, so Tigger decided to hang around. After the missile launched, Tigger flew fast to its launch site, and

there observed a covert Fleet military unit moving away
from the missile launcher – probably one confiscated at
the end of the War – about which Brumallian corpses had
been neatly laid out. The covert team was well away
before a laser strike from a hilldigger positioned far
above. Just enough evidence would be left to fully implicate the Brumallians.

Tigger separated completely now, his chrome Bengal
tiger form peeling away from the sphere and sending the
latter up into space, via which he observed the ship in
flames as it plunged towards the planet. Continuing to
listen in on com traffic, he discovered McCrooger was
aboard none of the escape-pods now spreading out into
space. Belatedly he detected one single pod splashing
down in the ocean, and realized it had been cut out of
the communication system. Tigger sent his tiger body
bounding in that direction, accelerating to just below the
speed of sound and occasionally grav-planing tens of
miles above the landscape. Then out over the ocean,
neutrally buoyant, paws slapping the waves and jaws
grinning a joyful grin.

– RETROACT 6 –

Rhodane – *in adolescence*

'Happy Assumption Day,' said Rhodane wryly.

Peering back at her from the flimsy screen, Harald –
clad in the foamite uniform of a chief engineer in Fleet
– replied, 'Ah, so all four of us are responsible adults now.
Words cannot express the extent of my indifference.'

Rhodane studied her brother, noting how much he

had changed in the six months since they last spoke. Back then he wore his blonde hair in the customary Fleet queue. Now he allowed his hair to grow long all over his head, and wore it tied back. His acerbic features were thinner, if anything, and his mouth was constrained in a strict line that failed to conceal his protruding canines. His pale blue eyes, however, seemed as cold as ever.

'It's all right for you, but then you escaped the net – as did Yishna,' Rhodane told him.

Harald acknowledged that with a slight tilt of his head, then added, 'Though not entirely. We have both been subject to rather patronizing supervision. I at least found the Fleet command structure so much easier to accept than did Yishna her regular psychological assessments.'

'Oh that.' Rhodane grinned. 'She's on her fourth counsellor now. I wonder how long this latest one will last?'

'And I wonder what complete change of career she'll convince this one to make. The first two returned planetside to study physics, but I'm not quite sure what happened to the third one. Apparently he irritated her immensely, and that was about the last I heard.'

'We'll be able to ask her directly – her comlink is now establishing.'

The display before Rhodane divided so that it now showed Harald and Yishna both.

'Happy Assumption Day,' said Rhodane.

'Yes, equally,' Harald added.

Yishna smiled seductively. 'It's a happy day now that I can apply myself completely and without interference to my research. My last psyche report was very good, apparently. I necessarily helped in writing it since my counsellor appears to be suffering a nervous breakdown. They're shipping him planetside soon and I suspect that, after a long rest, he will be taking an inordinate interest in cell biology . . . One for you, Rhodane.'

'We are curious,' said Harald. 'What happened to your third counsellor – the one before this one? Didn't she seriously annoy you or something?'

'She suggested my intelligence was not as high as I myself rated it since it was undermined by my being emotionally retarded. It seems I made the mistake of becoming too involved in my research and not paying sufficient attention to her. She was therefore preparing to recommend to the Director that I be sent to the Threel Asylum, where corrective measures could be undertaken.'

'What happened to her?' Rhodane asked.

'She's now a permanent resident of the Threel Asylum herself. My explanations to her of the nature of reality convinced her that there was no further point in her existing. She tried walking out of an airlock without a spacesuit, but since our mother's day the safety procedures developed have made that a difficult option.'

'As if the asylums aren't full enough,' muttered Rhodane.

'True,' said Yishna, looking slightly discomfited. 'What of yourself, Rhodane? How goes it?'

Rhodane replied, 'Now that I am officially an adult, I can freely accept one of the offers that have been made to me. Standing at the head of the list thus far are researching bioweapons with Fleet, or pharmacology and xenobiology with Orbital Combine. There are numerous positions being offered planetside, but as you must know, they don't interest me.'

'Which will you go for?' asked Harald. 'I hope you realize that bioweapons is not only concerned with new and interesting ways of killing Brumallians.'

'You *would* say that,' interrupted Yishna.

Before this turned into an argument, Rhodane continued, 'Whichever of those will get me to Brumal quicker. I have made them all fully aware of my main interest.'

'What fascinates you so?' asked Harald.

'Filling the gulf in my head, Harald. But what fascinates you so much with Fleet, and you, Yishna, with the Worm?'

Harald shrugged, and Yishna replied, 'We could always take the view that all life is empty, and so try to end it. We do what we do because we have interests beyond just our own personal existence. Why question this?'

'Because it is the one question we don't ask,' came a new voice.

The display divided again and Rhodane and the others now looked upon the ravaged features of their brother Orduval.

'Happy Assumption Day,' he added brightly. The shadows around his eyes had grown deeper since Rhodane last saw him, and his face appeared horribly thin, almost skeletal.

'Orduval,' said Yishna in acknowledgement, but no more than that. None of them bothered to enquire after his health. Why ask about the blatantly obvious and force him to tell comforting lies? She knew that Harald and Rhodane felt as she did, both guilty and relieved. It was ridiculous really: Orduval had fulfilled the mental illness demographic for them of one in four being committed to

an asylum, but that did not mean they were now immune.

'They are happening closer together now, aren't
they,' Harald pointed out succinctly.

'Three or four fits every day,' Orduval concurred.
'They won't tell me here, but it's not difficult to work it
out. If the fits continue at their present rate of increase,
and with their present adverse effects on my health, I'll
be dead within a year, either from heart failure or a cerebral haemorrhage . . . But let us return to the questions
we don't ask.'

'Those being?' Rhodane asked, though reluctantly.

'Why are we what we are?' asked Orduval.

Rhodane felt the gulf in her mind widen, a sudden
anger suffuse her, then pity. Orduval's mind was weak,
though the impulse that drove them all to excellence lay
as strong in him as in the other three of them. It was like
strapping a rocket engine to a sand sledge: now this
sledge was breaking up. Also, it could not have helped
that his consuming interest lay in subjects with no
certainty, no definition, which led to existential angst and
pointless speculation. Rhodane now felt contemptuous,
considering her brother ripe for plucking by one of the
planetside cults or the dominant religion down there, the
Sand Church.

'It has been interesting talking to you all,' Harald was
staring distractedly to one side, 'but I have fusion-pellet
injectors to strip and lengthy diagnostics to run. Stay
well.' His image blinked out.

'I too have much I must attend to, though I cannot
detail it over public com,' said Yishna, turned glassy-
eyed. Her image also blinked out.

'And you next, Rhodane?' asked Orduval. 'Some

urgent need to go out and study skirls, or to clip your toenails?'

So easy for him to say such things while confined there in that asylum. She really did have things she needed to attend to. There were those research offers from Combine and Fleet . . . Rhodane suddenly found herself hot and sweating copiously. 'I don't know what you mean.'

'You do, because of the gulf in yourself, and because sometimes you ask those questions that hurt you.'

Rhodane hesitated with her hand poised over the cut-off switch. With an effort of will she drew the hand back but, almost concurrent with that motion, the blackness in her head expanded. 'I can't . . . Orduval.'

'No, you can't, because you are constrained. You have no choice but Brumal, Rhodane. Once you get there, will you do something for me?'

'What . . . I . . .'

'Look into *your* gulf and admit to yourself what you see there.'

Rhodane's hand slapped down on the cut-off switch, and it seemed that same switch operated simultaneously inside her head.

Now, back to those offers from Combine and Fleet . . .

– Retroact 6 Ends –

McCrooger

Viral slippage . . .

Down on its side the pod moved in a way I recognized at once. Water slopping through the hole where I'd removed the hatch below the nose cone, now down beside me, confirmed that this had been a splashdown rather than a dustdown. I felt horribly sick but could not throw up, and feverish, while pain rolled through my body, yet was not centred around my greatest injury. I damned Iffildus and Earth Central, wondering if this was enough to finally tip the balance, then decided I must just continue without any expectation of death.

Iffildus was a haiman – a human highly augmented with computer hardware – an Earth Central agent and brilliant biophysicist who went rogue. Though the Spatterjay virus makes us practically immortal, as well as very strong and dangerous, on Spatterjay itself there is a natural substance, extracted from the bile ducts of large oceanic leeches, which can kill the virus. It is called sprine and is our get-out clause, our easy way out should the prospect of endless life become unbearable. The investigators supposed Iffildus did what he did because he felt hoopers to be a danger to the Polity. He mutated the virus using advanced nanotech to create a strain he called IF21. I received it in a bite from one of the leeches in his laboratory when I went to find him. Call it a mirror of the Spatterjay virus: it unravels where the original binds, it *deconstructs*, it produces sprine to kill the original virus, and it grows irrevocably. It is not yet certain that it will kill me, but then it is not certain that walking through the fusion flame of an interplanetary shuttle will kill; it's just very very probable.

With great difficulty I wrapped safety straps, attached to a couch, about each hand, then placed my feet against the couch itself and pushed back. The broken bones in both my forearms crunched and grated, and already there came some resistance from the rapid healing that had already occurred, but I gritted my teeth and kept pushing with my legs until both forearms seemed relatively straightened. I held them in that position and began slowly counting down from five thousand, which was usually how long it took for the viral fibres to rebuild enough bone to stand up against the tension of my muscles. All the time I seemed to gaze into a long dark tunnel that was ready to snap shut at any moment. Finally reaching the end of my countdown, I paused for a moment, then dropped back to the floor and unwound the safety straps. With some relief I felt the nausea and pain receding, the tunnel opening and light shining in. Now I really needed something to eat, because already what was known on Spatterjay as 'injury hunger' began hitting me.

Even without the added complication of IF21, hooper physiology is a strange and dangerous thing. The Spatterjay virus sprouts as fibres from the cells of its host, not destroying them but linking them together in a steadily toughening network. It is in fact mutualistic in that it actually increases its host's survivability. Thus a hooper can live forever and recover from the most hideous injuries. The downside of this is that the virus can actually alter the DNA and physical structure of its host. An eclectic collector of the genomes of all sorts of other creatures, the virus will use that mishmash of coding to increase its host's survivability. So a man who has lost his legs might end up with the slimy foot of a mollusc, or one who has lost his head might end up with a leech mouth sprouting between his shoulders. Unchecked, the virus will make such changes even though its host remains uninjured. Earth foods and many others will provide nutrition for the human body but very little for the virus, and thus act as a check upon its meddling. The food here in this planetary system, being very little different from Earth food, therefore served the same purpose. Injury uses up resources and if the ensuing hunger is not sated the virus moves into survival mode and can rapidly start making those physical changes already mentioned. The result can be monstrous, and not entirely sane.

However, other things first. I picked up the ceiling panel from where it lay on an acceleration couch, glanced outside at the familiar heave of ocean, then banged the panel back into place over its protruding bolt stubs. I then found a tool compartment beside the entry hatch, which was now above my head, and from this removed a small hammer which I used to rivet over some of these stubs to hold the panel in place. Now, at least, our danger of sinking decreased. I finally turned to my companion.

Of course, being a hooper, I got off lightly. He was not so lucky. The impact had snapped his spine so violently that bone protruded from his skin and blood had sprayed round inside his survival suit. Quick, anyway: he was spasming into death within a minute of our splashdown. I stooped down to pick him up, and laid him on one of the couches, securing him in place with the safety straps. There seemed little else I could do for him. So pathetic, so wasteful and stupid. I didn't even know his name. It was with a feeling almost of guilt that I started opening food lockers so I could tend to my own needs.

Noting how things were beginning to get a bit stuffy inside my ship survival suit, I removed it completely, since in order to eat I would need to remove the head covering anyway. Beyond its now depleted air supply it served little purpose, being composed only of a lightly reinforced plastic.

First I noticed the cold – my breath huffing vapour clouds into the air – then a smell like strong bleach hit me, and my lungs tightened. I recognized chlorine gas, though it was not very strong inside the pod, which would still be scrubbing its own air and adding oxygen. But should I need to leave the pod, I would be in pain for a while before my body adapted. And of course there would be the risk of further viral slippage, of further gains by IF21, and of death.

I munched my way through several ration packs containing compressed blocks of some kind of meat or of a chewy cake-like substance highly flavoured with vitamins. My hunger slowly receded but, with the repair of my body still ongoing, I knew it would soon return. Washing the food down with a litre of water, I then turned to the central column, sat astride it and began checking the pod computer.

The screen was still showing the schematic of the escape-pod. Though familiar with the touch controls of my palm screen, and these being similar, it still took me a little while to figure out just what this computer encompassed. Within half an hour I discovered that the pod was not transmitting a distress signal and that the radio was 'Access Denied'. Of course, this could be due to damage caused by the impact, but I rather doubted it. I searched for my gifts from Yishna and Duras, hooked both the gun and knife on my belt, and dropped the spare ammo clips into pockets around the waist of my shirt, then turned on the small palm screen. It certainly powered up, but provided no communication link. The Sudorians did possess their own com network or Internet, but this device was not finding it. I quickly discovered that it would work anywhere on Sudoria itself – its range being hundreds of miles – but here on Brumal it lay many thousands of miles away from the nearest relay transmitters, which were all aboard Fleet ships in distant orbit. Time to take a look around outside then.

From beside the pod's hatch a short ladder folded down to engage in sockets set in the column. It seemed evident from this that the pod must have been made to either float or come to rest in this sideways position. I undogged the hatch and hinged it up and over till it clanged down on the outer hull. The moment I climbed up and stuck my head out, an asthmatic contraction constricted my breathing and sharp hard pains grew in my lungs, as if someone were slowly driving in meat skewers. Hot pin-pricks speckled the skin of my face and my eyes began watering. My nostrils, sinuses and the insides of my mouth began to burn, then my sinuses totally closed up. I just held my position there and concentrated on breathing.

More slippage. I visualized the two viral forms inside me like two competing fig vines intertwined throughout the body of an ancient tree, one supporting it and the other strangling it. A dark sky seemed to lour over me, and again that horrible nausea overwhelmed me. I blacked out then, I don't know for how long.

The patter of rain woke me, and my exposed skin started to burn, then after a time to itch fiercely. I rubbed at blisters raised on the backs of my hands, and dead surface skin slewed away to expose new skin underneath with an odd slightly iridescent sheen. The burning in my mouth had eased to be replaced with a bitter metallic taste. It eased also in my nostrils and my sinuses, and I spat out grey slime, then snorted the same mucus from my nose. Some time after the rain stopped, the tight pains in my chest began to dissipate, and I started coughing up quantities of grey phlegm streaked with black. My body, though already adjusted massively, still had some way to go but at least I was functional again. And still alive, it seemed.

I gazed around at an ocean that disappeared into haze in every direction. The water possessed a jade hue much reminding me of the seas of home under stormy skies, while above me grey cirrus frosted a pale yellow sky. The swell wasn't too bad and, peering over the edge of the pod, I saw floats inflated all around it. Fortunately, whoever screwed the radio and the parachute had neglected to sabotage the floats too, else my escape-pod would be lying on the seabed by now. As I studied my surroundings something about them kept niggling at the back of my mind. Then I realized: everything was so clear, no displaced shadows, no weird distortion, no sense here that something might be peering over my shoulder. Had that been merely some physiological problem that the massive adjustment I had just undergone had dispelled? I could not know for sure, but was grateful to be free of it.

What to do now? Trying to swim to land, even if there was any in sight, was out of the question. Being a hooper from a world where swimming in seas swarming with voracious predators was the pastime only of the terminally insane or suicidal, I naturally felt some reluctance in that area. But even if land was in sight, I would still be unable to swim to it. Obese people float better than muscular people because fat is more buoyant. Being packed solid with viral fibres, my body was denser than ordinary muscle, and I weighed two and a half times as much as a normal human of equivalent size. If I abandoned the pod, I would sink like an ingot. I closed the hatch, dropped back down inside and found something more to eat while I pondered my options.

4

The fanatics of the Blue Orchid organization who climbed from the wrecked Procul Harum *and gazed for the first time on the arid desolation we now call the Komarl knew this world to be theirs, and wanted to experience it as humans first. More circumspect colonists aboard the ship quickly sealed the breaks in its hull and looked to what they could salvage, and what they needed to survive. The Blue Orchids, who were the prime instigators of the schism with those who went to Brumal, camped out in a desert night that was hot to them and discussed how their new world was going to be ordered. There are no records as to why* Procul Harum's *airlocks ceased to function for a couple of hours after sunrise. I rather suspect that those inside decided the first order of survival was to rid themselves of those now outside. When the airlocks were finally opened, and some wearing hotsuits stepped out onto sand hot enough to boil water, they found the Blue Orchids lying shrivelled in the sun. I guess the lesson to learn here is that though we now know how the desert can be a breeding ground for fanaticism, it can harshly punish the stupid kind.*

– Uskaron

McCrooger

Something thumped hard against the escape-pod, and I felt it beginning to move. My immediate thought, as would be the same for any erstwhile resident of Spatterjay, was that something nasty had just arrived from the sea in search of an easy lunch. I drew my gun and climbed up to peer out of the hatch, acknowledging that I must be feeling better now, since if I had still felt the same way as I had aboard Inigis's ship, I would probably have remained cowering in the pod.

The air outside didn't bother me so much this time, either because it did not contain so much chlorine or because of my adaptation to it. Nothing leapt out of the waves towards me, and I could see nothing large and sporting too many teeth hovering underneath them. The pod, however, was definitely leaving a wake behind it, as if now under power. It suddenly occurred to me that I must have overlooked some automatic system on board, so I ducked back inside, listened for motors, then once again checked the computer and, as half-expected, found nothing. I then considered a number of conspiracy theories: Fleet had hidden the pod's engine from its computer and were now controlling it remotely to take me somewhere for interrogation; or the Brumallians had learnt of my presence on the surface, and one of their submersibles had found me. Each theory struck me as wildly improbable, and each I quickly dismissed. But one quite simple explanation remained.

I climbed up to the hatch, then scrambled out so my legs were dangling down over the curved hull of the pod. Very carefully I began to inspect the sea around me, and finally began to note discrepancies in the wake as if I were viewing the part nearest to the pod through a slightly distorting glass. That I could perceive this was almost certainly deliberate.

'Okay, show yourself, drone,' I said.

'I wondered how long it would take you to figure things out,' replied a thuggishly insouciant voice.

'Perhaps I'm getting slow in my old age,' I replied. 'So are you going to show yourself?'

'They got satellites up there watching this place, but I guess I can show a little.' The head of a silver tiger materialized a couple of yards out and a little way down from me. It blinked amber eyes and grinned, making me think of Cheshire cats and suchlike.

'Nice to meet you . . .?'

'Tigger,' the drone supplied.

'Apt name. Satellites, you were saying?'

'Oh, lots of them.'

What were Fleet's options, and what were they doing now? Maybe they had just looked the other way while the pod descended, so they could claim I was killed in the initial missile attack. More likely they would want to ensure no incriminating evidence remained, so had watched the descent of this pod closely, intending to retrieve and destroy it later. Possibly they would not be able to cover up the fact that a pod had descended, since there were Orbital Combine satellites up there too. Two possible scenarios then occurred to me: the most drastic would be a weapons strike against this pod from orbit, but that would be really difficult to cover up. Fleet's most likely option, therefore, would be for them to rush to my rescue, but then sadly discover I had died during the splashdown.

But I did not need to speculate about this – I just needed to ask.

'Who's watching me now?'

'Oh, it's all getting very interesting up there. Combine have just informed Fleet of the ejection of a pod from the part of the ship where you were quartered. Fleet are claiming this was a misfiring, that no one was aboard, and that you died in the section of the ship struck by the missile; though, to cover themselves, they admit they may be mistaken and are supposedly searching for this errant pod right now. Of course they know where it is, and have been watching it for some time. Combine also knows where it is and are waiting to see what Fleet does next. With high satcam resolution on both sides, both sides know you are still alive.'

A nasty thought occurred to me. 'Of course if Fleet come to my rescue and find me dead, Combine will have enough evidence to roast Fleet and gain great leverage in the Sudorian Parliament. They could probably then ensure the establishment of a Polity Consulate despite Fleet.'

'Just a thought here,' said the drone, 'that won't make you any less dead.'

'A definite disadvantage.' I pondered my options. It had been my intention to come, at some point, to this world anyway. Any rescue by Fleet would probably prove unhealthy for me, so perhaps it would be best if I died for a little while. 'Can you cover this pod with your chameleonware?'

'Nope, an object that size is outside the range of my 'ware. But I could cover a human being, even such a large one. Like a ride?'

'Why not?' I gazed back into the pod, at its grisly

cargo. 'Sink the pod. If I'm being watched I'll have to go down with it.'

Black lines immediately cut across the flotation bags and with a *whoosh* they released their contents. The pod began to tip over and taking a breath I stepped off into the sea and went down like an iron statue. The brine was cold as death and soon, deep down in it, I could see nothing but black and green all around me. I tried swimming, just out of curiosity, but even with my strength it was a case of one stroke upward for every ten feet I sank. The drone suddenly appeared as a tiger-shaped blur underneath me. My boots came down on its back and I parted them to slide down astride it. Its back was slick metal only partially warmer than the sea, and there seemed nothing for me to take hold of unless I wrapped my arms around its neck or grabbed its ears. I was about to try one of these when tongues of metal clamped over my thighs, holding me in place. I touched that metal experimentally, surmising the drone's outer form to be a cell-form metal skin it could reconfigure at will. Then we were rising.

The drone broke from the water and began running across its surface, its paws occasionally clipping the wavetops – all for effect, of course, since it was gravplaning. I could see the machine entire now, probably because it was only 'ware-shielding itself from the satellites. It occurred to me that if any Fleet personnel saw or even recorded this, they would have a tough time convincing others of the reality. This was exactly the kind of technology Fleet commanders feared, yet were able to prevent from swamping the system only because Polity AIs allowed them to do so. An apt analogy would be that of a nation still only at the technological level of being

able to launch biplanes, laying down the law to a neigh-
bour geared up to fly stealthed Mach 10 jets and control
orbital laser arrays. Yes, as I had told Duras, we genuinely
did not want Sudoria turned into just another homo-
geneous addition to the Polity. Any more than we wanted
to utterly destroy the pride of these people, or terrify
them.

'How far to the shore?' I asked.

''Bout a hundred miles – we should be there in
under an hour.' As if to confirm this, the drone accelerated and the wind of its passage chilled my skin and
forced me back from my seat. I leant forward and oblig-
ingly a curved bar oozed up from the metal of its neck
for me to grip. I took hold, feeling slick cell-metal rough-
ening to my touch. We ran through a squall and I observed how stained my soaking clothing had become, and
that in places the cloth itself was parting. But all hoopers are aware that no clothing will ever be as durable as
their own bodies.

'How far then to the nearest habitation?'

'Another fifty. Do you want me to drop you right
there?'

'Get me within ten miles. I want to take a look at this
place before I go underground. I take it you'll be hanging around?'

'Well,' the amber tiger eyes peered back at me, 'my
instructions from Geronamid have been to keep a
watch here in this system, but to make my prime focus
Corisanthe Main, as it has been for the last twenty years.
I do have some cams positioned there . . .'

'So you are following those instructions,' I replied,
thinking some about the patience of machines – *twenty
years!* – and how even that wasn't limitless.

'Geronamid—'

'You know I've got carte blanche here, as the agent on the ground. I say I want your help, Geronamid can go suck on a black hole.'

'I think I like you,' said Tigger, facing forward again.

A while after that, land became visible as a lumpy purple-blue line separated from the sea by a line of mist. As we drew closer to shore I began to notice more life in the water below, and was reminded of home. The water remained a murky green but I began to see globular masses of something that might have been weed, and things swimming between them like foot-thick catfish: *wormfish* being the nearest translation.

'Herbivores,' commented Tigger. 'Nothing like on Spatterjay.'

Further in, I observed low rolling hills cloaked in bluey green. The beach consisted of boulder slabs, and through crevices in these white fumaroles of spume stabbed up into the air. An acidic chemical factory smell choked me and made my eyes water. By now, that mythical normal human would probably have been drowning in the fluid inside his own lungs. Tigger thumped down on these stone slabs, took a couple of almighty leaps, and came down again in a sandy cove.

'Take a break?'

'Yeah, why not.' Maybe my time schedule was tighter than I liked to admit, what with my viral problem, but I knew that ten years either way did not matter that much to Geronamid.

The two tongues of metal over my thighs withdrew and I stepped off Tigger's back down onto soft grey sand. Washed up in a tideline were numerous bones and mats of weed, though tides were rare here compared to Spatterjay or Earth, for this place possessed no moon. The tides only appeared during a few solstan months occurring three times every Brumallian year, when Sudoria passed close. As I recollected, such times were when many of the sea creatures bred. The wormfish then squirmed up onto beaches like these to bury their eggs in the sand. They hatched out between tides and the young headed inland, where they entered various pools and slow-moving rivers. By then they were carnivores, feeding on abundant pond and river life until attaining sufficient size to compete for mates in the ocean to which they eventually returned, transforming into weed-feeders on the way. No, not really like Spatterjay, for the only herbivores there were the land-based heirodonts, who were prey to just about every other life form they came into contact with. There seemed to be no predators feeding on these worms. As far as I knew they died of old age or from becoming loaded down with parasites. But the planetary almanac for this place was far from complete, so some as yet unknown predator might turn up.

'So, *you're* an Old Captain,' said Tigger.

Always that. Throughout the Polity there existed what I can only describe as an unhealthy interest in Old Captains. This stemmed from the part Spatterjay had played in the Prador–human war and other significant events much later that brought my world to the attention of Polity citizens. For it was the only world in the Polity where it was possible to attain immortality without technological intervention, and some of the sea captains sailing its oceans were the oldest humans in existence. This whole obsessive interest in us struck me as rather silly.

'Yes, I was the captain of a ship on Spatterjay, but I was never one of Jay Hoop's captives, and I arrived there a good few years after the Polity put in an appearance.'

'How old are you, then?'

'Old enough to be bored by that particular question.'

'Probably about the same age as me.'

'You don't even have to speculate, since the information must be available to you.'

'Okay, you're about fifty years older than me.'

The drone seated itself on the sand and began licking one of its paws. I gazed at it with renewed interest. On the whole, independent drones went out of fashion in the years after the Prador–human war. This was due to the rather lax quality control exercised then in the production of war drones, and because those that survived the war ranged from merely irritating and irascible to dangerously insane. They were not popular with either humans or the major AIs. After the war the big AIs no longer manufactured independent drones, but instead ones run by subminds recorded directly from themselves. However, over the years that changed as some of the subminds gained independence, and independent drones came back into vogue. There seemed almost to be a nostalgia for them, they being the product of a wild and raw time during Polity expansion. Many of the old ones achieved mythic status, like the war drone Sniper still resident on Spatterjay and still looking for trouble. Tigger was unusual in that he must have been made during the time when drones supposedly weren't being manufactured – some 200 years after the war.

'An unusual time for a drone to be made,' I suggested.

Tigger returned his paw to the sand. 'A drone is an AI, so when is an AI not a drone?'

'If language adhered to logical rules, it would con-
strain us.'

Tigger grinned. 'Now that's a quote from Gordon.'

I trudged a little way up the beach and plumped
myself down on a rock. 'Okay, as we define it now, and
probably not as we'll define it in fifty years . . . Those
that we don't call drones are permanently sited in large
structures, and though they interact with the world they
don't change their position in it. But that description
immediately falls down when you start talking about ship
AIs. Drones are merely smaller more independent AIs,
just like Golem androids are. Sildon created a more exact
classification based on power usage, processing power
and ability to move. I incline more to the idea that those
generally called AIs, and nothing else, control the world
and those defined as drones and Golem, and even
haimans and humans, interact with it. What's your point,
anyway?'

'I was incepted as a runcible AI, but some faults
developed as I expanded from base format towards that
end. I chose then to be a drone.'

'Why?'

'I wanted to interact with the world, not control it.'

'Then I wonder if what you now describe as faults
were truly such.'

'I try not to let the question bother me too much.'

I sat there and closed my eyes for a moment. I was
tired, since it had been a rather trying day. 'How long
until nightfall?'

'Eight hours.'

'Then take me inland now and drop me off.' I heaved
myself to my feet and stretched. 'I'll need some way of
contacting you.'

I don't know if Tigger had already made the thing in preparation, or simply made it right then as an extrusion from his skin. He flipped his paw at me, sending an object sailing across, which I caught. It was a chain with a pendant attached, the pendant depicting a leaping silver tiger.

'Just say my name close to it – I'll be listening.'

Technology indistinguishable from magic? In a word: yes.

– RETROACT 7 –

Orduval – *to the Desert*

It seemed the only way. His fits were becoming more frequent and the drugs being pumped into him, in an attempt to control them, ever stronger, till he could see himself soon joining the ranks of zombies he saw every day in the asylum. Orduval removed his arterial injector last, dropping it out of the window of the trans-Komarl maglev tram, along with the diagnostic device that linked him to the asylum's computer. Now back there an alarm would be ringing somewhere and the medtechs running to investigate his room. They would find it empty and they would find him gone. He had no intention of ever going back.

Hiatus.

'Hey, are you all right?' The woman leaning over him had the same concerned expression that Orduval had seen too many times before. As he blinked, everything seemed blurred around the edges, and fading light turned into a sharp pain in the centre of his skull. *Another fit*. He pulled himself upright and wiped bloody saliva from his chin, realizing he had once again bitten the inside of his cheek.

'I'm fine, thank you.'

The woman returned to her seat, obligation discharged. Orduval quickly checked the time display and the tram's current location on the screen display at the head of the carriage and realized, thankfully, that his latest fit had not taken him past the old outpost station. It would arrive there soon – hopefully before that same woman, now glancing at him with surreptitious concern, decided she was obliged to enquire further. It was always like this: first the immediate concern, then the relief once Orduval claimed to be okay, then a growing guilt impelling them to ask again after his health, to offer aid, to offer to *call* someone.

Sandposts indicated they were now approaching the station, and the tram began to slow. Orduval picked up his carryall and headed for the nearby doors, confident that another three or four hours would pass before the next fit struck him down. Peering through the window he observed a conglomeration of shacks with aluminium roofs sand-burnished and gleaming under the hot sun, their windows frosted by the desert wind, and their resin-bound sandstone walls carved by the same abrasive force into seemingly organic forms.

'Are you sure you want to get off here?' The woman again, standing up and peering out at the desolation.

'Yes, I'm sure. My brother is coming to pick me up with his sled.' Orduval turned to face her and projected as much confidence as he could muster. 'I made a small mistake with my medication, but have since corrected

that. Thank you for your concern, but I will be perfectly
all right.'

'I'm sorry to seem intrusive but—'

'Yes, quite. I'm sure you are,' said Orduval, and
turned back to the doors as the tram finally drew to a
halt and settled on the lev-road. He had deliberately
calculated his parting words to be just sufficiently insult-
ing to annoy the woman enough for her to think, *Damn
this uppity prick, I was only trying to help*, and then promptly forget the entire incident. Perhaps in some other
society she would have persisted in showing concern, but
nowadays it wasn't uncommon to see people suffering
Orduval's complaint, or something worse.

The doors folded open and Orduval stepped down
onto the worn sandstone platform. Glancing to his right
and left he waited for a moment to see if anyone else
would descend from the front or rear carriages. No one
did, and shortly the doors closed again, the tram rising
on its magnetic field before sliding away. He watched it
dwindle, raising a dust storm in its passage, and only
when it was reduced to a black speck in mirage shimmer
did he remove the gallon water bottle from his carryall,
kick the bag away from him, and set off into the old
outpost town nearby.

The wind stirred up dervishes in the dusty streets,
and moaned between the abandoned buildings. Orduval
stopped to peer inside one house and observed a beetle-
chewed floor collapsed inside, and glimmer bugs on the
walls airing their photo-active wings. Had he expected
anything else? Moving on down the street he soon reached
the outskirts and saw how orange dunes buried the road
a hundred yards beyond. Ahead of him the Komarl
desert extended, interrupted only by granite islands, for

2,000 miles towards the sea. He did not expect to reach that coast.

– Retroact 7 Ends –

McCrooger

We arrived at a clearing in the woodland, where a metal sphere six feet across rested on the ground.

'I thought *you* were the only drone here?' I said, as the tongues of metal clamping my thighs in place sunk out of sight, releasing me.

'I am the only one; that's the rest of me,' Tigger replied, as I dismounted.

My boots sank into soft loam and I peered down at a mat of damp rotting foliage subtly transformed to a bluish beige from the green-blue of that still growing on the trees. It looked like something produced by a paper shredder. Tigger padded over to the sphere and clambered up onto it; sphere and tiger then rose ten feet into the air.

'Now I must return to station before Geronamid starts shouting at me. The chief can get irate when I don't follow his instructions precisely, though he probably factors in both my disobedience and the effect of his shouting into his calculations concerning this place.'

'Doubtless,' I replied. Geronamid was a sector AI, a 'big' AI, but sometimes those of a lesser stature forgot what that status entailed. If he wanted *absolute* obedience he would have sent only those who absolutely obeyed. What I would do, and how I would react, he had already taken into account; as he had for Tigger. Predicted events here amounted to a formula inside Geronamid's ridiculously powerful intellect, with myself and Tigger as merely known quantities within that formula. Perhaps that kind of omniscience repelled Tigger, and had informed his decision to become a drone.

'Be seeing you, then, Old Captain.' The drone rose above the level of the treetops and faded out of sight as the effect of its chameleonware impinged upon me. I sighed, and then began to survey my location.

The trees – it was easiest to describe them as such – sprouted multiple trunks from large woody bulbs that ranged from three to six feet in diameter. The surface of each bulb gleamed like polished oak and the trunks like highly polished mahogany. About ten feet up they began branching and sprouting foliage. This consisted of small palm-like leaves whose separated fronds would eventually make up more leaf-litter like that I stood upon. Here and there above, I spotted dark globes up to a foot across. Perhaps they were some kind of seed or bulb that would be knocked to the ground to germinate when Sudoria's passing influence also upset the weather here and started the storm season? I didn't know for sure, even though I'd absorbed much knowledge concerning this planetary system. That knowledge still sat in my mind but, subject to the vagaries of human mentation, I had probably already forgotten about a third of it.

I set out on my way, knowing from Tigger that the forest extended for eight miles, cut through with streams and peppered with lakes, until reaching the summit of a buried Brumallian hive city. Moving into the shade of the trees, I noticed blue fungal spears piercing up through the ground cover, and began to hear the sounds of the forest: a weird chittering, something burping distantly, and a thwocking sound that could have been made by a woodpecker. To me the air still smelt of bleach, but with an additional slight undertone on the borderline between putridity and the smell of a rose – an odd combination. A few hundred feet into the forest I spotted one of the creatures making the thwocking sound: a large insectoid thing with a rectangular body, sprouting jointed legs at each corner. It clung to one of the tree bulbs, vibrating on the spot to emit that sound, and, as I passed, it extracted its tubular snout from a hole in the side of the bulb, turned its bird-like head towards me for a moment, then dismissively returned to its work.

As I trudged along I began to feel tired, and again hungry, so perhaps it would have been better had the drone dropped me closer to the hive city, but I needed time to think about recent events, and my response to them. I wanted to make my personal assessment of the Brumallians here, communicate with their ruling body – the Consensus – concerning their future course, for what the Polity achieved here depended upon them as well. After that I needed to get myself to Sudoria, intact. I could not use Tigger, since Fleet would pounce on that as proof of my having imported Polity technology. I would probably be unable to avoid the show trial Fleet was planning for me, but it being a media event, there might not be any overt attempts on my life, though the Fleet commanders would certainly try to keep me under tight control. Wondering how I might slip away from them, I did not notice the figure watching me until it emitted that same odd chittering sound I had heard earlier.

I stared across the intervening twenty yards at a squatting humanoid figure. Its skin was mottled dark green, black and creamy white and bore a chequered texture as if a net had been drawn over it tightly. Its hands were shaped little different from my own, but a spur thumb sprouted from the juncture of wrist and palm on the opposite side from its normal thumb, and another sprouted at the elbow, lying flat against its fore-arm. The creature's long neck extended forward, and connected to the skull in such a way that if it had risen vertically from the body, as with most humans, those wide total-green eyes would have been staring up at the sky. It possessed no nose and its face jutted forward at the bottom, terminating in saw-toothed mandibles that vibrated before its hard-looking mouth. It wore dun-garees cut off at the knee, and sandals, and metallic rings adorned the extended neck. A Brumallian.

While continuing towards it, I raised my hand in greeting and then signed the query, 'Correct course to the city?' gesturing ahead. The Brumallian language con-sists of a lot more than hand signing. There are numerous clicks, pops and sawing sounds I could not produce unaided, since I lacked their mandibles.

The Brumallian first stood there, eyes growing wider, then made a sound similar to that of a brick being thrown into a bush. Though I could not myself make similar sounds, I did recognize their meaning: 'What the fuck are you?'

I now tentatively identified this one as a female. Duras and his associates had transmitted holocordings to Geronamid. I had spent many hours studying them so that I could more fully comprehend Brumallian society and better recognize its components. I supposed my initial difficulty in identifying her sex might be due to her being just an adolescent.

'I'm a friend,' I signed. 'I am a Consul from the Polity.' Believe me, conveying that last bit made the joints in my fingers crunch. I then wondered if I'd got it wrong when abruptly she turned, dropping down on all fours, and hurtled away with a lizard-like gait. Maybe I'd unwittingly said something obscene or threatening. Then I reconsidered: perhaps from a distance she had mistaken me for a Sudorian, but as I drew closer my lack of a breather mask and sheer size must have become more evident. Being accustomed to living in hive-like conditions, Brumallians were probably a touch xenophobic – much preferring to face anything alien and new with plenty of their fellows around them.

I trudged on, and within an hour I reached a treeless area spanning both sides of a wide, slow-moving river. Here the soft ground showed a multitude of trails cut between spongy masses of growths resembling huge chanterelle mushrooms. These, standing waist-high to me, were coloured slick green on top and urine yellow underneath. I thumped the edge of one in passing and the whole mass of it vibrated, sending black crab-things the size of marbles scurrying out from their boreholes in it. I quickly discovered that I could not approach the river here since, after moving a few yards out on this soft ground, I began to sink. The closest I did manage to approach was by climbing up onto the mushroom growths and using them as stepping stones. However, upon reaching the ones nearest to the river, I saw that ten feet of glistening mud still lay between me and the water.

Then there was the murky water itself. Masses of weed like green caviar floated on the surface, things like black commas as big as fists shoaled everywhere, and quadruped insectoids, seemingly fashioned out of iron pipes and barbed wire, stepped from weed mass to weed mass. One of these, pausing too long astride a gap over the water, helped remind me that other creatures resided here too when a great yellow mouth engulfed it. The worm body of its owner then turned in the water like an ATV tyre, before disappearing with a final cocky flip of its meaty tail. I quickly returned to seek firmer ground.

Remembering how the Brumallian girl had fled over to my right, I turned in that direction in the hope of finding a river crossing point. Soon I came upon a trail worn deep into the ground and there turned back towards the river again. I don't know why I expected to find a bridge, since on Brumal it made perfect sense to instead find a tunnel burrowing underneath the river.

The oval brick-lined pipe speared down into the ground at forty-five degrees, its arched entrance poking up from the soft earth like the end of a Victorian sewer. The smell exuding from it reminded me of a damp shower cubicle recently scoured and disinfected by a Cleanbot. Leaning against the arch I peered inside. At first I assumed it utterly lightless down there, but as my eyes grew more accustomed to the gloom I discerned a pale blue glow, so I entered.

Just beyond the entrance, a series of steps led down, and there were hand grips grooved into the brickwork of the walls. As daylight began to grow dim behind me, I came upon the first of the overhead lighting units: a blue ovoid hanging from the ceiling attached to ornate black ironwork. Only when it shifted and repositioned itself did I realize my mistake, and now recognize the light itself as the body sac of a large tic, the black 'ironwork' comprising its thorax, legs and feeding head. I wondered what it fed on, and decided not to linger there in case I found out. Belatedly, as I moved on, I realized that what I had just seen was a biolight – a product of genetic manipulation, not nature.

Where the steps ended I was forced to wade on through about a foot of water. From somewhere nearby came a sloppy rhythmic sound, as of dinosaurs mating. Some kind of pump was preventing this tunnel from flooding, but after seeing that biolight I wasn't sure I wanted to *meet* this particular pump. To my surprise, at a point I estimated to lie directly under the midpoint of the river, I crossed a much wider tunnel that seemed to follow the river's course. Had I now reached the hive city's suburbs? I briefly considered turning left or right, but decided it would be better if I continued on towards the city overland, arriving in full view of lots of inhabitants. Judging by the reaction of the girl earlier, I didn't want to come unexpectedly upon any Brumallians down here – no telling how they might react. Another flight of steps came into sight ahead, and thankfully I ascended them. Once out of the water, my boots promptly disintegrated on my feet. As I stopped to kick off their soggy remains, I also noted long rips and spreading patches of yellow now decorating my clothing, and surmised that it would not be long before that fell apart too.

Finally I returned to yellow daylight, but my eyes did not even get time to grow accustomed to it before something big, heavy and smelling of boiled hammerwhelks, slammed me down into the mud.

– RETROACT 8 –

Yishna – *on Corisanthe Main*

After stepping from her quarters Yishna paused to breathe in the metallic air of Corisanthe Main, then turned to the two Ozark containment technicians. The OCTs were a power aboard this station, and wore their own distinctive uniform of sticksole slip-ons, knee and elbow protectors, and a garment tube covering them only from thigh to solar plexus. This tube of tough fabric sported numerous pockets and tool loops, and was cinched around the waist with a wide belt into which they tucked their armoured gauntlets – markings on the gauntlets denoting their rank. When she first saw these people it annoyed Yishna to feel herself reacting like any ordinary groundsider to their near-nakedness, for she understood their attire to be entirely practical for working in the hot confined spaces around the Ozark Cylinders.

'DalepanOCT. EdellusOCT.' She acknowledged them both, though her gaze lingered on Dalepan, the male. He nodded to her, his thumbs still hooked into his belt, but said nothing. Edellus grinned widely, and Yishna allowed her gaze to stray to the woman's large naked breasts overhanging her garment. She conceded to herself that though such attire was undoubtedly practical for their job, letting those two hefty objects swing free could only be a hindrance. Clearly practicality here had transformed into a fashion statement and a defiant assertion of lifestyle choices. Only later did she learn that Edellus was a member of the 'Exhibitionists' – one of the many subsects among the OCTs – while most

other OCT women kept their breasts strapped up, both
for decency's sake and to prevent them getting caught in
any machinery.

'Are you carrying any com hardware or storage
mediums?' Edellus asked Yishna.

'No, I am not.' Silly question really, since the importance of not taking anything along into a containment
cylinder that could be appropriated by a worm segment
had been hammered into her from the moment she
stepped off the inter-station shuttle.

'Are you mentally prepared for bleed-over?'

'I am prepared.' That one was easy since it required
a singularity of purpose, tight focus and no distracting
emotional problems: on the whole an attitude of mind
that described herself and her siblings only too well.
However, not having yet experienced 'bleed-over', she
did not quite know what to expect.

'Then follow us.'

Walking behind the two techs, she felt the almost
ceremonial air about all this. An intensity, a strangeness,
existed on this station, and people who stayed aboard for
any length of time changed in odd ways – the OCTs were
a good example – so that the society here differed considerably from that of other Orbital Combine stations.
Yishna wondered if this might be the result of bleed-over
occurring outside the Ozark Cylinders. She decided it
seemed likely.

Her quarters being located on the lower level of the
station, they had to take a lift tube up to reach Centre
Cross. The shaft was nil gee, so they had to pull themselves down into three of the four buggy chairs and strap
themselves in. After ensuring each and every buckle was
secure, Dalepan tapped a button on his chair arm, and

the buggy revolved to close off their entry point, before shooting up through the shaft, cramming them back into their chairs at one gravity. Only when the buggy slowed to approach the Centre Cross did the necessity for the straps become evident, as their bodies rose against them. After halting, the buggy then revolved towards the exit, and they unstrapped.

Yishna felt her excitement and trepidation growing. This was it: she was finally here. Stepping out after the two OCTs, she studied the Centre Cross Chamber. The roof was lit with star lights, giving the entire place a mystical air. Throughout the massive space, study units like lev-tram carriages were suspended on jointed crane arms, their occupants visible poring over touch-screens. Cables hung in liana loops between these units, and also connected to the four main ducts extending towards the containment cylinders. It was nil gee in here too, grav being maintained only in the study units, and then only when it would not interfere with research. Many OCTs could be seen at work in various surrounding areas: either maintaining or installing equipment. From the lift-shaft nexus, tubular cages extended to four quarters – reaching each of the inner caps of the Ozark Cylinders. Fortunately, these caps did not have to be opened for gaining access, since secure locks led through them.

The two OCTs demonstrated their facility in nil gee by going down on all fours and moving fast and easy along the tube cage leading to Ozark Three. Yishna felt clumsy and awkward as she followed them, receiving constant bangs to her elbows and knees which demonstrated why the OCT uniform necessitated those knee and elbow pads. Shortly they reached the secure lock where Dalepan and Edellus took out their control batons and relayed to it their input codes, then stepped back expectantly. Yishna pulled herself forward, hurriedly removing her baton from her belt cache, and twisted its ring controls to her input code, and sent that too. The heavy door – a great bung of solid iridium steel – thumped and hinged open. They passed through this, then through another smaller door – with similar security – finally reaching a small anteroom where breather masks were provided to cope with the inert gas that filled the containment cylinder they were about to enter.

As Yishna donned her mask, then allowed Edellus to check it fitted properly, she slowly became aware of a background murmur, as if she occupied only one room of many and crowds of people in the other rooms were conducting polite but insistent conversations. Then came an abrupt dissonance, as if a screeching lunatic was trying to fight his way through the same crowds. Briefly the tenor of the conversations altered, the strident madness infecting them all – till the atmosphere became suddenly threatening. Yishna felt a moment of panic, and realized she was tightly gripping Edellus's wrist.

'Some cannot feel it until they are right beside the canister itself,' Edellus informed her. 'We will have to watch you, for you are obviously sensitive.'

Yishna released the woman's wrist. 'Bleed-over?'

'We say it is the very thoughts of the Worm affecting us all by telepathic inductance. Those who style themselves more rational than us tell us telepathy is a myth, and that the Worm does not think, but they can offer no other explanation for the phenomenon.'

Yishna would normally have pointed out that such rationalizations were ever the excuse for religion, and when things remained unexplained that was simply because no rational explanation had yet been found. There was no need to attribute such phenomena to the kind of mystical sources beloved of cultists. But instead she said nothing, for now her normal rationality and love of empiricism deserted her.

Another door admitted them to the scanning area where station scientists conducted remote study of the Worm. Yishna inspected the giant heads of the multi-spectrum EM emitters and receivers poised around the giant canister below them, like thorns around a bug. Subversion-hardened machinery actually penetrated the canister: the heads of the nanoscopes, other emitters and receivers, and diamond probes and other mechanical tools. Intervening spaces were webbed with power and data cables and support frameworks. To perform maintenance impossible to conduct from outside, the OCTs always entered here in threes, so they could watch each other. Yishna now understood why.

The invisible muttering crowd seemed packed shoulder to shoulder all around her, but just slightly out of phase with the reality she knew. She heard occasional distinct words, 'location . . . compression . . . death . . .' and began to feel a terrible anger, yet Yishna had always considered anger a destructive emotion and had trained herself to avoid it. Thoughts started surfacing in her consciousness. She saw Orduval having his first fit on the floor of the Ruberne Institute museum, remembered eating sage cake with blueberry jam, began making random calculations, wondered about starting a lesbian relationship with Edellus and considered strangling Director Gneiss because he knew too much about her. She could make connections between these thoughts, and logically argue how they had proceeded into her consciousness, yet felt on a deeper level that some outside influence had forced them there. *Telepathic inductance.* She understood why the OCTs felt the way they did, and felt her own fear grow as members of that invisible crowd all around now fell silent and seemed to turn their regard upon her.

Bleed-over.

Station Director Oberon Gneiss, the man with the weird eyes and seeming emotional disengagement from the world, had stated that those studying the Worm must gaze upon it with their own eyes and feel its presence, for otherwise they could too easily fall into anthropomorphism and an expectation of the prosaic. Though Combine scientific communities frowned on the irrational, they valued imagination. Very well. Yishna tried to separate herself from the effect and to focus on her purpose here. She had come to study the Worm, so she forced her attention back to analysing her surroundings.

There were several scorched and melted places around the central canister. They called it an information fumarole breach when the Worm began to take over some piece of equipment, even equipment hardened to such attacks. A huge energy surge, tapped from massive capacitors lodged in Centre Cross, usually solved the problem, but to the detriment of the equipment that had been breached.

'Let us go down now,' said Dalepan.

Pushing off from the lip of the airlock, they descended towards the canister. It was fashioned of a ceramic-steel composite except for one end-cap, that one being optically polished diamond. A lattice of grip bars stood out only a few feet from the cap in question, the knurling cut into them worn smooth in places by the clench of sweaty hands. Edellus and Dalepan took hold on either side, leaving a space in the middle for Yishna. She noticed Dalepan was staring in through the cap, while Edellus kept her face averted. Catching hold of one bar and placing her foot on another, Yishna too peeked inside the canister.

Tangled bright complexity faced her: metallic ophidian movement squirmed across her optic nerves till she felt the need to scratch those places in her head, even though her eyes stood in the way. The mass lying underneath six inches of optical diamond seemed to be in constant motion, though when she focused on any part of it she saw no movement at all. This effect seemed to nibble at the periphery of her vision, at the edges of all her perception. At first she felt herself being observed, as she herself would observe a bug landing on her hand. But then the intensity of that observation increased, and it seemed a star-shaped crevice opened in her brain, and into that began to drain away all her self, all her will. There seemed a solution to all this contained in the patterns behind that diamond pane, if she could but stay a little longer to figure—

'Time to go.' Dalepan was gripping one of her biceps, Edellus the other.

'No, I just need to—'

They pulled her away from the bars and launched all three of them towards the airlock. She wanted to fight but, as the fascination broke, she realized how futile that would be since there was no way to get back there until she reached something to push off from again. However, by the time they reached the airlock, Yishna started to feel the fear, and did not want to return.

'We thought you might be a scratcher,' Edellus told her, as they unmasked.

'Scratcher?'

It appeared that one in fifty of those who looked upon the Worm would tear off their masks and try to scratch out their own eyes. The OCTs then warned her about after-images flashing in her visual field, and that if they occurred she must consult the doctor immediately, since the eye-scratching sometimes occurred *after* the visit to the canister. She also learned that her seemingly brief moment before the diamond pane had actually lasted for an entire hour. But now, with the formalities over, she could begin her apprenticeship, and decide the course her future research would take. Though, of course, Yishna had quickly decided her area of study would be *bleed-over*, as she searched for the god in the machine.

– Retroact 8 Ends –

5

Our ancestors here used biotechnology far in advance of what we Sudorians currently possess (though perhaps not in advance of that employed by the Brumallians). They used adaptogenic drugs and DNA-editing nanomachines, esoteric surgical techniques and viral-recombination therapies, but these weren't really enough. They knew with absolute scientific certainty that this world would kill them before they could enjoy grey hair. It was already killing them. Changed but not completely adapted, they took all that they and their machines could carry, and headed south out of the Komarl and into cooler climes. During the journey a quarter of them died, and a further quarter of them died while they set up their domed encampment where the city of Transit now stands. The survivors managed to endure simply because they limited the time they spent outside their specially cooled domes, where they worked quickly to raise the next generation. That next generation was created by drastic alteration of the embryos they had imported. The children inherited, and were free to walk outside but, as their parents and educators died around them, they did not inherit everything. Machines fell into disuse and technologies were lost, as these children tried to build a

society. They did not yet understand that the nuts and bolts of
civilization are more important than political infighting.

– Uskaron

McCrooger

Face down I could not see what had me trapped. It must
have leapt on me from the top of the tunnel exit. Just to
the right side of my head I could see one long jointed
finger the size of a banana, looking like it was made of
brass gone verdigrised on its upper surface, and terminating in a vicious though translucent talon. Chummy
growled with gurgling wetness beside my ear, which gave
me the benefit of its pickled-herring halitosis. I brought
my elbow back – not too hard since I did not really know
my assailant's intentions. It made a glottal *urf* and a long
red tongue slurped down the side of my face. I heaved
myself up, lifting it with me, reached back and grabbed
a thick wrist, rose onto one knee, then threw the creature
over my shoulder, slamming it down hard into the mud
before me. I then paused, somewhat at a loss on observing the form of my assailant.

About three hundred pounds of something looking
like a cross between a monitor lizard and a Rottweiler
struggled there on its back, panting for breath. Its chest
was a ribbed shield of yellow and green, its dog's head
and the rest of its body was that same verdigris-and-brass
colour, without fur, reptilian. Its thick lizard tail whipped
back and forth, and it gazed up at me with mismatched
eyes – one blue and one brown. I stood up, not recognizing this creature from the Brumallian planetary almanac.

It was also not alone.

I pretended indifference for a moment. Most of

my upper garment now hung bunched over my right shoulder and down that same arm. I slowly retrieved the ammunition clips from the waist pockets and tucked them into my belt caches, along with the gun and the palm screen – the belt being the only part of my attire that did not seem to be deteriorating the same way as my boots and top – then I tore away the soggy decaying cloth and dropped it to the ground. Finally I turned my attention to the four Brumallians who were now stalking towards me.

They wore uniform clothing: bulky camouflage fatigues to match our surroundings, and strangely shaped helmets to fit the odd structural angle of their heads. They were armed with long double-barrelled guns holstered across their stomachs. One of them carried four rings attached by lengths of wire: presumably manacles to be placed upon me once their pet had subdued me. The pet which now, finally regaining its feet, sped away to slink around about behind them. Now two of them drew their weapons.

I held up one hand and signed, 'No need for that. I am not here to cause harm.' I wished I'd spotted these four earlier, because then I could have remained 'subdued' and let them manacle me. Now they had witnessed my strength and might be scared of me – which was never a great thing when the one fearing you held a gun.

They halted, and one of those pointing a weapon at me buzzed and clicked, 'Should we kill it?' accompanying this question with one-handed signing almost too fast to follow: interrogative, myself plus two names, consensus request in rhetorical mode.

The one with the manacles replied, 'Not yet.'

'It must be a splicing, but it talks,' added the gunman.

'Not yet,' said another gunman.

'It talks,' added the last.

It took me a moment to realize 'splicing' meant 'gene-splicing' – something which, judging by their decidedly odd pet and the pump and the lights in the tunnel behind me, they obviously knew how to do quite well. I also noticed how their speech seemed to be blending together, and realized this was a sign of underlying pheromonal communication which had to be slower than sound.

'Do – you – understand – us?' asked all four of them together, speaking that language of stones in a food processor nice and slow for this retarded creature. The sentence seemed to slide from each to each of them, all of them speaking the words but emphasis on each separate word coming from different individuals.

'I understand,' I signed, 'but for obvious reasons can only use hand signals.'

They needed to discuss this:

'Could it be a splicing –'

'– from the Sudorians?'

'We doubt it. They couldn't splice a grug –'

'– with a froud –'

'– without making shollops.'

No equivalent translation in any language I knew. The first two items mentioned I vaguely recollected as being some kind of mollusc, though I did not know what a shollop might be. This equally shared comment was obviously amusing, for they near split their cheekbones with their clattering and buzzing laughter that followed.

'Or gloms,' one added, obviously slow on the pheromonal uptake. The laughter became tentative – there's always one who tries to stretch a joke too far, even when shared so closely.

'Do you think he'll put on the manacles voluntarily?' asked one gun-waver, surprising me by speaking this entire sentence alone.

'Will they work?' asked two others. The one holding the manacles wound up the connecting wires and hung them from a belt hook. They turned and eyed their pet, which seemed to have now taken a special interest in a nearby tree and commenced some kind of strange backwards and forwards dance beside it, before finally raising its leg and urinating copiously, raising dense clouds of steam. Its eyes crossed as it missed its target entirely. The two turned back to me, the one with the manacles now drawing his gun.

'You will first remove your belt. You will walk between us, then ahead of us,' said he.

The others added, 'If you try to run we will shoot you.'

'If you try to attack us, we will shoot you.'

'And if you disobey an order we will shoot you.'

That seemed to cover all bets, so I removed my belt and let it drop, then, while holding up my ragged trousers with one hand, I signed with the other, 'I am a Consul from the Polity.'

'Polity?' all four again. 'And when did you come up with that idea?'

My problem here was that the word 'Polity' in their language came across as 'political unit not of Sudoria or Brumal', hence my difficulty in signing it. And now that they were parting ranks and waving me ahead of them, I could not explain, since even doing the hand signs with both hands before my chest was difficult enough.

As I strode ahead of them, the dog thing moved through the trees off to my left and occasionally bark-growled ferociously as if to cover its embarrassment at its earlier pitiful performance. My captors meanwhile chatted amongst themselves.

'He's a big splicing, and very strong.'

'Yes, but increasing muscle mass like that you always lose out in the cerebral area.'

'Did you see the way he threw Tozzler?'

'Is that why he thinks he has no loyalty to either world?'

'We should think so.'

'Probably escaped from some secret breeding pro-gramme.'

'Yeah, some idiot trying to make quofarl again.'

'No use in a space war.'

'You need brains for that, not brawn.'

It was easier for me not being able to see them, for I could pretend to myself that each comment found its source in a separate individual, despite this not being the case. I noticed how infrequently they used the word 'I' as in that 'We should think so.' The first question prob-ably found its source in one or more of them and the answer came back the same. Communication was going to prove difficult for me, and that same difficulty was per-haps one of the underlying reasons for the war between them and the Sudorians.

After trudging through yet another rainstorm, which turned into lime-coloured hail that beat at the trees like falling gravel, we eventually reached the edge of a lake. By a jetty was moored a fan-powered boat. I halted before reaching the shore, and turned round carefully. The one carrying the manacles now placed some kind of com device below his ear so it lay along his jawbone. His mandibles clattered and I recognized segments of the communication: code language, like Morse, but rattled out so fast I could barely pick up the occasional word or vague meaning.

'I am surprised,' he finally said in speech I *could* understand.

'We are surprised,' the others added, putting away their weapons.

'This Polity –'

'– is real –'

'– but remained Consensus-denied until the information reached proving threshold.'

The four moved closer to me, and one of them held out a bag made of some material similar to canvas. I accepted it and nodded my thanks – not being able to sign my gratitude since if I did that what remained of my trousers would end up around my ankles. Shaking the bag open I found it contained my belt, its caches open, and my gun, palm screen and spare ammo clips. The belt still seemed okay, so I used it for what it was designed. Surprisingly the gun remained gleaming and pristine, as did the clips – probably designed for warfare down here in this acidic environment. The screen, however, was warped and stained, and when I tried to turn it on it made a buzzing sound, part of the screen then melted, and the device emitted a puff of smoke. I tried detaching the control baton, since that might still be workable, but it just snapped in half. With great reluctance, since these devices had been an invaluable source of information, I tossed them on the ground, then passed the bag back to its owner.

'We will await Consensus Speaker,' two of the Brumallians informed me.

'So my story been confirmed?' I signed.

'Sudorian individuality,' they decided, 'from Earth. We are out of Consensus until update. Part of the job. You will not be shot. Go full speak – one individual.' What followed I could only assume to be some chemical debate in the air, then the one with the manacles spoke alone: 'Why are you here?'

'To establish relations between the Polity and the humans living in this system,' I replied.

'*All* humans?'

'Yes.'

'But why are you *here*?'

'Because the ship taking me to Sudoria was hit by a missile. I landed in an escape-pod – incidentally one that was sabotaged.'

'Fleet?'

'Quite possibly.'

All four now said, 'We must await the Consensus Speaker. An update is imperative for us. We cannot communicate with you while uninformed, since this encounter is too important.'

Four sets of mandibles snapped shut, then all four of these . . . individuals? Difficult to decide really . . . all four of them abruptly sat down cross-legged on the ground. I realized I would get nothing more from them and so sat down too. Tozzler edged his way over from the trees, came and paced around me stiff-legged, then abruptly sank down between me and his masters. Thus we remained for about an hour – the only sound being a rustling from the trees, the lapping of waves in the lake behind me, and the occasional thunderous rumbling of my stomach.

– RETROACT 9 –

Director Gneiss

Gneiss sat in his chair gazing at a screen display which, divided into four, showed views through the diamond pane end-caps of each Ozark canister. The tangled complexity within appeared ever on the point of movement, like some simple optical illusion, and seemed to offer him answers to questions – but questions he did not know how to pose. He felt as if the images he saw pressed on his eyeballs, and sometimes wondered if that pressure lay within the skull behind them. But Gneiss had always been stubborn, and so resisted something he could not even identify.

The only child of parents who had remained desert nomads despite all pressures to join 'civilization', he had inherited their pig-headedness and forever been a trial to them. He had in his early years learned all they taught him about desert survival, but then, before he even reached his teens, he decided their lifestyle was not one for him. Informing them of his decision had perhaps not been the brightest idea, because it developed into a contest of wills with them, often culminating in physical violence. They did not win in the end, for at the age of thirteen he packed up his meagre belongings and fled, taking himself off to the nearest city to acquire a 'proper' education. His parents came after him but, having rejected the society they now entered, they did not know how to fight the systems that would keep Gneiss from them. Despite having obtained what he had apparently wanted, Gneiss remained an outsider even within the Sudorian orphanage and schooling system. But ensuing years of conflict opened his eyes to the fact that his stubbornness, candour and uncommon intelligence would have made him an outsider in any society. Those same intransigent qualities finally secured him his promotion to the overall directorship of Corisanthe Main.

The view of the four canister end-caps was one Gneiss called up regularly to remind himself that he was only human and must never *again* become complacent about his charge. He gazed frequently at the mind-distorting patterns so as to accustom himself to them, to toughen his mind and harden himself against their influence. Leastways, this is what he assured himself when given time to distance himself from the hypnotic experience. For during it he felt himself to be pitting his will against that of the Worm. Sometimes, as on this occasion, he felt himself locked in a conflict he could not resolve but which, oddly, enabled him to remain obstinately himself.

Standing abruptly, Gneiss turned away from the images and walked over to a mirror inset in his apartment wall. He noted the even spokes radiating his irises, like two small wheels inset in his eyes, and remembered a time when they had not been like that – some months before Yishna Strone was born. Upon first noting this change, and suspecting some strange influence from the Worm, he had them medically checked but found that nothing else untoward could be detected. He reached out and palmed the carved head of the snake swallowing its own tail which formed the mirror frame, and stepped back while the mirror itself turned sideways into the wall to reveal the cavity of a small lift, into which he stepped.

As the lift carried him down, he opened a small hatch and took out a visored breather mask to place it over his face. The direction of the lift's acceleration changed, then changed again, and he clasped a handle beside him as he became weightless. Shortly afterwards the lift slowed to a halt, and then revolved partially to open into a gloomy chamber.

None of the sensors here in Ozark One would report his presence, since he had long ago instructed them to ignore him. He pushed himself down in an angled trajectory he was well accustomed to, and after a few moments of weightless flight closed his fists on the hand bar positioned before the transparent end-cap of the Ozark canister. Now, without an imaging system inter-vening between him and the Worm itself, the effect upon him was distinctly more powerful, as was the effect of that muttering madness called bleed-over. It almost felt as if something was reaching out physically from within the canister, to push the patterns shimmering before him through his eyes and deep into his head. His customary response was instant: a solid mulish stubborn resistance. This was his parents trying to shape him into what they envisaged was a more perfect version of themselves. This was his political teacher trying to impress on him some ideology obviously at variance from reality. This was the constant pressure of Sudorian society showing him the easy path to conformity. And it was Combine society trying to deform his mental shape to fit a particular niche. He resisted with the flat negativity of an iron wall.

Gneiss remained obstinately himself.

Gneiss accepted that this conflict prevented him from being anything else.

– Retroact 9 Ends –

McCrooger

While studying my erstwhile captors I remembered how their body chemistry was weirder than their appearance. They could breathe atmosphere such as once killed soldiers in the trenches of ancient Earth battlefields, and could eat bivalve molluscs and worms containing enough sulphuric acid to burn through hull plating. But, as I saw it, their main difference to 'normal humans' was a mental one, stemming from the hive-like set-up of their society and the consequent ways they had of communicating. It seemed as if, when together, their minds partially conjoined.

This sort of thing had happened back in the Polity once or twice, when certain groups using cerebral augmentations tried to set up gestalt societies, which never lasted since each individual had been originally *raised* an individual. Such societies would inevitably break apart, often with many of their members needing psychiatric help for a long time afterwards. I wondered if here the formation of a gestalt had been a matter of necessity, or just resulted from their severe genetic modifications. It may even have been planned by some or all of the original settlers, but I would probably never find out for sure.

After about an hour the sound of an engine alerted me to another fan-driven boat approaching across the lake. As it drew closer, I saw that it was another four-man vessel like the one waiting by the jetty, but with only three individuals aboard. Turning hard, it slowed by the beach and then drew up to the jetty. I noticed that the two in the front seats were very different from those waiting alongside me, and this difference became even more evident as they climbed out – one quickly securing the mooring rope to a bollard.

These were bigger, heavier, more stooped and ape-like. Their heads seemed like boulders and what I at first took to be helmets I shortly realized were chitinous plates. Then I noticed similar growths extending over the rest of their bodies. The new arrivals were armoured, not by artifice but by biology, or rather by the artifice of genetic manipulation. Both of them lacked spur fingers, had eyes sunk into hollows, and were wearing green dungarees. They carried heavy carbines suspended across their stomachs, from which cables extended to packs resting on the near horizontal part of their backs just behind their shoulders. Their mandibles were huge and, upturned like tusks, were obviously intended for more than simply gustation.

Standing up, the four with me in unison announced, 'Quofarl.' I glimpsed hand signals implying both trepidation and amusement.

Soldiers, I realized, created by a society dependent on genetic manipulation and under the intense pressure of war. I wondered if these two creatures had been fashioned back then, or if the Brumallians still created them.

One of the quofarl remained by the boat, while the other one, dropping down onto all fours in the disconcerting way of these people, accompanied the third figure as she headed towards us. She proved to be a Sudorian woman clad in some kind of tight-fitting envirosuit.

Halting within a pace of me she inspected me from head to foot from behind a flat visor, then said in Sudorian, 'Remain standing right there until I come back for you.' At her beck my four companions followed her to the edge of the forest. I couldn't hear what was being said, nor could I see any sign language, for the quofarl stood directly in the way, glaring at me. Even when I tried to shuffle to one side to see more, he shuffled across to block my view.

'How are you?' I signed to him.

'I have a headache and it makes me tetchy,' he immediately replied.

'Is she a Consensus Speaker?'

'She is,' he replied.

'I couldn't help noticing she's Sudorian,' I signed.

'You got a problem with that?' he asked.

'Why should I have a problem?'

'Just checking.'

The woman returned, while the other four headed down to their boat and climbed in. Tozzler leapt in last, lying across the laps of the two sitting in the rear seats. The fan started and they pulled away. I raised a hand and four hands were raised in return. Strange people, these Brumallians, but I felt I could get along with them.

'Consul Assessor David McCrooger,' said the woman, 'I am to take you to the ReconYork. Meanwhile I would like you to explain to me how you came to arrive on Brumal.'

'You're what they describe as a Consensus Speaker, yet you're Sudorian,' I countered.

A hint of a wry smile crossed her features. 'My race

has not prevented me becoming a member of Brumallian society. Are things very different in your Polity?'

'No,' I admitted.

She led the way down to the boat, the quofarl falling in behind us. 'Perhaps if you would continue?'

'Well,' I began, 'my intended destination was Sudoria . . .' and then related to her the events resulting in my presence here on Brumal, though omitting Tigger's part in it all, merely saying that the escape-pod had washed into the shallows. As our boat pulled away, the fan became too noisy for me to be heard, so I then tried Brumallian signing, to which she responded easily. I had finished relating my story by the time we approached the far shore, where the quofarl at the helm shut off the fan, then turned on some grumbling electric motor within the boat's hull to chug us into the mouth of a canal.

'What's your name?' I asked.

'Rhodane,' she replied.

'You already knew my name when you met me, so I'm presuming you know a fair amount more about me and where I come from. Perhaps you can tell me what you've learned so far, and I can fill in the gaps?' I suggested.

'We've known for some time that my former people have been communicating with the Polity, but we learnt only recently that a Consul Assessor was being sent. Only within the last day did we hear what you've now con-firmed.'

'Your *former* people? Do you now consider yourself a Brumallian?'

'I do.'

'That's . . . unusual.'

'Not as much as you might think. Many Sudorians

have come here, abandoning their old allegiances to join the Brumallians. This place is an oasis of sanity. Now, perhaps you could explain the exact purpose of a Consul Assessor?'

On considering my own experiences before arriving here, I wondered if 'oasis of sanity' might be more than just a throwaway comment.

The canal cut its way through land cloaked with tough thorny bushes of gnarled grey twigs laden with red and green spheroids which were either berries or something equivalent to leaves. Ahead squatted two pylons, rising either side of where the watercourse cut through a ridge. They were topped with elliptical structures rimmed with windows – likely either watchtowers or weapons platforms. To my right something suddenly rose squalling from the bushes. It looked like a huge headless bat with a whip tail and light blue skin. I briefly glimpsed a folded-in mouth pouting horribly from its forequarters, before it dropped from sight again.

'The title "Consul Assessor",' I told Rhodane, 'is an amalgam. I'm ostensibly here to set up a Consulate on Sudoria, though it is quite possible I won't manage that very quickly. During the interim I am to assess the situation here, and report on it back to the Polity.'

'How will you report to the Polity?'

'Through the comlink established on Sudoria.'

'You could have set up a Consulate here, so why there?'

It was a rather silly question, but I have known for longer than I care to think that even silly questions can elicit useful information. I decided to be brutally honest. 'Because the Sudorians nearly bombed the Brumallians back into the Stone Age and' – I glanced at her – 'your new compatriots are no longer a power in this planetary system. To establish a Consulate here, the Polity would need Sudorian permission, which we would not get.' I studied her for a reaction, but behind that visor her expression remained opaque to me. 'Were we to establish a Consulate here without Sudorian permission, that would only lead to conflict.' I left it at that, not adding that conflict was something we wanted to avoid, because I did not want this conversation to lead to questions about what circumstances might provoke us *not* to avoid conflict.

We passed on through the ridge below the two pylons, and slowed to a halt in the first of a system of locks. Below us lay an area forested on its further rim and circled by the distant jut of pylons like those behind us. Within this lower area were many mounds of spill, chimneys belching smoke or steam, and large oblate buildings muscling from the ground like fungi. Canals and roads, busy with barges and wheeled transport, networked all of this, in places disappearing underneath some of the buildings, or spearing off into the forest. I saw all of this only briefly, as once the first set of gates closed behind us, the water inside the lock began to drain, quickly raising twenty-foot lock gates to cut my view. These eventually opened to allow us into the next lock, from where I now noticed huge earth movers working the spill piles down below, before my view was again cut off. Another three locks followed before the system finally released us out onto the canals I had spied from above.

'Tell me about the Polity,' Rhodane instructed.

This I did, though not painting the Polity in too glowing colours. The general populace of Sudoria must still resent the Brumallians, so I did not want this

Consensus Speaker – and adopted Brumallian – enthusi-
astically advocating further contact with us, since that
might cause just the opposite reaction from her 'former
people'.

The canal cut straight through a muddy landscape
on which grew fungal growths like those I had first
encountered beside the forest river, but here speared
through with stands of plants similar to horsetails. The
bleach reek became stronger, but there were other odours
as well: a farmyard smell consisting of decaying excre-
ment and warm animal bodies on a winter morning;
something resinous as in a pine forest, probably from
those horsetails; and other astringent odours usually
associated with some sort of chemical plant. The air was
also noticeably warmer – the temperature having risen by
at least five degrees – which of course tends to make
things smellier.

We finally drew into the shadow of one of the oblate
buildings glimpsed earlier, chugged through an arch into
the interior, which was lit by the pale sunlight shining
through thin translucent walls. The building was filled
with the sloshing, sucking racket of water being shifted.
Great clams opened and closed rhythmically, spilling
foot-wide pipes like a vomit of spaghetti, and all exterior
smells were soon drowned out by one I recognized
from home: the meaty smell of open molluscs. Our craft
motored to a halt in a circular pool, more gates closed
behind us, and the water level began to drop fast. Then
down a mile-deep pipe we descended into the organic
gloom and cacophony of the hive city ReconYork.

Harald

As he entered the *Ironfist*'s Bridge, Harald observed
with his uncovered eye crewmembers becoming con-
spicuously busy at their stations. Many feared him, for
which he felt both gratified and ashamed. From the
moment of his arrival on *Ironfist*, Harald had climbed
with almost unhuman brilliance through the ship's ranking
system, so it had been quite predictable to Fleet commanders that, out of the many candidates, he would be
the one to attain the rank of captain-in-waiting. Not so
predictable had been his successful pursuit of the role of
ship's tacom. He felt that most other Fleet personnel just
did not understand the power inherent in the position of
ship's communications, logistics and tactical officer. But
perhaps, after he had finally centralized those various
duties aboard *Ironfist*, creating for himself the rank of
Fleet Tacom Commander, some understood too late.

Harald's other eye – the covered one with its surgically altered lens, grid-division of the optic nerve and
channelling in his visual cortex – gazed upon four separate scenes displayed on the eye-screen shrouding one
side of his face. The earphones of his com helmet played
audio information he could call up by using the control
glove on his right hand, in conjunction with the eye-
screen. He could play messages as text, and reply easily
by using programs created in the computer modules
imbedded in his foamite suit. The non-standard surgical
alterations within his skull enabled him to multi-task to
a degree unknown to the tacoms aboard other ships, for
he could also easily interact with his immediate environment. Still studying those around him, he called up new
displays from the multitude of satellites positioned around

Brumal. Flicking through views showing nothing but cloud, he paused to study others showing Brumallians moving about on the surface, then moved on to find the one he particularly wanted. This showed a leaf-shaped craft settled down on the ocean, the waves hammering its outriggers.

'Com 324 – status?' he whispered into the helmet mike, after selecting the correct channel for his demand.

'We are in position. Sonar indicates a depth of one mile and we have found the escape-pod. Difficult retrieval since the weather is kicking up and images from below not so clear, but we are lowering a robot now,' replied the tacom officer aboard the craft he observed.

Harald paused, realizing he was clenching his teeth, and deliberately relaxed his jaw before speaking: 'Let me know the moment you find it,' and was at once annoyed with himself for having issued a needless instruction. He offlined the relevant screens and comlink, did a personnel search checking the location of Admiral Carnasus, then resumed his walk across the Bridge to the spiral stair leading up into the Admiral's Haven – Carnasus spent much time up there nowadays, as Harald increasingly shouldered the burden of the old man's command. Since the Admiral's attitude to invasive new technologies was not the best, Harald removed his coms helmet and control glove, along with his side arm, and left them in the security box situated at the foot of the stair. Nothing he could do about his surgically altered eye, since it comprised no single pupil, but a honeycomb of fibre-optic lenses below its flat surface. He climbed up to speak with his superior.

'Ah, there you are, Harald, so what's the news?' Carnasus sat in an old wooden chair upholstered with hide that was now worn and cracked. He had moved it to where he could gaze out through the narrow windows overlooking the body of the hilldigger *Ironfist*. Harald eyed the Admiral's cooling hat, resting on the floor beside the chair, and surmised Carnasus must have removed it upon hearing him mount the stair. Sympathy and contempt for the old man warred for predominance inside him.

'Good and bad,' he replied. 'The Polity Consul survived the Brumallian attack, to reach the surface of the planet intact. We detected him with one of our satellites.'

The Admiral grimaced at this news. While Harald knew that Carnasus would never have countenanced a direct attack on the Consul Assessor, he would make no objection to the Polity intruder dying inadvertently.

Harald continued, 'Our spies informed us that a Combine' – Harald sneered his next words – 'geological survey satellite, which we positioned for them, also detected him. However, his escape-pod then sank in deep ocean, so we do not expect to recover him alive. Obviously, since that Brumallian attack, Fleet combat alert has been raised, and Parliament has since restored to us certain wartime prerogatives.'

'The parliamentary vote?'

'Most Orbital Combine representatives voted against, of course, but those planetary parties voting with us gave us a marginal win by two votes, despite the recent changes in public opinion caused by that damned book. Our new prerogatives will remain in place for the duration of the emergency.'

'That's good?'

Harald explained, 'We, being on the front line, can decide when the emergency is over. For the duration of the emergency, we can reinstate our current weapons, and manufacture of new ones at *Carmel*.'

'Yes, I see.' Plainly the Admiral did *not* see.

Harald strode up beside him and leant against the thick steel window frame to gaze out. 'What are our aims, sir?'

Eyes glazed, Carnasus recited, 'To keep this damned Polity out. We fought long and hard for our freedoms, and I do not intend to see them given up lightly.'

Harald kept his face expressionless. For the moment he remained loyal to Fleet, and Fleet sat embodied in this man beside him – who nevertheless often needed to be guided along the correct course. But the idea that they had fought then, or now, for 'freedom' was laughable at best. A hundred years ago, many sitting in Parliament were industrialists and authoritarian politicians who benefited greatly during the first twenty years of conflict. When the economy nearly collapsed, those same pluto-crats began to turn up drive-bolted to rocks out in the Komarl desert, and thereafter the war became one for survival only. And now that damned Uskaron, and his wretched book, had raised questions about why the war had started in the first place, and who was to blame.

'Our first problem,' he rejoined, 'is Combine.' He turned and gazed directly at Carnasus. 'Their laudable project for building orbital planetary defence platforms is undermining our position as defenders, and to keep the Polity out we *must* retain power.'

'Yes, Orbital Combine can be very irritating,' the Admiral observed.

Harald continued relentlessly, 'I understand from Captain Inigis's report that this Polity Consul was very tough, both physically and mentally. The Polity will certainly send another like him, and this time Combine will make sure he gets through safely by sending one of their own interplanetary ships to collect him.'

'They've got their own ships?'

'For fifteen years now, sir.'

'Oh . . . yes, indeed.'

'They've been challenging our monopoly on inter-planetary travel. Now, in order to sway Parliament against us, they're sowing stories that imply that Fleet is somehow culpable in the death of this Consul. But they wouldn't even need to do that, since everyone planet-side is asking the same question. Also, some Combine concerns are loudly advertising the fact that they're building working passenger liners to operate throughout the system, and that too is swaying public opinion, and Parliament, against us.'

'But *we* are the only space power . . . we must retain power.' The Admiral began to push himself up from his seat, but settled back readily when Harald stepped for-ward and pressed a hand gently on his shoulder.

'And we will,' said Harald calmly, 'but you have to understand that you will soon need to make some tough decisions about Orbital Combine, its ships and those planetary defences.'

'But why the defences?'

'Because with them,' Harald explained, 'Combine can *protect* its ships and its industrial satellites.'

Orbital Combine's power bases were many – the industrial satellites, their new ships, the defence plat-forms – but Harald's focus remained on their heart, which was Corisanthe Main. Because of the alien arte-fact aboard that station, it was the source of many new technologies, therefore the focus of Combine and its *main* power base. He needed to get his own people aboard – no easy task what with that place's elaborate defences and armaments. That his sister Yishna would be aboard, so might be killed in any fighting, just did not impinge upon him at all.

'I will begin making some arrangements. First we must see whether this Consul did indeed die. Apparently the satellite image showed him exposed to the atmosphere down there yet unharmed. We must also recall Captain Dravenik on hilldigger *Blatant* from Corisanthe Watch, and replace him with Franorl on hilldigger *Desert Wind*.' Harald turned to go.

'Why's that?'

'Because, in your own estimation, Admiral, they're the right people for the job that lies ahead. During this heightened state of emergency we should be able to wrest control of the defence platforms from Combine. Ships they can be allowed to control, but those platforms come under *our* remit. Parliament will certainly agree.' He continued on his way, the lie tasting sour in his mouth.

– RETROACT 9 –

Orduval – *in the Desert*

Where the orange sand lay thick across the compacted hogging of the rough track, Orduval paused, the strap of his water carrier already cutting into his bony shoulder. He hoisted the vessel up and studied the display on the solar-powered chiller unit: water temperature thirty Celsius, external temperature eighty-five Celsius. He uncapped the bottle and gulped some of the brackish

electrolyte-mixed water, then moved on, his boots sinking an inch into the sand.

By his estimation the water would last the rest of this
afternoon and into the next day; thereafter the heat
would swiftly kill him. But to die that way would be
unpleasant and only the choice of the most despairing
suicide. He would save at least a few mouthfuls of water
with which to swallow the pills in the tube that weighed
heavy in his pocket, and then only after achieving one
other thing: a moment of clarity.

In many writings they spoke about the trammelling
effects of the desert heat and how, near the point of
dying, people achieved huge insight and a beatific
moment of revelation. Orduval felt sorely in need of
such, and thought one of those experiences would be a
fine chaser into the abyss. What was he, and what were
his siblings? Sometimes, usually just before suffering a
fit, he felt himself coming to grips with that mystery, but
after the fit ended all surety left him. Only a few days ago,
on their Assumption Day, he had spoken with his brother
and his sisters about all this, but now, already numerous
fits later, he recollected the conversation only vaguely.

Orduval halted and asked the desert a question:
'What are we?'

The star in his mind seemed somnolent now, so perhaps his choosing to die relieved it of its responsibility to
keep him quiet. Walking on, he spoke now to the sky: 'I
need to know that, before the end.'

He and his siblings forever drove themselves to
excellence, and in his estimation some of them had
driven themselves beyond their own mental limits, hence
Rhodane's forever nascent depression and his own fits.
Why were they like that? Irrationally it seemed to him

that it had to be something to do with their mother and her death.

Orduval halted on the crest of a dune and gazed across the sand sea. Distantly, a rocky mount seemed to float on heat shimmer. He chose this as his destination and tramped down the dune face, sending a skirl wailing ahead of him. Some hours later, the sun low in the sky, the shimmer began to fade, but the mount looked no closer. And now only three-quarters of his water remained. He gazed down at the bottle for a moment, then . . .

Sand in his mouth and clogged around his eyes, to where his nictitating membranes had cleared it. Sand in his clothing and two skirls sheltering in the shade of his body. The water carrier lay still-stoppered down at the bottom of the dune, so it was lucky he had not been drinking from it when the recent fit struck. Orduval crawled down the dune face to retrieve the precious carrier, the skirls skittering away with their usual racket. He drank thirstily, noting that, with half the water gone now, the chiller worked better on the smaller quantity remaining. Not that he particularly needed cold water now, with the desert temperature plummeting as the sun sank behind the horizon, for the night-time should provide a chilly but bearable fifty-five degrees Celsius. He hauled himself to his feet and climbed back up to the dune peak he had been following. With the stars coming out and his eyes adjusting, he decided to continue towards the mount, since it still remained visible.

Why did their mother die? Apparently it had been a miserable accident, though Orduval had suspicions about that. Had Orbital Combine been conducting some kind of experiment that went wrong, and then swiftly concealed the evidence?

'Did they kill you, Mother?' he asked, his mouth already dry again.

He desperately wanted to drink more water, but decided he must reach the mount first and so he trudged on. A Sudorian human needed to consume an estimated gallon of water every four hours, to survive here in direct sunlight, so after his day under this sun he was now severely dehydrated. His clothing felt crusty – sand and salt combined – and he began to feel damp with a sweat that would have earlier quickly evaporated. It seemed as if shadows now accompanied him on his trek – the expected hallucinations were beginning to arrive.

'But who was our father?' he asked the desert night.

Amenable to his request, the silvered darkness provided a shadowy figure, though not located in that same darkness but somehow standing just aside of it. He tried to discern its features and could not. He and his siblings had once asked Utrain about their father, but their grandmother could provide no answers: Elsever had formed no permanent attachments on Corisanthe Main. A brief liaison, then? Perhaps even a brief liaison with something *not human*. The figure changed into an unknowable spectre poised on the edge of his perception. *The Shadowman?* Orduval shivered and turned away, to find himself falling into his own abyss.

An unknown time later, voices called him out of it:

'With all your understanding of the human condition, is this the best solution you can find?' Harald sneered.

'I am saddened,' said Rhodane. *'But I understand.'*

'Get up, Orduval,' Yishna urged. *'The mount is not so far.'*

He was lying on his side, and the salty taste in his mouth was blood from where he had bitten his tongue.

It occurred to him that in his weakened condition he might not even need the pills, for the next fit might kill him. He struggled to his feet and moved on.

'Pathetic, weak . . . are you sure you are one of us, Orduval?' Harald taunted.

It was so unfair. He wanted to cry, but his body lacked sufficient moisture to allow him tears. Immediately after the moment of self-pity, he grew angry. Yes, pathetic, weak, but what other recourse did he have? Staying there in the asylum was no life, and the fits so disrupted his thinking that he could pursue no selected subject as deeply as he wished. He could have chosen to just keep on existing, but to him *that* was displaying weakness. He cursed and shook his head . . . and his siblings fragmented into the night. Clasping his failing body under an iron will, he forced himself onwards. Hours later, when his boot finally came down on stone, he considered that a victory, allowed himself a celebratory drink of water, then began to climb the rocky slope ahead. Hundreds of feet above the desert, weariness finally clubbed him. He drank once again, then curled up in a sandy hollow in the rock, and slept.

Morning; the sun rougeing the horizon and glimmer wings twinkling in the twilight. Up on his knees, Orduval drank more and now felt ravenously hungry. New day, new perspective? He felt suddenly optimistic, as if he could continue living. But this feeling was precisely why he had walked out here, the previous day and night, since there could never be any return. He stood and peered up the slope above him. He would climb to the very top, watch the desert for a while, and then ease his way gently from life with the pills. But the moment he moved, dizziness washed through him, and it was on unsteady legs

he began to negotiate the slope. And with a degree of
reluctance – where was his moment of clarity? That
strangeness during the night was already fading in
memory. So unfair—

Blackness slammed him down.

Orduval woke to utter agony. Perhaps his suicidal
impulse was working, with him climbing such a difficult
slope when he suffered from fits. With vision blurring he
gazed at the shards of bone poking from his right shin,
the dislocated fingers of his left hand, the rips in his
clothing and the blood. The sun, now shining straight
down on him, burned acidically into his wounds, and
thirst lay like a twisted knot inside him. His water carrier
was nowhere in sight, but maybe he could summon up
enough saliva to swallow the pills without water. He
groped into his pocket with his right hand, searching for
the pill tube. Couldn't find it. Summoning the will to lift
his head and look, he saw the pocket was torn open. He
moaned with self-pity, then the ensuing anger drove him
to crawl on. At least he could find some shade where the
sun did not burn so.

Harald came to taunt him, the sun a halo around his
furnace head; Rhodane came to sympathize, and Yishna
to offer pragmatic advice. Utrain called him in to supper
and stood some way to one side, holding out a chilled
glass of fruit juice. Memories surfaced and fled and
another fit took him away for a while. How many hours?
How many hours did he make animal sounds of pain?
Shade then . . . cool . . . and was that trickling water he
heard? He lay still, sliding in and out of consciousness.
A kind of relief settled on him, and a calm, for he felt the
worst suffering had passed and death was now coming to
embrace him. The hallucinations seemed to lose their

potency . . . but for one appearing near the end. His fevered mind painted a metal beast out of surviving biological files from Earth, squatting at the mouth of the cave in which he lay.

'Screw non-intervention and screw Geronamid,' grumbled the silver tiger. 'I'm not going to let you die, Orduval.'

– Retroact 9 Ends –

6

The colonists of Brumal required very few adaptations – and those mostly concerning toughening their bodies to the acidic environment and a mild amphidaption to their watery surroundings. Their leaders instituted building programmes – quickly setting up a domed encampment much like the one we set up at Transit. Exploration led to the discovery of deep cave systems, huge forests and massive river systems. The leaders were preparing to build their communal and socially just isocracy, whereupon they would of course relinquish control. However, then the first out-gassing occurred upon the first close pass of the planet Sudoria, and for frantic days the Brumallians thought our predecessors here were gas-attacking them from orbit. But then they discovered, in the mountains, the geothermal vents spewing out pure chlorine gas. The atmosphere became rapidly intolerable, and their technology began to corrode and decay around them – the landing craft they had so congratulated themselves on retaining becoming unusable within a matter of weeks. Salvaging what they could, they retreated into the shelter of the cave systems. The first Brumallians – as we know them – did not step outside until seventy years later. What changes they made to themselves and their society in the intervening period we know to *have been radical, and occurred almost certainly because they never managed to lock their fanatics outside like we did.*

– Uskaron

McCrooger

Injury hunger was again churning up my insides by the time we reached the bottom of the brick-lined shaft. It persisted because of the broken bones I had suffered aboard the escape-pod, and was exacerbated by the constant physical abuse this environment subjected me to. If I did not eat something soon, IF21 would kill me or I would change horribly. The change would begin by me starting to go a little crazy, then chewing plates would begin to harden inside my tongue and its tip begin to hollow prior to it turning into the feeding mouth of a leech. I would then turn violent, and it would be others who would die.

'I need something to eat,' I informed Rhodane.

She glanced at me, then after a moment removed her visor. Dropping it into a pocket in her belt, she then pushed back her hood to release tousled blonde hair. I noted how her dark skin displayed a greenish cast, the same hue even evident in the whites of her eyes. Hard skin ran along the line of her jaw bone, divided into segments like the scales on a reptile's tail, and ran up before her ear to terminate in rough fibrous patches.

'You'll be provided for once we reach our destination,' she said.

I kept my complaints to myself and hoped we would reach there soon. Right then I did not feel up to frittering away time by asking how she managed to breathe atmosphere that would leave any other Sudorian writhing, coughing and retching on the ground.

Riveted steel gates opened to admit us to an underground marina. Biolights clustered on the rocky ceiling a hundred feet above, and the chamber ahead was packed with all manner of watercraft moored to floating jetties. Leading off from this chamber were numerous tunnels, some containing canals with paths down either side, and some leading directly to stairs. Far to my left I observed cargo being craned from a barge onto motorized pallets, which in turn were driven by Brumallians right into a huge lift, whether to go up or down I could not guess. As we chugged through into the marina, one craft nearby particularly drew my attention. The thing looked alive, insectoid, with legs folded along its sides, antennae sprouting from the weirdly shaped bowsprit, and a rudder that looked more like a tail than anything else.

I pointed. 'What's that?'

'Something made before the War,' Rhodane replied.

I mentally compared the biolights and those pumps on the surface with all the other simple mechanisms up on the surface and down here. When a society adopted the biotechnology route, its results tended to fill every niche, gradually displacing all those objects and processes that used to be the products of plain manufacturing. On a world called Hive, right on the far edge of the Polity, the AIs only kept passive watch, for that world had fallen under the control of another race (another story) and the small human population there was ruled by the CGs, or Chief Geneticists. Once, when visiting there, I saw an organism whose sum purpose was to produce nails and screws. I asked the designer of this thing, whose life work it had been, why for so prosaic a purpose she had made something so complex and in need of such nurturing, when simple machines were easily available for the same task. She replied, 'But simple machines cannot be bred to replace themselves.' I guess she had a point.

'Do Brumallians still possess the capability to produce such things?' I asked Rhodane.

'Should the Polity concern itself with such matters?' she countered.

Any complex technology is the product of many antecedents. Destroy the infrastructure of a society supporting such technology and, though the knowledge itself might not be lost, the society would lose the basis on which the tech was built. Members of a human civilization bombed back into the Stone Age are hardly going to be able to build computers from flint and wood.

Rhodane then relented. 'Much was lost during the War.'

Our craft motored into a space alongside a jetty, whereupon one of the quofarl leapt out to secure the mooring rope. Rhodane stepped out ahead of me, and as I stood to follow her a sharp hunger pang stabbed through me. I peered down at my hand and spied the shade of blue presaging a horrible transformation, and inside I felt a churning sickening sensation as the two viral forms competed for predominance. The quofarl still onboard reached out and prodded my shoulder – just a nudge to indicate I should now go ashore.

I turned on him. 'Touch me again and I'll knock those fucking mandibles through the back of your thick skull.' He did not understand me, since I spoke a language not known in this Solar System, but he understood my tone. He began to lean forward, mandibles grating together and eyes narrowing. Luckily the surge of pure rage passed and I managed to get myself under control, abruptly turning away to step ashore.

'Rhodane, I *really* need something to eat.'

'There is nothing suitable here. We've got supplies of Sudorian food over in Granitesville, and should be there within the hour.'

'You don't understand. After recent changes I've undergone to adapt to your environment I need to eat substantial amounts, regularly, or my judgement and reason can be impaired. I can become . . . dangerous.'

'He can –' began the quofarl on the jetty.

'– become dangerous,' finished the one still aboard the boat.

Much clattering mandipular laughter ensued, and Rhodane chuckled too.

'Please let me explain,' I continued doggedly. 'This is not a usual condition with me, but one brought on by recent injuries and my adjustment to your environment. Additionally, I can eat Brumallian food.'

'Whoo, Mr Dangerous –'

'– wants to chew –'

'– grobbleworms.' The last came from Rhodane who seemed to have been caught up in the joint communication. It only dawned on me then how she easily managed the clicks and rattles of spoken Brumallian, and I realized this had something to do with those physical changes evident on her face. But I did not feel inclined to satisfy my curiosity about that right then. My left hand began to quiver, and I really *really* wanted to put my fist through the nearest quofarl's head – the one on the jetty. I needed to get this sorted fast before I lost control. I decided on a half-measure.

'Let me illustrate.' I grabbed the chosen quofarl by the front of his dungarees, since the material looked strong enough, hoisted him from the jetty one-handed and hurled him over the boat into the water beyond. Turning to Rhodane, I said, 'If I lose control, people will die.'

She stared out to where the quofarl had now surfaced and began swimming back towards us from about twenty feet out. She glanced down at the other quofarl on the boat, whose mandibles were hanging wide apart, then turned to study me cautiously.

'Follow me,' she instructed abruptly.

The grobbleworm seller occupied the first stall of a market running alongside a canal that tunnelled off from the marina. Even as we approached, a fisherman brought his catch to the stall – a basket full of the same armoured worms making a racket like snakes writhing in a barrel of stones. Their pincers extruded through the basket mesh, sharp tail fins stabbed out like knives. The stallholder extended one mandible, directing him to a stack of similar baskets ranged to one side, then turned her attention towards us, or rather to me. She stared, mandibles hanging wide in what I now recognized as an expression of surprise or shock.

'Give me your attention,' Rhodane said in Brumallian, though the subtext she signed went something like, 'Consensus Speaker business – stop staring at the weird human.' She continued out loud with, 'I want ten worms – six of them overcooked.'

Once the stallholder got over her surprise she pulled on gauntlets and began the dodgy task of pulling arm-thick worms from a nearby basket and threading them

onto long steel skewers, before plunging them into a pot
of boiling water.

'Why overcooked?' I asked.

'It weakens the acid content, which is more acceptable to me, and I presume would be more acceptable to
you?'

'You presume right.'

Six skewered worms squirmed and thrashed in the
boiling water. The stallholder paused for a while before
dropping in the remaining four, long enough only for
them to stop thrashing about. I felt a surge of nostalgia
for Spatterjay, where similar monsters met a similar end
in similar pots. By this time the quofarl I had thrown into
the water had turned up. I expected some display of
anger or resentment, but he showed none I could
identify.

'Grobbleworms –' he rubbed his meaty hands
together.

'– good,' his companion completed.

Meaty hands continued, 'You weren't joking –'

'– about being hungry,' the companion supplied.

Rhodane took the four minimally cooked worms
from the stallholder and handed them to the two
quofarl, who, holding the skewers in their right hands
whilst pulling off shell with mandibles and left hand,
began stuffing the gristly meat into their mouths. Observing them, I realized one did not really need mandibles,
since these worms looked no more difficult to eat than
say a lobster or a prill. When at last the six overcooked
worms were ready, Rhodane took two for herself and
handed the remaining four to me. I placed three of the
loaded skewers down on the stall and impatiently started
on the other, pulling the worm apart and stuffing chunks

into my mouth and sometimes chewing up shell as well as flesh. It took the skin off the inside of my mouth, burned like jalapeño chillies and caused such an eructatious racket in my stomach that those passers-by who stopped to gaze at me hung around to listen to the symphony until Rhodane shooed them away. But my body's need took over, quickly regrowing damaged skin in my mouth and adjusting itself to this acidic nutriment. By the time I sucked the last piece of meat from the last piece of shell, the worms tasted like chilli-flavoured frog-whelk to me, and I was hooked.

'Less chance of you turning dangerous now?' Rhodane asked, eyeing the remnants of shell and the discarded skewers about my feet.

I glanced longingly at the pot, but the worms had taken the edge off my hunger so I decided not to push my luck. 'That will sustain me for a little while,' I conceded.

She handed a small black rod to the stallholder, who pressed it into some kind of reader before handing it back. Some transaction had obviously just taken place. I knew nothing about their economic system here, but supposed they must use some form of currency since few human societies ever have managed to survive without it. We moved on, stared at all the while. As I walked, feeling a little calmer and more able to assess my situation, I considered what I had seen back at the stall. The Brumallians didn't really need mandibles to handle their food, so were they a result of inefficient recombinant techniques, or had some bastard in their past saddled these people with mandibles to make some obscure ideological point? Again, one of those things I would probably never find out.

– RETROACT 10 –

Yishna – *on Corisanthe Main*

The screen showed the distinct words:

HATE . . . SKIRL SAND . . . IMPACTED . . . FIRE

Keleon, the OCT who had heard those words in his mind, had told her in detail the sensations and thoughts accompanying them. He had experienced the usual fantasies, some violent, some sexual. He described to her how he imagined setting at each other's throats two OCTs he knew had had him thrown out of the Cognizants – yet another sect aboard this station – then went on to describe to her how he had vividly visualized buggering her over a console in a study unit. After this Keleon had taken the opportunity to suggest that this might be something they could try – strictly in the interests of research. Yishna had subsequently dismissed him and had used her consoles for more prosaic activities.

The workings of the human brain were intricate indeed, sometimes annoyingly illogical to Yishna when compared with computers; but thus far that lump of pinkish organic matter was the only instrument sensitive enough to detect bleed-over. In her first year aboard Corisanthe Main she had worked on developing ways of recording the workings of the brain. Delving into the research of others, she mapped its function and learnt how to interpret electrical and biochemical readings as thoughts. From this she managed to create audio recordings of bleed-over and listened with growing disappointment to the disconnected and sometimes half-formed words that seemed merely the product of random selection from some lexicon. Further studies revealed that these thoughts arose out of deeper functions of the brain; the words being merely the bubbles bursting at the surface of a pool, and therefore only an indication of deeper activity. She did, however, create complex linguistic programs in order to analyse these first recordings by comparing content with source. Some interesting connections arose, but never enough to understand the purpose of bleed-over, if it even possessed one.

Keleon had become the source of more information, for he was the first to volunteer for surgery and try out the new hardware. A year ago Yishna had designed both hardware capable of surviving in the hostile environment of the human body and the surgical techniques for installing it. She often went back to his file in search of inspiration, or in the hope of seeing something new. As she studied the cladograms of synaptic activity, applied comparative programs and mapped the course of thoughts through his brain, she mused and speculated. Perhaps bleed-over, weakened almost to non-existence outside Ozark Containment, was the actual cause of all the flourishing sects aboard this station? In fact she felt sure it was the cause of most of the strangeness aboard Corisanthe Main. Telepathic inductance, the OCTs called it. She did not believe that was what it was, but for her it was no longer the issue. The Worm affected humans who got close. She also felt certain that the definitely emotional elements of bleed-over indicated the Worm was self-aware – *that* was the issue.

Yishna closed the file, stood up and walked to the window of the study unit, to gaze down into Centre Cross Chamber. As always, there was much work in progress: old equipment in the containment cylinders being replaced, refurbished; new designs of scanner being brought in for trial; and as ever the perpetual checking of security. After watching for a little while, she returned to her touch-screens, keyed into the networks, and began checking on published research and looking for news of new developments.

Unlike others working here Yishna frequently published her research for, unlike those others, knowledge not status was her goal, and by publishing quickly she received much useful feedback. It did not concern her that other scientists frequently took her work and ran with it, that around her a whole network of R & D had sprung up, and that some of them awaited her publications with something approaching desperation. Only recently had she learned that both Fleet and Combine scientific teams were developing her hardware – surgically implanted inside the brain – for the purpose of controlling ship and satellite systems, for the fast analysis of information, for many operations that shortened and made more efficient the link between thought and action. She had watched with interest the trials of new surgically implanted communications hardware; how Fleet tacoms – ship's communications, logistics and tactical officers – became capable of comprehending multiple visual and audio inputs, and then acting on them with computer speed.

There was some breaking news about the surgical division of certain brain functions and some further development of the synaptic connection. Though both of these were of interest and directly applicable to her own work, Yishna felt a sudden weariness and unaccustomed boredom. Idly working her touch-screen, she allowed her mind to wander. Remembering something Dalepan had said earlier, she wondered what would actually happen here if the Worm broke free? During fumarole breaches, those computers affected ended up scrambled and running some decidedly odd code, but even that – like bleed-over – seemed only to hover on the point of making sense, but never did. Dalepan had told her about a physical breach occurring near the end of the War, when the unlikely failure of three reactors simultaneously resulted in a brief power outage to Ozark Three. This in turn resulted in the similarly brief collapse of the magnetic containment field inside the canister itself, and the Worm directly touching the sidewall. He had elaborated no further.

Yishna looked up and realized that, almost without thinking, she had dropped from accessing the networks and instead opened a port into Corisanthe Main's library. Her interest stimulated, she began to do some research.

The touch against the side of the canister had resulted in the slow spread of something like a metal-eating fungus. That was the kind of nano-technology they studied endlessly, very often understood, but simply had no way of creating for themselves. It was, many opined, something you could not build without it having been created as a part of your science. A desert nomad could understand a computer, but without the infrastructure, the tooling and much else beside, he could never build one. Such creations were the culmination of a long chain of development.

The reports she read then went on to detail how, avoiding the implementation of any of the main 'Emergency Ozark Protocols', an OCT had entered the affected cylinder and sterilized the infestation with a laser. Later, OCTs cut away this section from the canister and replaced it with new metal. They also replaced all the equipment within the surrounding cylinder and thereafter ran constant checks for nanite infestation.

Emergency Ozark Protocols . . . Yishna searched the library for further mention of them. She found only one: *EOP Three would only be applied if we were unable to evacuate the station—*

It was just that one line remaining from a partially deleted file. Further searching referred her to 'Gneiss eyes only' files stored in the system under heavy encryption, beyond the scope of the access codes in her control baton. She had encountered these files many times before and knew that any foolish tampering with them would result in station security officers dragging her off to face the Director. However, on those previous occasions she had felt insufficiently curious to know what was hidden in them. Now she was, and when it came to cracking encryption there was probably only one person better at it than herself, and he was busily climbing the ranks aboard *Ironfist*.

Yishna stretched her fingers, smiled to herself and went to work. It was exhilarating, and using programs she had created during her research she easily sidestepped all the traps and was soon browsing the Director's database. Private reports he had compiled concerning herself soon distracted her. It pleased her to note comments like: *If it were not for the importance of her research, I would immediately recommend her for a position on the Oversight Committee. However, I am loath to turn such a mind away from research and employ it in the prosaic managerial and political aspects of running Combine.*

A further distraction for her was the archived

material concerning the original building of Corisanthe Main while the four segments of the Worm were held in a stripped-out cruiser hastily converted into the role of a magnetic bottle. It seemed at this time the Worm showed little activity. *In a state of shock, perhaps?* It only began to become active after they transported it from the cruiser to the newly completed canisters which would hold its separate segments inside the Ozark Cylinders. *As if it knew where it was being taken?* But eventually Yishna found what she was looking for, and then it felt as if something juddered to a halt inside her mind.

There were three of them. Protocol Three detailed *'Actions in the event of physical containment breach should there be an inability to evacuate the station'*. It seemed that it was possible to eject the Ozark Cylinders entire from the station. Protocol Two detailed the *'Evacuation of the station in the event of physical containment breach and the thermal and EM sterilization of the Ozark Cylinders'*. Protocol One talked of evacuation, massive physical breach beyond the cylinders and the infestation of the station itself. Six thermo-nuclear warheads had been evenly placed throughout its structure, and their detonation would vaporize everything. It also seemed evident to Yishna that, in some cases, the protocol demanded their detonation even without evacuation of personnel.

She stared at this dry set of rules and felt a sudden overpowering anger. *This cannot be allowed.* The thought sat leaden and incontestible in her mind. They should not be able, out of fear, to so easily destroy all or part of the Worm. It was a trust. It belonged to all and itself. It belonged to *her*!

Now she began to really tear into the station's

computer systems. With both hands to her touch-screens she created and modified programs, hunted down and absorbed. Inside her skull she felt a bloated heaviness, and knew she was moving into one of those almost sublime moments of mentation. She quickly located all the warheads, and discovered they could not be physically disarmed – were in fact regularly checked for readiness. The lasers and thermite explosives it would be impossible to get to, since they lay actually inside the cylinders and none could go there without accompanying OCTs. But, as always, there was another way.

The command would come from Director Gneiss himself, after ratification by the Oversight Committee. The answer lay in a bit of rerouting, so that when Gneiss ordered one protocol the system employed another. Without hesitation she made the alterations. Now, if the Director ordered EM and thermal sterilization as detailed in Protocol Two, or the detonation of the nukes as in Protocol One, in both cases Protocol Three would be employed and the Ozark Cylinders would be ejected. *All of them* would be ejected.

When she was done, Yishna sat back and just stared at the screens. After a moment she triple-wiped memory so nothing of what she had done could be detected. She then turned everything off, stood up, and headed for her quarters. Dropping fully clothed onto her bunk, she fell immediately into a deep sleep.

Four hours later she woke in utter panic. *Why did I do that?*

Deep inside she somehow knew why, but could not allow herself to consciously admit it. She felt the terror of madness – of her mind not being her own. And from that moment Corisanthe Main seemed filled with dangerous shadows, and the nightmares began.

– Retroact 10 Ends –

Harald

As he headed for his quarters aboard *Ironfist*, Harald seethed. Had David McCrooger remained unthreatened throughout his journey here from the edge of the system, people would then have believed that Fleet had honourably discharged a duty it found distasteful and been extremely embarrassed at subsequently losing McCrooger to unprovoked Brumallian aggression. Inigis's foolish attempt to rid them of the Consul Assessor straight away had changed that scenario by exacerbating public suspicion already driven high by Uskaron's book. It was lucky that despite that idiocy, parliamentary vote had allowed Fleet to recommission its old weapons and begin to manufacture more, just as Harald required. However, supposed threats to Sudoria needed to be highlighted and brought closer to home, and Orbital Combine must be implicated.

Harald halted by his door and, without the intercession of a control baton, sent the access code direct from the hardware in his foamite suit. The door unlocked and he pushed it open. Sensing that his quarters were occupied, he drew his side arm, then quickly darted in and to one side, the weapon levelled at the figure occupying the chair beside his console.

'Have you so many enemies, Harald?' asked Yishna.

Harald kept his weapon sighted on his sister, while

eyeing the small pistol she held. She watched him for a moment, then glanced down at the pistol.

'Combine manufacture,' she said, placing the weapon down then sliding it to the back of his desk. 'Surely Fleet possess better weapons?'

Returning his side arm to its holster, Harald closed the door behind him and advanced into the room. To obtain that little Combine gun, she had obviously opened the code-locked storage compartment under his desk – not a serious problem for her, of course.

'To answer both your questions, I *do* have a few enemies. There are some in Fleet not averse to using assassination as a means of gaining promotion, though there're few like that here on *Ironfist*. Hence my reaction to you just then, and hence the presence of an unregistered weapon here in my quarters.' He walked over to his samovar and tapped himself a cup of the same pungent tea Yishna was presently sipping. While doing this he tried to relax the tension that seemed to entwine steel springs through his body.

'I had not realized,' said Yishna, looking dismayed.

Harald immediately understood that she referred to his tacom alterations, and not the fact that he had enemies. 'Communication is the key, sister. It always has been.'

'Some might consider it mutilation.'

Harald grimaced, carefully placed his cup down by the samovar, then removed his helmet and glove, placing them down beside it. Taking up the cup again, he finally turned and seated himself on his divan. 'Perhaps you should be the last to make such observations, since this technology stems from your own research.'

'Perhaps.'

'So why are you here, sister?'

Yishna stared at his adapted eye. 'Interesting. It merely looks like you've received a poke in the eye, yet we both know the largest alterations are behind it.'

'I asked you why you are here.'

Yishna stared at him a moment longer, then said, 'I'm here because, apparently, some suicidal Brumallians fired a missile at the ship I was aboard. Those surviving the attack were picked up by *Ironfist*'s rescue boats. Seven others died, including, apparently, the Consul Assessor.'

'Regrettable,' said Harald. 'I was looking forward to interrogating him during Inigis's trial.'

'I suspect you would have found it an illuminating experience.'

'Doubtless.'

'What happened to Inigis's ship?' Yishna asked. 'I know it was hit by a Brumallian missile and that there was a detonation in one of the silos aboard, shoving it into a decaying orbit, but that's about it. No one here seems inclined to tell me any more.'

'It nearly went down, but Inigis, ignoring the order confining him to his cabin for his *alleged* attempt on the Consul Assessor's life, took command again and saved the day by detonating a second weapon in another silo, thus changing his ship's trajectory. His actions will of course be taken into account when he comes to trial.'

'What are you up to, Harald?'

'I'm not sure I understand your question.'

'We two are driven; we studied hard and we learned, and have now attained high positions in Sudorian society. I have only one more step yet to make to become Director of Corisanthe Main, but my work sufficiently satisfies me that I'm prepared to wait until Director Gneiss steps down.' Yishna frowned as if remembering something unpleasant, then shook her head and con-tinued, 'What are *you* waiting for, Harald – and are you waiting at all?'

'The stratified ranking system of Fleet will not allow me to take the position of Admiral, since Captain Dravenik gets precedence. However, as Fleet Tacom I now hold more power in fact than Carnasus holds in name. Standing at his shoulder, I've reached the highest position I can attain without a major readjustment of the ranking system.'

'And killing the Polity Consul Assessor helps this how?'

'I don't know. Perhaps you'd better ask the Bru-mallians that.'

Yishna just stared at him for a long moment before going on: 'It may be that the Polity does not represent as much of a danger as you might think.'

'Our affairs here are complicated enough as they are without outside interference,' Harald snapped, not sure why he suddenly felt so angry.

'David McCrooger was a very interesting person . . .' Yishna trailed off, staring at something distant. 'I . . . I thought I would be able to easily play him, understand his motivations and the true intent of this Polity, but every time I began to feel I knew what he was all about, some new level to him was revealed.' She focused on Harald. 'Like sometimes when you talk to someone intelligent and old, you keep uncovering layers of complexity.'

'Perhaps that is precisely what he is,' Harald replied. 'We don't know how good their medical science is, so he may have been much older than he looked. I in fact think that rather likely.'

'I asked him about their policy regarding imprisoned sentients, should the Polity take over here.'

Harald felt something go quiet inside him, waiting. Every sound in this room suddenly became intense and every object clearly defined and subject to his full perception.

'His reply?' he asked casually.

Yishna's nictitating membranes flicked closed, giving her eyes an opaque sheen. 'He told me that in the case of corrupt totalitarian regimes they grant a full amnesty to all prisoners, though those guilty of capital crimes are checked for socio- or psychopathic tendencies. But because our regime is not such, cases would be individually reviewed under Polity law, and those found innocent of any crime would be released. But Polity intercession is unlikely.'

'Reviewed under Polity law,' Harald repeated. 'Your impression?'

Now, in a noticeably flat tone, his sister replied, 'I am sure that those unjustly imprisoned would be released no matter who or *what* they are.'

Harald felt himself returning to a more normal level of perception. Yishna's nictitating membranes opened and she looked about with annoyance.

'It happened again,' she said.

'It often happens when we meet after being apart for some time.'

She glanced up at him. 'It's some sort of communication – non-verbal.'

'It is,' Harald agreed, 'but I fail to divine its purpose.' He paused for a moment then asked, 'How goes your research into the Worm?'

Yishna shook her head as if dispelling idiocy. 'I can

record bleed-over now – not telepathic inductance after all, but some inductance phenomena related to under-space.' She was now fidgeting, as if bored with this conversation.

'Which the Polity would know all about, of course. It is a shame that David McCrooger is now dead, for he could perhaps have helped you in many ways.'

'Yes, a shame.'

Harald continued, 'However, I rather suspect that David McCrooger is not the Polity's only envoy here within our system, and for my purposes I would rather there were none here at all.'

'Your purposes?'

'Yishna, much as it's pleasant to chat to you, perhaps we can take this up later?'

'What are your *purposes*, Harald?'

'I am not at liberty to discuss Fleet matters with some-one so high up in Orbital Combine, sister.'

'Would that I could believe "your purposes" concern only Fleet.' Yishna put aside her cup and stood. 'We should discuss this further.'

'Yes, perhaps later.'

Yishna glanced at his coms helmet and glove, then turned and departed.

Harald sat for a long moment with the polished wheels of his mind turning. Some input in the recent conversation had changed his attitude to McCrooger, but that did not alter his overall plan, and his feeling that the Consul Assessor was best out of the way, perma-nently. He stood and went to retrieve his helmet and glove, donning them almost with relief. Opening a com channel he waited. After a moment a woman's face peered at him from his eye-screen – cropped grey hair and bitter mouth, and a thin face deeply grooved with lines and a permanent look of disapproval. He rather suspected her sour mien was due to years of fighting her way up through a patriarchal organization.

'Jeon,' he acknowledged. 'Update?'

She glanced at something to one side then said, 'I am still analysing the data. The trace separated on the surface – one part of it remaining inland, and the other travelling fast over land and sea to the escape-pod, then back again.'

'So there is either one conjoined object or two separate objects that have remained together until now?'

She nodded. 'So it would seem. It also strikes me as likely that, whatever it is, it rescued the Consul Assessor.'

Harald sat back. 'I will ask Special Operations on Brumal to . . . solve that problem. They will enjoy the challenge. But that is irrelevant for my purposes right now. If the Polity is interventionist, it seems this unknown object is the greatest danger to us. You have detected nothing else?'

'Nothing so far, but that's not to say there's nothing more here. It was pure luck that we picked up on this thing – luck and the application of some recent research results from Corisanthe Main.'

'I must work on the assumption that there is only this one . . . maybe two.' Harald grimaced – he did not like making assumptions. 'You're still tracking?'

'The trace is sitting five hundred miles above the ReconYork, holding station there.'

'Very well, Jeon. I want you to prepare a five-megaton warhead – fully shielded and EM hardened – for simple contact detonation, and allowing coded detonation from here.' Jeon frowned her puzzlement, and he explained,

'There will be a retaliatory strike made against the Brumallians for their attack on Inigis's ship. We will then see if the Polity is prepared to intervene, and perhaps we can remove their ability to do so.'

'I see.'

'Let me know when you're ready. The missile is to go into Silo Fourteen.'

Harald cut their communication and opened another channel. After a moment, a man gazed out at him.

'Captain Franorl, you will shortly be receiving instructions, through the usual channels, to replace Dravenik on Corisanthe Watch,' said Harald.

'To whom do I owe this honour?'

'To me, as always.'

'I see.'

'As per the agreement between Orbital Combine and Fleet, Combine observers will be sent over to your ship while you are on station watching Corisanthe Main. You are to know where they are at all times, because at a certain time they will attempt to sabotage the *Desert Wind*.'

'If we've evidence of this, why can't I just throw them in the brig?'

'You misapprehend me. They will all be killed while making this sabotage attempt, and therefore no evidence will be required. Suspecting attack from Combine, you will then move your ship out of range of Corisanthe Main's armament.'

Franorl smiled. 'At last.'

'Out.' Harald cut that connection and quickly made a new one. After a short delay a different male face gazed at him from the screen. 'Captain Dravenik, you will shortly be replaced on Corisanthe Watch by Captain Franorl on *Desert Wind*.'

'This is from the Admiral?' Dravenik asked suspiciously.

'It is. You will also be receiving orders to position yourself just out from Planetary Defence Platform One. It seems we may be having a little bit of a problem with Combine.'

'The nature of this problem?'

'It would appear there may be some connection between the Brumallian missile strike on Inigis's vessel and certain factions operating in Orbital Combine. We have yet to obtain clear proof of this, however.'

'Combine and Brumallians collaborating?' said the Captain disbelievingly.

'Unlikely, I agree,' said Harald. 'It seems more likely to me that these factions in Combine deliberately tried to implicate the Brumallians so we would be distracted.'

'Why would Combine want to take down the ship transporting the Consul Assessor?'

'Factions *within* Combine, Dravenik.'

'This is all very well,' said Dravenik, 'but I'd get all that through the usual channels. Why are you contacting me privately like this?'

'I have a favour to ask of you.'

'Oh really.'

'Attempting to keep the peace, the Admiral will order you to hold station there, but to keep your weapons systems offline. I am not entirely sure if he understands the seriousness of the situation. I am not entirely sure if I do either, so I want you to keep your weapons systems online.'

'Provocative.'

'Yes, but not sufficiently so to cause an incident, unless an incident is what Combine wants. Should such circumstances arise I would rather you were ready.'

Dravenik paused for a moment, before replying, 'I'll consider your request.' His image blinked out.

Harald sat back. Dravenik, whose dislike of Harald never wavered, would now assume Harald was trying to undermine his position as the senior candidate to replace Carnasus. The Admiral would never order him to take his weapons systems offline, though that was standard peacetime practice, but would leave that decision to Dravenik. The Captain, however, would most certainly keep those weapons offline now simply because Harald asked him not to. Dravenik would still be able to respond to an attack, but only belatedly. Fleet needed substantial motivation to turn on Orbital Combine, and Dravenik would soon be providing it.

– RETROACT 11 –

Orduval – *in the Desert*

The moment Orduval woke he felt reduced – honed down to a smaller point in existence. With his body comfortable and warm, he dared not move for fear of stirring pain. Gradually he became aware that his head rested gently on padded fabric, and daring to turn it he eventually focused his blurred vision on a large water chiller standing beside him – precisely the sort found inside municipal buildings. Then, inspecting his close surroundings, he realized his head was resting on the pillow of an inflatable mattress and that he was lying naked in a sleeping bag. Still he dared not move excessively, know-ing that, no matter what drugs his rescuer had pumped inside him, the compound fracture of his leg was going to hurt.

'You're safe now, Orduval,' said a voice nearby.

Immediately analysing that voice, he found it scared him badly. He detected a dearth of humanity behind it, like something heard from a voice synthesizer. Slowly now, he drew one hand up out of the sleeping bag and inspected it. It was bruised but hurt surprisingly little. His rescuer had relocated his fingers, so perhaps had also set his leg?

As he slowly pulled himself upright, more of the interior of the cave became visible to him. On a canvas sheet laid on the ground nearby rested an assortment of packaged foods, a solar-power store and cooker, some medical supplies and a stack of clothing. With his vision clearing properly, it seemed to Orduval as if all these objects became more real to him, more substantial than anything he had ever seen before. With a sudden panic he recognized the clothing as some of his own he had left behind in the hospital.

He looked round for the speaker. 'Where are you?'

'Outside the cave at the moment – well, mostly. Why don't you get dressed and come and join me?'

Orduval paused a long moment, then ran a finger down the stick-seam of the sleeping bag and peeled it open. He then inspected himself more fully.

His bony frame felt tender, bruised, but he could see no open cuts or grazes. When last he saw it, bits of shattered bone protruded from his leg, but now the dark skin was pristine, without even a scar. He swung both legs to the side and cautiously stood up. He still ached, all over, even the crown of his head. With care he stepped over to the water chiller, found a cup hanging on the side, and filled and drained it three times, before turning to his clothing.

Definitely from the hospital, for he recognized the tabard his grandmother Utrain bought him years ago, also the hospital-issue undergarments and his loose trousers and cotton shirt. His desert boots resting beside these garments were the same ones he wore in getting out here, yet he distinctly remembered the right one having been split. Picking it up he tried to find a mend, but it was as invisible as the repairs made to his body. Glancing round, he then observed his old clothing piled over by the wall, bloody, ripped and filthy. He dressed in the new.

Upon first waking he had supposed some desert Samaritan had rescued him, but factoring in the renewed state of his body, those intact boots and a fuzzy recollection of something significant before he had lost consciousness, he knew this situation to be abnormal. Once dressed, he rummaged through the food supply until he found several bars of compressed fruit and jerky, two of which he gobbled swiftly, taking his time over a third. Despite the bruising, he decided he had not felt so good in a long time, and it was then he realized that his body must be clear of the anti-convulsives. He decided to just enjoy the moment – until the next fit struck him – and stepped outside the cave.

The midday sun had heated the surrounding rocks to oven temperature – warm enough to fry meat and boil water. An arid breeze blew and dust misted the horizon. Orduval studied the object at the edge of the small clearing before the cave, and recognized the basic shape of one of the big cats of Earth, though which genus he could not guess. It was fashioned of silver metal and utterly still, so logically had to be some kind of statue placed here by his rescuer, and his earlier vision just another hallucination. This logic shattered as the statue turned, jointless as mercury, and regarded him with amber feline eyes.

'I projected a pretty picture that finally lured the searchers to find and save the kid who fell through into an abandoned skirl nest,' it announced suddenly. 'No problems there, and the only minus point being the mother getting infected with religion – she thought the images had been sent by the Shadowman. No one saw me, either, when I holed a water tank to put out a fire in a burning building in Transit, or when I pushed a foundering shrimp boat ashore on Brumal.'

Orduval suppressed his abrupt fear and odd feeling of dislocated loss. This . . . thing just did not fit into his perception of reality. However, here it was, so his perception of reality must be wrong.

'Was that building you mentioned the Sunlight Tower?' he ventured. 'They said it was lucky the water all poured down the correct lift shaft, and that it was surprising so small a quantity put out the fire.'

The cat shrugged. 'I squirted in fire-retardant gas as well, and it broke down into base gases before the investigators got to work. Anyway, those are three examples of how I occupy my time here, within this system, whenever I've got the time to spare, of course. But you, Orduval—'

'What are you?'

'Me – I'm Tigger.'

Orduval tasted the name, ran it through the processor

that was his brain, checking the ancient languages he knew. 'Like . . . tiger. You're a tiger?'

'Not exactly,' Tigger replied.

'Well, you appear to be made of metal.'

'Yup, cell-form and pliant,' said the tiger proudly.

'You still haven't answered my question. I want to know –' Orduval froze, blankness occupying his mind, though he retained an awareness of time. Minutes passed, but he felt disconnected enough from them to not become too concerned '– what you are.' His body ached and slowly his muscles unlocked. The scene had changed. Tigger was now right in front of him.

'Yes,' said Tigger, 'there'll be no more falling off mountains for you, which is, I have to say, a pretty unhealthy occupation – nor anti-convulsives either. I placed a block to stop the clonus, so the fits will eventually fade. I've got to admit I can't yet figure out what's causing them.'

Orduval felt his legs grow weak and shaky, and he slowly sank down until he was sitting in the dust. 'What are you?'

'You're a bright spark, Orduval, just like your brother and your sisters. Let me ask you this: do you think that after you lot left it, Earth just ceased to be?'

No more anti-convulsives.

Orduval clamped down on his feelings and tried to understand more clearly what he had just been told. Really, he should have fathomed this being's source once it gave him its name. 'You are a technological product of the human race . . . from Earth.'

'Close enough.'

Orduval narrowed his eyes, stared at the cat, and

made an abrupt reassessment. 'You're a product of a product.'

'Startlingly fast.'

'Does humanity still exist?'

'Now you're getting ahead of yourself. Yes, humanity, in all its wonderful and sometimes repulsive variety, still exists and has spread throughout many star systems, and will soon be coming here.'

Orduval began to feel bolder. He stood up. 'And do humans tell *you* what to do?'

'Sometimes they do, though not very often. Generally, the machines rule the Polity. We're better at it.'

'Polity?'

'Empire, dominion . . . call it what you will.'

'Why do you *bother* to rule?'

Again that tiger shrug. 'Why not?'

Orduval closed his eyes. He could feel himself absorbing this new data and placing it on hold, ready to apply it to the huge body of knowledge resting in his narrow skull, before making massive reassessments. He replayed the conversation thus far, then asked, 'Why am I different? You inferred that rescuing me was a different matter from rescuing all those others.'

'I was instructed not to reveal myself or to interfere here. I've been ignoring that order and until now got away with it. You were one of four people – you can guess who the others are – I decided to watch very closely. You would have died here, either quickly from exposure or your injuries, or later from your fits. My intervention will be discovered, though perhaps not for some time.'

'You did not need to actually show yourself to me. I'm sure you could have anonymously engineered a scenario similar to the others.'

'Similar, maybe. But then there were those fits . . .'

'What about them?'

'Well, I interfered a bit more than can be covered.' Tigger looked to one side, exposing his teeth, then turned back to centre his gaze on Orduval again. 'Your problem was interesting to neurologists on Sudoria, in the Orbital Combine stations and in Fleet – mainly because of the notoriety of your three siblings. No engineered scenario would prevent those neurologists getting a bit uptight after seeing the first scan made of your brain after your return home.'

'That block you put in?'

'More than that.'

'You've done something else?'

'Where's your star, Orduval?'

Looking inward, Orduval felt his mind was closed like a fist. The white star, that point at the centre of his being, seemed now to be missing.

Tigger continued, 'I made surgical alterations – very small ones. I've stuck a device in your skull that shifts the balance of your neurochemicals closer to that possessed by your brother Harald. From this device a mycelium is growing which will finally complete the job. I designed it all myself.'

Orduval felt an instinctive urge to protest, but immediately rejected it. He held no love for experiencing the alternative to what this entity had done to him.

'So what now, you're going to keep me prisoner?'

'No, you can bugger off if you want, and we won't meet again for some years.'

Orduval knew he could not walk away from all this, so wondered just how well this entity knew the workings of his mind. The questions were building up inside him, like the preparatory quakes before a volcanic eruption. 'What do you want me to do, then?'

'I want them to think you dead. If you like I can give you a new identity, though I'd have to give you a new face too.'

Orduval smiled at the metal tiger and gestured back towards the cave mouth. 'If you can continue to provide for my more prosaic needs, Tigger, I will be happy to stay here for now.'

The cat grinned back.

– Retroact 11 Ends –

7

After the first two generations of Sudorian pioneers, the technology for tank-growing human beings was still in use, but with an increasing lack of expertise in that area and a dearth of resources it became a risky affair, with a less than fifty per cent chance of success. We needed people, though, for without a certain population density the establishing of many of the basic requirements of civilization becomes impossible. In those early years women were applauded for their contribution to society as mothers. There was no real marriage at the time, though casual partnerships were formed and, continuing with the system used for the tank grown, children were communally raised in crèches, whilst the mothers went back to work and to further pregnancy. Inevitably patriarchalism raised its ugly head and things began to change. The first such change was when the Planetary Council made abortion illegal. The second change was when the Orchid Party – highly patriarchal from the beginning – and the growing representation of the Sand Churches attempted to extend the law further to prohibit contraception. For eighty years women were incrementally and increasingly restricted by new laws and amendments to existing ones. It was only during the War, with the formation of the Woman's League and its landmark *inclusion in Parliament, that this trend was reversed. However, patriarchalism is still prevalent, mostly among the personnel of Fleet.*

– Uskaron

McCrooger

From the grobbleworm stall, Rhodane led the way alongside the canal. The noise of the hive city was a continuous roar in the background and it seemed to mostly consist of Brumallian chatter. I supposed that those living here came to tune it out like any other city dwellers tune out noise, but Rhodane soon disabused me of that notion. Halting shortly after we left the stall, she tilted her head, listening for a moment, then informed me, 'The Consensus acknowledges and accepts your presence.'

'As a Speaker for the Consensus do you also speak for all the people here in this city?'

She glanced at me, raising an eyebrow. 'No.'

'I see, do you then speak for a council of representatives of these people?'

'No.' She was smiling now.

I guess until then I had not truly considered what this 'Consensus' might be. In the back of my mind I had toyed with the idea of it being some democratic council of regional representatives, rather like the Sudorian Parliament, and that, as is always the case in politics, the term 'consensus' was distorted to fit reality rather than being used to actually describe it.

'Rhodane, what *is* the Consensus?'

'It is the Brumallian consensus.'

'So you speak for *all* Brumallians on this planet?'

'No,' again that smile, 'I speak for the consensus of all Brumallians on this planet.'

'So there are no real rulers?' I suggested.

'None.'

'I am surprised.' An understatement, as I simply did not believe her.

'What then do you have in the Polity?'

'Rulers and ruled – just like everywhere else.'

As we moved on, I noticed Brumallians studying me, but without surprise now – more out of curiosity regarding something about which they had already been informed. It occurred to me that if news travelled so fast in the hubbub, and in the pheromones in the air, there would be no need of media here to ill-inform public opinion. It tired me even thinking about it. Where were the controls? Could a touch of xenophobia spread amidst the citizenry, and thereby cause the Consensus to decide – or rather to *be* – that the best place for a Polity Consul Assessor was the bottom of the sea with lead weights tied around his feet?

We reached a stairway, cut into the rock and leading up from the canal path. The two quofarl stepped ahead of us and began to climb.

'I have to admit,' I told Rhodane, 'that I'm not entirely sure that I yet grasp how this society works. How would such a society initiate action that is good for the society as a whole, yet disliked by most of its members?'

'Ah, but what is good for Brumallian society is never disliked by it.'

'What if there was a plague here and it became necessary to kill three-quarters of the population in order to save the remaining quarter?'

She shrugged. 'Either the three-quarters would die

to save the society, or there would be a Consensus schism.'

'A schism?'

'It has been theorized but has never yet happened.'

'Are the mentally deficient part of the Consensus?'

'Yes, though the irretrievably retarded are not allowed to live beyond their first year.'

'Do the more intelligent Brumallians wield more influence in the Consensus?'

'Yes.'

Ah . . .

'Good ideas spread,' she added.

Oh.

'How are false memes controlled?' I asked.

'Consensus factual comparison destroys them.'

I thought about that for a while, then asked, 'Do Brumallians ever lie?'

'Yes.'

'But lies cannot survive Consensus?'

'They cannot.'

I considered some of the political ideologies that had caused massive human suffering a thousand or more years ago on Earth. Those ideologies arrived before their time, and it seemed their time was here and now. I could see just one tiny aberration in this classless, democratic, communal society, and she was walking beside me.

'So you need speakers like yourself to communicate with non-Brumallians. That such a position even exists indicates that not all Brumallians can understand the likes of myself. That's something I think reinforced by the fact that you, a Sudorian, have risen to such a key position. A speaker could easily lie about what I say, and what she says to me.'

Rhodane ran a finger along the ridging on her jaw-line. 'All 840 speakers can both hear and see us.' She then gestured to objects mounted on the walls: hemispheres with spirals of holes cut into them, of woody composition and slightly distorted, organic. 'Machines can auto-translate Sudorian, so those interested can sense our exchange.'

'Who decides what to broadcast?'

'It is all broadcast, and available to all. Individuals can decide what they want to listen to.'

'Who decides when to act if . . .' I paused, realizing I was heading for a circular discussion. 'Don't tell me: the Consensus decides.'

I realized that I would be much interested in learning more of the history of these people, since they must have gone through some traumatic upheavals before the controls – like the weighted governors on ancient steam engines – were firmly established in their society. But, of course, it was more than that. Most human societies within the Polity still carried the burden of having evolved from small hunter-gatherer communities. Here their alterations had been so drastic that little of that original blueprint might remain, and all those things imposed on previous human societies, to maintain order, here might be integral to the people themselves. What would be their next evolutionary rung to achieve? I wondered. How to improve further the well-oiled machine of Brumallian society? As I saw it, individuality needed to be removed, turning each of them into something little better than an ant functioning on hard-wired imperatives, so the society became the individual: a single mass mind.

A few Brumallians passed us as we climbed the stair. A clatter of mandibles:

'They didn't get the –'

'– smell right.'

'It's changed –'

'– clothing decaying and –'

'– physical change and –'

'– dubious –'

'– personal hygiene.'

'Hey, I'm standing right here and I can understand you!'

My comment just seemed to accelerate their conversation which, from the moment they appeared, also drew in Rhodane and the two quofarl:

'Very Sudorian –'

'– slow as a –'

'– gnubbet.'

'And really *really* dangerous.'

Laughter.

As we left the stair the noise increased and I realized, on looking around, that we must now be entering a high-density living area. The huge upright cylinder cave was filled with light provided by powerful lighting bars mounted in a framework that cut across a hundred feet above the floor. The surrounding walls glittered with windows, and out jutted numerous balconies, many of them filled with greenery. Vines laced the walls too, though I saw very few flowers and wondered if flowers, in view of one of the Brumallian methods of communication, might be considered too 'noisy'. The smell here was one I would describe as complex, and only here did I notice its subtle changes reflected in the rise and fall of audible Brumallian chatter. I felt thousands of pairs of eyes observing me, knew myself to be the subject of many local conversations, as well as the topic of a huge conversation being conducted by millions.

'We go this way,' said Rhodane, gesturing along a path nearby.

This gravelled walkway turned sharply to the left, where it met a canal and ran alongside it. Only upon seeing the waterway did I realize that what I first took to be buildings scattered about the cavern floor were in fact the deckhouses of barges crowding a canal network. Intervening spaces were filled with gardens, gazebos, circular hothouses and thousands upon thousands of Brumallians: men, women and children, who were often riding on the backs of creatures like, but never entirely like, the one that had earlier pinned me to a muddy riverbank. Many of these people walked upright but, when convenient, some went down on all fours to put on speed. I found that particularly disconcerting, since this method of locomotion seemed to dispel what remained of their humanity. Walking along with Rhodane and the two quofarl, I constantly expected us to end up trapped amid curious crowds, but the way ahead always remained clear.

We reached a bridge, crossing above barges on which goods were being loaded and unloaded. Someone nearby played a musical instrument rather like a violin, and someone else on a balcony far above supplied a clattering beat either with drums or mandibles. The aroma of boiling grobbleworms wafted across to us, then a smell like roasting chestnuts. Was that the smell of pheromonal communication or just of food? Distantly I observed a procession, with red flags flicking. A funeral, a wedding or something entirely else?

The path terminated in a stair winding up through

the cavern wall, with many exits on all sides into the surrounding accommodations. Hemispheres like a phero-mone tannoy system dotted the rock walls all the way up. We entered a low corridor with many arches opening off from it into living quarters, curious residents peeking out at us. No doors, of course. Then, surprisingly appeared a door – which opened to admit Rhodane and me into an airlock swirling with warm air. A second door admit-ted us into quarters warmer still, where the air seemed finally to take its foot off my chest.

'So how is it *you* can breathe the air and understand their pheromonal communications, Rhodane?' I asked, turning to her.

She touched that ridging on her jaw. 'Because I am now both Sudorian and Brumallian, in every sense.'

– RETROACT 12 –

Yishna – *on Corisanthe Main*

The armoured shields had been raised from a quartz window overlooking the outside area between Ozarks One and Two, and a crowd of OCTs had soon gathered there to watch the installation of the fourth quadrant gun. During Yishna's first months aboard Corisanthe Main, she had swiftly learnt just how secure the station had been made, and just how strange and insular the population aboard had become. But now she was at ease with it all. She surveyed the crowd around her, who by their dress seemed some barbarian horde out of ancient Earth history, spotted Dalepan and Edellus and walked over to join them.

Dalepan was pensively gazing down at his co-workers outside as they bolted in place the lower section of the massive gas-propellant gun. Edellus, bare-breasted as usual, rested one hand against the quartz window as she peered up towards a crew bringing in the weapon's five-hundred-foot barrel. Yishna accepted the woman's naked mammaries with equanimity now, for she had soon discovered Edellus to be the least exhibitionist of the Exhibitionists. Some of those gathered around her here wore garment tubes even cut off above the waist. This was mainly the females, though, since the way a man's genitals flapped about in zero gee put them in serious risk of damage.

'Dalepan, Edellus.' She smiled at each in turn. Now having successfully applied for research permissions, she no longer needed to add the OCT title to their names when addressing them. She fully realized how much of a privilege this was, since it meant she was now one of the elite. That set her over and above tens of thousands aboard who would have loved to attain a similar position. Nodding down towards the gun site, she said, 'Rather excessive that, don't you think? Surely the Brumallians no longer represent much of a danger.'

Dalepan did not turn round. 'The Brumallians were a serious danger once. Who can say who or what *will be* a danger?'

Paranoia was easily engendered in this cloistered and weird environment. Combine security here on Corisanthe Main consisted mainly of OCTs, who were usually more qualified for the job than anyone else. New arrivals from outside either became part of this society or swiftly transferred out, and over time the place had grown somewhat distinct from the rest of Orbital Com-

bine – almost a dictatorship under the distinctly strange
Director Gneiss.

'Four big guns, the shielding tech, missile launchers,
and twenty one-man attack craft . . . oh, and of course a
defence platform being built almost within sight of us . . .'

Now Dalepan did turn round. 'You are remarkably
interested in Main's defences.'

'Yes, I'm probably a spy or saboteur.'

Edellus chuckled. 'Maybe the former, but definitely
not the latter. You would never want this place damaged,
or for anything to come between you and the Worm.'

It was true, since her obsessive studies of bleed-over
were only interrupted by sleep, occasional periods of
relaxation like this and those damnable visits to the
psychologist some Combine do-gooder had foisted on
her. She grimaced at the thought of that individual. She
had learnt that Director Gneiss was on her side, since he
also would rather not have such people aboard and was
only acceding to the wishes of his fellows on the Combine Oversight Committee. It struck her as quite likely
that she herself was an excuse to get a psychologist
aboard, and that the real aim of Oversight was to obtain
a professional assessment of the entire population here.
And Gneiss appeared even more on her side, now that
she had uncovered part of the mechanism of bleed-over,
and found a way to record it. Apparently her recordings
were now also being copied and passed around by
the OCTs, who studied them with something akin to
religious awe.

'Agreed,' said Dalepan humourlessly. 'But we must
always remain aware of danger, for we have a great
responsibility here.'

'But what dangers are there *now*?' asked Yishna.

'Fleet, the Groundstars, the Orchid Party – and even some elements of Combine itself,' Dalepan replied.

'And now, of course, there is also the object on Corisanthe III to be taken into account,' added Edellus.

'You mean the space liner they're building?'

Edellus shook her head pityingly.

Realizing her mistake, Yishna persevered, 'Object?'

Dalepan grinned. 'No, you are no spy or saboteur, Yishna Strone. Either one would have been thoroughly aware of recent events and I see you haven't a clue.'

The gun barrel was now descending directly past the window, while suited figures fired gas thrusters attached to its surface to manoeuvre it into position.

'What object?' Yishna felt suddenly desperate. Something major had occurred and she had missed it. She must not allow herself to go uninformed.

'You tell her,' said Dalepan to Edellus, before turning back to the window.

'You can call up the full text of their message from the system, but in essence it was: *We are peaceful and we want to talk. You will find the U-space communication device at these coordinates.*'

'U-space?' Yishna felt as if she had been strolling calmly along a pavement, only to suddenly find herself teetering on the edge of a cliff. 'Who wants to talk with us?'

'The human race . . . the rest of the human race we left behind in the Sol system and on Earth, and the artificial intelligences it created. They now call themselves the Polity, though that seems a vague description. Parliament is presently debating where to site this device; Combine is fighting to retain it up here, and of course Fleet is demanding it be either handed over to them or destroyed, and that we then begin a full mobilization.'

Yishna could not speak. She felt locked in place as something seemed to tear inside her head. It felt utterly strange to suddenly find herself taking interest in something not directly related to her studies of the Worm.

'I have to find out more about this,' she said, only belatedly realizing that those overhearing her did not know what she was talking about, since she was already walking away from the two OCTs. Leaving the crowd behind, and unable to contain her impatience, she broke into a run. The terminal section where she analysed bleed-over lay nearest, so she went straight there and quickly keyed into the public information network. Soon she was reading the text of the message. It was plain Sudorian, and Edellus had accurately given the gist of it. Some considered it a hoax but, as well as arriving on just about every entertainment console on the planet, this same text apparently also turned up in the secure computer system of the new parliamentary Chairman, Abel Duras.

The given coordinates were checked and there, orbiting Sudoria, was a sphere made of a kind of chain-molecule glass that though not beyond Sudorian science, had simply not been created by it. Taken aboard a ship, this sphere was opened to reveal a communication device that could project holograms, sound and even smells. The first hologram it projected was a three-dimensional blueprint of itself, along with the warning that no one should be too eager with a screwdriver, since some of its components weren't exactly made of matter. Yishna studied the blueprint intently, then felt a sudden overpowering moment of epiphany. She understood it because it related to her work.

U-space.

Yishna immediately contacted Director Gneiss. 'U-space, that's the answer, not telepathic inductance! That's what bleed-over is!'

Gneiss gazed at her impassively from the screen, then cracked an insincere smile as he played the part of a man quite accustomed to dealing with erratic brilliance. 'As you must be aware, that has already been theorized.'

'It can be the only rational explanation,' said Yishna, calming down.

'Prove it, then,' said the Director, and cut the connection.

– Retroact 12 Ends –

McCrooger

'How does it work?' I asked as I stepped from Rhodane's bathroom, clad in Brumallian dungarees and a thick shirt of canvas-like material. The boots had not fitted me, but my feet were tough enough to manage any surface.

'You'll talk and we Consensus Speakers will listen and question you. Originally there used to be twenty Speakers present, but this was found to be too confusing for anyone not a Brumallian.'

Rhodane was sitting in one of the shell-shaped chairs, and gestured to the other one facing her across a low table. I sat down, and eyed the drink and two large dishes of food on the table before me.

'Please, help yourself. I've already eaten.'

Sliding the two dishes over towards me, I decided to dispense with the eating bowl and just hunched over and tucked in. In the typical manner of hosts everywhere she had provided more than she expected me to eat. Broiled creatures looking like crayfish steamed on one dish while the other was heaped with segments of some potato-like vegetable sprinkled with stuff like grated carrot but peppery and hot.

'We usually remove their shells before eating them,' she noted wryly. She herself sipped something similar to the cool minty concoction she had provided for me, though the temperature of hers must have been higher, judging by the steam.

'I'm very hungry,' I told her between mouthfuls.

She nodded – perhaps considering me barbaric – then stood up and wandered away for a while. Had I continued without food for long enough, she would then truly see my barbaric side. I ate literally everything, noting her bemused expression when she returned. I licked my fingers clean and wiped them dry, then with a muted belch pushed the dishes away.

'Including yourself, how many Speakers will there be?' I asked.

'Do you need any more to eat?' she asked in return.

'For the moment, no, thank you.'

'There will be five of us. We'll maintain our link with the Consensus by wearing earpieces and through the pherophones in the walls. The others are trained to respond to you as individuals – hence my being able to become a Speaker so quickly, since I didn't require that special training. However, you'll have to accept that when it comes to important decisions, or ones requiring further analysis, any response you receive will not be the definitive one. We Speakers might say *yes*, but the

Consensus *no*. It's quite difficult for the Brumallian Consensus to communicate down on the Sudorian level.'

'Down?' I sat back, feeling my digestion writhing as it went to work.

Rhodane grimaced. 'Even I am only now beginning to understand the true range of Brumallian language. One spoken word can possess all the same verbal inflexions of a similar word spoken in Sudorian, but in the process of speaking it they can load it with additional nuances and twist its meaning further by signing and emitting pheromones. One word in itself can contain everything a Sudorian would need an entire sentence to convey.'

'And their sentences?'

'Enough meaning to fill a small book. But it's the precision that's important to Brumallians; they don't often misunderstand each other.'

'Hence their success in creating a society without leaders?'

'Yes.'

She paused to sip her drink – and I to sip mine and contemplate her.

'Why are you actually here, Rhodane?' I eventually asked.

'Why're any of us here?' she countered.

I winced, not wanting to play that silly game.

She gave a tired smile. 'Many Sudorians come here to carry out research, or to work in the Fleet ground bases. It's not that unusual to find people like myself here.'

I didn't believe her for a second. She had yet to explain her comment about being both Sudorian and Brumallian. I rather suspected I knew the explanation already, and that no other Sudorians here would be Speakers as they did not possess sophisticated biotech growing on and inside their faces.

'You're a researcher, basically?'

She stared at me very directly, then said, 'My brother Harald is Admiral Carnasus's top aide and therefore wields a great deal of power. My sister Yishna is similarly the right hand of Director Oberon Gneiss on Corisanthe Main. Orduval, my other brother, could also have been very influential had it not been for the constant fits he suffered. He disappeared. I too have disappeared, in my way, and can be considered a failure too.'

'I've met Yishna. Your elder sister?'

'We're all precisely the same age: quadruplets conceived on Corisanthe Main during an information fumarole breach. We were born there, then transported planetside after our mother, Elsever, died in some stupid accident.'

She had just told me something important, yet I could not decide what it was. Perhaps I could integrate it at a later time. 'Did you feel a need to disappear . . . to escape some kind of pressure?'

Rhodane set her drink down on the table and sat back with her fingers interlaced below her breasts. She gazed up at the ceiling for a moment, then directly at me. 'So how is it, with Fleet's ban on Polity technology, that you manage to watch us so closely?'

I raised an eyebrow. 'Why do you suppose we do?'

'I've already analysed much of what you've said and done, and it seems quite evident that your knowledge of us extends beyond what has been transmitted via the U-space link on Sudoria.'

'If you're capable of such analysis, then surely you can answer your own question?'

She nodded mildly. 'Of course, while we regressed and had to start over again after arriving here, you kept on progressing? So you possess technology we are unable to detect?'

'Small regressions, but nothing on the scale of what happened here. And as for the technology you mention, I can't comment.'

'I see . . .'

I was slowly coming to realize I was dealing with a formidable intelligence here. I felt her analysis of me went beyond that comparison between my overt knowledge and what I could have learnt from the transmissions from this system to the Polity. As we had talked she had been providing just enough for me to grasp a point, where she wanted me to. This showed she had made a deep assessment of my intelligence, and perhaps knew more about me than I would like. 'You still haven't answered my question, Rhodane.'

'Why am I here?' She smiled, reached up and began running her finger over the ridged skin on her jaw-line. 'Well, I am here because here is where my driving force impelled me, just as Yishna's impelled her to Corisanthe Main, and Harald's sent him to Fleet. I was not *trying* to "disappear", but I feel I've managed to do so.'

'What is this driving force you mention?'

'I think it only fair that I ask some questions too.'

'Ask, then.'

She leant forwards. 'There used to be much dispute amidst Sudorian biologists about what the human strain was like before we began tampering with ourselves, but in recent years we've agreed on a basic format. Yet my contacts on Sudoria tell me you're not even close to that format. I've learnt from them that you are strong enough to toss about Fleet personnel and snap the locking mechanisms in armoured space doors, and I myself saw you toss a three-hundred-pound quofarl about twenty feet. You can eat grobbleworms and breathe the poisonous atmosphere beyond that door. What are you, exactly?'

'Human.'

'Not good enough.'

'Very well. I am both human and hooper. I was born and lived a substantial portion of my life in the Sol system, but I eventually made my home on a world called Spatterjay. On that world an alien virus infects all indigenous life forms. Humans can become infected too. This virus roots inside us and grows as a fibre connecting to other cells, gradually networking through the body in a fibrous mass and at the same time perpetually maintaining it. But the virus also caches, and engineers, the genetic blueprints of its various hosts. Should I be harmed or my environment change, the virus can change me to its optimum physical form for survival. For me those changes could be very nasty, because the bulk of additional genetic material the virus has cached – and uses for such changes – is of its original hosts, the Spatterjay leech and other creatures on that world. A mutality exists between leech and virus: virally infected prey becoming a perpetually reusable food resource for the leeches, whilst the leeches themselves continue to spread the virus.'

'So by coming here you risked that "nasty" change?' Rhodane could not keep the fascination out of her expression.

'It can be staved off, slowed down, by my eating foods lacking in any nutrition suitable for the virus.' I gestured to the empty dishes. 'In that way I retain my humanity. Drugs also inhibit it, but I don't have any of those with me. Without either, infected humans can transform into chimerical creatures that are a random combination of Spatterjay fauna.'

'But that's not all, is it? There's some additional problem . . .'

I had no idea how she worked that out. 'I believe you are one question ahead of me already. My question remains: what is your driving force?'

Rhodane tilted her head as if listening to something. The Brumallian chatter remained audible in this room, though muted. I had already noted the pherophones on the walls and wondered just how deep was Rhodane's understanding of their complex language. 'The answer to that will have to wait,' she announced. 'The other Consensus Speakers are almost ready for you.' She stood, then beckoned to me as she headed for the door.

'Finishing on your question,' I said. She turned to gaze at me as I stood up. 'My problem, Rhodane, is caused by a second virus that's killing the first. In essence my problem is mortality.'

Her eyes widened in shocked appreciation, or maybe disbelief, as she absorbed the implications. She then gave me this quid pro quo: 'And your question, David. I don't know the answer, yet I cannot shake the feeling that you yourself are perhaps the best person to discover it.'

'Yes . . .' It was opaque to me at that moment, yet I knew the answer lay within my reach. *Information fumarole breach . . . Corisanthe Main . . .*

'When we return I have something you should see,' she said.

'Let's hope I'll be allowed to return.'

'Yes, let's.'

She opened the first door of the airlock, and we stepped inside. After a moment the temperature abruptly dropped, as if someone had just opened a fridge nearby. Shortly the outer door clonked and she pushed it ajar. As we stepped out, my lungs tightened and my eyes began watering. Two quofarl stood waiting for us.

Rhodane led off and I followed, the two big guys falling in behind me. My lungs began to ease; I wiped my eyes, cleared my nose. It seemed almost like a touch of hay fever that quickly passed. Rhodane led me in the opposite direction to the one we came in by, heading towards a stone stair that wound up and up. Eventually we turned off that to enter a short corridor terminating at an armoured door. I noted a lot of cable trunking and sealed boxes affixed to the walls on either side, probably control circuitry, fuses or relays, I surmised.

Rhodane halted before a pherophone located beside the door, inclined her face towards it for a moment, whereupon the door immediately unlocked and she pushed it open. Inside, three Brumallians were sitting on a low horseshoe-shaped couch semi-circling a single low steel chair with head rest and arms. I noted the eyelets and metal tags on the chair for affixing straps and guessed its previous occupants did not always enjoy their sojourn there. No straps in evidence now, however. Scanning the room I noted a square port positioned directly above the chair and others positioned around the walls, so wondered what weapons would be trained on me while I spoke.

As well as the pherophones ranged around the walls, there were many other devices pointing probes and recording heads towards the chair. I guessed they were going to do more than broadcast just sound and vision footage. Doubtless there was instrumentation here to measure the beat of my heart, the electrical activity of my brain, every smallest movement, and even my pheromonal emissions. The place felt like a combination of interrogation chamber, hospital scanning room and holovision studio. Without awaiting further instruction, I went over and sat down in the chair. Rhodane walked past and joined the other three on the couch, while the two quofarl squatted on the floor right behind me.

Silence fell. I considered breaking it, then turned aside on hearing the door open, and watched as the last of the five Speakers entered. Now they could begin.

'What is your name?' asked the male sitting just to Rhodane's right.

'David McCrooger.'

'What is your title?'

'On this occasion, Consul Assessor.'

'What are you?' asked another.

'That is a question you will have to elaborate.'

They did, at length, even going into biological detail. My extended reply in turn contained more detail than I had given Rhodane. They then moved on to ask me about the Polity and my position within it, about the AIs that govern it, about Geronamid, the full extent of the Polity and its history since their ancestors departed. Every now and again they threw a completely outfield question at me like, 'Is St Paul's Cathedral, in the City of London on Earth, still standing?' To which I replied that indeed it was, though much of its original stonework was

covered by diamond film and much of its structure supported by nano-carbon filaments. I realized they were
then confining themselves to historical stuff so as to build
a picture of the present-day Polity. When it seemed they
had that sufficiently pegged, they moved on.

'Does the Polity need to expand in order to maintain its stability?'

'Not any more.'

'Why, then, did the AIs send you here?'

Motivation? Damn! Why did the AIs do anything?
Why did they stay to rule the Polity when they could
move on into realms of mind that humans could hardly
understand? 'Expansion is no longer required for
economic reasons, but humans and AIs both need to
expand their horizons. I suppose that doesn't really answer
your question? OK, it has become our policy that when
out-Polity civilizations are encountered, we first establish
dialogue with them, assess them carefully, then offer
them inclusion. If they reject this offer, we leave them
alone.'

'But being rejected here by Fleet, you have not
departed,' Rhodane observed.

'The dialogue we establish is not just with the few
who rule.'

'As we understand it, you only have one line of
communication open, and that's with only a select few
of the ruling class on Sudoria.'

'Dialogue can take many forms, and has yet to be
fully established, and I am still assessing.'

'One man cannot see everything.'

'Yes, I'm aware of that. We abide by the strictures
imposed by our hosts because that is a price we are prepared to pay to gain a foothold amongst them, so as to

properly establish a dialogue and to make a full assessment. Approached in any other way, the cost in human suffering could be great.'

'Why does Fleet so fear you they're prepared to destroy one of their own ships in order to be rid of you?'

'I think you can work that out for yourselves.'

'Why has the Polity not tried to establish dialogue with us here on Brumal?'

'I believe I already covered this ground with Rhodane, but I shall reiterate. You are not irrelevant to the Polity,' I explained. 'But making you a relevant issue in the eyes of the Sudorians, by establishing an apparently independent dialogue with you, would put you in danger from Fleet and endanger our chances of establishing a foothold on Sudoria.'

From then on the tenor of their questioning slowly began to change. They became more keenly interested in my knowledge of the situation here, specifically my knowledge of Sudorian technologies and capabilities, and the politicizing between the various power blocs on the other world. I started to feel rather uncomfortable with all this, since the information they sought was obviously more of a military nature than that relating to me.

'If we were to be attacked by the Sudorians, would the Polity support us?'

'No.'

'You would support the Sudorians?'

'No.'

'What would you do?'

'One of two things: either leave you to kill each other, or stop you killing each other.'

An abrupt gear shift occurred then with, 'How do Polity citizens entertain themselves? Do they like music?'

Weird, but I was beginning to sense how Consensus thinking outside this room swayed the questions they posed, and realized that such abrupt changes resulted from the speakers here catching up moment by moment with Consensus opinion. It reassured me to learn that the Brumallians, as a whole, had now become bored with the subject of war and instead wanted to know about music. There followed a long question and answer session about the arts. The sciences next, with many attempts to obtain hard facts from me, which led on into medical technology. But then the questioning abruptly segued into history and the Prador War. It all now seemed more like general conversation than interrogation. By the time I started fidgeting in the chair and was looking round to see if there was a toilet nearby, the session came to an abrupt end with a single question.

'Why should Brumallians want to join the Polity?'

I had been waiting for that. 'Because there are now no wars in the Polity, and very little crime. Every citizen is wealthy beyond measure and our medical technology is such that everyone there has a good chance of living forever.'

They fell silent for a very long time, then Rhodane stood up. 'Thank you, Consul Assessor David McCrooger. The quofarl will conduct you to your accommodation. We have much to consider now.'

And so I was escorted away.

– RETROACT 13 –

Gneiss – *on Corisanthe Main*

The station OCTs came here to the Blister to relax, as did security personnel and researchers. But that separation by definition of the groups within the station was something imposed by Orbital Combine and never really adhered to here aboard Corisanthe Main. This nil-gee area seemed a microcosm of the entire station, visibly displaying its oddities. The furniture within the Blister had been transformed beyond the exigencies of gravity and turned into baroque tangled sculptures in which the personnel lolled while drinking, eating, smoking strug and occasionally coupling. This exotic environment all surrounded a vaguely globular central swimming pool at the juncture of numerous cables, which also bound together the surrounding chaotic tangle. In the mass of water, naked figures swam, their features obscured by masks and breathers. People occasionally drowned there – a strange way to die aboard a space station – but Director Gneiss, who stood at the door viewing the scene, had never contemplated closing it down. He calmly surveyed the occupants of this area, and defined them, but not by their Combine titles. There the first-stage Exhibitionists, there second- and third-stagers. There Suffocant Supplicants, Endurers and Indolants. And over there was Dalepan, who had once been an Exhibitionist and had moved on to become a Cognizant. Of course, Gneiss had often felt the pressure to fall too easily into one of these groups. He resisted this and in the end his classification had remained simply 'Station Director' – a seeming subcult all its own.

The Director launched himself from the grav floor of the corridor, rising up into the tangled and comfortable chaos. He grabbed a curved strut resembling the horn of some ancient beast, pushed himself through a structure seemingly fashioned of a giant's bones, then settled down beside Dalepan, hooking his legs around the curving beam on which the Cognizant OCT rested with a hexagonal glass drinking cell, like a section from a large quartz crystal, clutched in his hand.

'Director,' said Dalepan lazily. 'I would offer you alcohol but I know you'd never take anything likely to soften that shell you live inside.'

'I thought Cognizants avoided that *poison* too?' Gneiss observed.

'I'm a neophyte, so I'm allowed my lapses.'

'How generous of them.'

'Yes.' Dalepan rolled his eyes. 'But returning to the subject of your shell, Director, how can any of us know if there is anything inside it?'

Gneiss did not reply, that being a question he often posed to himself. He was also thoroughly aware that the drink Dalepan had been imbibing contained intoxicants beyond mere alcohol. He gazed steadily and coldly at the man, wondering if he would still be able to get any sense out of him, or even if he might be able to obtain *more* than sense.

'What can I do for you, Director?' Dalepan asked, finally sobering up a little under Gneiss's wintry gaze.

'The Polity is sending a Consul Assessor here,' Gneiss replied.

Dalepan pushed himself upright, as best he could in relation to the curving beam, set his drink cell spinning weightlessly beside his head, and obviously made some effort to return himself to a more sober state. This struck Gneiss as very unlikely to happen, since he had now recognized the seared plastic smell of a particularly powerful hallucinogen based on a combination of strug extract and a cortical stimulant. Dalepan probably even thought he was hallucinating both Director Gneiss and this conversation.

'We use a slightly altered form of coconut oil on the surface of our pool.' Dalepan pointed to where a swimmer frog-kicked his way through blue water. 'It cuts down on evaporation and also increases refractivity.' He gestured to a nearby cable. 'Some of these are hollow, and through them water is removed, then cleaned and returned. If we left it untended and prevented swimmers from using it, this pool would soon turn stagnant.'

Stagnant? Gneiss analysed the unfamiliar usage of the word, and shortly realized why it was unfamiliar. Pools never grew stagnant on Sudoria, for they evaporated long before that could occur. The Sudorian language still contained a lot of words like that, because they derived from Earth languages: words that now seemed surplus to requirements. Of course, such a word would find much use on Brumal, where pools lasted longer.

'And why do you think this is of any interest to me?'

'We are submersed in a stagnant pool, drowning, trapped.' Dalepan fixed a pinpoint pupil gaze on Gneiss. 'You more so than the rest of us.'

'Someone to stir the water?' suggested Gneiss.

Dalepan nodded sagely then grabbed his drink from the air and took a pull from it. For a short while he seemed to be utterly unaware of the Director's presence.

'Do we need the water stirring?' Gneiss wondered.

'Many in Combine definitely want further contact with this Polity, but what about us here . . . and our charge? Should I contest this? Should I fight for the status quo?'

Dalepan's gaze wandered back to him. 'Of course not – we're suffocating in here and we need to find the way out.' He focused on the Director completely. 'We need to break our stasis – find a way to become fluid again.'

Gneiss nodded and felt something ease inside him. It suited him that by doing nothing, by allowing those others in Orbital Combine to get what they wanted, he might at last be given the opportunity to become freely himself rather than have himself defined by a stubborn resistance to a manipulation he barely comprehended. He smiled to himself – a rare occurrence in itself. It seemed that things might be about to change, quite possibly in a radical manner.

– Retroact 13 Ends –

8

Much to the disgust of Fleet personnel, many Sudorians have gone voluntarily to Brumal to study and better understand our old enemy. That they have even been able to do so is one indication of both waning Fleet influence and the increase in its perpetual search for a purpose. When Parliament voted for civilian researchers to be allowed to travel there, Fleet commanders could not argue against using warships for transporting those civilians, since the War was undeniably over. The request also enabled Fleet to find a new use for these vessels, and thus seek funding for their maintenance. This steady migration of researchers nearly ended when a typically naive faction of the Orchid Party detonated a nuclear bomb inside a Fleet ground base on Brumal, as a protest against Fleet oppression. Believing the indigenous population to have caused this explosion, the response of the captain of the nearest hilldigger was to launch a missile down into the nearest Brumallian town, incinerating its entire population of 5,000. This shamefully misguided act was then used by Parliament to prevent Fleet clamping down on further migration. A memorial stone was erected in memory of the personnel who died in the Fleet ground base. The burnt-out Brumallian town, however,

was quickly filled in and, if you ask now, no one is entirely
sure where it was located.

— Uskaron

Defence Platform One

With puzzlement, Kurl studied his screens for a moment
then raised his gaze to the thick glass window above
which girded the entire operations room. Outside, in the
black of space, he could just make out the shape of
the hilldigger.

'So what's this all about?' asked Cheanil.

Kurl grinned. 'When Fleet start giving me notice
of what they'll do next, I'll be sure to let you know. Until
then I'm as bewildered as you are.' He paused, checked
his displays, then asked, 'Who have we got out there?'

'Dravenik on the *Blatant*. Last I heard he was on
Corisanthe Watch.' Cheanil studied something coming
up on one of her screens. 'Apparently he has been
replaced there by Franorl on *Desert Wind*.'

'Dravenik is next in line for Admiral,' Kurl observed,
'and apparently Carnasus has started wearing a cooling
hat.'

Cheanil glanced at him. 'And what's that got to do
with anything?'

Kurl leant back, shaking his head in irritation. 'It
may be nothing . . . I don't know. Can you open a com
channel to him?'

'I am not sure the Commander would be best pleased.
Maybe we should inform him about this, and *he* should
speak to Dravenik.'

'Come on, Cheanil, I've been on this station longer
than the Commander and I know what I'm doing. I'll

just make a polite enquiry.' He paused for a moment. 'Do you want to go and wake up Commander Spinister?'

Cheanil grimaced, input the required information, and one of Kurl's screens blanked for a moment before a channel-holding graphic appeared. Then that abruptly disappeared and a young man wearing a coms headset peered back at him. Kurl realized that this image was also computer-generated, since he was talking to a tacom.

'Hello,' said Kurl. 'I'm calling from Defence Platform One, and am obviously curious about why you have positioned yourselves so close to us.'

'I'll pass you on to Lieutenant Crastus.'

The screen blanked again, the holding graphic reappeared and remained in place for some minutes before the officer in question appeared.

'You are calling from Defence Platform One?' asked the Lieutenant.

'I certainly am.'

'And you wish to know why we are holding our present position?'

'I certainly do.'

'Well . . . I did not get your name?'

'Kurl.'

'Well, Kurl, when Parliament decides Orbital Combine must be informed of every Fleet manoeuvre, then you will have every right to pose such questions. Until then, such questions are not only impertinent but a security risk.'

Kurl shrugged. 'I'm only asking what Commander Spinister will be asking Dravenik sometime soon.'

'That is Captain Dravenik to you, civilian.'

Tightly, Kurl replied, 'It may have escaped your notice, but this is a military defence installation.'

'Yes, though it would seem there are those who do not consider it as efficient as a hilldigger. For your Commander's information, we are here for planetary defence as an added precaution since that Brumallian missile attack on one of our ships. This has been approved by Parliament. Thank you for your interest.' The screen blanked again.

'Approved by Parliament?' said Kurl, leaning back in his chair with his hands behind his head. He glanced across at Cheanil, then looked at the display she was studying. One screen showed the present locations of all the personnel aboard the platform. 'I guess I should inform the Commander,' he added.

Cheanil shook her head and began groping under her console for something. 'No, I don't think you'll be doing that.'

'Huh?' Kurl wondered what she was now doing. If she was having trouble with her equipment, she should get Grant up here. Then again – Kurl checked her display – Grant was in the refectory with some of the other techs, and probably halfway through a bottle of kavis by now. 'Why won't I be doing that?'

'Because you'll be dead,' said Cheanil, sitting upright and pointing at him the silenced handgun she had retrieved from under her console.

'What do—?'

The gun made a triple thunk and an iron fist slammed into Kurl's chest hurling him from his chair. Lying on the floor, struggling for breath, he just could not believe this was happening. Cheanil came to stand over him, pointing the gun down at his forehead. Brief light ignited inside the barrel. It dropped a blackness on Kurl that would never end.

★

Cheanil returned to her seat and pulled the two spare clips from where she had taped them under her console two hours earlier. She had rather liked Kurl and therefore regretted the necessity of killing him, but she did not feel the same about the others. Commander Spinister, the other officers and the station techs were all definitely and arrogantly Orbital Combine people. All of them felt that Fleet, which had kept the Brumallians from their throats for a century, was now obsolete. Cheanil felt that the ease with which Harald had organized her penetration of Combine, her promotion to coms officer aboard this station and her smuggling of arms aboard were all proof of how wrong they were. Though, admittedly, Harald was no ordinary Fleet officer.

Cheanil picked up her console and checked its screen. With the radio link established to the station computer, she could now see clearly where everyone was, and thus plan her actions accordingly. Grant and eight other technicians occupied the refectory, Spinister and four others were in bed, and a four-person crew was conducting maintenance on the maser array outside. Cheanil entered the lift to the rear of the operations room and took it down to the living area. Stepping out she could hear Grant and the rest of them roaring with laughter or speaking with that stepped-up volume that bottles of kavis tended to provide.

Entering her own quarters she quickly pulled out her case from under her bed, input its lock code and hinged it open. As she hoisted out the Fleet-issue disc carbine, power pack and spare magazines, she again wondered at Harald's brilliance. Combine Security was by no means a pushover, yet he had gone through it like it just wasn't there. There seemed something almost supernatural

about his abilities . . . not that Cheanil believed in anything like that. Strapping on a harness to carry the power
pack and the magazines, she considered this further affir-
mation of Fleet superiority, and some sign of just what
Fleet could achieve under the right leadership: in other
words Harald.

Cheanil plugged in the carbine's power lead and
watched the indicator lights on the weapon step up
to optimum. Selecting a magazine of fragmentation
discettes, she slotted it into place underneath the tongue-
shaped barrel, and felt a whirr as the load backed up to
the breech. She took a slow, calming breath then opened
her door and peeked out. No one in the corridor.
Another check of her console revealed that one of the
techs had retired from the drinking session and returned
to her quarters. Hopefully she would have collapsed into
drunken sleep, but Cheanil would have to be careful
since the doors to those quarters would be at her back.
Walking quietly she advanced down the corridor to the
refectory entrance and looked inside. Grant and the rest
were playing cards, some of them were smoking strug
and tobacco, and thankfully, at tables drawn together and
cluttered with bottles of kavis and bowls of snack-beetles,
they all sat as a close group.

'Cheanil!' Grant spotted her and began to stand.

Cheanil replied by stepping inside and opening fire,
drawing her weapon across. Twenty discettes hissed from
the flat barrel, unravelling into razor peelings of metal as
they travelled. Two of the group, sitting with their backs
to her, slammed forward, their heads disappearing in a
shower of brain and bone. Three next to Grant shot
backwards, their chairs toppling over, pieces of gory
flesh, broken glass and game cards hailing beyond them.

Grant's guts and most of his backbone exploded out behind him, and he hurtled back to land in two separate halves. Only one man now remained alive – still sitting at his chair at the table, his mouth gaping. He had time only to glance down to see his entire arm missing below the shoulder before Cheanil fired again. Then he, his chair and part of the table turned into a cloud of bloody splinters that coated the wall behind.

'Will you please keep the noise—'

Turning, Cheanil notched down the firing rate and triggered once. The woman, who only yesterday had tried to proposition her, slammed back inside her sleeping quarters, leaving an extended star-shaped splash of blood and flesh particles along the corridor wall. Cheanil checked her in passing: no need for another shot. Now for those hopefully still asleep.

Heading back down the corridor, Cheanil called up a new display on her console: this one showed the locking code to each set of quarters – obtained by another of Harald's wonderfully intricate programs. Three died on their sleeping mats, the fourth as he was vomiting kavis and snack-beetles into his toilet. Saving Commander Spinister for last, Cheanil was disappointed to find him still in his bed. It seemed to her that she should at least say something.

'Commander,' she began. 'Commander, I've come to wake up both you and Orbital Combine.'

He turned over and stared up at her bleary-eyed. 'What are you doing in here, Cheanil?'

'I just told you.' She raised her weapon.

His arm came round and up. Something fisted her kidney and spun her back from the doorway. Recovering, she fired back blind into the room, then kept firing as she staggered towards the door again. Spinister managed to rise to one knee before she finally spread him all over the walls. Stepping back, she gasped and looked down at the hole that had been ripped through her just above the hip.

Damnation, she should not have been so unprofessional.

Four yet to deal with. Cheanil wiped blood from her console screen and saw they were still outside, working on the maser. Even if they came in now, it would take them half an hour to unsuit. It meanwhile took her a quarter of an hour to find a medical kit, plug her wound and seal it under a sticky patch, and then inject a local anaesthetic and anti-shock drugs. Returning to the control centre she took the weapons-control chair – the Commander's place – and on one screen viewed the four figures gathered around the maser. They were all inside the forty-foot-wide dish, replacing some of the reflective cells. It was a minor job, however, that would not affect the functioning of the weapon. Cheanil plugged in her console and, using more of Harald's programs, took control. A small test burst to check positioning of the central unit was all she required. Cheanil watched the sudden frantic motion of the four figures. Their suits grew fat and taut, and by the time steam and smoke burst from developing leaks, the four were no longer moving. Microwaved above boiling point, their own fluids impelled them tumbling away from the station.

Now Cheanil opened a secure communications channel.

'I am in position,' she said, 'though I am injured and estimate I will only remain useful to you for a maximum of five hours.'

Harald gazed coldly at her from the screen. The

image was a recorded one, animated to suit his words, since she knew he would really be communicating with her via his coms helmet. 'Disappointing, Cheanil. How did you manage to get yourself injured?'

'I allowed myself a moment of grandstanding, and for that I apologize.'

'Very well. It is fortunate that the timing I require should still be within that period. Tune into the media channels and keep watch. I will try to contact you again, but if I am unable to, I confirm that you must attack immediately after our retaliatory strike against Brumal.'

'Understood,' Cheanil replied, but now found herself talking to a blank screen.

McCrooger

I waited with a degree of trepidation, but that didn't last, and soon all the effort of the last few days came down on me and I closed my eyes. Some hours later the sound of the airlock opening jerked me out of a deep sleep, as Rhodane entered.

'How did it go?' I asked.

She shrugged. 'They asked the questions and you replied.'

'But what is their response to my replies?'

'It will take some time for it all to be processed by Consensus, but there are no quofarl standing guard outside, so it seems you are not considered a threat.'

'I see.' I sat upright, trying to clear my mind. 'You told me earlier there is something I should see?'

'Yes, there is.'

'Then perhaps I should see it now, before any quofarl do come to guard me.'

'Yes,' she agreed, with some reluctance, I thought.

She led the way back out into the Brumallian city, turning to the right along the main corridor, then into a side corridor terminating against another spiral stair. Here I noticed the stone was coated with a fine lattice of something like lichen, and saw how the stair was eerily lit by those insectile biolights. Climbing ahead of me, Rhodane began to speak.

'When depression controls the mind, its power increases when the mind remains inactive. It is like a computer virus spreading to occupy unused processing space. You can fight it by keeping busy. There are other ways to fight it: exercising releases endorphins to counter it, or manufactured drugs can be used. Those who suffer learn many such techniques to defeat it, or they go under.'

I could not see her face but understood she was using some rather oblique analogy about her own condition, about what she was. I told her, 'In the Polity, few suffer from depression, having had the original genetic fault corrected. Whenever it stems from a later physical or mental problem, microsurgery and nanoscopic techniques can be used to correct it.'

I don't know how high we had climbed by then, but I noticed now a lack of any corridors branching off from this stair, and also a lack of pherophones on the walls.

'So it is always organic?' she asked.

'Usually, yes, though otherwise reprogramming and memory adjustment can be used.'

She halted for a moment. 'We don't have the benefit of such technologies.'

The stair finally ended under a cramped dome, where we entered a long cold tunnel running through damp clay that was braced with numerous beams and with sheets of mesh.

'We're not talking about depression, here, are we?' I asked as we strode along.

Ignoring my question she continued, 'I suffered from the black pit all my life. Whenever I slowed down, relaxed or stopped, the pit opened and I began my descent. It was related to and part of my other condition, and is an affliction from which neither Yishna nor Harald suffer. It *drove* me. Orduval was likewise driven and suffered a similar malady, though his problem lay in some other part of his psyche. In his case he just kept overloading and crashing like a computer asked to do too much.'

'It drove you to what?'

'Carnage,' she replied succinctly.

'Why?'

'I don't know . . . or I am unable to let myself know.'

The tunnel terminated at a single exit door, which was secured by a pherophone and keypad lock. Rhodane stooped for a moment before the pherophone, before inputting some code into the keypad. She then spun a wheel positioned centrally on the door, to admit us to a warmer place, but with air just as lethal to normal humans as that left behind us.

We stepped out on a balcony overlooking an immense dark hall. How far it extended I could not say, since before me the curved surface of some giant object rose to the ceiling, its skin hexagon-patterned over shifting veins, and scaffolds laced all over it. I could, however, see that another of its kind lay beyond it, and more beyond that, until the curve of the side wall concealed all further on. I realized we were just below the planet's surface now, for ceiling panels admitted a glimpse of night sky.

'Let's go down.' She pointed to a nearby stair of prosaic metal, bolted to stone.

'What is this?'

'When I came here I knew only how to sign-speak. They did not allow me down into one of their cities until I could understand their vocal language as well. Their language underlies everything that they are – how their minds develop, and how their society has developed. I didn't realize until recently how language underlies everything that I am.'

'As with us all,' I replied. 'How we describe our world informs our perception of it – but I again sense you are hedging around the point.'

She ignored that, continuing with, 'Have you read Uskaron's book?'

'I have.'

'I did not really need to read it, because I felt immediately sympathetic to the Brumallians and came to value them more than my own people. What the hilldiggers did to this place angered me, that hideous loss of life angered me. I wanted vengeance.' She turned and looked at me. 'But as you must realize, David McCrooger, what I want is not necessarily what *I* want.'

We had by now reached the floor. I gazed at dormant biomechanisms clustered like huge iridescent beetles about the base of the nearest of the huge objects, all of which I now saw bore a teardrop shape. The pumps sounded louder here and I could feel their titanic vibration through the floor. Reams of peristaltic pipes entered the base of each object – forcing in nutrients and evacuating waste. To one side, on a large trailer, rested a mechanism consisting both of some biofactured and some plainly manufactured components. It took me only a moment to realize this was a fusion engine, though one of esoteric design. I began to understand what this place was, and wondered what my chances were of getting out alive if we were discovered here.

'When I originally found this, they had no interest in it at all,' Rhodane told me. She smiled and gestured for us to move on down the lengthy hall. We walked in silence for a while, finally coming athwart a side cavern in which squatted something I could only assume to be some kind of cannon.

'They abandoned this place after the hilldiggers struck. When I asked about the weapons they used during the War, a Speaker directed me here. No attempt was made at concealment, and clearly no Brumallians had come here in a long while. I knew that to get things running again, to be able to right the terrible wrong done to the Brumallians, I needed them to feel the same way as I did and for that I needed to become more like them.'

'They had sufficient expertise left to physically change you?'

'I found it in their records, but it took me some time to create the recombinant viruses. They watched my work with some interest, and sometimes they even helped.'

I looked at her and tapped a finger either side of my face where the fibrous patches were positioned on hers. 'Those are for the pheromones?'

'To emit them, yes. My sense of smell increased till I could read them just like any other Brumallian.'

I studied the weapon and the other things surrounding me. The teardrop objects were evidently biofactured spaceships – warships – and though there seemed little activity here now, there had definitely been much recent activity.

'You persuaded them,' I suggested.

'I became part of the Consensus, but a rogue part. I could influence it and yet not be influenced myself, or so I thought. I stated my opinions again and again. At first nothing much happened, then slowly one or two of them came to help me. After a year I had a thousand Brumallians working here, and the meme I had sown began to spread.'

I guessed what was coming next. 'But the language?'

'Yes . . . filling up my mind with its intricacies. Communication itself slowly becoming more important than what I was communicating. The Brumallians began to trickle away, lose interest, and their lack of interest began to affect me. Perhaps by changing myself I have overwritten basic codes implanted into my original DNA at the moment of my conception. One day I just walked out of this place and knew I was free.'

As I studied her for a long moment, the spectre of the war she had tried to resurrect seemed to crouch in the shadows here. I shivered, now knowing the frightening efficacy of Rhodane, and by extension that of Yishna and Harald.

I asked, 'Will you eventually grow mandibles?'

She did not reply, because just then came the racket of heavy feet descending on the stair far behind us. I glanced back to see many quofarl and other Brumallians charging down, armed, and looking none too happy.

– RETROACT 14 –

Orduval – *in the Desert*

He counted thirty-two fits occurring since his first meeting with Tigger, each much weaker than the preceding one, the most recent causing a mere thirty-second stutter in his life. With the anticonvulsives no longer impeding him he felt healthier and much more alert than at any time since he had walked into the Ruberne Institute as a child. Sometimes he questioned his choice of remaining out here in the Komarl, but never for long. The information Tigger imparted to him each time it came here kept him hanging on eagerly for the drone's next visit. He also realized that a large proportion of his life had been a kind of aversion therapy and that, illogically, he felt a return to civilization somehow related to a return to his previous mental and physical state. He stayed. And he loved the desert.

On his twentieth day he found a metallic sphere resting in the clearing outside the cave. Recognizing it as being fashioned of the same metal as Tigger, he felt no fear as he stepped out to inspect it. However, he did jump when it addressed him.

'Let me introduce you to my other half,' said Tigger's voice.

Orduval stared at the sphere and considered for a moment, quickly working out what the drone meant. It then occurred to him that this fast grasp of meaning was a complete conversation killer, so decided to ask the obvious question: 'What do you mean "your other half"?'

'I reckon you understand perfectly, Orduval, but I'll tell you anyway,' Tigger replied. 'Being a manufactured entity, it's not necessary for me to have a discrete body. I consist of two parts: the tiger part which I use for planetary environments and to chat with the likes of you, and this sphere which, on the whole, I use extra-planetary. It's the larger part of me, in that it contains the most memory and other resources – tools and the like.'

'Weapons?' Orduval suggested.

'Those too. They're only a kind of tool.'

'So why have you brought your other half here?'

'To use the more prosaic tools,' Tigger replied. 'Your accommodation here is merely one-star and I intend to correct that. Why don't you pack some supplies and take a walk for the rest of the day? I've got work to do here.'

Orduval returned to the cave, filled a backpack with a water container, some food and a small console – which also contained a direction finder – and then did as suggested. Under the pounding sun he chose the desert outpost as his vague destination, but did not expect to reach it. As he tramped across boiling sand, he considered all Tigger had told him about the Polity; he similarly considered his own world, and compared philosophies. At one point he sat on the ridge of a dune and gazed across the shimmering sea of sand before him. Those dunes, stacked up by the wind and driven across the landscape, were like waves, maybe ripples on a pool? Each wave of colonization from the Sol system was just like such a ripple, the cast stone that formed them being human sentience centred on Earth. He made some notes in the console about this, and considered other analogies: humans like grains of sand; swirl patterns of dust storms compared to the turmoil of newly forming societies. It was a game, a game of analogy, and one he knew had been played many times before.

Surprisingly, he reached the outpost station before the morning was done and before consuming even half of his water. By this feat he realized just how unfit he had been when first setting out from this place. After wandering around the dusty buildings, he went to gaze at the maglev road – his link back to civilization – and watched one train shoot past raising a dust cloud, before turning to head back towards what had begun to feel like home to him.

Only now he could not find it.

Climbing the mount to reach the place where he first saw Tigger, Orduval found no cave entrance behind the familiar clearing. For a moment he thought the drone had sealed up the cave with the intent of driving him out into the desert to die, but quickly rejected the idea.

'Tigger,' he called.

A stone door hinged silently open and the drone sphere floated out.

'I think you'll like it once I'm done.'

When Orduval entered the cave he wondered at the power and efficiency of the tools the drone employed. It had carved out branching rooms, with no sign of the stone debris removed, had smoothed walls and cut shelves, levelled the floor and installed lights. Everywhere protruded wiring and pipework, ready to be connected to familiar domestic appliances.

'Where will the power and water come from?' Orduval asked, as he inspected his newly fashioned abode.

'I have drilled down to ground water, and behind the rear wall I have installed a small fusion reactor – enough for your needs.'

Over the ensuing months the drone brought in appliances, furniture, carpets, installed sanitary facilities, filled a food store and cooler. When it brought him a desk and a chair, Orduval sat down, opened his console and typed *The Desert of the Mind: A History*, and appended his own name to it. After a moment of consideration he deleted his name. Then, remembering stories of one of the early colonists, he appended the pseudonym *Uskaron* and began to write.

– Retroact 14 Ends –

Harald

Harald felt the vibration of the *Ironfist*'s drive through his chair. It was not leaving orbit, merely repositioning to deliver Fleet's violent reply to the attack on Inigis's ship. Right now Fleet surface installations were being abandoned, and communications with the Brumallians being cut. Harald smiled coldly and returned his attention to the Lieutenant seated opposite him.

'A detailed and extensive report,' he pronounced, then closed off the segment of eye-screen that had displayed it. 'Now you must give me your conclusions.'

'With respect, Tacom, it is not within my remit to come to conclusions,' Lieutenant Alun replied.

Harald grimaced. 'And those who stick too diligently to their remit are doomed to languish in the same rank in Fleet until they retire. Let me put it another way, I would be most interested in hearing your opinion on this matter.'

'Which I should append to this report?'

'If you so wish.'

Alun stabbed a finger down onto the deck between them. 'The launcher was of wartime Brumallian construction; the dead were certainly Brumallians, and those available satellite pictures of the action seem to indicate they did fire the missile that struck Inigis's ship. This being so, to have remained undetected the launcher must have come up through BC32 – the small underground city they call Vertical Vienna – which lies only twenty miles away.'

'But?' suggested Harald.

'Some believe this was a preliminary strike preparatory to full conflict. I cannot see how this could be true, since we know they hardly possess the ability now to even get into space, and there has been no follow-up aggression from them. Had the attackers been Sudorians, we could have supposed them to be renegades, but Brumallian society acts in consensus, so there are no renegades there. I can only suppose that they felt the Consul Assessor himself to be a threat or . . . this was *not* an attack by the Brumallians.'

Harald leant back. 'Interesting theory. Who then?'

Alun kept his voice bland as he explained, 'There are elements here in Fleet who considered the Consul Assessor much more of a threat than the Brumallians.'

'That is a very serious accusation.'

'Opinion merely,' insisted Alun.

'Which you will append to the report?'

'I *shall* append an opinion,' said Alun carefully. 'It seems to me that elements as yet unidentified intended this action to be blamed on Fleet – suggesting that we used some Special Operations team to set it up, in our usual warmongering manner. The implicit sophistication of the action leads me to suppose that some powerful organization has used one of its own Special Operations teams – meaning a Sudorian organization . . . perhaps one even as powerful as Orbital Combine?'

Harald studied Alun. 'I think you can neglect to mention Fleet Special Operations teams, but I would agree with the theory that some Sudorian organization plotted with the Brumallians of BC32 on this. Evidence has since become available indicating a schism in Brumallian society, centring on that city, and that Sudorian agents of the aforementioned organization are active there.'

'Evidence?'

'Oh yes, plenty of incontrovertible evidence.'

Alun just stared at him for a long moment, then shrugged.

Harald continued, 'Both parties would benefit from smearing Fleet and thereby reducing its power. The Brumallians would benefit from our reduced vigilance, and others would be able to seize some of our prerogatives in controlling the defence of Sudoria.'

'Yes, that seems reasonable,' said the Lieutenant.

'Thank you, Alun. I look forward to the additions you will make to your report, and will watch with interest your advancing career.' Harald gestured to the door.

Alun stood up, saluted with his closed fist over his side arm, and moved to depart. However, he halted at the door and turned back. 'May I ask a very direct question, Commander?'

'You may. I think you have earned the right.'

'It *was* one of our teams down there, wasn't it?'

Harald smiled. 'I don't think Orbital Combine or

any other organization possess the professionalism – so of course it was our men.'

'And we're going to bring down Orbital Combine?'

'Yes, Alun, we are going to bring them down – and hard.'

Alun grinned fiercely and departed. Harald's smile evaporated as the door closed behind him.

The man was now on his way to make his *other* report, and on his way to a bitter destiny. Harald focused on his eye-screen again, and ran through a recording of this most recent meeting with Alun. There was plenty there he could use, plenty he could change, distort and edit together. Afterwards he checked the time, then speed-read another five reports. He moved on to check the programs he had made to track events. Franorl was now in position off from Corisanthe Main, and the party of Combine observers was aboard *Desert Wind*. And any moment now . . . Harald observed the com icon light in the corner of his screen, initiated it and read the expected text summons from Admiral Carnasus. He stared at it for a long moment, then abruptly gave his response before wiping the summons, and then opening a secure com channel. He observed a white and sickly face, framed by black hair, turning towards him.

'Are you still ready, Cheanil?' he asked.

'I am still ready,' she replied.

'Stay ready. Your time comes within the hour.'

– RETROACT 15 –

Yishna – *leaves Corisanthe Main*

A vision arose in her mind of steel hearts beating in darkness, the spaces between them crammed with folded layer-upon-layer of reality, programs chewing through the folds like metallized bugs and long segmented worms, and the feeling of being smothered inside this mass . . . Yishna woke with panic heavy in her chest and lay motionless on her sweat-soaked mattress. Every clink or distant sound caused this panic to surge sickeningly. Slowly a feeling tingled in her legs, a restlessness. She had to move them but felt frightened to do so. She fought against it, slowly overcoming the paralysis. But moving her legs didn't seem to help. Carefully she reached out and put on the light, then lay there gasping, for even the bright sunny glow did not dispel the inner darkness, rather seemed thinly layered over it. Abruptly she sat up, swung her legs to one side of her sleeping mat and stood up.

The same nightmare had been recurring in every period of sleep for some time, so that she had now become afraid to close her eyes. Trying to stay awake did not help, since even then the nightmare eventually crawled into her conscious mind, or otherwise loomed at the periphery of her perception. Drugged sleep merely held it off for a little while, then it returned with redoubled force. Trying to remain rational, she analysed her condition, but the fear that she knew precisely its source caused her to veer away from making any conclusions.

Standing leadenly in her room within Corisanthe

Main, it took Yishna some minutes to notice the flashing icon on her touch-screen. She keyed it and found a summons from Director Gneiss, but timed for an hour ago. Though dreading this summons, now that it had come she felt relieved. Still dressed in the clothes in which she had slept, she moved quickly out into the corridor and strode woodenly towards the Director's office. Seeing OCTs and researchers bustling about around her offered a welcome distraction from the shadows. Finally she came to stand before the curtain drawn across his office entrance, and there lost her impetus. After a moment Gneiss himself drew the curtain aside. She tried to tell herself that he must have been on his way out, but knew deep inside that he had somehow sensed her presence.

'Yishna,' he looked her up and down, 'come in.' He gestured her over to his divan, then sat down beside her, peering at her intently, the spoked wheels of his irises seeming almost on the point of revolving. 'You know why you're here?'

'I think so,' she managed, though she felt his question contained several perilous levels of meaning.

'Can you explain?'

Stay at the surface. Don't go any deeper . . . it's dark down there. Why was she here in his office now, not why did she exist.

'I just can't seem to . . .' Yishna could not go on. The nightmares had started after she interfered with the emergency protocols, and from then on she had felt her condition steadily worsening, until, over the last year it seemed all she could manage was to drag herself to a convenient research unit. But, once there, she had discovered nothing new, and often found herself just staring at the screens for hours. She knew that no psychologist could have helped. How could she explain to them her fear that the territory of her mind had been invaded? How could she now tell Gneiss? Or did he already know?

'You need a break. When was the last time you left Main?'

Entirely unexpected. She looked at him in puzzlement. *Leave* Corisanthe Main?

Gneiss leaned back. 'I have recommended you for a position outside the station. You'll still be working for me, but must report directly to the Oversight Committee. We need somebody of your . . . potential, in at the ground level.'

What was he talking about?

He continued flatly, 'We don't know when this individual is going to arrive but we definitely need an established Combine representative in this matter.'

'Representative?'

'We need a representative in place when this Polity Consul Assessor arrives.'

'Oh.' She recollected hearing something about that, but could not summon any emotional response. Gazing down at her grubby clothing and the dirt under her fingernails, she said, 'I'm a mess.' The words seemed to cause a moment of disconnection, a lessening of the intensity between them. The moment became almost humanized.

'Do you think I don't understand?' Gneiss stood, paced over to his workstation and picked up a console. 'It gets to some people. Dalepan said you were sensitive to it.'

'To what?'

He gestured about him with the console he held. 'All

of it: bleed-over, the oppressive claustrophobic atmosphere, the downright strangeness . . . Stand up now.'

Yishna got up, realizing with some disgust that she
had not washed her hair for longer than she cared to
think about.

'Yishna Strone, you will be the Orbital Combine representative designated to meet the Consul Assessor when
he arrives. Get yourself cleaned up and your belongings
packed. You leave on the next shuttle heading over to
Corisanthe II, and from there you will take the next
landing craft groundside, where you will be taken to
meet Chairman Abel Duras.'

'But why?' Yishna could not understand why he had
chosen her. Surely he, as well as many others, must consider her a burnout.

'I have every confidence in you, and I know the
power of your mind. It goes away, you know, once you
are back in the real world.' He seemed almost wistful, his
strange eyes gazing beyond Yishna to some other place
or state of being.

He was right. Aboard the shuttle, as it headed for
Corisanthe II, Yishna felt as if she was pulling out into
sunlight from underneath some bleak shadow. And in her
mind suddenly flashed an image of Gneiss, black and
toad-like, with Corisanthe Main clutching him like a fist.

– Retroact 15 Ends –

9

The War properly ended when Fleet employed its gravity disruptors against the remaining Brumallian warships and their orbital support industry. The near-genocide committed thereafter from orbit and through the deployment of ground troops underlined that ending of conflict in so sordid a fashion as to begin a major shift in Sudorian public opinion. There are only so many broadcasts about Brumallians being conquered that any civilized human being can cheer. We grew uneasy at seeing images of yet more quofarl being incinerated in tunnels or disc-gunned into bloody fragments in forests. Seeing ordinary Brumallians trapped on shores or river-banks, and then shelled into non-existence, increased that unease. 'They won't surrender,' we were assured. 'We have no choice,' said those GDS troops and Fleet marines, their expressions haunted. We grew sick of seeing piles of worm-riddled corpses being pushed by bulldozers into pits. We grew increasingly suspicious of Fleet's censorship of certain broad-casts. But, even then, many of us had grown desensitized to the images, and the real turn in public opinion was instigated by a simple audio recording that was smuggled out. There are few of us, as a result, who have not heard the terrible sound that ensued after phosphor bombs were dropped into an underground

Brumallian town with a population of ten thousand. It was
a sound often reproduced in the protest songs that followed;
that concerted shrieking rose like a symphony of Hell recorded
from the Pit.

– Uskaron

McCrooger

The quofarl first surrounded us, then closed in. Two
grabbed Rhodane, thrust her down on the floor and
pinned her there. As two grabbed me, I allowed them to
shove me to the floor, and as I went down I felt something rip across the back of my hand, probably the edge
of a quofarl carapace. They searched us, thoroughly, then
grudgingly hauled us back to our feet.

'What's going on?' Rhodane finally demanded.

The quofarl responded only with an irritated click-
ing of their mandibles, and aimed their weapons more
deliberately. Now Rhodane began to look really worried
as she observed other Brumallians spreading out through
the surrounding area. It was not just quofarl arriving, but
others laden with equipment. Abruptly lights set into the
walls came on, and the hum of power permeated the air.
Some of the biomechanisms around the bases of the
ships began showing signs of movement, the pumps
accelerated, and light and heat began to emit from the
ships themselves.

'Are you picking up anything from the Consensus?'
I asked.

'Something is definitely going on,' she said.

'No shit?'

She held up her hand, listening intently to the
chatter of the other Brumallians here. I guessed she was

also trying to interpret the chemical messages in the air.

'Perhaps you should never have brought me down here?' I suggested.

'It's not that. Something about Fleet . . . and an evacuation. I think the Speakers—'

The quofarl abruptly parted.

'Come –'

'– with –'

'– us,' they said, and a couple of the hand gestures I read indicated: *Move now, urgency, danger, outsiders, protect citizens.* The butt of a weapon smacked into my back and I started to turn in anger, but Rhodane grabbed my arm and began towing me after the two quofarl who led off. 'Keep moving, don't question their orders, don't disobey – and don't do anything stupid.'

'Danger?'

'They are confused and scared, so will kill us at the slightest provocation. There's a threat to—'

'Silence,' ordered the quofarl, and that's what they got.

They did not take us out the way we had come in, but into a tunnel to one side, then at its end through two sets of heavily armoured doors and out into the open air. The ground lay hard underfoot – mud frozen solid and blistered with shell-ice – and snakes of aubergine cloud occluded the starry firmament. To my right I observed more quofarl shoving ahead of them another figure in an envirosuit like Rhodane's. I also noticed that one of them carried a similar figure slung over his shoulder. So it was not just us, and I guessed this was some instinctive or preplanned reaction to threat.

Finally they brought us to the edge of a canal where a massive cargo barge sat on the steadily freezing water.

By now Rhodane had put on her helmet and gloves, so looked little different to the other Sudorians being forced into the barge. Typical: round up the aliens and intern them. I guessed some things would never change.

It was crowded inside, people sitting with their backs against the outer walls or scattered in groups about the cold alloy floor. I estimated there to be at least 200 people gathered here. Frightened chatter filled the area, but it always dropped to silence when the doors opened and more people were shoved inside. I supposed these Sudorians were used to dealing with Brumallians and well aware of how dangerous quofarl could be, but I also wondered how many had died already, for the one I had seen being carried over a shoulder had not been brought here with us but taken towards a barge moored further along the canal. Standing head and shoulders above everyone else, blatantly not wearing protective gear and evidently neither Sudorian nor Brumallian, I became the focus of much attention.

'What's he?'

'That Consul Assessor from the Polity.'

'I thought he was dead.'

'Looks very much alive to me.'

'Is he anything to do with this?'

Finally seals thunked down in the doors, fans started running, and the temperature began to rise. After a little while someone called out, 'It's safe!' and people began to remove their atmosphere helmets.

'Have you any idea what's going on?' I asked Rhodane once she had taken off her own.

'Not yet.' She raised her hand in greeting to a woman just across the room, who began to make her way towards us. 'Shleera will know.'

'So this is him.' Shleera looked me up and down, and I studied her in return. I realized that her bulk was not all due to her envirosuit. She was overweight and wore spectacles – both of which were never seen in the Polity unless as a matter of choice.

'It certainly is,' Rhodane replied. 'Shleera, meet the Polity Consul Assessor, David McCrooger.'

'I would rather have met you under different circumstances,' she said.

'Do you know what's going on here?' Rhodane asked.

'Fleet,' Shleera spat. 'What do you think?'

'Have they attacked?'

'Not yet.' Shleera glanced around at those who were gathering closer. 'Consensus Speakers have been in contact to deny any responsibility for the missile strike on his ship' – she gestured at me. 'They investigated and retrieved enough evidence to refute Brumallian involvement but, before they could pass it on, Fleet cut communications. Now Fleet are pulling their personnel out of the ground bases.'

'I have heard nothing about this.' Rhodane was looking puzzled.

'Perhaps you're not as close to them as you would like to think,' Shleera replied.

'We did hear something about an evacuation,' I interjected.

'Evacuation,' Shleera shook her head. 'That's not the ground bases, that's Vertical Vienna. It started in secret shortly after the missile strike, and is now being conducted with some urgency.'

'Fleet wouldn't dare,' said Rhodane.

'Parliament has allowed Fleet to take the caps off its

guns. You do realize the *Carmel* space station is working again?'

'Shit,' said Rhodane, or rather used some nearly untranslatable Sudorian equivalent.

'Vertical Vienna?' I enquired.

She glanced at me. 'The subterranean city nearest to the missile's launch site.'

I considered that, and found my hand straying to the tiger pendant on my chest. After a moment I coughed into my hand and said, 'Tigger.'

Rhodane looked at me, 'What?'

'Nothing. "Tigger" is just an expletive in my language.' The pendant moved against my chest. I casually took hold of it, and looped the chain off over my head. As soon as Rhodane returned her attention to Shleera, I opened my fist and glanced down to see that the miniature tiger now held one paw over its eyes and seemed to be wincing.

'You were saying Fleet would destroy an entire city in retaliation?' I asked.

'They'll call it a military excision,' Rhodane replied. 'And it will all look very neat in the media, because all anyone will ever see is a hole in the ground.'

'Or not even that,' Shleera added, 'if they use a gravtech weapon.'

'So you're saying that Fleet may very soon be launching an orbital strike against the Brumallian city called Vertical Vienna?'

The pendant squirmed in my fist. Rhodane gazed at me with a blank expression, but Shleera's look gave me the distinct impression she thought me rather thick.

'Yes, that's very likely,' said Rhodane, before Shleera could comment.

I raised my fist, rubbing one eyebrow with my forefinger, opened my hand as I lowered it, then quickly closed it again. The tiger lay on its back in my palm, paws in the air and eyes crossed. In my own tongue – the language spoken on Spatterjay for a millennium and on Earth for a similar period before that – I said, 'Tigger, stop those fuckers from destroying that city. Use any means necessary.'

'What was that?' asked Rhodane.

'I believe in a supreme being,' I replied, 'and I just prayed for intercession.'

– RETROACT 16 –

Tigger – in the Past

With his two halves joined together Tigger gazed down at the river, tracking further along its course to where it poured into the fifty-yard-wide mouth of the underground pipe. Seismic mapping had shown only two breaks in the pipe, where water seeped into the surrounding limestone and sought out its previous natural routes from the time before the Brumallians had diverted it to New Pavonis – a city named after one on Mars that lay in the shadow of Pavonis Mons. *New* Pavonis had been one of Brumal's largest underground cities, its population topping five million.

'Okay, graverobber,' said Tigger to himself, 'let's take a look.'

Still remaining combined, because for this task he felt he would require *all* of himself, Tigger descended alongside the massive waterfall into misty depths, tracking his progress by radar once the light from above ground began to fail. Two hundred yards down, the pipe began to curve, the waterfall becoming a torrent that gradually filled the entire pipe as it narrowed. He submerged, initiating sonar and switching on his headlights. Here he came upon the first rupture; the pipe being sheared through and displaced to one side by half its width. Some water had flowed into crevices throughout the surrounding rock, gradually widening its escape route, but not enough to make a visible difference to the main torrent. Five hundred yards further on, the pipe began to widen again, to level out, and here the flow hit a series of generator stations and baffles. Emerging from the main flow of water again, he kept his lights on as he cruised along above the surface. Some Brumallians had escaped from here through exit tunnels leading to the surface. Many others had not. After their exit tunnels were blocked by collapses they tried to head downstream back towards their city. Only death had lain in that direction.

Some 300 yards beyond the last generating station, Tigger entered a wide slice through the rock, where only a few remnants of the pipe remained, the river now spreading out into a wide shallow flow that disappeared off into darkness on either side. Ahead, he eventually came upon a continuation of the pipe again, bone-dry and high up in a rock face. He entered this and cruised along to where the pipe terminated in a canal bed, now roofed with stone where there had been open space. Either side of him there had once been a glittering grotto of underground tower blocks, homes, factories, shops: all the panoply of human civilization. After the attack it had all been compressed down to a layer about three feet thick in which the humans had become thoroughly melded with their civilization. He passed a barge lying on the canal bed, disconnected skeletons scattered all around it, the distorted skulls of Brumallians presenting nightmare mandibles. Further skeletons revealed broken bones. He wondered if they had died of their injuries here or drowned before the water drained away. There was no way of telling without some forensic work, and that was not what he was here for.

Tracking through the canal system the drone eventually reached a point where a crevice opened above him. Closer now to this feature he had often scanned from above, he scanned it again to confirm his supposition. Tigger mapped the weaknesses in the rock then after a short while rose to a preselected point, before extending a metallic protuberance from his body which flashed and emitted the turquoise glare of a particle beam. After a few seconds the light went out. He withdrew the device then in its place extended a tentacle holding a brushed aluminium cylinder which he inserted deep into the glowing hole he had just cut. Then he dropped back down to the canal level and sped off a mile away before sending the detonation signal.

Even at that range the blast wave knocked Tigger back a hundred feet. After a cautious pause he advanced again, ultrasound scanning the rock above him for weaknesses. Finally returning to his original position he peered at the huge slab of rock that had dropped down into the canal. Above this the crevice was now much wider, opening up into darkness above. He rose up into this gap, testing the air with his sensors. It smelled foul, still full of organics, still redolent with the stench of death after all this time.

Even though much of the section of city above – the

ceiling of this section – had fallen, still some buildings
had remained standing. Giant boulders and tons of
rubble jammed the rest of the tubular city above. It was
a shame the populace trapped here had not thought to
drill downward rather than up, for then they might have
escaped via the route Tigger had entered.

The dead were stacked in their tens of thousands
along the course of a dried-up canal. At first the survivors
had filled the ground in above the corpses, then – perhaps as water, energy and hope ran low – they ceased to
cover them. Tigger observed the heavy drill they had
been using to cut right through one wall to one of the big
vent pipes – to their minds their nearest possibility of
escape – and did not have to speculate on how they must
have felt upon finding that the pipe itself had simply disappeared, closed up by the massive quakes caused here.
He cruised along, studying the temporary accommodations the survivors had made for themselves, the
equipment salvaged, the food supplies – soon emptied –
the attempts at making water condensers and air
scrubbers. And the little huddles of bones representing
those who had survived long enough so as not to have
anyone else to throw their corpses in the canal.

After a few hours of surveying this mass grave, and
recording all of it, he eventually headed over to one
particular building, whose upper floors had been crushed by the falling ceiling but whose bottom two levels
remained intact. He entered the foyer through a space
for wide doors that now lay some distance behind him,
having been blown off by the compressive effect of so
many levels above being crushed. After scanning for a
little while he settled to the floor and detached his tiger
half from his sphere. This tiger form was small enough

to negotiate the narrow corridors inside. There were bones evident here, but none belonging to the survivors. He supposed the place had not been considered safe. Eventually he entered a room where, surprisingly, a mummified and perfectly intact Brumallian sat in a chair by one of the cylindrical storage containers. No clue as to how he had died, until scanning revealed the effects of massive compressive shock. Strange how this particular container was the one Tigger sought.

The drone did not need to search now, for he understood precisely how Brumallians filed things. He reached up with one extended claw and flipped open a quadrant drawer. From this he removed a single recording disk. He slipped this into his mouth, shunted it through, played it inside himself, and confirmed that he had what he wanted.

Whether Orduval would be pleased with this trophy was debatable, but hopefully it might prevent further graveyards like the one presently all around Tigger.

– Retroact 16 Ends –

Harald

As Harald stepped onto the Bridge, he glanced around at the replacement personnel he had organized and concealed his satisfaction. Everyone was now in position, and the Bridge was abuzz as *Ironfist* slowed to its new position and prepared for the retaliatory strike against the Brumallians.

He walked over to Firing Control and stood behind the officers operating the instruments aligned there.

After a moment he set his headset to route his voice through the ship's public-address system.

'Everyone, I want you to listen closely.' The buzz of activity cooled and everyone on the Bridge turned towards him. 'We have now confirmed that the missile strike against Captain Inigis's ship was instigated by a rogue schism within the Brumallian society designated BC32 – otherwise known as Vertical Vienna. It has also been confirmed that this dissident group was assisted by as yet unidentified agents of a Sudorian organization.'

Harald scanned the room as a disbelieving mutter arose from many – but many more just waited, hard-faced and patient. He considered how most of those here had been children during the War, and how they would react to his next words.

'Parliament, having reinstated our wartime preroga-tive of independent crisis management up to and including the use of lethal force, therefore approves of the action we must perforce take.' He glanced down at those looking up at him from Firing Control. 'Let us now remember why Fleet exists. Many of you here did not fight in the War. I did not either. But many did, and many more died for the freedoms we enjoy today. Millions of Sudorian citizens died, millions lived lives of privation and died never knowing peace. We cannot let that happen to us again. It is our *duty* to prevent it happening again, and to that end we must be harsh and uncompromising.'

He pointed to the Munitions Officer. 'Prepare for a warhead launch from Silo Fourteen, back-up in Thirteen.' Now he pointed to the Targeting Officer. 'Target BC32.'

Looking around the room, Harald registered the expressions of shock.

'It is a terrible thing we do here today, but the consequences could be more terrible still if we did nothing. We cannot allow this provocation to pass. We cannot allow the war to begin again.' Harald paused. 'I will now obtain confirmation from Admiral Carnasus himself.' Stripping off the headset he headed for the stair, knowing that many would question his orders, but none would disobey him. As he reached the stair he glanced across at the four Bridge guards near the main doors. Two of them immediately detached from their group and slowly, casually, began making their way over. It was all working perfectly to plan – perfectly visualized and now being exactly executed – yet now the reality was beginning to bite. Harald felt his stomach tighten and a sudden onset of nausea. He paused, removing his side arm, as protocol dictated, then felt the sudden need to just turn and run. But he also felt like simply one cog in the unstoppable machine that was his own plan. Teeth gritted, he climbed, finally stepping up into the Admiral's haven.

'So, Harald, is everything prepared?' asked Carnasus.

Harald eyed him, realizing the Admiral was in his more lucid mode. The old man stood with his hands behind his back, gazing through the narrow window across the body of the hilldigger, which now stood in silhouette against the backdrop of Brumal. Harald glanced around and noted Lieutenant Alun seated on a couch just in front of the glass case containing the Admiral's collection of trophies and awards.

'It is all prepared,' Harald replied.

Carnasus turned. 'So why a five-megaton warhead?'

'Because, though Parliament will accept our necessary excision of BC32, it would not be prepared to accept the damage a larger warhead or a gravity disruptor might

cause to BC31, which is indirectly linked by tunnels to
our target.'

'But you think they will accept the destruction of
Vertical Vienna itself?'

Harald paused for a moment. He had expected
Carnasus to be more lucid than usual now, since the
exigency of the situation could produce no less than that
effect, but the old man seemed worryingly *sharp*. Here
then was a hint of the Carnasus who had commanded
this ship during the last five years of the War. A man to
be admired, and not just . . . Harald could feel the sweat
slick on his hands. He closed his eyes for a moment and
felt something shift inside his head. Yes, what happened
now was inevitable, and regret was merely wasted energy.
He opened his eyes, dried his palms against his foamite
suit – and knew they would now remain dry.

'They will have to accept it,' he confirmed.

'Yes, they would have . . .' Carnasus blinked, looked
momentarily confused, then hardened again. 'Return to
the Bridge, Harald, and cancel the strike.'

'Why do you—?'

'Are you questioning my orders, Tacom?'

'Yes, I am. I am questioning the orders of a man who
is obviously no longer fit to be Admiral. We cannot let
the Brumallians get away with this.'

Carnasus glared at him, then slowly his expression
softened. Harald noted Alun stand up and begin moving
over. Like Harald he appeared unarmed – having left his
side arm down below.

'Harald,' said the Admiral, 'I have always wanted to
see Fleet remain pre-eminent in the Sudorian system,
and I have always felt that we should have exterminated
all the Brumallians. But I would rather see our hill-

diggers scrapped in the sun than stand by and watch you start a civil war.'

Harald could not believe that he now wanted to cry. Angrily he clamped down on the feeling. 'Then you are a fool.'

Carnasus just looked tired as he raised his arm and spoke into a wrist communicator. 'Guards, get up here now.' Lowering his arm he stepped closer to Harald. 'The loss of the Consul Assessor is no particular loss to me, and I could even accept that you used a Fleet Special Operations team to accomplish it. But Combine, Harald? A civil war between Fleet and Orbital Combine?'

'I'm so sorry,' said Harald, something catching in his throat – and he truly was. Hearing the sound of boots on the stair leading up, he stepped sideways, spun, the edge of his hand cracking hard against Alun's temple. The man dropped instantly, without a sound.

'So sorry,' Harald repeated, reaching inside a belt pocket to withdraw the small Combine-manufacture pistol he had obtained many months before. Two shots spun the old man off his feet. Harald stepped over, glancing back as the two guards entered. He stood over Carnasus and shot him twice more, through the head, then turned as his guts suddenly twisted up. After a second he staggered to one side, abruptly crouched and vomited on the floor. This physical reaction had been unexpected. He gave himself a moment to recover, then stood up again and wiped his mouth. One of the guards, he saw, was staring up at the recording heads mounted in the ceiling. 'Don't worry about them. They'll show exactly what I want them to show.' Walking over, he dropped the pistol down beside Alun. 'Just as the recordings of this one's interrogation will.'

One of the men stooped to turn the unconscious officer over and cuff him.

'Now,' said Harald, 'I have some terrible news to deliver about the assassination of our Admiral by Orbital Combine. And I have a missile to launch.'

Tigger

Right, stop Fleet from destroying Vertical Vienna, thought Tigger.

Preventing the first missile reaching the planet's surface was no problem, but what about the next one? He could introduce some massive fault into *Ironfist*'s systems to prevent further firings, but then there were still five other such ships within a day's travel of Brumal, so what about them? If Fleet proved utterly relentless in its purpose, Tigger's continued actions would eventually reveal his presence, then the problems would really start.

Accelerating up through atmosphere, Tigger separated into his two parts – his tiger aspect dropping back down towards the planet's surface. Of course, even without McCrooger's instructions, Tigger would have intervened to prevent such wanton death and destruction, for he had seen the bitter results, close up, when he retrieved that disk for Orduval. Descending from the sky his tiger half landed on an icy canal path leading towards the ground-level cap of Vertical Vienna. His sensorium divided – since his consciousness also occupied his sphere half – he also left atmosphere and distantly observed the hilldigger *Ironfist*. Listening in to com channels he realized the launch of a missile was imminent.

On the surface, the cat half of Tigger scanned down inside the hive city and realized, with some relief, that the Brumallians were rapidly evacuating it. He estimated that within two hours not a living soul would still occupy the tunnels. This made his task somewhat easier, since he only needed to delay things that long and then Fleet would be destroying an empty city. Of course, there was nothing to prevent them then firing on other Brumallian cities. If that proved to be the case, Tigger decided he must come out into the open and yell for help from Geronamid. The AI, though against taking overt action, would not countenance blatant genocide here.

Still listening to com channels, Tigger then heard about the assassination of Admiral Carnasus. Apparently a Fleet officer had gunned him down in his Admiral's Haven. When Tigger learnt that Harald Strone had assumed command until Captain Dravenik could be recalled, he felt a deep disquiet. He needed to find out more, but that would have to wait, since he could now see the tops of two missile silos opening on the body of the hilldigger *Ironfist*.

Scanning, Tigger learned just enough to ascertain which missile was the main one and which the back-up. He focused on the main missile but found shielding and hardened systems defeating his probing. A lot of that shielding lay within the silo itself, so best to wait until after the missile was launched. Cruising 1,000 miles down, and to one side of the hilldigger, the drone decided his best option would be to introduce a fault into the guidance system, then return to the ship and tamper with those systems that loaded guidance to the missile. This way Fleet's inability to destroy Vertical Vienna right now would be seen as just one random fault, and thus be less likely to arouse suspicion.

The missile launched and Tigger began vectoring in on it. Scanning again he realized the missile itself was hardened against informational attack. It therefore looked like he would have to physically intercept it to introduce the fault. He sighed and accelerated. He would have to drill through the casing and inject micro-manipulator tentacles to tamper with its hardware. Merely pushing it off course would not work, since the guidance system would automatically correct. As he closed, he wondered at the degree of paranoia within Fleet – at them using a missile as difficult to interfere with as this. Did they think the Brumallians still possessed the ability, or the will, to maintain electronic warfare devices? If so, it showed that those in command of Fleet did not understand their old enemy at all.

Eight hundred miles from *Ironfist*, the missile's drive shut down. Tigger closed in on it, extending four cell-form metal grabs to close around the armoured cyclindrical body. A rosy glow bloomed from the missile's nose cone as it entered thin atmosphere, and streaks of orange fire spat past the clinging drone. He extruded a chainglass drill and began cutting through metal. Then a sudden horrible and aberrant thought occurred to him and he put together some wildly disparate facts. There was that certain recent research undertaken on Corisanthe Main, which Fleet had access to despite its hostility towards Combine. And Harald, like his three siblings, was never to be underestimated.

'Oh shit.'

A second sun ignited high in Brumal's stratosphere, rolling out nuclear fire that skated on lightnings around the curve of the globe. On the surface, a running silver tiger howled and coiled in on itself, crashed into hard ground and skidded into the nearby canal, breaking ice as it entered the water, and sank.

Harald

Frowning, Harald studied the telemetry on his eye-screen.

'I don't understand, sir,' said one of the officers at Firing Control. 'The missile was set for impact detonation and was hardened against interference.'

'I can only suppose, then,' said Harald, 'that the Brumallians have developed some way of getting through our shielding.'

He stood upright, inspecting a view only he could see, then ran it again. Now the shadows looked right as well. The scene showed Admiral Carnasus interrogating Lieutenant Alun in Harald's presence. It showed Alun pulling out a gun and shooting Carnasus, then stepping over and pumping further shots into the Admiral's head. Harald needed to work on the interrogation next, altering stored footage of previous interviews with Alun to suit his purpose. Of course it still might be possible for an expert programmer to divine the falsity of these recordings. However, Harald intended events to move too swiftly now for anyone to get a chance to inspect them too closely.

Switching his headset to general address, he began, 'I have an announcement to make,' then paused until everyone was facing towards him. 'Evidence has been accumulating that the Brumallians were not working alone. It would now appear that Lieutenant Alun was in the secret employ of Orbital Combine.' First a shocked silence, then sudden heated debates all around him. Now Harald opened a channel to Ship's Security, 'Order all Combine personnel aboard confined to quarters for the present.'

'Yes, sir . . . Erm, your sister, Yishna? She is now aboard the transport heading back towards Sudoria.'

'With Chairman Abel Duras?'

'Yes, sir.'

'Let her go. We certainly don't want to aggravate our parliamentary Chairman.'

He cut the link to Security, then addressed those at Firing Control. 'Maybe Combine technology was used to stop that missile, so I want one prepared for simple mechanical detonation as used during the fourth battle Arkan. Keep me informed.'

Quickly departing the Bridge and reaching his cabin he seated himself on his divan and opened a secure channel. His eye-screen immediately lit up, but it took a moment for the individual he was calling to respond and sit down to answer.

'Jeon, what do you have for me?' he asked.

'One part of it – whatever it was – tried to intercept the missile. The detonation destroyed it, however. I last detected the other part in the region of BC32 but have since lost that trace. Maybe destroying one half of it somehow damaged the other half?'

'Let us hope so. Inform me if you pick up on it again. If not we can always hope our next strike against BC32 will deal with it.' He cut the link, quickly opening another. 'Cheanil?' The woman looked very ill and Harald realized he should wait no longer. 'First give me Combine visuals of Defence Platform One and Dravenik's ship, and then fire on my order.'

'I have it all ready for you, Harald.' She reached out for something and Harald's eye-screen display instantly divided into four. Two of the views were of the defence platform, one of Cheanil herself, and another of the hilldigger *Blatant*. He cancelled one of the two views of the station and opened communications with the *Blatant*.

'Commander Harald,' said a tacom officer, gazing at him from one screen quarter.

'I need to speak to Captain Dravenik, at once.'

A holding graphic appeared, and Harald impatiently rattled his fingers on the divan arm. He checked the time display in one corner of his view, but Dravenik did not seem inclined to keep him waiting.

'What the hell is going on out there, Harald? I'm told the Admiral has been attacked and that you have fired on Brumal. If Carnasus is incapacitated, you must put on hold all further actions until I have reviewed the situation.'

'Carnasus is dead,' said Harald.

Dravenik drew back as if Harald had spat at him. 'Dead?'

Harald considered the possibility of this communication being recorded. If that was the case, the recording would be aboard *Blatant*. Maybe it might be recovered, but Harald was prepared to take the risk of that just to enjoy the satisfaction of his next words.

'Yes, he is dead. I killed him, just as I am about to kill you . . . Cheanil, fire now.'

The view of the defence platform showed very little,

just a faint hazing of vacuum and then some interference on the image. Dravenik's face winked out of existence as the microwave surge wiped out all com from his ship. *Blatant* seemed to ripple, or perhaps that was just interference too. Such a small image in one quadrant of his eye-screen. He enlarged it to fill the entire screen, but still it did not seem real enough. He saw out-gassing and stars of fire spread all along the hilldigger. Missiles were being fired, swarms of them. Dravenik had managed to get some of his weapons systems online, but not nearly enough, nor quickly enough. Then the multiple explosions began to tear *Blatant* apart: white balls of fire blasting out and wreckage spewing into vacuum. As he had expected, the intense microwave hit was detonating the shaped charges in the nukes and other chemical munitions. He had calculated that at least one of the shaped-charge explosions among the hundreds of missiles aboard, though not precisely timed, would lead to a thermonuclear detonation. So it occurred. His screen blanked for a second, then returned in negative with hazy lines across it. Debris spread. He observed something mangled passing down to the right, and the image shuddered.

'Cheanil . . . Cheanil, reply.'

Three returned images, all shadows under heavy interference, then nothing. Lit-up icons indicated he had lost the signal. Harald did not suppose Cheanil had survived Dravenik's reply to Defence Platform One, just as calculated. He felt she had performed her duty adequately. Now, during this emergency, Harald could take full charge of Fleet.

McCrooger

A dull grumble grew into a roar, and those of us within the barge fell silent. I felt something lurch in my stomach. That first explosion, a few hours before, I had been optimistic about. I was not feeling so sure now, for the pendant in my hand no longer bore the shape of a tiger, but had become a smooth ovoid as if the drone's direct link to it had been somehow cut. It was then that I also noticed something else, something strange. There was a crusty black substance on my fingers that I assumed was mud until, on closer inspection, I saw a partially closed rip in the flesh of the back of my hand, caused when the quofarl had captured us.

Blood?

I had not bled in more years than I cared to count – the last time being when I received a serious slash from a chainglass knife that had cut through my biceps right to the bone. Even then the quantity of blood would not have filled a shot glass, and the wound had closed very quickly. But here, what I previously ignored as a mere scratch, had bled copiously, and the wound had still not closed. I realized I was now seeing the physical results of the war being fought between the two viral forms occupying my body.

'That could have been thunder,' Rhodane commented, eyeing me tentatively.

'You don't really believe that, Rhodane,' said Shleera. 'I would guess that was another nuke exploding. If they'd used gravtech, we would have felt more vibration through our feet.'

I could only hope that Tigger had obeyed me and somehow diverted the strikes launched against Vertical

Vienna. Within the barge much angry argument ensued and a woman, sitting nearby, began sobbing. Everyone here believed the worst, including me – the sight of that cut on my hand had dispelled my usual optimism.

'What did the Brumallians do with any prisoners they took during the War?' I asked, and then wondered if the question sprang from sudden feelings of mortality.

'There weren't that many captured,' Rhodane replied. 'Some survived, some were tortured, and many others interrogated by means that left them drooling and mindless. The Sudorians were no better.'

Great.

I abruptly seated myself on the deck. I could easily break out of this barge, but what then? Or *could* I in fact break out of this barge? As a test I drove my finger down hard against the floor. It made a satisfying *donk* and left a dent in the metal. Okay . . . though my finger did ache a bit afterwards. But back to the initial question: I was just another of the dispossessed all wars produced – one of the millions driven here and there by events we could not control. How would the Brumallians react? They possessed some ships, as I saw, but I doubted they could put up much of a fight against the superior forces of Fleet. I considered how such a unique society as theirs might respond. A normally governed society could perhaps hold back from trying to retaliate against its attacker, realizing there was little chance of succeeding, but here society's actions were the direct result of Consensus. Would they want vengeance and would that want immediately turn into action? In response to a possible threat, they had immediately begun work again on their spaceships. But now they had actually been attacked.

Perhaps half an hour passed before the door seals

whumphed open. Those around me immediately began pulling on their helmets and surging away from the opening doors. I thought it telling that no warning had been given, for that simple lack of consideration could have killed people in here as the poisonous air from outside flooded in. Rhodane kept her head bare.

Quofarl stood out on the ramp. They now wore extra armour and carried heavy weapons. Two of them immediately marched inside, the occupants of the barge quickly parting before them. I stood and observed them focus in on me, whereas before they had been concentrating on Rhodane.

'You two –' they intoned.

'– come.'

I was surprised to recognize the same two who, with Rhodane herself, had accompanied me into ReconYork. We stepped forward, perhaps expecting to be shoved on our way, but the two quofarl just gestured us towards the doors and waited for us to move off.

Rhodane quickly turned to Shleera. 'I'll see what I can do about all this.' She made a gesture encompassing the interior of the barge, which already was beginning to smell of human sewage.

'Do what you can,' Shleera replied, 'and try not to get yourself killed.'

As we left, all the quofarl fell in behind us rather more like an honour guard than the kind that might be too liberal with the rifle butt. Many of those we left behind called out their best wishes to Rhodane, and some even to me, before the doors closed.

'What now?' I asked Rhodane.

She was coughing, eyes watering, and it took her a

moment to reply. 'Let us hope they are correcting a per-
ceived error.'

Upon hearing that I realized I still did not know
enough about Brumallian society. I realized the Consensus could not decide everything, and that there had
to be levels of decision-making below that to tighten the
essential nuts and bolts of their civilization. Yes, the Consensus might decree that non-Brumallians should be
imprisoned, but I doubted it had specified where or how.
Did individuals make such lesser decisions, or perhaps
subgroups of the overall Consensus?

'Do you yet have any idea of what happened?' I
asked.

She glanced at me, expression bland, and nodded to
one side. 'I can't pick up very much out here, but my
sense of direction is fine and I know *that* is not the
sunrise.' An orange glow etched out the dark horizon. It
told me nothing – Tigger could still have diverted the
attack. She added, 'That's where Vertical Vienna is . . . or
was.'

The cold finally drove Rhodane to put her helmet
and gloves back on. Beside us on the canal path grew
plant life resembling blue cycads. Where guards brushed
against the overhanging leaves, pieces snapped off and
tinkled to the ground. As we trudged over frozen mud,
I studied these quofarl and picked out one of the two I
had met before. 'You, quofarl.' He glanced towards me
and I signed a question, asking his name. It was short and
pithy with a nuance of meaning conveying hard relentless striving. In my mind I translated it as 'Slog'.

'Slog, can you tell me what has happened?' I signed
as he stepped up beside me.

'Fleet destroyed Vertical Vienna,' he replied.

'We heard *two* explosions,' I suggested in the interrogative.

'One missile detonated before reaching the ground.'

'Was the city fully evacuated before the second missile hit?'

'No.'

'Damn them,' muttered Rhodane. 'Damn all Fleet to the hells they create.'

Finally we cut away from the canal, heading along a path through the vegetation. Fluted mollusc shells like old porcelain crunched underneath our feet. Upon reaching another canal where a small barge was moored, much debate ensued between the quofarl escorts. I guessed this sort of thing might be a problem without someone appointed to give orders. Eventually they came to the conclusion that the ice lay too thick for them to commandeer a barge from there to the city and down, so on we trudged. Dawn lit the sky by the time we reached the underground city's head. In its light I saw the large catfish forms of wormfish writhing under the ice and peering up at us with bemused eyes. The temperature above the city grew noticeably warmer and the ice thinner, and in places broken. We clambered aboard another barge, motored into the top of one of those watery lift shafts with living pumps labouring ceaselessly all around us, then plummeted down the descent tube. I was getting very hungry now and starting to feel a bit strange, but we did not come upon any grobbleworm stalls this time. We were quickly whisked from the barge and guided through corridors and hallways until I thought I vaguely recognized our surroundings. Having removed her helmet and tested the air, Rhodane told me, 'Eighteen

hundred dead, and the entire city of Vertical Vienna
gutted.'

Eventually they brought us to a room, into which
Slog and his companion accompanied us while the rest
of the quofarl departed. Glancing around I saw this place
was furnished, but with oddly grating discords in the
layout and the furnishings themselves. A cylindrical shelv-
ing unit occupied the central space, loaded with a
seemingly random collection of screens, pherophones,
mollusc shells and curiously shaped glass tanks containing squirming life forms. Plants, which were all dark
green leaf interspersed with bright orange tendrils, were
arrayed around the walls, growing from polished woody
spheroids I recognized as the husks of things I had seen
on some of the trees up on the surface. There were paintings too, displaying bizarre Brumallian landscapes or
crowded city scenes. Triangular wooden tiles covered the
floor, upon which was scattered various geometrically
shaped mattresses, and similarly shaped low tables of
verdigrised metal sealed under a glistening skin. Putting
aside some device which apparently fitted over her face
– I suspected it to be their version of a VR mask – a
Brumallian woman rose from one mattress and turned
to face us. It took me a moment to recognize one of the
Speakers who along with Rhodane had questioned me.

Without much ado she informed me, 'Fleet is not
listening. It is in fact jamming all communications. You
must present our case to the Sudorian Parliament, but
let me first present our case to you.' She gestured to a
large chest standing open nearby.

Feeling somewhat tetchy, I replied, 'You had better
feed me first.'

In their terms, the evidence was incontrovertible,

though it took me some time to understand this since much of it could be easily falsified back in the Polity, yet not here. The Brumallian Speaker, whose name referred to some flower found in this acidic environment and who I called Lily, showed me a picture of the missile launcher in question, then gestured to a nearby table on which lay a piece of metal with something like a barcode etched into it.

'There are some launchers stored 8,000 miles from here, but they are the only ones we have left. This was one of the last seized by Fleet and taken into the ground base nearest to Vertical Vienna, where it was supposed to be destroyed,' she told me.

This proved Fleet was last in possession of the missile launcher and, before using it, neglected to file off the serial number. There was more evidence: footage, obviously taken from concealment, of a Fleet Special Operations team transporting a bulky cargo out towards the launch site; Brumallian remains found at the site DNA matched, perfectly, with Brumallians who had disappeared during the War; and a chemical analysis showing that the propellant used in the missile was of Fleet manufacture. But it was not just that: there was lots of linking evidence, lots of detail, carbon-crystal storage filled with information. As I ate roasted molluscs off a gold-plated spike I assessed it all throughout the many ensuing hours.

'You understand that this proves the remnant of the launcher definitely came from that launch site,' Rhodane pointed out while I studied a particular recording. Without her I would have missed a lot of stuff like that.

Finally satisfied and somewhat weary, I realized that here lay proof of the innocence in this business of the

Brumallians, and that here also was a weapon the
Sudorian Parliament could use to politically castrate
Fleet. Of course the evidence lay here while those who
needed to see this lay some millions of miles away, with
Fleet sitting directly in the way. And political castration
was not quite the same as the physical kind; Fleet might
be put firmly in the wrong and voted down in Parliament, but votes, and being in the wrong, did not
necessarily take fingers off triggers.

'And how am I supposed to present this evidence to
the Sudorian Parliament?'

'We have ships,' replied Lily.

'So do Fleet – large powerful ships sitting in orbit
above us.'

'They are withdrawing towards Sudoria. It has become
apparent that *we* were not the real target.'

'Real target?' Rhodane queried.

'Orbital Combine,' Lily replied.

10

Technologies and knowledge were being rediscovered – not discovered for the first time – so the process was a whole lot faster. As the third generation of Sudorians was growing up, small but thriving industries and agricultural concerns had been established and our society had wealth to spare for more than just survival. The first crossing of the Komarl was made on foot, or rather the first successful crossing, and those adventurers reported finding the wreck of the Procul Harum. Within a few decades we had taken to the air and built ground vehicles capable of negotiating the desert sands, and soon the first expeditions were being made out to the ship. The secrets of the ship were being quickly rediscovered and much of its physical structure was transported back to our then small civilization. This caused something of a renaissance, and no little degree of that thing called arrogance. The final expedition made was the one sent to retrieve one of the U-space engines. We know that the expedition party planned to try firing up a ship's fusion reactor to provide power during this task. We know that they were preparing to dismount the one engine protruding above the desert sands. The ensuing explosion caused a dust storm out of the desert that lasted for days. An observer flight reported just the nose of the ship remaining,

*and that a perfectly spherical part of a nearby granite mount
was missing.*

– Uskaron

Yishna

She watched the image displayed on Chairman Duras's
cabin screen, first feeling contempt for Fleet's military
posturing, then a growing horror. Seeing the multiple
launches from *Blatant*, she assumed it was making an
unprovoked attack on Orbital Combine, and only when
the first explosions began to tear the hilldigger apart did
she realize what was really happening. In blank shock she
watched the final detonation that obliterated the great
ship, then tracked the descent of the missiles it had fired
down onto Defence Platform One, and watched the subsequent detonations turn that platform into a burning
ruin. Then Director Gneiss was back gazing at Duras
with an implacable indifference.

'Those last images were recorded from the transport
being used by a Combine orbital assault team. They had
to pull out quickly, though, because there were still more
of *Blatant*'s missiles on the way.'

'I served aboard that ship,' said Duras, a catch in
his voice. 'I even remember Dravenik attending the engineering lectures I gave to new recruits on board . . .' He
cleared his throat and continued, 'Why was an assault
team there?'

'We'd lost communication with the platform for two
hours, and some very sophisticated software had meanwhile locked us out of its systems.'

Gneiss spoke factually, hinting at no suppositions.
Yishna felt that on the surface he was doing the right

thing, for only by being utterly frank, and making no accusations, would he gain the Chairman's respect and thus ensure a fair hearing. But, as ever, to her it seemed as if the Director was merely playing his chosen part in some drama.

'I am told,' said Duras, 'that the Combine observer team attempted to sabotage *Desert Wind*, and that now Captain Franorl has withdrawn his ship from Corisanthe Main.'

Gneiss replied, 'All of that same team were killed by Franorl's people during this alleged sabotage attempt, and the only proof of it he presents is some hazy recording of a gun battle taking place in *Desert Wind*'s engine galleries. None of the observers was armed when they went aboard – having been checked by Franorl's own security officers.'

'Equally, I have no positive proof that Combine was locked out of the defence platform's systems,' observed Duras, 'or was at any time out of communication with the personnel aboard.'

'True, but what would Combine have to gain by firing on a hilldigger?'

'One might suppose Combine feels itself in a strong enough position to go up against Fleet, and that these are the initial shots in some power bid. The assassination of Admiral Carnasus would seem to confirm this hypothesis.'

Gneiss nodded acknowledgement. 'Equally, one might say that a faction in Fleet does not want Combine to reach such a position of power, so has manufactured this present conflict deliberately. The Admiral, though fighting to retain Fleet's powers, always acceded whenever Parliament took away any such powers. Combine is also prepared always to accede to the will of Parliament, but I wonder if the same applies to Fleet now it is under new command.'

Duras glanced at Yishna, then asked Gneiss, 'What are you doing now?'

'I have just come from a meeting of the Combine Oversight Committee. We have decided that security teams will be sent immediately to the remaining eleven platforms. We are also requesting that wardens from Groundside Defence and Security join those teams.'

'That seems reasonable.'

'We also wanted to send a team to Brumal to investigate this claim of our complicity with the Brumallians in the death of the Consul Assessor. We suggested that this team be provided by GDS, but of course needed Parliament to grant us permission to do this, since we would be entering Fleet-controlled space.'

'This request was presented to Parliament?'

'Yes, but only minutes before Fleet had suggested using one of their own transports, crewed by their own people, for the same purpose. Paranoia is running high at present, so both ideas were kicked out and now Parliament is wrangling over a compromise.'

'Such is politics.'

'Yes, and meanwhile Fleet is bringing all its capital ships towards Sudoria.'

'And this concerns you?'

'Fleet are deliberately sowing discord and suspicion. We feel their ultimate aim is to seize control of the defence platforms, either through Parliament or by force. It has also been mooted by some parties that Orbital Combine can no longer be trusted with projects critical to Sudoria, like the study of the Worm.'

Duras sighed and shook his head. 'In the past,' he said, 'a hilldigger was placed on Corisanthe Watch, ready to destroy the station should its captive become a danger. In recent years that watch has been in essence merely traditional, since you and I both know that a lone hilldigger is now incapable of destroying Corisanthe Main.'

'True.'

'I must consult with my colleagues and with Parliament entire. Until such a time as we come to some decisions on this, I am presuming you can defend yourselves?'

'We can.'

'It has been good speaking to you, Director Gneiss. Let us hope all this can be resolved without further bloodshed.'

Gneiss inclined his head once, just before Duras cut the communication. Now the Chairman turned towards Yishna. 'So, what do you think are your brother's intentions?'

Yishna sat back in her chair. 'I no longer know my brother's mind, but I do know what he is capable of. It was convenient, don't you think, that the first main casualty of this crisis was the Consul Assessor, who was a possible threat to Fleet power, and that the next two were Carnasus and Dravenik, both of whom stood between Harald himself and the position of Admiral.'

'Under emergency powers he has now seized that position,' said Duras, 'but that will still have to be ratified by the other Captains.'

'If Harald seized power, that means he is capable of holding onto it, believe me.'

'So you think this crisis to be limited to Harald's ambitions in Fleet?'

'No, like me, Harald does not want power for its own sake – he only wants it if he has a definite use for it. He has always been attracted to Fleet, and the *idea* of Fleet, and seeing it rendered impotent must gnaw at him. I suspect he's preparing to destroy Orbital Combine – so as to make Fleet the ascendant power, beyond Sudoria.'

'But then what would he do with *that* power?'

Yishna bowed her head and considered. She felt sure Harald's aims were inward-looking – power and control within the system – but could see nothing beyond that. 'I really don't know.'

'Control of Sudoria itself?' Duras suggested.

'That seems logical, but I just don't see it as being of any real interest to him.'

Duras frowned. 'In three days we should arrive there, but I wonder if Fleet will even let us pass through.' He stared at her directly. 'You realize that which side actually caused these events is of little matter. That one of them wants conflict means there *will* be conflict, and there is very little Parliament can do about it.'

'Yes, I realize that.'

McCrooger

The other quofarl I named Flog. This name seemed appropriate because of its similarity in sound and meaning to his tank twin's name, Slog.

'I am not so sure that having two quofarl bodyguards just for me would go down very well on Sudoria,' I suggested. There had been no Brumallians on Sudoria ever since the War, and even those encountered there during the War had not been seen often, since they were prisoners.

'You misunderstand me,' said Lily. She pointed to the heavy chest containing all the evidence the Brumallians had collected. 'They will accompany you at all times solely to carry the evidence.'

With that, Slog and Flog hoisted up the chest and headed for the door.

Turning towards Rhodane, Lily added, 'You, of course, will be going with him.'

'I rather suspected that,' said Rhodane, adding with a hint of bitterness, 'You need a Sudorian on your side to add some veracity.'

I felt this to be a distraction from my own point. 'Excuse me, I did not misunderstand you about the bodyguard thing. I am quite capable of reading the sub-text of your communications.'

Lily hissed and rattled her mandibles. 'It is the will of the Consensus that you be protected. Should Brumallians arrive at Sudoria with all this evidence, without one of your standing aboard, it is unlikely we would even be allowed to land – even with a Sudorian aboard.' She gave a glance of acknowledgement to Rhodane. 'Also, without you, it is unlikely we could get it to the direct attention of the Sudorian Parliament.'

I decided to accept gracefully – mortal thoughts again – and followed the two quofarl from the room.

I still hadn't quite located where we now were in ReconYork. To begin with I had not expected so long a journey from the holding barge to the city head, and now wondered where we must go to reach that place where the spaceships were stored. This particular room opened onto a stair leading down the side of the central cylinder, and I stood for a moment wondering whether I was meant to climb or descend.

'We go up,' said Rhodane, divining my indecision. 'A workable vessel has apparently been moved to the surface.' She added, 'Fast work – I myself never got anything done so quickly.' This then must have been the substance of one of her earlier conversations with Lily while I was studying the evidence.

'Perhaps their heart wasn't really in it,' I suggested.

'Most certainly.'

We climbed side by side, with the quofarl traipsing along behind.

'I thought he –'

'– was dangerous –'

'– and strong,' muttered Slog and Flog.

I glanced back.

'Polity Consul Assessors don't –' began Slog.

'– have to carry their own luggage,' finished Flog.

I turned and signed to them, 'It's not my bloody luggage – it's all of yours.' I finished with a gesture to encompass all of Brumal.

Their words descended into an indistinct grumbling and mandipular scraping.

As we ascended further, other Brumallians began to join us, many of them lugging bags and cases. Their conversation ran fast and excited, and I very often found it difficult to understand those few snatches that were audible, but surmised that this lot were the crew of the spaceship we were heading for. I also felt a strange kind of locus, a sense of those around me separating as a kind of encystment from the rest of the population. I was beginning to pick up the undercurrents and the feel of this society, yet now I was leaving it. I decided then, if I survived, to return here and learn more.

I assumed the top of this cavern was also the top of

ReconYork, with open air just above, but I was very much mistaken. The stairway wound up through the few hundred feet of rock of the roof, then we left it through an arch leading into the base of yet another cavern. From there we traversed a pathway of crushed shell to a canal edge, where a barge awaited. Whilst the large group of Brumallians that had joined us clambered aboard, I gazed around wondering if this part of the city was the one I had first entered. No way I could tell. Finally we boarded and moved to the foredeck where a helmsman sat behind a triangular helm and archaic-looking controls.

'How long will we be on this barge?' I asked Rhodane.

'An hour and a half.'

I moved back and plumped myself down with my back resting against the deck cabin. 'Wake me up when we arrive. It's been a rather busy day for me and I need my rest.'

I closed my eyes, expecting to find sleep a problem – ever since being infected by the Spatterjay virus I had never needed more than a few hours a night, and sometimes neglected even those. While I waited hopefully for sleep, it crept up behind me with a heavy club. The next thing I knew Rhodane was shaking me by the shoulder, and I opened my eyes to a Brumallian morning.

The spaceship crewmen made a considerable racket as they disembarked. I blinked, feeling listless and heavy and wanting to close my eyes again. I gazed at the back of my hand and flexed it. A scab lifted to expose scar tissue, pink and new, again something not produced by my body in a very long time. Heaving myself upright, I looked around.

Our barge was now moored by one bank of a watercourse perhaps a mile across. To my left it stretched to
the misty horizon – a smooth gilded snake. To my right
it seemed some structure had been built across it – docks
or a pier – but on closer inspection I realized I was gazing
upon the front end of an immense barge nearly a mile
wide. Upon the deck of this rested one of the spacecraft
I had seen below. It looked less like a living thing now,
its surface a bland grey with many additional protuberances and steely triangular section bands caging its
surface. Huge pylons reared around it, conveying
immense pipes and elevators to various openings in its
hull, and probably also preventing the vessel from rolling
away.

We followed the crew ashore, then along a path
running between the canal bank and a wide concrete
road along which presently cruised a low heavy truck
consisting of three carriages – probably carrying further
supplies for the vessel. Beyond the road rose mountain
slopes cloaked with forest cut through by many churned
mud tracks, on one of which had been parked a large
treaded vehicle. Was it pure luck or providence that made
me upgrade the magnification of my eyes to take a closer
look at this machine? In doing so I identified wide pincer
jaws, a saw tongue and logs stacked behind. Then I
spotted something sprawled in the mire before it: a
Brumallian, the mud all around him bloody, half his head
missing. Just back from him, by the machine itself, something glinted in the hands of a crouching figure.

Turning I shouted, 'Get to cover!'

Rhodane looked at me blankly, and I then realized
I had used my own language. As I stepped forward to
push her down, a bullet smacked me hard in the back. I

staggered forward, something spraying out ahead of
me . . . pieces of me. Rhodane jerked back and made a
horrible grunting sound, then dropped and rolled neatly
over the bank into the water. As I came upright another
shot cracked viciously past. It is not a sound you forget
and one I had heard many times before. Squatting, turning. A spray of automatic fire lifted two crew off their
feet, chunks of their bodies flying away like confetti
dropped before a fan. I forgot about mortality, vulnerability, and launched myself across the road. Hitting a
hedge of green twigs and spade leaves, I pushed through
to land between clumps of multiple trunks supporting a
canopy like the scaled underside of a lizard. Shortly afterwards two figures crashed through to either side of me:
Flog and Slog. They scanned around, peering down the
sights of their heavy rifles – stooped low, bestial.

'This way,' I signed, and ran diagonally upslope to
the left, where lay the track leading up to that tree-felling
machine.

We reached the track, but did not step onto it, since
that would expose us out in the open.

'What have you seen?' asked Slog.

I signed, 'One figure by a machine up at the top of
this track.' Delving into the front pocket of my dungarees I took out the gift Duras had given me, and loaded
it. Slog grunted noncommittally, then set out upslope,
Flog behind him. At no point did they take their eyes
from the sights of their rifles – the weapons seemed
sealed in place and they perfectly comfortable with them.
I coughed, breathing raw, spat blood and mucus, then
looked down at the fist-sized hole below my collar bone.
Blood seeped, and raw flesh layered with purplish woody
bands lay exposed. It felt numb, as such wounds had felt

for me for a long time, but I knew this one would not heal in just a matter of hours, and that at some point it would begin to hurt like hell. I followed them.

The two quofarl obviously possessed some idea of the machine's location since, as we drew close, they began advancing one at a time, covering each other with professional care. Then there, glimpsed between the tree clumps, loomed open metallic jaws and that saw tongue. A whistling crackling caused me to fling myself to the ground. Pieces of brown and yellow bark rained down. I looked around for my companions but could see no sign of them, so crawled on towards the machine. A low drumming *thump* sounded. A tree clump exploded and a human figure spun away, loose-limbed and broken. A human figure – but not quofarl-shaped.

Reaching the forest edge, I dropped down onto the track and ran towards the logging machine, automatic held out in front of me. A figure darted out and, identifying it as one of the attackers, I tracked it across, firing all the time. Returning fire spewed up gravel towards me, then Slog appeared and hit the figure from one side. The attacker shrieked, slammed into the logging machine's cowling, and bounced away. Then, on all fours, Slog disappeared into the trees again. Running up, I glimpsed the man on the ground. He wore an insulated suit – Sudorian – one of his arms was missing and his throat was torn out down to the spine. More firing from all around. Back in the trees I crouched behind a woody clump.

Brumallian speech, mandibles only, a woodpecker clattering: 'One left – do we want him alive?'

The reply, 'Yeah.'

That familiar sickening squirming began inside me,

and looking down at my wound revealed the sensation to be utterly accurate, for my flesh was shifting and shuddering. More firing from an automatic weapon, followed by a thoroughly human bellow. I stood and headed towards the source of the sound, soon finding Flog suspending a Sudorian up off the ground by his ankle, and Slog standing to one side picking gobbets of flesh from his mandibles.

'How did we lose against these?' wondered Flog.

'They got lucky,' Slog replied.

I found myself down on my knees, everything seeming to grow dark around me. Next I was hanging over Slog's shoulder, in such pain I felt sure I was dying. Then the blackness became entire.

– RETROACT 17 –

Orduval – *in the Desert*

The corpse lay spreadeagled on the rock, anchor bolts driven through between the bones of the forearms and of the lower legs. It had been stripped naked, and had not decayed, but dried out – skin and flesh turned hard and woody, eyes sunk away. Orduval rapped a knuckle against the victim's chest and was rewarded with a hollow thunk.

A piece of history, he thought.

Here lay one of those who had dragged them into the War against the Brumallians and benefited as a result rather too much . . . initially. He, yes a *he*, had been bolted here to the stone probably seventy or eighty years before Orduval was born, and just after the economic

collapse resulting from the first two decades of the War.
He wondered who this person had been, an industrialist
or one of the politicians in the pay of the industrialists?
The collapse, he recollected, resulted in a putsch – the
old oligarchy being ousted and replaced by people's
representatives from the various Sudorian states, from
Fleet and from the then-nascent Orbital Combine. Only
the threat from Brumal had prevented a total collapse of
the civil system too. Orduval now knew a great deal
about all this, though some years back had not known
nearly so much. But then, since being in the desert he
had needed to learn how things were before the War,
right from the beginning, so he could translate it in full,
make it contemporary, enable people to understand. He
remembered a conversation with Tigger, back then.

'It is almost as if I contain a surfeit of words, and
that if I can write them all out of my mind I will find a
cold centre point of understanding,' he said.

'But these are not *your* words,' the drone replied,
dipping its muzzle towards the stack of book disks it had
deposited on the floor.

'Yes, but I need to translate them and understand
the underlying meanings in order to get to *my* words.'

'Could it be that the cold centre point you seek is
that star you once described to Rhodane as lying at the
centre of your mind – the source of your fits. Are you not
trying to write your way back to your previous condition?'

It had worried him at first how much Tigger knew
about him, and he still felt uncomfortable with the idea
that throughout his life this Polity drone had watched
him and his siblings so closely. Tigger's contention also

bothered him, for he still did not really know his own mind, or purpose.

'That is entirely possible, but I have to find out for myself,' he replied. 'Now, will you be able to connect me into the Sudorian net?'

The tiger shrugged. 'Certainly.'

Considering how much he had learnt since then, Orduval turned away from the dried-out corpse and began making his way back towards his cave. His history of the colonization and the years leading up to the War, now published by the Ruberne Institute, had caused a media furore and questions to be asked in Parliament, and now there were those in the media prepared to pay a small fortune to anyone who could locate him. Tigger assured him that his netlink was untraceable with current Sudorian software, and that equally no one could trace him through the private account he had set up – that was until he withdrew any money from it. He did not need to.

Orduval estimated that his take on the War with the Brumallians would be ready for the Institute sometime soon, but he was finding himself distracted by the news of, finally, open contact with the Polity. Tigger had informed him long before that this was going to happen, but the content of and reactions to the communications Parliament published fascinated him. He had been living a hermit existence here and so, disconnected from his world, the reality of Tigger and the Polity did not seem so real until now.

Finally reaching his cave, Orduval saw the door standing open. For a moment he wondered if he had been discovered, and wondered too if he any longer considered that a problem. However, when he stepped into the cave he found Tigger waiting for him beside the desk.

'You must finish this,' said the drone.

'I know I must – remember that surfeit of words?'

'Yes, I remember . . . but it is important that you finish this soon and get it into the public domain.'

'Why the urgency?'

'You've been listening to the recordings and reading the transcripts of the communications between Parliament and the AI Geronamid?'

'I have.'

'Then you must understand that contact between you people and the Polity will not continue to remain limited to this . . . conversation?'

'Yes, I see that.'

'Publish your book, then . . . and perhaps you would like to include something from this.' Tigger raised a paw holding a recording disk. He continued, 'Already, much of what you have written throws an entirely new light on your old enemy, and the people of Sudoria are now utterly ready for that illumination. Opinion is changing fast, and people now indulge in painful speculation about culpability during the War. Some brave souls have even gone to Brumal to try and learn more about your neighbours. Your sister, Rhodane, is one of them.'

'Yes, I found a news item about that.' Orduval stepped forward and took the disk held out to him. 'What is this?'

'You could make it the culmination of your book. This disk contains the schematic of *The Outstretched Hand*.'

'The first ship we sent to Bruml.'

'Yes, it also contains information obtained from Bru-

mal: recorded footage of the arrival of that ship and subsequent events there.'

'I think you can tell me a little more?'

'Look at the recordings, Orduval. To stretch a
metaphor to breaking point: *The Outstretched Hand* contained a knife. It was a warship, and it did not approach
Brumal with anything like friendship in mind.'

Orduval felt gut-punched. He walked shakily over to
the chair and sat down. He had suspected something
to have been a little off about that first mission, but this?

'Why . . . now?' he asked.

'Sudorians need to know their real history, and to
lose the long-fostered idea that they fought and won a
just war. They need to know because, in no less than
a year and no more than five years, the Polity *will* be
coming here.'

Orduval inserted the disk, viewed it . . . and then
began to finish off the book that would change so much
but, as always with paper and words, never enough.

– Retroact 17 Ends –

Harald

From the Admiral's Haven, Harald gazed out across near
space. Four hilldiggers and various support ships were
visible, as was the arms factory station *Carmel*, bearing a
grim resemblance to a metallic skull hanging there in the
void. All but three of Fleet's hilldiggers were assembled
– two more of them were due any time now to join the
eight already here. The remaining hilldigger, Captain
Grange's *Dune Skater*, had suffered a major engine fault

way out in the system – where Harald had earlier
assigned it – and, unless the crew could repair that
fault, it would take the ship months to limp home. So
unfortunate that, Grange being a great friend of
Dravenik and so utterly hostile to Harald.

Harald grimaced. Of course he should not become
complacent. Three of the captains here, Ildris, Lambrack
and Coleon, objected to his assumption of the Admiralship, and others remained undecided. If a total of six
captains objected the whole issue would have to go
through the laborious Fleet electoral process. Harald had
no patience with that possibility. He turned from the
window and headed for the stair.

The Bridge now worked with smooth efficiency,
despite the many replacements Harald had made. Ship's
Security had been totally under his control for some
years now, and though its officers had found it necessary
to break a few heads and confine some members of the
crew, only three deaths had resulted since he took
control.

Jeon now sat before her own console at Firing
Control, and he stopped beside her.

'Still nothing?' he enquired.

'Nothing – we have a clear run.'

Harald nodded, unclenched his teeth, then called up
data from *Carmel*. He saw that six of the captains were
now aboard, so it was time for him to get over there
before they had a chance to talk to each other face to face
for any length of time. He was sure of his power aboard
Ironfist, and was now ready to confirm it over Fleet.

From the Bridge, Harald headed down to one of the
transport bays, where he picked up his retinue of Ship's

Security personnel. Aboard the shuttle, during the short journey over to *Carmel*, he considered his future actions.

Long before recent events, groundsider opinion had been turning against Fleet, especially with Orbital Combine now offering the possibility of travel throughout the system. Immediately before those events, Parliament was debating about how to conduct an investigation into the missile attack on Inigis's ship, and Combine was proving open and amenable. However, the murder of Admiral Carnasus and the destruction of *Blatant* by Defence Platform One would inevitably swing public opinion to Fleet's side. It may have been twenty years since the end of the War, but paranoia still held sway on the planet Sudoria. The change in opinion would in turn influence those groundsider representatives who held seats in Parliament, and the majority of the vote. Harald fully expected to win the vote he had ordered Fleet representatives to call for in Parliament – and for control of the defence platforms to be handed over to Fleet. Of course, Orbital Combine would refuse to actually hand over control, which meant Harald could then do what needed to be done.

The *clonk* of docking clamps snapped him out of his reverie. He unstrapped and pulled himself through the nil-gee vessel towards the airlock, but allowed his guards to move out ahead of him and secure the immediate area. He clambered through the lock, and beyond it dropped to the wide gravity floor, where he eyed stacks of equipment and squads of station assault troops – probably awaiting their ride aboard *Desert Wind*. Then he turned and focused his attention on Station Supervisor Harnek, who awaited with a pale and worried expression.

'There's been a killing,' said the man.

'Who?'

'Captain Ildris was found dead in his quarters only minutes ago. Poison, we think.'

Harald absorbed that and wondered just what to make of it. Ildris was one of those firmly set against him assuming the Admiralship, but Harald himself had not ordered the man killed. It struck him that there were those in Fleet who might be rather too enthusiastic in their support of him.

'Have you any idea who did it?' he asked, while tracking information himself via his headset.

Harnek looked wary. 'I was preparing to start an investigation, but thought it best to wait until you arrived. Perhaps you would prefer your own people to conduct it?'

Harald felt himself tensing up again, and glanced down at his clenched right fist. He carefully unclenched it, breathed evenly and summoned calm. Of course Harnek wanted Harald to conduct any investigation – the man obviously thought Harald had ordered the murder of Captain Ildris.

'Be assured, Harnek,' he said tightly, 'that I have every confidence in you and want no less than the truth to be revealed. Investigate this murder and be certain that if you find the culprit he will be punished.'

Harnek looked doubtful. 'As you will . . . Admiral.'

'Now, the other Captains?'

'They're waiting in the Desert Lounge.' Harnek gestured to the door to a nearby corridor and led the way.

As they moved off, Harald immediately instructed *Ironfist*'s Security to get teams aboard Ildris's ship, *Resilience*. He then checked on the whereabouts of Franorl, and discovered the *Desert Wind* was not due in for another day. He opened a link to that ship and was shortly speaking to Franorl himself.

'No great loss,' Franorl replied upon hearing the news.

'It could turn others against us,' Harald replied. 'When you get in, I want you to check out the Captain-in-Waiting aboard *Resilience*.'

'But of course.'

Harald took the lift at the end of the corridor, which opened into the foyer of the Desert Lounge. He handed his headset and glove over to one of his guards, then forced a relaxed mien before entering through the foamed steel doors. Immediately general conversation subsided and a silence descended. Harald saw five Captains present along with some of their staff. Lambrack was one of them, but Coleon seemed to be missing. Harald headed over directly.

'It's good to meet you again, Lambrack.' Harald fist-saluted over his side arm, then held out his hand.

Lambrack returned the salute but ignored the hand. 'Yes, it's interesting to meet you again, Harald. You've risen in the world.'

'Not entirely through choice,' Harald replied, lowering his hand.

'You know, I knew Lieutenant Alun well, and last I recollect he would have laid down his life for Admiral Carnasus,' said the Captain.

Harald was thoroughly aware that everyone else was listening intently.

'That was the appearance he liked to give, certainly. But Alun was attracted to power and wealth. He would have done nothing so drastic, I suspect, had not the

Admiral found out he was passing information to Combine.'

'And no doubt you, being so able with computers, discovered this?'

'As it happens, no. The Admiral found out through his own agents in Combine. I suspect Alun had been given orders concerning the Admiral that he was not following, and Combine wanted to push him into action. What I've since discovered is that Combine wanted the Admiral dealt with quietly – only Alun's ineptitude led to the shooting.'

'You have proof of this?'

'I do.'

'Quietly . . . like poison. Perhaps a potion similar to the one that made Ildris tear out his fingernails against the floor of his quarters?'

'What are you suggesting?' enquired Harald. 'That I would know?'

Conversation had risen to a mutter, but it was now abruptly stilled.

'Far be it for me to suggest such a thing.'

Harald stared at him for a long moment, until the man started to look edgy, then said, 'I've had enough of such innuendo. If you have accusations to make, then make them. You can present your evidence, and a quorum can decide on it, and then we can move on.' Harald paused, still unblinking. '*Do* you have evidence?'

'I have none . . . yet.' Lambrack began to turn away.

'Do not turn your back on me,' said Harald quietly.

'Believe me, that's not something I would ever feel comfortable doing.'

'Very well,' said Harald. 'Thank you, Lambrack – you have made your position clear. And should Fleet come under the control of Orbital Combine, and they replace you with one of their own lackeys, I hope you will still be happy with that position.' He turned away.

'And now you turn your back on me.'

'I am prepared to trust honourable men, even if they refuse to trust me.'

Lambrack found no reply to that.

Harald moved on through the crowd, working those in it like any groundsider politician. Two more Captains arrived and upon speaking to them he realized that, despite Lambrack's hostility, there would be no vote concerning his assumption of the Admiralship. He learnt in passing that, after the murder of Ildris, Coleon had returned to his hilldigger and taken it away from the station. He had run, and it did not seem likely he would be coming back any time soon. They were all scared, it seemed, scared of Harald, and only Lambrack possessed the nerve to show he resented feeling that way.

'It would appear that there is not sufficient objection to my assumption of overall Fleet command,' he said later, addressing them all. 'So let me give you a summation of the situation: it would appear there are those in Orbital Combine who feel ready to displace Fleet. They first attempted to sway public opinion against us by conniving with the Brumallians in the assassination of the Polity Consul Assessor, perhaps rightly expecting the groundsiders to blame us for this. They then beheaded us by murdering Admiral Carnasus, and around Sudoria have made their first direct moves against us. I suspect the destruction of the *Blatant* was also intended to remove another possible leader for Fleet. In such a situation Fleet definitely needs firm leadership.' Harald paused and gazed at them all in turn, before continuing:

'My qualifications took me to the position of
Captain-in-Waiting on *Ironfist* – the highest rank possible
with a Captaincy as yet unavailable. Admiral Carnasus
made it known that I was to be viewed as an Admiral
Candidate. I would like to add that he was also prepared
to demote one of you in order to give me such a position
– which strategy I refused. Only Dravenik stood higher
than me in the ranking system, and he is gone. So I have
now assumed the position of Fleet Admiral. I understand
that four of you, one now departed in his ship, have
lodged objections to my claim. Under Fleet law, six
objections are required. I am now Fleet Admiral, and
whether you object to this or not, I expect your obedience, and hope in time to gain your respect.' Again he
paused, studying those captains he knew to have
objected.

'Since Parliament reinstated our wartime prerogatives, *Carmel* has been brought back online and is now
processing materials stored here for twenty years. Over
those twenty years all our hilldiggers have depleted their
stores of spare parts, weaponry and fissile fuels. My
orders to you now are that you make your ships ready,
suckle on *Carmel* and grow strong, for soon we will be
going to Sudoria to bring Orbital Combine to account.'

Applause followed, some overly enthusiastic, some
desultory.

It was enough.

11

In the century before the War we were growing wealthy and most of that wealth lay in the hands of industrialists and agriculturalists. They used this wealth, and consequent power, to form their own 'parties' and thus gain representation in the Planetary Council. The old parties were pushed aside till the largest proportion of representatives belonged to powerful corporations – their voting strength coming from workers who had signed up to the corporate parties out of fear of losing their jobs or of losing the protection afforded by their corporation's security force. There were also other forms of coercion: 'If you leave, remember that our fire service won't be able to help you should your house inadvertently burn down. If you leave, you'll have to find a school for your children and the best schools are those funded by the corporation. And if you decide to join another corporation, well, think again about that fire risk.' Though we can criticize this unfairly coercive society now, it's well to remember it created the wealth to take us back into space. It was also this wealth that built the spaceship called The Outstretched Hand. *And it was also the drive to acquire more such wealth that equipped it, and that worded the secret orders to its crew.*

– Uskaron

McCrooger

I woke up suffering pain even worse than during the brief while I spent slung over Slog's shoulder. My mind seemed to be replaying a random selection of memories as if to entertain itself while I had been unconscious. Someone had enclosed my body in a lead suit and dropped it down into the dark hold of a Spatterjay sailing ship, where the motion made me nauseous – that, and the snakes writhing inside the suit along with me. A dark place loomed and I knew I just needed to relax into it and everything would go away, but every time I started to do that, something jerked me out, like that rasping snore which snaps one out of a doze.

'You are dying,' someone said matter-of-factly. 'The best analogy I can give is that the cold war inside you between the two viral forms has now turned hot. They are eating up your physical resources in order to destroy each other.'

'Thanks for that,' I slurred, my mouth sticky and foul, since a rat seemed to have crawled into it and died.

'Sprine seems to be the only answer.'

I considered that often an answer that older hoopers retained as an option, but one they spent their very long lives avoiding. For some reason I remembered my mother calling up viral codon repair options on our house computer, since I was then of an age to decide whether I wanted to suffer the old genetic throwbacks of acne rosacea and asthma, to which I was prone. Of course I chose to be perfect – don't we all.

'Don't really want to die just yet,' I muttered.

'Then sprine it will have to be.'

I tried to yell then, but it came out as a whimper. I

tried to fight free of my lead suit, but to no avail. Then came some kind of schism: the me fighting for life and another me analytically inspecting past memories. I remembered that terse individual aboard a sailing ship on Spatterjay telling me, *'Now you're buggered.'* Then, with seemingly no transition I was standing on *Crematorius*, the Mercury station from which they launched the bodies of the dead into the sun.

'Why?' I asked.

'That is not a question you need to ask,' my father replied.

No, it wasn't – just one I would have to face in the future. It was accepted wisdom that, though it was possible to live forever, people reaching their second century often got bored with life. Ennui killed them. Sometimes it was utterly conscious – a quiet suicide at home or else something often spectacular and messy – other times it manifested in an impulse towards increasingly dangerous pursuits. My mother took up free climbing without aug link, locator or any of the usual safety equipment. She did Everest, many of them do, but her attempt at the Eiger resulted in the mess now sealed inside a glass coffin, ready to be fired into the sun.

Of course, born to my parents when they were in their fifties I hit my similar watershed fifty years after that funeral. I lost interest in U-space mechanics, which I had been pursuing avidly for about thirty years, and decided I would like to go sailing. Inevitably I chose to go sailing on oceans full of lethal predators, which were located on the planet Spatterjay. But I survived and, after a further 400 years, discovered that 'long habit of living' of which the Old Captains there are so fond.

I did not want to die. I didn't want sprine. Sprine

means death to those infected by the Spatterjay virus. Sprine on the blade of a dagger . . .

'Screw you! Screw you and your shag-nasty woman. I'll eat your fucking eyes!' He was big, a 300-year-old hooper who had thrown his Captain's wife over the side of the ship, so it wasn't exactly murder. She would continue drifting through the ocean, body stripped down to bone, but alive and forever suffering, unless someone rescued her, or until her mind went. The penalty remained the same, however. The Captain stepped up to him as he struggled against chains and manacles thick enough to hold an elephant, and drove the sprine-tainted dagger up under his ribcage.

'Oh,' said the hooper. 'Oh bugger.'

Black fluid flowed from the wound. He began shuddering as if being electrocuted, splits developed throughout his body and slowly he began to fall apart, like a building being dismantled brick by brick. And in the end all that remained of him was a pile of steaming offal.

Sprine.

My suffering lasted four days, every hour filled with hallucination and many memories I would rather not recall. Slowly, very slowly, I began to return to myself – disparate fragments of my mind slowly melding together until I became conscious. My body burned. Someone had sanded off the outer layer of my skin and injected chilli oil into my depleted veins. Gritty eyes finally open, I surveyed my surroundings.

The room looked like the inside of a walnut shell, but green and yellow, with light permeating the walls. Nil gee, I noticed. I was strapped down to some organic pulsing object that smelt of clams. Something sucked at my anus and I could feel the intrusion of a catheter. Hoisting myself up a little, I saw a ribbed tube snaking down from between my legs and disappearing into the living mattress. But this wasn't what riveted my attention, for I hardly recognized my own body. It was starveling thin, ribs plainly evident under sagging skin, and jaundice-yellow. *Great.* Only as I lay back did I feel something squirm on my face and at the back of my throat. Tubes retracted from my nostrils and flipped aside like beached sand eels. I saw them being sucked back into the grey veined flesh pillowing my head.

'Hey,' I managed weakly. 'Hey.'

A vaginal door opened in the wall and Slog stuck his head through. I raised a hand to try sign language, but it shook so much I gave up.

'I'll get someone,' Slog clattered, and disappeared.

My thoughts ran clear but I felt incredibly weak. Obviously I was aboard a Brumallian ship, and that ship was now in space. Had I hallucinated that voice talking about sprine? I thought not, but couldn't fathom what had happened. The vaginal door parted again and Rhodane entered, pulling herself along by struts jutting out from the wall to reach over beside my bed.

'You're alive,' I said.

She pressed her hand to a bulky lump concealed under her clothing, just over her right hip. 'The bullet lost much of its momentum, and broke apart as it passed through you. Some fragments penetrated, that is all.'

I wondered what else might have penetrated her. Like many viruses of Earth the Spatterjay virus could not long survive outside its host. However, a bullet passing through me first and then entering her might serve to infect her with it, or with IF21, or both.

'She is not infected with either virus . . . probably,' said a voice.

I recognized it as the same voice that recently talked to me of sprine, and now recognized it from before that. 'Are you going to keep on hiding?' I asked in English.

Tigger materialized at the foot of my living bed. 'Their own surgeon removed the pieces of the bullet. I used nanoscopic techniques to ensure the removal of any viral fragments, and then screened her blood and other bodily fluids.'

I tried to hoist myself up again, but could not seem to find the strength even though I was not fighting gravity. Rhodane reached down and touched something beside the bed. The part behind my back folded up smoothly to bring me into a sitting position.

After a rush of dizziness I said, 'Perhaps you'd better start with Vertical Vienna,' switching to speak in Sudorian for Rhodane's benefit.

'It would seem that Fleet has obtained technology enabling it to detect me despite my chameleonware.' Tigger now spoke Sudorian too. '*Ironfist* fired a missile at the city – one deliberately hardened so I could not interfere with it from a distance – and when I closed with it, someone aboard that ship pressed the detonation button.'

'Yet you are here,' I said.

'The smaller portion of me is here,' Tigger replied. 'As you will recollect, this form you see before you is not all of me.'

'The sphere,' I managed.

'Yes. By the time I was again able to move, a second missile had already been fired into Vertical Vienna.

Through Brumal coms I was able to track you down and came here to this ship as they were bringing you aboard.'

I glanced at Rhodane, who was staring at Tigger intently. 'He revealed himself to you.'

She turned towards me. 'You were dying. We sealed your wounds as best we could and made the most of the medical technologies aboard, but to no avail. Tigger then appeared, told us what he was, and took over.'

'What did you do, Tigger? I heard something . . . about sprine.'

'As you have known for some time, any injuries done to you enable IF21 to gain headway within your body. Your gunshot wound caused something like open war-fare between IF21 and the Spatterjay virus, both of them using up your physical resources in the process. Had I left matters as they were, nothing would have remained of you but the two virus forms, and perhaps a few bones. One of them had to go. I could do nothing about IF21, but sprine effectively kills the Spatterjay virus. I showed the Brumallians how to synthesize that organic chemical, then we fed it to you in very small doses, killing off the Spatterjay virus and enabling IF21 to win the war.'

I tried to absorb that news, but felt so very tired. 'But sprine kills . . .'

'It kills the virus. When given in large quantities, the breakdown is so sudden and catastrophic that the body supported by the virus dies as well. However, the small quantities I gave you killed the virus at a rate your body could support. As it died, IF21 then took over the Spatterjay virus's role in your body, displacing it.'

'So . . . I am no different now . . . just another form of the same virus?'

'I cannot even speculate on that. IF21 was based on

the Spatterjay virus, but it is unaffected by sprine and in fact produces it. The changes Iffildus introduced to enable it to do that were substantial. In fact, less than ten per cent of it remains the same as the original virus.'

'So I could die?'

'I just do not know.'

'A risky strategy.'

'It was either that or death. You chose not to die.'

I closed my eyes. Iffildus's aim in making IF21 had overtly been to create something that killed the Spatterjay virus, but had he intended anything beyond that? The Spatterjay virus could cause some horrible transformations; so had that aspect of IF21 been changed? Even if not, IF21 might just die within me, poisoning my body in the process. But at the moment there was nothing I could really do about that; I just had to live with the possibilities. I drifted mentally, only half aware of the bed levelling out again. Then I slept.

Yishna

Sudoria now lay within view as the transport decelerated. Gazing through the polished quartz windows, Yishna could just see the thousands of gleaming satellites that made up Orbital Combine, and though glad the journey was over, she felt some trepidation about arriving at her final destination.

For the *Vergillan,* a transport for short insystem flights, the run from Brumal to Sudoria had been a long one. As the journey progressed, Yishna began to notice a change in attitude amongst its small crew of twenty Fleet personnel. First polite but distant, they now tended to either avoid her, or were unhelpful bordering on insolent. She suspected that without the Chairman aboard their treatment of her would have been even worse. She recollected a recent conversation with Duras on this subject.

'Just smile and bide your time, Yishna,' said Duras. 'Had Pilot Officer Clanot received other instructions concerning you, I believe he would have carried them out by now.'

'That he has not received any other instructions I put down to your presence,' Yishna replied.

'Undoubtedly.'

'But that may change when we reach Sudoria, since Franorl, aboard *Desert Wind*, awaits there at Corisanthe Main and, judging by what happened to the Combine observers, he is not averse to taking very direct action.'

Duras gave an empty smile. 'But his actions were in response to attempted sabotage by those same observers.'

'Do you really believe that?'

'I have yet to decide what I believe,' said Duras, 'but you may put your mind at rest about Franorl. *Desert Wind* is presently on a course that takes him wide of us, heading out from Sudoria.'

'You learnt this from Clanot?'

'I did. Apparently Fleet is grouping at *Carmel*.'

'Oh no,' Yishna felt her legs grow weak. She abruptly sat down in one of Duras's chairs and tried to figure her way through this latest news. Obviously Harald must be securing his position in Fleet, but that he chose *Carmel* – the factory station that had supplied much of the munitions during the last few years of the war – was ominous.

'What are you thinking?' Duras asked.

'I am thinking we are on the verge of something regrettable,' Yishna replied.

'That has been implicit since the moment the Consul Assessor's ship was struck, and subsequent events only confirm it. I can only say that at present Fleet and Combine still seem to heed the will of Parliament.'

'What do you intend to do when you reach Sudoria?'

'I will continue pushing for an extensive investigation, and in undertaking that try to keep Fleet and Combine from each other's throats. I will play the political game in the hope that both sides will hold off because of the chance of getting what they want without resorting to bloodshed. I will feed and nurture that possibility for as long as I am able.'

'I don't think Harald will have much patience with that.'

'Then, as you say, we are on the verge of something regrettable.'

And there the conversation ended.

Standing by the viewing windows, Yishna hoisted up the bag containing her few belongings. Since first contact with the Polity and the arrival of the Consul Assessor, Director Gneiss, whatever his own aims, had positioned her at the fulcrum of events, here at the Chairman's side. Now, with McCrooger dead and war seeming almost inevitable, it was time for her to return to Corisanthe Main, to where she had invested her life. She felt a surge of dread at the prospect – remembering nightmares and darkness – then grew angry. Her feelings back then must have been an aberration, for Yishna could hardly recognize as herself that person sent off from Corisanthe Main to accompany Duras. She quickly dismissed those past episodes from her mind. On Main she would throw herself into the defence of Orbital Combine's interests, and if that meant her going up against her brother, so be it.

The Corisanthe stations lay in a widely spaced long triangular formation travelling in orbit. They were originally built as just one station, then were broken into three and shifted to their present orbits shortly after the end of the War. At that time they had been small, but with the previous addition of the Worm canisters and containment cylinders to Main, and the rapid expansion of Orbital Combine since the end of the War, and the growth of all three stations to house burgeoning populations, they were now immense. Soon Yishna saw that their transport was approaching Corisanthe II – a huge cylinder, once the central part of the original single station spun up for gee in the days before the Worm provided them with the technology for artificial gravity, and now nearly drowned in accretions. Further deceleration caused her to reach out and balance herself against the wall.

'Yishna Strone.'

She turned to see four Fleet personnel awaiting her. 'Yes?'

'I'm to escort you off this ship,' said the Lieutenant in charge, his hand resting on the butt of his side arm.

'I already know the way, so that seems hardly necessary,' she replied.

'Come with us,' he insisted, and at that moment Yishna wondered if she *would* be leaving the ship. The man added, 'Neither yourself nor Chairman Duras will be leaving by the main airlock. A shuttle is coming out to pick you up.'

'You're not docking with Corisanthe II?' Yishna began walking with them, two of the crew, armed with disc rifles, falling in behind her.

'We have little inclination to leave ourselves open to Combine treachery.'

They reached a lift and descended in it for a couple of floors.

'What do you have in the bag?' the Lieutenant asked.

'Personal effects.'

'You understand we must check?' he said.

'No, I do not understand.'

They drew to a halt and the snouts of their weapons wavered in her direction. She sighed, unshouldered her bag, but before she could pass it over a door opened behind her and they crowded her through it. The bag was snatched from her and slammed down on a nearby table.

'Strip,' ordered the Lieutenant.

Yishna eyed him for a long moment. She could protest, she could make demands, try to assert her authority, but she realized he would not have placed her in this position if he did not think he could effectively carry through a search. He did not meet her eyes, merely fixed his attention on her bag as he opened it and began sorting through its contents. She glanced at the guards, two of whom were grinning, the other two looking embarrassed. With as much dignity as she could muster she removed her clothes and stood naked before them. For a second she considered making some sarcastic remark about how Fleet personnel found their entertainment, but refrained. Perhaps they were just waiting for some kind of provocation from her.

'Check her clothing, Marks. The rest of you check her personally – make sure she has nothing concealed.'

They grabbed her firmly and began running a hand scanner over her body. She remained silent and seemingly without reaction even when they dragged her to the table, bent her over it, and conducted an even more intimate search. Finally allowed to stand upright again, she observed one of the guards stripping off a glove.

'You may dress now.'

Yishna picked up her clothing, observing that the Lieutenant had now separated her belongings into two piles. One of those piles contained anything written or containing data storage, including her control baton. The rest, after a perfunctory scan, went back into her bag.

'I would guess that the Chairman has not received similar treatment,' she observed.

The Lieutenant stepped out from behind the table and slapped her, hard. She took it calmly, then just raised her head and stared at him. She knew she could easily take him down, and perhaps one or two of the others, but would probably end up badly beaten or dead. She also knew that if this went any further she would have to do something drastic, because many prisoners had died in such situations, foolishly waiting for them to improve.

'Orbital Combine!' he spat. 'We fought and died for Sudoria while you nestled around the planet growing fat and wealthy. Now you think you're better than us. Worse even than the groundsiders, you lie about the War and you smear Fleet. Now the Brumallian is painted as the poor victim, with Fleet's boot on his neck.' He stabbed a finger. 'You forget what we did!'

Yishna could feel herself flushing with anger. 'Hardly *you*; I should think you were still pissing your bed when Fleet destroyed Brumal.'

He swung at her again, but this time Yishna raised both her forearms, scissoring them with his wrist between. Bones broke with a satisfactory crunch. She grabbed and pulled him into her and, turning, spun him

over her hip into two of the guards behind her. Still turning she raised her foot off the ground and cannoned it
into the temple of another guard. To her left: a weapon
being raised. Leaping in close, she drove the heel of her
hand into that guard's nose, and he flew backwards over
the table. Behind her, the others were recovering. Probably she would be gunned down as she went for them,
but—

The door slammed open. 'Enough!' bellowed Pilot
Officer Clanot. 'Lower your weapons!' Struggling to his
feet the Lieutenant did not seem to be listening, as he
tried to draw his side arm left-handed. Clanot drew his
own weapon, stepped in close and brought it down hard
against the side of the man's head. Now Duras entered,
followed by two more crew and a third figure Yishna
recognized at once.

'You four, return to your berths right now!' Clanot
ordered. He reholstered his gun, his hand shaking. As the
four guards exited, he turned to Yishna, keeping his
gaze fixed firmly upon her face. 'Please clothe yourself,
Yishna Strone.'

'I didn't know you had joined the Exhibitionists,'
said Dalepan. The Ozark containment technician, clad in
a spacesuit, leant back against the door jamb with his
arms folded.

Yishna shot him a wry look and began to pick up her
clothing.

'It is precisely this kind of behaviour,' observed
Duras, 'that causes people to fall out of sympathy with
Fleet.'

'They will be punished,' said Clanot, gazing down at
the unconscious Lieutenant.

'Will they? After we have left this ship?'

Clanot looked up. 'There are those in Fleet who do not like what is happening now.'

'Not nearly enough of them.'

'Yes.' Clanot looked down again.

Now once again dressed, Yishna tossed her belongings into her bag and shouldered it. 'It's time for us to depart, I think,' she said.

'Yes, I'm very much afraid it is,' Duras replied.

Orduval

He gazed out at the setting sun, its light hazed above the desert like angel dust, and a weary sadness infected his mood as he reviewed recent events. His book had very much changed public – and thus parliamentary – opinion about the Brumallians and about Fleet. He understood how the effect of its publication had killed Fleet's political manoeuvring to have the U-space link closed down, and that, without that same effect, Fleet would have had the power to prevent the Consul Assessor coming here. But in the end it had been too late, for he calculated that if he had published it five years earlier, things would have been very different now.

'Oh, Harald, what are you doing?' he asked the desert, but the question was rhetoric into the abyss, for he knew the answer.

Had public opinion been swayed only a little more against Fleet and in favour of the Brumallians, Parliament would not have returned to Fleet its wartime prerogatives, and Fleet would not then have been able, without consultation and a vote, to bomb a Brumallian city. On such little things turn catastrophic events.

Orduval wished Tigger would return, but supposed

the Polity drone was wrapped up in business more important than keeping Orduval informed. He did not himself believe the Brumallians had launched the attack that resulted in the Consul Assessor's death. He understood that many on Sudoria did not believe it either, and like him could not decide which of the two, Fleet or Combine, was the guilty party. Tigger could tell him, and had already told him so very much.

'I have finally ascertained the cause of your debility, and I am amazed,' Tigger informed him during their last meeting, just before the drone's departure for Brumal.

'If you could explain?' Orduval suggested.

'You knew I was coming today, even though I did not tell you I would be coming.'

Orduval felt a moment's bewilderment. Yes, Tigger was right. He had turned off his console, put it to one side and walked out here fully expecting Tigger to be waiting – and never questioned that impulse.

'Some structures in your brain are sensitive to U-space,' the drone explained. 'Interestingly, the first fit you ever experienced happened precisely on one of the occasions when I arrived back here from Brumal.'

Orduval knew that Tigger contained in his sphere part a U-space drive which he used in order to zip back and forth between the two worlds.

'So it's all your fault,' he wryly suggested.

'Not entirely. My arrival on that occasion may have triggered the first feedback loop that resulted in your fit, but the weakness was already there, and such a loop inevitable.'

'I feel a bit more explanation is required.'

'So do I. Far in the past, on Earth, there used to be a long-running debate, often quite heated, concerning so-called psychic powers. Those being the ability to see into the future, to move objects by thought power, to read minds or communicate from mind to mind. It was only some years after the advent of U-space technology that the debate was partially resolved. Most psychic phenomena were then found to be related to a brain configuration that made them sensitive to U-space, and theoretically able to cause localized phenomena related to it.'

'Theoretically?'

'Cases of the strictly mental phenomena have been documented, but none has been documented regarding the physical phenomena.'

'So I am in some way sensitized to U-space, and this causes my fits – a phenomenon you say is already known about in the Polity. Why then are you amazed?'

'Because the structures in your brain grew from your DNA blueprint, as do most basal structures in most human brains – meaning nature not nurture. Everything that forms afterwards is nowhere near so dramatic.'

'Biology is not my main interest, but I do know enough to understand that.'

'Without her knowledge, I visited your grandmother Utrain, and sampled her DNA. What I found there led me to a rather risky penetration of Corisanthe Main, where I managed to obtain a stored blood sample taken from your mother. I discovered that the difference in your DNA, resulting in those unusual brain structures, cannot be accounted for by your ancestry.'

Orduval nodded slowly to himself, realizing that at some level he already knew that someone had tampered with his DNA.

'This is something I must investigate further,' Tigger

told him, 'but now I must prepare for the arrival of the Consul Assessor.'

Their conversation continued for a while, as it always did, while they discussed current events and Orduval's eventual return to Sudorian society. But he felt himself to have shuddered to a bit of a halt, contributing only little to the conversation as on some other level his mind chewed over the latest information. After Tigger departed he returned to his cave and sat and thought for a while, then opened up his console and began to use programs provided by Tigger for research, in order to penetrate Corisanthe Main. He began looking at the time when his mother had first arrived there, and speed-read files feverishly, looking for some clue to what dangerous genetic experiments Orbital Combine had been con-ducting then. For two days and two nights he found nothing, and began to realize that his conjecture about experiments might be wrong. Then he found something significant – right near the end.

Combine claimed that a fumarole breach was merely when an energy surge from the Worm knocked out a piece of equipment, and like everyone else he had always accepted this. Now a simple manifest transference showed that Fleet occasionally boosted cargo crates, for Orbital Combine, towards the sun. Tracking this manifest back to source, because he thought Combine might have been destroying evidence, he discovered the crates contained equipment damaged by fumarole breach on Corisanthe Main. For a while he tried to believe that he had genuinely discovered the concealment of evidence, but from previous reading he knew that the crates did indeed contain such affected equipment. Why such caution about equipment merely damaged by an energy surge?

Obviously fumarole breaches were something more than Combine was admitting to.

We were conceived during a fumarole breach. Tigger had told him how that conception, according to heavily edited and often hidden station records, had actually taken place inside Ozark One *during* the said breach. He wished Tigger had been here to ask more about this. He wished he'd asked the drone about fumarole breaches before, but it just hadn't seemed so important then.

Now the implications terrified him and he knew he must find out more, yet felt a terrible reluctance to do so. He now had to talk to someone, perhaps Yishna. Yes, it would all become clear . . . somehow. Orduval would have liked to share with Tigger this strange discovery, but the drone would not be returning any time soon. Orduval closed up his console and began to pack those belongings he felt he would need, then finally set out across the boiling sand. He had a tram to catch, and a story he needed to tell.

Harald

It was an awesome sight: including *Ironfist*, nine hill-diggers were now parked around *Carmel*, the gaps between them no more than a few miles wide and support ships scattered throughout like glimmer bugs about a herd of sand cows gathered round their barn. Harald regretted that he could not see the view entire, only through the quartz windows of the Admiral's Haven and on his eye-screen. Apparently Polity ships were not limited like this, or so he understood from what had been learnt from the Consul Assessor and from information imparted via the U-space comlink. Their Polity ships carried panoramic

windows fashioned of the same chain-molecule glass as
the spherical vessel in which the U-space comlink had
arrived. Aboard them it was also possible to enter a
virtuality from which ships could be viewed via external
probes, so to the viewer himself he seemed to be standing
out in vacuum. Harald had already instructed Jeon to
allocate some of her research staff to investigate such
possibilities. He considered further the implications.

Chainglass was very strong, stronger in fact than
some of the hull metals of older Fleet ships. But lasers
could pass through it, as could other radiations further
along the electromagnetic band. Also, no matter how
strong such a window, by inserting one in a hull you
created a weakness. So did this mean their ships were not
often involved in conflict, or else possessed some shielding technology that rendered strength of hull irrelevant?
Or were these just passenger ships being referred to –
information about Polity warships being deliberately
withheld? Harald suspected all this was something Fleet
would be learning about in years to come. But not yet,
not until he had done what needed doing.

He turned away from the Haven windows and
headed for the stair leading down into the Bridge. The
two guards who stood below, armed with disc carbines,
stepped aside as he descended and alertly eyed the
surrounding Bridge. Like many other personnel in Fleet
they were eager to show their loyalty and demonstrate
the quality of their service to him. Such dedication was
admirable, within limitations. The two guards fell in
behind him as he headed for the exit. As he left the
Bridge, the two guards manning the door also fell in
behind. He did not really like having such an armed
retinue, but in the present situation, and with him having

known enemies inside Fleet, an attempt on his life was not unlikely. And on this particular occasion their presence might be very necessary.

He took a lift down to the ship's forward transport station, then took one of the egg-shaped carriages, travelling between three evenly spaced rails, along the length of the ship's body to the docking area amidships – the mile-long journey, in nil gee, taking only a few minutes. He pushed himself out, weight returning over the gravity floor of the platform. Here one could gain some perspective of the sheer scale of *Ironfist*. There were four sets of similar rails for the entire length of the ship, two located below and one beside this one. Alongside each of these ran continuous platforms, and spaced every few thousand feet along these were lift stations to take people and cargo up and down to other levels. The rail lines below were not used for people, since those ran to and from the ship's docking area, shifting fuel for the engines, fuel for the reactors and various ship's transports, munitions, supplies of food and water, and numerous spare parts. Gazing at these over the platform rim, Harald observed crates being loaded into a large cargo cage and guessed they contained the tons of optic cable required for refitting some of the engineering sections of *Ironfist*. Another cargo cage, just arriving, held some huge item of machinery to be hoisted from the ship. Checking via his headset, he discovered it was a worn-out generator destined for *Carmel*, where it would be fully reconditioned.

A lift arrived and Harald strolled across the platform towards it. After a moment out stepped Captain Franorl accompanied by four others, two of whom were armed guards marching one other man between them. The fourth man strolled to one side, appreciatively studying his surroundings. Like Franorl, he was clad in the foamite suit of a Captain.

Franorl and Harald approached each other with a degree of wariness, fist-saluted then clasped hands. Harald eyed Franorl's two guards and then their prisoner. His own guards had quietly moved out to either side, to give them a clear view.

'So at last we are here,' said Franorl. 'I did wonder if we would make it.'

'You should have more confidence in me,' said Harald.

'Oh I have confidence in you, Harald, but fate can deliver some mean injustices.'

'I've never believed in fate,' said Harald, 'but let us consider injustice, and its opposite.'

Franorl nodded minutely, then turned, clapping a hand on the shoulder of the other Captain. 'Let me introduce Jalton Grune, the new Captain of Ildris's *Resilience*' – he waved a hand at the prisoner – 'and Captain-in-Waiting Orvram Davidson.'

Grune smiled and nodded. 'It is a pleasure to meet you at last, Admiral.'

'Admiral,' said Davidson, fist-saluting over the empty holster at his hip.

In utter contrast to Grune's quiet confidence, Davidson stood very correctly, and he looked frightened. This was perfectly understandable. The man had been utterly loyal to Ildris and supported his Captain's objection to Harald assuming the Admiralship, and being brought here under guard would certainly make him suspect the worst. Grune, however, was a supporter – a fanatical supporter.

'Well, let's not draw this out any longer than necessary,' said Harald. He drew his gun and let it hang down beside his hip. 'What do you have to say for yourself, Davidson?'

'Do you give me your permission to speak freely?' asked Davidson. He looked stunned, as if this was all happening too quickly. Perhaps the man had expected a court martial before all the other Captains, and some chance to prove his innocence.

'I do, though you should be aware that all of this is being recorded.'

Davidson glanced upward, noting the sensor heads set in the ceiling high above. He again focused on Harald. 'I have very little to say. My Captain, as you know, was not an advocate of your assuming the position of Admiral. He was subsequently poisoned aboard *Carmel*, which I imagine suited you quite well—'

'Yes, that poisoning,' Harald interrupted. 'Fleet has an unfortunate history of some personnel using such methods to climb the promotion ladder. The removal of Ildris has placed Grune here in the Captain's chair, and moved you another step closer to it. As Admiral, I can no longer countenance such methods.'

'I would not murder my own Captain,' said Davidson. His face was pale now, and despite this area of the ship being cool, he was sweating.

Harald shrugged. 'I possess incontrovertible evidence – supplied by Station Supervisor Harnek.' It had taken Harald little time to track down the incriminating evidence, somewhat longer to surreptitiously bring it to Harnek's attention.

'Yes,' said Davidson, a touch of a sneer in his voice. 'I suppose you do.'

Harald could see the man was ready to do something drastic, perhaps try to grab a weapon, so it was time to wrap this up.

'Under Fleet law, in an emergency, I, as Admiral, possess certain powers, which I intend to exercise now.'

As Davidson began to turn, Harald raised his gun and fired once. Davidson staggered back into one of his guards. Pieces of flesh and blood were spattered over his suit. The guard pushed him away, then after a pause Davidson straightened up, wiping a hand down his face and smearing the blood further. He turned and gazed down at Grune, who now lay quivering into death on the floor, with half of his head missing.

'What . . .? I don't . . .?'

'You have my deepest apologies, *Captain* Davidson,' said Harald. He nodded to one of the guards. 'Return his side arm.'

The guard handed the weapon to Davidson, who took it but just stared down at it in confusion.

Harald holstered his own weapon and continued, 'As I said, I will not countenance murder as a method of climbing the promotion ladder. Harnek's evidence proved to my satisfaction that Jalton Grune poisoned Captain Ildris. This subterfuge was necessary to extract him from *Resilience* without having to send in a combat team and risk bloodshed there. He was showing a reluctance to come at my invitation until the matter of Ildris's death could be resolved.' Harald nodded to Captain Franorl. 'Franorl here went aboard to arrest you, informing Grune that we now possessed sufficient evidence to accuse you of the murder. Franorl being very persuasive, Grune then lost his reluctance to come aboard.'

Davidson looked up. 'But he was one of your keenest supporters.'

'I will see Fleet kept clean and pure and sharp as a dagger,' said Harald. 'I will have no dirt in it. You, Davidson, return to your ship, set it in order and be prepared to receive my instructions, and to *obey* them.'

Davidson straightened up, saluted, then after a moment turned on his heel. Franorl still gazed at Harald expressionlessly. He possessed more sense than to grin triumphantly or laugh uproariously while the sensor heads recorded these images.

'Get this mess cleared up.' Harald gestured to the corpse. 'We have work to do.'

12

Human embryos weren't the only organic cargo of the Procul Harum. We also brought with us the components of whole ecologies in what was called a 'genetically plastic' form. The huge efforts involved in establishing our agriculture are often neglected in many texts, so let me restore the balance. Thousands of Terran animals were altered to survive here, in much the same way as we ourselves were, along with plants and the whole support ecologies right down to the bacterial level. Some were only partially adapted, hence the large specially cooled underground complexes used to grow much of our food. Areas of desert were stabilized using tough local flora, then the thin but increasing topsoil converted to support Terran crops. The tools we used to achieve all this were developed on Mars and under the domes of Earth's own moon. It is worth remembering that a large proportion of our food is produced in vats by bacteria that was also designed before we even set out from the Solar System. There has been much research into the impact of ourselves and everything we brought on the indigenous environment of Sudoria. Many thousands of species have been wiped out, on both sides, but thousands of new ones have been created and introduced. Much recent research has focused on creating

Terran-Sudorian hybrids, which now seem to be filling all available niches and finding new ones. Suffice to say that, with the level of our present genetic technologies, we are some way beyond the environmental disasters that plagued Earth a thousand years ago.

– Uskaron

McCrooger

A town in a cylinder world, the inner curve of that world giving the illusion of the buildings leaning into each other, as if complicit in some plot. I gazed around, sure I had been here before, but only recognized it on finally peering down to see the skull-cobbled street. Then the figure was standing before me, and I told it that it could not be my father, for he had died long ago. It made no pretence of trying to be him, merely stared, its face a shining wormish tangle that seemed to project pure malice. I turned away and sought consciousness . . .

I awoke feeling a little better and a little stronger – approximately the strength of cardboard as opposed to wet tissue paper. Reaching down to the straps securing me to the bed, it took me a while to figure out they clung to the mattress below with some kind of organic Velcro. Finally managing to pull them away, I lay exhausted for a while before sitting upright. That exertion set me drifting away from the bed, catheter and sucking anal tube trailing after me like umbilicals, so I pulled myself back down using one strap then secured it over my skinny legs.

Studying myself I realized that the loose skin made me look a lot worse than I actually was. I'd shed about a quarter of my body mass and now carried the musculature of a 'normal' human. Even so, I wondered how I would stand up under gravity, or if I would be able to stand up at all. We were heading now for Sudoria, which was about 1.2 standard gees, and I did not relish the prospect. Something else I did not relish was having to accept that my surroundings seemed slightly distorted, with the shadows out of place, and that the malady I had suffered aboard Inigis's ship was back to add to all my other ills.

My shoulder was stiff, with a dressing like cured hide around it which extended down to cover my collar bone at the front and scapula at the back. I was naked and not particularly proud of that nakedness. I drew out the catheter, wincing, then slid back on the bed and removed the other tube, gagging at the smell.

What now?

I just sat there for a while feeling like shit, until a sucking exhalation alerted me to the opening of that door.

'Rhodane,' I said.

'Consul Assessor.'

'Be a good girl and get me some clothing will you?'

She snorted at that, but departed nevertheless. I must have drifted out of consciousness for seemingly only an eye-blink later she was back, accompanied by Slog and Flog. She had brought along some Brumallian dunga-rees, underclothing and a shirt that looked to be made of the same foamite that Fleet personnel wore. I was grateful, for the shirt was thick and would go some way to conceal my debility. I sat upright and reached for the garments.

'You are not ready,' she said predictably.

'Is that Tigger's medical opinion?' I enquired, as I took the clothing from her then struggled to dress.

'No, it is mine.'

'I need something to eat and drink,' I said. Though I did not feel particularly hungry I was anxious to get myself functional again – working on the premise that this might even be possible.

'Do you feel ready to enter the spin ring?' asked Rhodane.

'You'll have to explain that.'

'Brumallian ships do not possess artificial gravity, but an internal ring of compartments is kept spinning to give the—'

'Yeah,' I interrupted. 'I get the idea. I don't know if I'm ready, but there's one way to find out.' I realized I was not my usual cheerful self at this point, and really did not care.

'Come, then.'

She led the way to that disconcerting door and I followed. Slog hovered about me as if ready to assist. I gave him a look he interpreted rightly and he hovered no more. The door brushed over me smooth and dry as snakeskin. On the other side was something I'll call a corridor, but which looked more like an intestinal tract. The walls, however, were not soft – bearing a resemblance in feel to grainy wood and the look of cloudy glass. Light permeated this corridor, as I was to discover it permeated throughout the ship – emitted by layers of luminescent bacteria similar to that found in the body of one of their multi-legged biolights, which were thankfully absent here. After two branchings of this corridor I became increasingly aware of a bubbling sucking sound. Finally we came to its source: a wall I could see slowly revolving about a centre point. Rhodane pressed her hand against some fleshy nub and that same centre point slowly opened wide a sphincter.

'Here,' she said, and launched herself through.

I wondered if I was ready for this, since I had a good idea of what to expect. Gritting my teeth I moved ahead of the two quofarl, then pushed myself through. Hollow shafts, like the spokes of a wheel, revolved about me. Rhodane had pulled herself into one of them and there clung to a ladder. She held out a hand, which I grabbed, and she pulled me in. For a moment, because I could still see beyond the door, I felt a surge of nausea as I revolved. Closing my eyes I clamped down on that reaction and began to push myself backwards along the ladder. After only a short distance, centrifugal force began to impinge, and I was no longer pushing myself along the ladder, but descending it. Looking up I saw Flog come through the opening and now, from my perspective, it was he who was revolving. He too grabbed the ladder and began to descend behind me.

At first it was easy, but with each step I felt my skin and flesh beginning to sag on my bones, and breathing started to become an effort.

Pausing, I asked, 'When we reach the bottom will the spin acceleration be the same as Brumal's gravity?'

'Yes,' replied Rhodane from below.

I had hoped otherwise.

Nearing the bottom of the ladder the soles of my feet hurt as they came down on the rungs, and for a moment I visualized myself walking along that skull-cobbled street, then my hands began to ache from holding up my abruptly enormous weight. It felt to me as if my internal organs were being sucked down towards the bottom of my torso, only suspended in place by threads and weak sheets that could tear or break at any moment. My leg muscles burned with lactic overload and my testicles seemed to have turned into lead shot. Finally reaching the floor, I swung round to the wall and rested my back against it. I really wanted to sit down, but knew that if I did so I would not be able to get back up again.

'Can you continue?' asked Rhodane.

I nodded very carefully, frightened that too vigorous a response might damage my neck. She stared at me for a long moment until I realized my gesture had been wasted – not being emphatic enough for her to recognize.

'I can,' I said.

As she moved on, I stepped out from the wall and turned to follow her. Slog and Flog, recently departing the ladder, moved in either side of me and gripped a biceps each. I felt that protest now would be foolish, because it seemed unlikely I would be able to manage any distance at all down here on my own.

Rhodane led the way into a kind of dormitory, with beds jutting from the wall like bracket fungi, and sporting those familiar organic mattresses. Tottering through the door after her, I could think of nothing to say, I was so unutterably weary. She merely gestured to one of the beds, onto which Slog and Flog released me. I hauled up my legs, then . . . nothing.

Yishna

Leaning her forehead against a port of the inter-station shuttle – the cool glass soothing the burn inside her skull – Yishna observed a landing craft departing Corisanthe II, and knew Duras was aboard and now on his way back to the planet's surface. He might well achieve all he intended down there, but she suspected it would not be enough. A conflict between Fleet and Combine seemed unavoidable, no matter what votes were won in Parliament. As the shuttle turned, she took her head away from the port, then pulled herself over and down into the chair beside Dalepan, and strapped herself in.

'What preparations are being made?' she asked.

'All the quadrant guns are now operational,' said Dalepan, as he guided the shuttle towards the distant speck of Corisanthe Main. 'Presently all other weapons systems are being checked, as are all the safety protocols.' He gestured to the spacesuit he wore. 'Everybody works wearing one of these now.'

'If it comes to us ever needing them, we'll probably have lost,' said Yishna.

'Perhaps so, but we also have a few surprises awaiting the hilldiggers – should they attack. Gneiss has only just informed me that Orbital Combine has been working in secret to build and develop gravity-disruptor weapons, which are also being installed on the Corisanthe stations and on some of the defence platforms. We are also launching stealthed space mines, and Fleet is being ordered to stand off by a million miles.'

'Which Fleet will not do.'

Dalepan nodded, then went on, 'I think the largest imponderable concerns directed and undirected weapons. All the stations of Orbital Combine are a sitting target so Fleet could remain far out and pound us with inert missiles fired by linear accelerator. If we reply in kind, the hilldiggers merely need to be moved.'

'Collateral damage,' said Yishna, understanding at once.

'Precisely. If they bombard us from a distance, a proportion of their missiles will inevitably strike Sudoria. Is Harald prepared to countenance that? How far is he prepared to go to win?' Dalepan gazed at Yishna queryingly.

'I don't know,' she replied, and then began to consider what might be her brother's objectives, and just what he might do to attain them.

Upon their arrival at Corisanthe Main, they were forced to wait until sufficient precautions were taken before the shields shut down. While this was being done, Yishna observed a maintenance vessel approaching the station, clutching in its multiple grabs some kind of massive engine. Space all around it was filled with suited figures and installation pods. After the shields shut down, a computer-controlled maintenance sphere mounted with a missile launcher came out to escort them in. Upon docking, five heavily armed OCTs came aboard to check over their ship before she and Dalepan could disembark.

Once inside the station, he told her, 'Stay healthy,' before moving off. She smiled her thanks, but had to wonder about that comment. Certainly she had not been too healthy when last she left this place, and now, upon her return, felt a growing fear that she might once again become the troubled person she had been then. Shaking her head angrily she set out, two of the armed OCTs staying to escort her to the Director. From them she discovered that all Worm research had been stopped – the containment cylinders locked down under a security protocol, but thankfully not one for a physical breach, she realized, because, after her own interference, that would have meant the containment cylinders had long departed the station. Everyone she saw on the way was wearing either spacesuits or emergency survival suits and seemed to be moving at an accelerated pace.

In his office the Director had the same question for her as Dalepan had asked aboard the shuttle.

'I've considered this,' she replied, 'and come to the conclusion that, just like myself, my brother is prepared to do anything to attain his goals.'

Director Gneiss gestured to the seat before his desk, swung a screen scroll across on a pivoted arm, extended the flimsy screen, then tapped something into a console before him. Yishna sat eyeing the sensor head mounted in the wall behind him, then his suit helmet resting on the desk beside him. She had yet to collect a suit for herself from the stores. After a moment he gazed across at her, and once again Yishna was struck by how she somehow knew him, yet could never read him. Having been away for a while she had nearly convinced herself that her prior opinion of him had been distorted somehow. But here, now, upon her return, she found him just as unnerving as ever.

'We have defences against conventional weapons, and possess many such weapons too,' he stated. 'We also have gravtech weapons of our own; however, there is as yet very little defence against them, and in the end, should they be deployed by either side, very little will remain around Sudoria but the wreckage of the hill-diggers and our stations.'

'But don't the same rules apply to gravtech weapons as to missiles that aren't self-directed, like those fired by linear accelerator?' Yishna interlaced her fingers in her lap and attempted a relaxed mien. She had no doubt that members of the Combine Oversight Committee were watching very closely everything that occurred in this room and logging questions on the screen the Director kept flicking his plastic gaze towards.

'Your point?' he asked.

'A gravity-disruptor burst expands like a torch beam – by the inverse square law – so to hit one of our stations without striking Sudoria, that weapon would need to be fired at or below the orbital level of the station.' Yishna shrugged. 'Should a hilldigger manage to attain such an advantageous position, that would mean it no longer needed to use such a weapon.' Gneiss just stared back at her so she continued. 'What Harald could do in close with gravity disruptors, he could also manage at a distance, with little danger to Fleet, with missiles fired by linear accelerator. To go back to your original question: I feel my brother will be quite prepared to inflict con-siderable collateral damage on Sudoria while attaining his goal. But I feel the real question to ask is how much collateral damage to their home planet are those under his command prepared to tolerate?'

'You make some interesting points,' said Gneiss.

'Harald is not Fleet,' Yishna added. 'And it is well to remember that there'll be few under his command who do not have family down on the surface, and even aboard some of the Combine stations.'

'What does Harald actually *want*?' Gneiss asked. It was another of those questions posed by him that seemed to contain too many perilous levels of meaning.

'You know the answer to that as well as I do,' Yishna replied, deciding to give as good as she got.

'We are supposing that, like many in Fleet, Harald resents Orbital Combine's growing power?'

'So it would appear.'

All surface . . . all ephemeral . . .

'He instigated recent unfortunate events so he could use them as an excuse to take away our control of *our* defence platforms. We are supposing, from his recent actions, that if he cannot attain this end through Parliament, he will resort to force.'

Yishna shook her head. 'I feel you're missing the point. If Harald cannot take control of the platforms through Parliament, he'll know that he cannot ultimately take control of them by force. His aim will be to take control of them out of our hands, so he'll attempt to destroy them.'

'And having done that, he will cease?'

'Of course not. We built the platforms . . .' Yishna paused, realizing that during this discussion she had come to properly understand Harald's aims. 'I think that what Parliament decides has become irrelevant. Harald knows that, even with a parliamentary vote going against us, we'll not hand over the platforms.'

'Conflict cannot be avoided, then?'

'I think not. I think it my brother's intention to smash Combine and then absorb its remnants into Fleet. I talked to Duras about this, who feared his next target might then be Sudoria itself. I doubted that then . . . now I am not so sure.'

'Do you feel any sibling loyalty?'

'I am loyal to Combine because it allows me to do those things that most interest me, involving research of the Worm, and now to stand at the fulcrum of events concerning our contact with the Polity. During his petty games, my brother killed the Consul Assessor, and I can never forgive him for that.'

'Your brother will attempt to seize the Worm for Fleet?'

'If possible. And if not, he'll destroy it.' Even as she said the words, a sudden outfield thought occurred to her: *It has prepared for this possibility.* A simple containment breach, which would be almost inevitable if Corisanthe Main came under heavy attack, and her alteration of the protocols would result in the Ozark Cylinders all being ejected. Then she shook her head. *Madness, surely?*

After a long pause while he studied his screen, Gneiss said, 'You should go now and draw yourself a spacesuit from stores.'

'What do you want of me now?' Yishna asked, standing.

'There is much work to be done and you possess so much expertise.'

'*You* might trust me, but will the Oversight Committee let me stay here?'

'I have always trusted you, Yishna, for I know what you hold most dear. As for the Committee, they heed my advice. You will now take charge of the research body and find useful employment for it, and you will also act as my troubleshooter, as problems are sure to arise from the new . . . installations.'

'Thank you.' She turned and headed towards the door.

'One other thing, Yishna,' said Gneiss, and she paused and turned enquiringly. 'It seems likely that the Consul Assessor is not dead, after all.'

'What?'

'Though Fleet are now blocking all communication, analysis of some pictures earlier transmitted from our geosurvey satellite clearly shows him on the planet's surface, accompanied by some Brumallians, a short time after his escape-pod sank.'

Yishna felt at first glad, then bitter. What difference

did it make to her, to any of them, with what seemed now almost inevitable?

'That's good news, I guess,' she said.

Gneiss waved a dismissive hand.

Harald

Harald sat back, headset placed to one side, smiling gently as he watched the feed arriving direct from Parliament to a screen here in the Haven, then frowning when the image hazed momentarily.

'What's causing that?' asked Franorl, sprawled in a comfortable chair.

'Overspill from the EM chaff, presently blocking com to and from Brumal,' Harald replied.

'Can you do anything about it?'

'Not without ordering the com-block raised.'

They returned their attention to the screen.

Already four delegates had been expelled for unruliness, but none of them represented either Fleet or Combine. Clearly the delegates on both opposing sides knew that the issues being discussed and soon to be put to vote were vitally important, and expulsion meant a loss of voting prerogative for this day's session.

'Whose idea was it for them all to wear their uniforms?' Harald asked.

'Julian felt that, despite the low opinion of Fleet in some quarters at present, the nostalgic attachment to what our uniform once meant would be helpful,' replied Franorl.

'It could backfire on him – many might look upon it as a threat.'

'True, but should we let that worry us?'

Harald glanced at him. 'If Parliament does order Combine to hand the defence platforms over to us, that will ensure obedience amidst our own ranks to the orders I give, once Combine refuses to comply.'

'You still feel your position insecure?'

Harald relaxed his jaw muscles, since it now felt as if a steel ball had been inserted into each, then smiled and nodded. 'Let's say I am not going to make too many rash assumptions. Ah, here's Julian now . . .'

They sat back and watched while Lieutenant Julian, like so many delegates before him, stood to deliver a speech that began by decrying the cowardly Brumallian attack on the Fleet ship carrying the Consul Assessor. He then moved on with: 'In the interests of Sudoria we have had to take a hard line with the Brumallians, and punished them for their—'

A Combine delegate interrupted, 'Yeah, frying a Brumallian city is always the best option when—'

Fleet: 'Under our restored prerogatives, the retaliatory strike—'

Combine: 'Convenient that any evidence of Combine complicity got—'

Uproar ensued, and Harald directed his attention towards Chairman Duras, who was sitting with his chin in his hand, his other hand resting on the head of his cane. Finally the Chairman said, 'I will have silence now or there will be further ejections.' Though he spoke quietly, Combine and Fleet representatives quickly resumed their seats. He then pointed his cane at Julian. 'Fleet claims Orbital Combine is complicit with the Brumallians in their attack upon the Consul Assessor's ship, this being an attempt to blacken Fleet and reduce its power. In support it presents evidence implicating

Combine in the assassination of Admiral Carnasus, in the alleged attempt to sabotage *Desert Wind* and in the destruction of *Blatant*, and now demands that Combine hand over control of all its defence platforms. However, all of this evidence has been gathered and presented by Fleet itself. Orbital Combine claims these events have all been instigated by Fleet, and the evidence implicating Combine has been falsified, because Fleet is jealous of the growing power of Orbital Combine. Let us return to the point: we have no *independent* evidence of either of these claims.' He lowered his cane and sat back and, almost as if being given permission, the delegates began shouting at each other again.

'He is still highly respected,' said Franorl.

'He would not have been appointed Chairman otherwise,' said Harald.

'We have already voted upon and agreed what seems to be the best course of action following recent events,' said Duras, and quiet fell again. 'A Fleet intersystem transport, crewed by Fleet but commanded by GDS wardens, will be sent first to the hilldigger *Desert Wind*, then on to Brumal. Whatever investigations might be required will be conducted by a team provided by GDS. There will also be Orbital Combine observers aboard.'

Franorl glanced at Harald. 'Well, we knew that would be the one they'd go for,' he whispered.

Duras finished, 'Of course the question remains: what must be done in the meantime?'

Julian stood up abruptly. 'Combine cannot be allowed to retain control of their defence platforms,' he insisted. 'Though you may doubt the evidence, we in Fleet are absolutely certain of their complicity with the Brumallians.'

'Do you suppose Combine might use those platforms to fire on Sudoria?' asked Duras.

'That is not out of the question,' Julian replied.

'Why would they attack our home planet if their aim is to displace Fleet?'

'That is the assumption we make, but it may not be correct. It is our primary duty, has always been our duty and one we have fulfilled well, to protect Sudoria. We cannot allow such an obvious threat to this planet's citizens to go unchallenged.'

Duras nodded slowly. 'Then this issue must now, without further debate, be put to the vote.'

Harald abruptly leant forward, something tightening in his stomach. 'He knows something,' he hissed.

'Why do you say that?' asked Franorl.

'He's been delaying that vote all morning, deliberately circumventing Julian every time he's called for it.' He glanced at Franorl. 'We might lose this.'

'But Duras himself served in Fleet.'

'Yes, he did, but I suspect that subsequent contact with the Polity has changed many of his opinions.' Harald sat back. He felt suddenly hot – a stickiness of sweat forming under his foamite uniform. In this one small thing it seemed he had miscalculated.

'Those in favour of handing over the defence platforms to Fleet, vote now,' instructed Duras.

Harald checked the figures at the bottom of the screen.

'Those in favour of Orbital Combine retaining control of the defence platforms vote now.'

More figures.

'That doesn't add up,' said Franorl.

'Some of our own delegates voted against us,' said Harald bitterly.

Duras stood up to close the debate. 'Combine will retain control of their orbital defence platforms. But let me remind Parliament that Combine have requested teams of planetary wardens to board each platform. May I suggest that Fleet Security teams also be—'

Standing up, Julian interrupted, 'Having earlier received instructions from Admiral Harald Strone, I now have something to say.' He paused and gazed about the room.

Duras used the pause to interject, 'Might that be something to do with the alarming news that the entire fleet is now on its way here from *Carmel*?'

Julian ignored him. 'Under our restored wartime prerogatives, we cannot accept the result of this vote' – other Fleet delegates were by now also standing – 'and must now withdraw from Parliament.'

Chairman Duras abruptly sat down, suddenly looking very old and tired.

'Franorl,' said Harald, 'it's time you returned to your ship. As of now we are on full alert. I will broadcast the attack plan and general orders directly.'

Franorl grinned. Harald just stared impassively at the screen.

Orduval

This was the fourth delay on the maglev – it just settled down on its lift plates, with no explanation forthcoming from the tram service, but someone back at Central Control put up on the carriage screen the feed coming from one of the news services.

'. . . refused access to wardens and threatened to open fire if they attempted to enter Fleet property. GDS forces consequently placed a cordon around the base. It has not yet been confirmed that the missile was fired from within that cordon.'

The image showed a badly wrecked street, with the remains of what looked like a landing craft strewn down it. As the camera focused in on the logo displayed on one piece of smoking cowling, Orduval felt a sudden tired disgust. The downed craft belonged to Orbital Combine. It had started.

As the news story continued he began to get the gist. After Fleet's refusal to acknowledge the parliamentary vote, with the subsequent walk-out of its delegates, those members left behind decided action must be taken. There were many Fleet bases located on Sudoria and, it seeming likely that Fleet intended some kind of attack, GDS wardens had rapidly moved in to take control of whatever arms caches the Fleet bases still contained. Working in conjunction with the warden force, a Combine surveillance craft overflew the particular base this report was about, and was blown out of the sky. Now more disturbing images: rioting, gunfire, an overhead shot of the city showing a massive explosion and fires burning here and there. It seemed those factions supporting Fleet were already fighting those supporting Combine, while GDS wardens were trying to restore order.

Orduval sat back disgusted. This could all rapidly run out of control. Fleet sympathizers, though outnumbered on the surface, were usually of a military bent, therefore very well armed, trained and organized. Those opposed to Fleet tended to be less aggressive, yet there were lunatics amidst them – like the group causing the nuclear blast on Brumal that destroyed a base there. If they now began attacking Fleet ground bases, there would soon be many more deaths and much more damage, and quite probably the rioting would spread as other groups joined in, but ultimately everything would be decided beyond the confines of Sudoria.

The maglev tram continued on to the next station, where most of the passengers got out and moved across to the other platform – most of them obviously deciding that a trip into the city was not such a great idea today. Perhaps he should join them in that? He thought not. Most of GDS's warden forces would have been deployed in the city, so that was the place he wanted to be.

To the rumble of a distant explosion the tram finally pulled into the city station, where Orduval was now the only one to disembark. While walking up to the exit barrier, he removed his control baton from his pocket, along with a bank disk Tigger had brought to him some years back. Pushing the small disk into the side slot of his baton, he finally connected a large bank account to his own identity. An irrevocable move. Standing before the barrier, he waited while the station computer logged his ID – which had also been logged when he stepped onto the tram. The price came up on a screen, with below it a small map indicating where he had boarded and his subsequent route. He confirmed this and pushed his baton into the slot – this was the first time he had used *that* particular bank account to pay for anything. The machine returned his baton and the barrier opened – no security alerts, no attempt to detain him. He supposed that apprehending him to ask some pointed questions about where he had obtained information about *The*

Outstretched Hand was not high on the agenda of Groundside Defence and Security right at the moment. But his presence here would be logged, and sooner or later someone would come looking.

Outside the station a city bus lay sideways across the street, ablaze. Beyond it he could see rioters hurling rocks at two armoured cars advancing towards the bus, ahead of one of the modern floating fire tenders. Why the saucer-shaped vehicle remained at ground level he did not find out until later. The missile bringing down the Combine craft had not been fired from the nearest Fleet base, but from the city itself, and a second missile had also brought down a tender similar to this one. Orduval turned and started walking in the other direction.

Gunfire sounded from along a sidestreet. In another street a group of youths was busy dragging sand scooters out of an emporium, over the wreckage of its doors. Everywhere lay a litter of rocks, broken glass and the empty shells of stink gourds. A balloon-wheeled ambulance – normally used only for desert work – sped past and then, as if in pursuit of it, came two people, one staggering while holding a cloth to his face, blood spattered down his front and on his shoes. Orduval stared at them, recognizing the tough canvas overalls they both wore, with tie-straps and sewn-in metal links, as institutional garb made for the easier handling of patients. But clothing like this was worn only by the more dangerous residents. Orduval just hoped these two were the only escapees, and that the asylum they fled remained locked down. During his own time in asylums he had encountered some seriously dangerous lunatics, and the prospect of the likes of them running free was not a pleasant one.

Every hostelry Orduval passed had its storm doors firmly closed. He even tried banging on some but received no response. Then finally he saw a teahouse still open, for there were people sitting drinking in the vine garden situated to one side. Glancing through its windows he recognized the uniforms of wardens inside, then returned his gaze to the steps leading up to the main doors, guarded by two heavies whose clothing seemed stuffed with rocks. He felt a sudden nervousness but, understanding this was mostly due to not having spoken to another human being in years, he forced himself to walk up to them.

'Risky, staying open now?' he suggested, his voice sounding rusty to his ears.

One of the men shrugged. 'Everywhere else is closed. We haven't had sales this good in two years.'

'May I enter?'

The man looked him up and down for a moment. 'Certainly, but any trouble and you leave head first.'

Orduval smiled to himself as he entered. Before his sojourn in the desert, no one would have bothered to give him such a warning, but now he had bulked out a little, and looked capable of more than merely standing up.

Strug and tobacco smoke fugged the air inside, and only a few tables were free. Conversation rose and fell in counterpoint to the news items continually displayed on a couple of screens. Two service counters were open, one automated and one staffed, while a robot – a simple cylinder with a carousel for glasses girding its exterior and a flat top to carry a tray – trundled between tables accepting empty glasses and tea flasks from the clientele or taking the occasional order. Orduval stood still, indecisive and tense at being surrounded by so many

people, until he spotted yet another staff member opening the gates accessing a staircase leading to the upper
floor. Relieved, he hurried over and began climbing, just
ahead of some others heading upward.

The upper floor, as well as overlooking the inside of
the teahouse, was glassed all around the outside so it also
overlooked the vine garden and the street. He chose a
table where he could view both and took a seat. Still feeling nervous he avoided heading over to the just-opened
counter and waited until a robot trundled past nearby,
then clapped his hands to bring it rolling over to him.
Pressing his baton into the relevant aperture caused it to
settle and revolve its upper section until a menu screen
directly faced him. Orduval selected herb beer and a
snack of roasted honey beetles with preserved sausage
and chilled salad. After a moment the robot beeped and
poked his baton back out. He retrieved it and the robot
rolled away.

When the six wardens climbed the stairs, all that
remained of his meal were discarded beetle-wing cases
and the waxy ends of the preserved sausage. The wardens
wore body armour, helmets and carried stun-bead shot-
guns. Three of them moved quickly out amidst the
tables, one guarded access to the stair, while the two
remaining stepped over to the counter to consult the
woman tending it. She called up something on her console, then nodded in Orduval's direction. His stomach
clenched, but he tried to keep calm. Concentrating on
keeping his hand from shaking, he picked up his drink
and took a sip. The two officers headed over and, by the
time they arrived at his table, a watchful quiet had
descended on the room, and many were openly staring
at him.

'If I could see your ID,' said the older of the two. He wore his grey hair plaited in a queue, and a nasty scar ran down his left cheek from beside the eye – both of which strongly suggested he was a Fleet veteran. Despite his own nervousness, Orduval immediately realized this man was very unsure of himself, from the way he kept glancing around at those occupying the other tables. His younger companion just stared silently at Orduval, clutching a shotgun to his chest as if for comfort. Orduval took out his baton and handed it across. While the older warden placed it in a reader, Orduval heard snatches of conversation from nearby tables.

'. . . fraudulent . . .'

'Probably thought he could get away with it while . . .'

'. . . bit heavy-handed.'

'Maybe others in here.'

The warden removed the baton from the reader and handed it back. 'Where did you obtain the bank disk, Orduval Strone?'

'From my bank – where else?'

'So the account is yours?'

'It certainly is.'

'But we have evidence connecting this account to . . . another.'

'My pseudonym.'

The younger warden seemed unable to contain himself upon hearing this. 'Then you are . . . Uskaron?'

'Shaddup, Trausheim,' said the older one, but it was too late. The name was repeated at nearby tables and rippled out in excited whispers. People further away began to stand up. Suddenly Orduval understood: the wardens were here to control the city riots, and had suddenly been sent to a crowded bar to apprehend someone who had now become something of a legend.

'Please stand up and come with us,' said the older warden.

Orduval wasn't so sure he could stand at that moment, his legs felt too shaky. 'One moment.' He drained his glass, then tried to force inner calm upon himself.

Looking at his companion, the older one said, 'Now.'

Trausheim seemed reluctant, but obeyed. The two of them moved to either side of Orduval and hauled him to his feet. His chair went over with a crash as they hurried him from his table and over to the stairs.

'Hey!' someone shouted.

He glimpsed another of the wardens shoving a woman back down into her seat. Orduval's feet could not seem to find the steps, but no matter, since the two men were nearly carrying him anyway. More customers were rising, and a large group of people had begun arguing with some of the wardens.

'That's Uskaron!' A shout followed from the gallery as the other wardens piled down the stairs, quickly pushing customers out of the way. Then they had their captive out into the street, and being hustled into an armoured car. He glimpsed a crowd pouring out of the teahouse behind him as armoured doors closed and the vehicle pulled away.

'I'm sorry we had to do it like this,' said the older warden, turning to his younger companion. 'Trausheim, I recollect giving a specific order that no one was to mention that name.'

'I'm sorry, sir, it was just . . .'

'Yeah.' He turned back to Orduval. 'Are you really . . . Uskaron?'

Orduval leant back in the padded seat. 'Yes, I am.'

'Why here, *now*?'

'Part providence, but mainly because I have some . . .' Orduval frowned, not entirely sure what he intended to do now, since certainly his chances of getting to see Yishna now were remote '. . . some research to conduct,' he finished.

'Into what?'

'That being my business.'

'Well, before you can go about your business, you've got some explanations to make.'

'Who to?'

'Chairman Duras.'

McCrooger

The weird perceptual effects I was experiencing seemed to fade in and out, as if they originated from beyond the ship and then sometimes something about my surroundings managed to block them. But though these nightmares were weak, they also sometimes slid into my consciousness while I was awake. Occasionally the feel of the floor would remind me of that skull-cobbled street, or I would turn expecting to see someone behind me, but find no one there. Things flickered at the extremities of my vision, and sometimes I would see a dark figure retreating around a corner ahead of me. Usually all these effects were preceded by an apparent distortion of my surroundings. It all combined to add to an air of menace, so when Rhodane summoned me to the interrogation I felt edgy and angry.

His cell was much like the medical area I had found myself in when I woke up: looking like the interior of a walnut shell, only green. The Sudorian soldier, however, did not lie strapped to a comfortable bed but was instead ensconced in a chair. He shivered occasionally, probably because they had removed his helmet and the temperature in there must have been chill to a Sudorian. Something like a melted crab clung to the side of his head, with its leglike protrusions penetrating his skin. Blood had crusted around the wounds.

Slog and Flog squatted against the wall over to one side. I did not think they were there to guard him, since with his insulating suit epoxied to the chair he wasn't going anywhere, but were watching out of curiosity. Slog, who I now identified more easily by a blotch resembling a birthmark on the side of his neck, was sharpening his mandibles with a small hand-held rasp. The Sudorian soldier kept glancing at him, whether out of fear at the implicit threat or just through irritation, I couldn't say. The prisoner otherwise seemed pretty self-possessed.

'I thought it might be a good idea for *you* to question him,' Rhodane suggested.

I hesitated, then abruptly stepped forward. 'What's your name?'

He stared at me for a long moment, then winced and jerked his head, replying, 'Erache Turner.'

'What is that thing on the side of his head, Rhodane?' I asked.

'The broud encourages him to answer quickly and discourages him from lying,' she replied. 'It uses pain, certain neurochemicals, stimulation and uninhibitors.'

Rather unpleasant, I gathered, but I wasn't feeling particularly sympathetic right then since, as well as the nightmares and other weird effects I had been experiencing, I still felt nauseous most of the time, aching from head to foot as if from unaccustomed exercise, and my shoulder still hurt, a lot. In fact, at that very moment my right leg started to develop a case of the shakes. Looking round I noted a shelf-like protrusion beside the door, stepped back and rested my weight on it.

'Why did you try to kill me?' I asked him.

Again that pause then wince. 'I didn't try to kill you.'

I glanced at Rhodane. 'But he can obviously resist it.'

'The absence of further discomfort shows that he did not lie.'

The prisoner looked rather smug all of a sudden, and I realized my questioning required more precision. 'Why did one of your companions try to kill me?'

'I don't know—' His head snapped back and he grimaced. The broud shifted slightly against his temple. 'You were in his sights when—' His jaw locked into a line and his eyes squeezed shut. 'Fuckit! We were ordered!' Panting, he opened his eyes. A little trickle of blood ran down his cheek.

'Who gave the orders?'

'Admiral . . . Carnasus—' Gloved fingers clamping onto the chair arms. 'Fleet!' He started shivering.

'Did your orders come directly from Admiral Carnasus?'

'No.'

'Did your orders come from Harald Strone?'

'. . . Yes!'

My mouth suddenly arid, I glanced at Rhodane. 'Any suggestions?'

She had been standing, arms folded, staring pensively at the prisoner. Her mouth had a slight twist, as if she had tasted something bitter. Of course – Harald was her brother.

'Why were you sent to Brumal?' she asked.

The man stared at her. 'Traitor, how can you . . .? We were sent . . . we were sent.' He yelled and thrashed about as much as his glued-in-place suit would allow. He started gasping again, and despite the room being cold for a Sudorian, sweat beaded his face.

'Answer me,' said Rhodane, 'and the pain will stop.'

'Harald sent us.' He managed this through gritted teeth. 'He sent us—' His head snapped back and his eyes closed – apparently the broud was as impatient with pro-crastination as it was with prevarication. 'We were sent to scout—' He shrieked. This performance went on for some minutes until eventually it started to all come out. The missile launcher came from a Fleet ground base, and they moved it using antigravity lifts, camouflaged and at night. The bodies had been stored in the same ground base: Brumallians killed during the last stages of the War or during the subsequent occupation, and put on ice for further study. The missile they had fired was guided in by a beacon on Inigis's ship, a beacon in the viewing gallery which someone activated once I was in there alone.

'I don't think there's much else I want to ask,' I said, standing up.

'I will obtain further details,' Rhodane informed me.

I left that place, clamping down on my need to vomit.

13

*The first five hilldiggers were built during the first twenty
years of the War and it was this effort that pushed the
economy of Sudoria into collapse. The Planetary Council
plutocrats had of course gathered to themselves a huge proportion of Sudoria's wealth, and lived sybaritic lifestyles utterly
at odds with the famine and want experienced by the
majority. The revolt, when it came, was led by workers in
the space industry and by Fleet personnel returning groundside.
Chaos ensued and many of those sybarites turned up in the
Komarl, bolted to rocks with the kind of fixings used in
the construction of hilldigger skeletons. Things settled down a
little, but there was much argument about what kind of regime
should come next, how wealth should be distributed, who
should be in charge of what . . . The list just kept growing.
The old planetary parties began scrabbling for power, and
some infighting ensued. The people lost focus and indulged in
some rather silly squabbling. The fifty-megaton Brumallian
warhead that annihilated the city of Cairo-Desit came as a
timely reminder. It took just ten days to form Parliament after
that.*

— Uskaron

Harald

Feet thundered on the deck plates, the racket of machinery was constant. A hot metal smell permeated the air, as did the drifting smoke from welding whose arc flashes lit the interior of the engine galleries. Standing on a high catwalk, his guards deployed around him, Harald was hardly aware of this commotion. He instead stared at the code scrolling down in one segment of his eye-screen, while clenching and unclenching his hand to stretch his fingers inside the control glove. One of the other two screen segments, either side of this main one, held his cracker programs, worms and viral decoders – a toolkit he had built up over many years of breaking into Fleet com. He began working the glove, selecting out lines of code to copy and then apply his programs to, before dropping the results through analytical sieves. It soon became evident to him that Lambrack was using a standard randomizing protocol, but obviously running a book code behind that, for the third screen divided itself into blocks displaying parts of images, and from the speaker issued something sounding like an alien tongue. He made the obvious selection – Uskaron's damned book – and felt a cynical contempt when two more screen sections lit up to show Captains Davidson and Lambrack, and their voices became clear.

Lambrack: '. . . to come over to his side. In a way I admire that. It shows a degree of ruthlessness we need in an Admiral, but I still cannot agree with his obvious intent. The purpose of Fleet is to defend Sudoria, obeying the dictates of Parliament. If we follow Harald, we'll end up with a military dictatorship.'

Davidson: 'I understand that probability, but

wonder if that is really his intent. It could be that he feels, as do many in Fleet, that Parliament is making a mistake in its dealings with this Polity.'

Lambrack: 'Maybe our politicians *are* making a mistake, but it's theirs to make. Yet think about it. Sudoria's defence is not weakened by Combine continuing to run those defence platforms. The only question is one of centralized command, which is always preferable in conducting a war. Do you think that is a question worth internecine conflict – worth killing our own people over?'

Davidson: 'It won't necessarily come to that.'

Lambrack: 'Davidson, you're only giving him the benefit of the doubt because he cleared your way to the Captaincy of the *Resilience*. Don't be naive. He's manipulating you.'

Davidson: 'But he still could have killed *me* rather than Grune.'

Lambrack: 'No one would have believed you guilty and Grune innocent. This way, all the other Captains who were wavering are more likely to take Harald's side.'

And so Lambrack continued to work on Davidson. Harald began recording their exchange in case anything useful to him arose. With Lambrack being a long-established and respected Captain, Harald could not employ the same peremptory justice he had used against Grune, but with the present recordings he had sufficient to bring the man before a Fleet court. The problem would be extracting him from his ship, and that Harald did not have time for currently. However, there was an alternative.

Harald wiped the code screens and put through a direct call to Captain Lambrack. Watching the man, he saw him glance to one side and frown.

'We'll have to cut this now, Davidson. It seems Harald would like to speak to me. Just consider all I've said. We will need to act quickly and decisively to prevent an all-out firefight with Orbital Combine.'

Harald would have liked Lambrack to elaborate on that, but the man cut his connection with Davidson, then his image appeared alone.

'Admiral Strone, what can I do for you?'

'I note,' Harald replied, 'that you and Captain Davidson have been rather stretching the definition of the "diamond formation".'

'We wished to conduct a private conversation,' replied Lambrack.

The two ships had pulled back only a little way, to a position where they could use com lasers without any possibility of interception of laser reflection from their own hulls. Harald had not intercepted the lasers; he had simply subverted Davidson's onboard com system remotely. It would certainly come as a surprise to many hilldigger Captains just how well he had penetrated the security of their ships, both informationally and physically.

'I have to wonder what you needed to talk about that required such privacy,' he said.

'Yes, I imagine you do.'

Harald knew he was not going to get anywhere with this so decided to take a new tack. 'No matter. We have some more immediate concerns that I'll get to in a moment. But first, I understand that your brother is a senior researcher aboard Corisanthe II and that you have recently been in communication with him?'

Lambrack glanced to one side, then returned with,

'I note this is not encoded com. A rather shoddy attempt to smear my name, don't you think?'

'You misunderstand me. How could I use such a fact to smear your name when my own sister ranks so high aboard Corisanthe Main? I am merely seeking to confirm some rumours concerning equipment recently moved from II to Main.'

'Equipment?'

'Weapons.'

'That's not the kind of thing my brother and I would discuss.'

'Then what do you discuss?'

'Our recent conversation centred around events in Parliament and how they may affect us both. I imagine this was a subject raised by many officers in Fleet who have relatives in Combine and on Sudoria itself. Or rather, it was something undoubtedly raised until you restricted communication.'

Harald awarded Lambrack that point and smiled and nodded for the benefit of those who would certainly be watching this or would view a later recording. Inside he seethed, however. By not pretending loyalty to Harald or his aims, Lambrack placed himself in an unassailable position. Harald could accuse the man of sedition, but that would only cause more problems than it would solve.

'It's an unfortunate situation and of course I would perfectly understand any reluctance you might have to obey any orders putting members of your family in danger.'

'I have not disobeyed any of your orders, Admiral Strone,' replied Lambrack firmly.

'No, you haven't as yet.'

'Are you implying that I intend to?'

'I would never question your loyalty to Fleet.'

'I am so glad. Now what were these "more immediate concerns"?'

Harald paused for a moment. The fact that Lambrack had a brother aboard Corisanthe II with whom he had recently been in communication was now firmly established in the minds of any listeners. Yes, his own sister Yishna occupied a high position aboard Main but, since he was Admiral and the initiator of Fleet's present actions, his own motives would not be questioned. Lambrack's would – however, that was a lever he could use at another time. His aim now was to get Lambrack away from Davidson, and away from this entire mission.

'I have a task for which you are best suited,' said Harald, 'in view of your probable reluctance to be involved in what lies ahead.' Lambrack just stared at him in silence so he continued, 'Our satellites around Brumal have detected the launch of a ship from the planet's surface. It is a Brumallian biotech vessel and its course is presently taking it towards Sudoria.'

'What?' Lambrack looked shocked.

'Yes, those who question whether the Brumallians have been complicit in recent events, or even capable of involvement, perhaps need to examine their assumptions. One doubts that such a ship – flying in flagrant breach of the surrender terms – has anything but hostile intentions. What would you think, Lambrack?'

'I think this is certainly something that needs to be checked.'

'You'll do more than check, Captain Lambrack. You'll intercept and destroy this vessel, then you will progress to Brumal to destroy its launch site, which lies above BC30 – the city they call ReconYork.'

'You're sending *me*?'

'You're right for the task, Captain, and here is an enemy about whom you'll have fewer reservations.'

Lambrack swore and cut the connection. A little while later, as he continued his inspection of Engineering, Harald watched the Captain's ship dropping out of formation and turning to head back towards Brumal.

McCrooger

A long intestinal corridor ran right around the ship's internal ring, the walls braced by cartilaginous bulwarks, and ceilings and floors either held together or apart by pillars of a substance like glass heavily streaked with impurities, and through which ran capillaries with lucent fluids flowing inside. With little else to do once I could manage to stand for more than a few hours at a time without falling poleaxed into sleep immediately afterwards, I walked this ring, Tigger pacing at my side, the ship wheezing and glubbing around us like a hungry stomach. *Convalescence,* I tasted the word and found it bitter. I had never needed to convalesce since my first visit to Spatterjay, and now found weakness abhorrent. Six days remained until we arrived at Sudoria, and by then I needed to be fully ready.

'Still no luck trying to get a transmission through?'

'Not much,' said Tigger. 'The EM chaff broadcast from Fleet satellites swamps everything. I could probably get something through, but it would be *loud,* and everyone would know where it came from.'

I noticed how his heavy paws and my booted feet left

bruise-like marks in the translucent floor behind us, which had faded by the time we came round full circle to this same stretch of floor again. I couldn't shake the feeling that someone else was following us just out of sight, and kept looking out for the imprints they must leave. 'I think we should hold off on that for the present, though I wonder what the general reaction would be to a Brumallian ship arriving unexpectedly in orbit, if we don't get something through to them beforehand.'

'The least of our worries,' the drone stated.

'Um.' I grimaced. 'Fleet?'

'Fleet ships are a long way off right now, but watch stations will still spot us, and Harald could get a hill-digger out to squash us before we arrived at Sudoria.'

'That will depend upon how much he considers us a threat.'

'We won't worry him at all, but he might think it handy to tell everyone he destroyed a Brumallian ship that was heading for Sudoria. That'd make him look like the good guy.'

'And what is the plan should they send such a ship?'

'There is none – as yet.'

It wasn't particularly comforting to know that the virus left inside me might not, in the end, be the cause of my death.

'You must have studied this ship carefully,' I said. 'How well would it stand up to a hilldigger?'

'There's an old expression . . . a snowball's chance in hell?'

'You seem decidedly unworried about it all.'

'The emotional range of a tiger's facial expression isn't huge, but like yourself I find little to recommend mortality – even more so now I am . . . diminished.'

'Does it hurt to have lost your other half?'

'I've lost my ability to travel through space, many tools, weapons and processing space, so my loss is like yours, one of strength. Didn't lose much memory and knowledge – just a few seconds.' Those amber eyes fixed on me. 'Given time and materials I could easily rebuild my other half, with all its previous advantages. I might have lost a lot, but I still do *possess sufficient tools*.'

I realized, as Tigger spoke, that he was gently prodding me in some direction. I replayed our recent conversation in my mind and asked, 'So how could this ship be saved in the event of Harald sending one of his hilldiggers against it?'

'With current Brumallian technology, not a chance.'

Ah.

'And how well do you understand Brumallian technology?' I asked.

'Better than them.'

Tigger halted, sat back on his haunches, raised a paw and, peering down at it, extended one claw at a time for inspection. I halted as well and rested my back against a pillar, feeling a muted vibration through the ship's bones. Guessing where this conversation was leading I took a leap ahead.

'Providing the Brumallians with any technology that would give them a definite military advantage would seriously piss off Geronamid, but obviously having that AI angry with us is substantially better than being dead.'

'Oh, I agree.' Tigger raised his head to meet my gaze.

'Were you waiting for permission from me?'

'Well,' Tigger shrugged, 'I'd then only be following orders.'

Tigger, who could have been a major AI but chose

to be a drone, was clearly not a great lover of responsibility. He wanted me to take the rap. I considered then who we should talk to, since this being a Brumallian ship, there was no Captain aboard.

'Tell Rhodane,' I said. 'She can put it to the Consensus.' I wondered if that would be limited to a consensus of the present crew, for Fleet's blocking of signals prevented communication back to Brumal. I saw then how their system might not work so well in some situations.

Only later did I find out how they got round that one. They asked the ship.

Harald

With AC hum permeating the air and vibrating the catwalk below his feet, Harald folded his eye-screen to one side and peered over the rail down at the linear accelerator. Having finished the final checks, the gunnery crewmen were now moving into position on their monitoring platform above the aseptic gleam of the machinery surrounding the vacuum breech. The 800-foot-long accelerator – six feet wide, wrapped in heavily insulated coil sections and cooling jackets, and trailing massive power cables – slanted down through the body of the ship, its mouth opening directly below *Ironfist*'s nose. A conveyor belt crammed with resin-encased iron projectiles snaked down to the breech machinery. Unlike the solid projectiles fired at the military infrastructure around Brumal throughout the war, Harald knew that inside their bullet-shaped cases these consisted of a block of irregularly shaped iron fragments bound together by the resin.

'It will be interesting to see how closely fact matches theory,' he commented.

Standing next to him, with her hands folded behind her back, Jeon grimaced. 'The ballistics formulae incorporate a degree of error, but on hitting an orbital target these projectiles should break apart like antipersonnel bullets to inflict maximum damage. Missing the target and entering atmosphere, they should quickly burn off their cases, then break apart and burn up before reaching the planet's surface.'

'Should?' Harald repeated.

'We can't be entirely certain with a ton of iron travelling at such speeds. At the worst, one in ten will forge-weld into one single lump on atmospheric impact, and retain coherence long enough to strike the ground as a plasma column, but thereafter there's a less than point one per cent chance of hitting a major population centre.'

Harald nodded slowly, then pushed his microphone across in front of his mouth. 'Run test,' he ordered.

After a moment the hum dropped to a lower note, which it held for a couple of seconds before rising back to its previous level. Through Harald's headset, his gunnery officer informed him, 'Resonance in coils four and fifteen, but within operational parameters.' Harald flipped his eye-screen back into position and read the data feeds from the other five hilldiggers chosen for this chore. Four of them were ready, but one had detected major faults in its linear accelerator. How surprising that one should be Davidson's *Resilience*. However, Harald had already factored in that at least one hilldigger would be unable to fire.

'Estimated damage such a forge-welded lump could cause?' he enquired of Jeon.

'About five hundred kilotons.'

'Enough to take out a small city, then.'

'Yes.'

Harald stared down at his hands and observed how he was white-knuckling the rail. He deliberately relaxed his fingers. 'Commence firing,' he ordered over general com.

Down below, a snake of missiles advanced one segment down a conveyor, an arm slid one translucent yellow bullet – in which could be seen dark iron bones – into one of the two inner breech sections. With a hiss this section slid down into place in the vacuum breech. The hum dropped to a low note. Simultaneously the second inner breech section clonked across, and another projectile was fed into that too. The hum rose as the first section retracted, dropped again as the next fed in. So it continued for the first five shots – the motion similar to that of a simple pump. Then, after these second-stage test shots, the firing accelerated until the hum never rose again; the breech sections were in constant motion with projectiles being fired once every second.

Harald summoned up an exterior view of the fleet, but there was very little to see as the projectiles departed at near relativistic speeds other than the occasional spurt of a drive flame to keep the hilldiggers in position. The time until the projectiles reached their targets was one hour, but within only a few minutes Director Gneiss and the rest of the Oversight Committee would know Combine was being fired upon. Harald now keyed into feeds from Fleet stations all around Sudoria and flicked through multiple views, observing landing craft in the process of evacuation, as ordered previously. Accounting for the transmission delay, those craft should already be on their way down to the planet's surface. Quite probably the personnel aboard would be arrested once the wardens managed to reach them, but that was a problem to be resolved later. Those personnel would be safer in custody on the surface, for most certainly, knowing it was under attack, Combine would react fast to remove Fleet eyes from orbit. He waited, constantly checking the time display.

The smell of heating metal filled the air, and the accelerator's loading gear continued to produce its fast metronomic racket. Over the last three minutes the five ships had fired over a thousand projectiles. Gun technicians constantly monitored their displays, hands at rest as the machinery did its work. A pause. Misload. One of the breech sections dropped down and swung aside, as one of the five spares slid into place. Harald observed a hydraulic plunger shoving the misfire out of that particular section. The resin body of the projectile was cracked, exposing the iron inside, and when it crashed into the reject shoot, it fell in half. That would have to be investigated but Harald was not over concerned, since errors were certain to arise when using a new design of projectile like this. At least no manual intervention had been required. As the end of the load came in sight on the conveyor, it became easier to see how fast these objects were being fired. Harald tracked the last one down, saw it safely on its way, listened to the hum rise again, steady, then slowly fade.

He was utterly committed now; there was no way to recall those shots.

Again he checked his time display; in a few minutes'

time he would know Orbital Combine's response. When it finally came, it was not unexpected.

One display feed from Sudoria blinked out, while another showed the reason why: a Fleet supply station – a cylinder 4,000 feet long and half as much wide – hung in space now ripped open, gutted by incandescent fire. Harald guessed some hot-burning chemical warhead had been used. Then another station – a trans-shipment base for Fleet personnel consisting of four similar cylinders joined end to end – flew apart in a fusillade of rail-gun strikes directed from above. Internal atmosphere exploded into vacuum and something detonated inside one of the cylinders, tearing it open and causing all four of them to separate. Harald could see how Combine was using methods that reduced the chances of too many fast-travelling, dangerous chunks of debris going into orbit, as the previous firebomb, and now the rail-gun missiles were fired from above, so any misses or pieces of shattered station would travel on downward to burn up in atmosphere.

Coverage then became even more intermittent as Harald lost feed after feed. He felt a twisting in his gut upon seeing a watch platform destroyed just moments after a lander had departed it. There the evacuation had been tardy and the lander, struck by following debris, tumbled out of control. He never saw if the pilot regained control; suspected the first Fleet casualties.

'Reposition to second strike point,' he ordered over general com. 'Evasive course correction on *Ironfist*'s lead. Prepare second loads.'

He felt the rumble of drives starting, followed by a sideways drag of acceleration. In the Bridge the gravity floors would correct for the latter, but not down here. On his eye-screen he observed multiple drive flames igniting; the main fusion engines of hilldiggers and support ships, and the blue-red spears of steering thrusters. His diminishing view of events around Sudoria showed nothing being fired in this direction just yet. Perhaps they were not prepared to fire on the fleet itself until there were no more Fleet observation posts left in orbit, but more likely Combine considered it not worth wasting the ammunition, knowing their targets could move out of the way long before anything had a chance of reaching them.

The last feed from Sudoria orbit winked out, but there were still telescope views from the surface on nightside. As expected, the tacom aboard *Wildfire*, to whom Harald had assigned the task of monitoring Sudoria com, contacted him.

'I am receiving messages from our groundside bases. GDS wardens are now withdrawing from any of those bases they haven't taken. In those they have captured they are closing down all feeds. All the commanders of bases still in our control have received a message from Combine that they are to hand over control to GDS immediately. Otherwise, all those bases remaining under Fleet control will be destroyed. Their commanders have half an hour in which to comply.'

'What about bases in urban areas?' Harald asked.

'Nothing about them. Either Combine is hoping to bluff them into surrender or intends to take them out anyway.'

'Don't waste bandwidth stating the obvious. Anything for us from Combine Oversight?'

'Yes, sir. I have a message addressed generally to all of us, followed by an eyes-only one from Director Gneiss on Corisanthe Main for you. Relaying right now.'

Harald frowned. He really needed to hone down these tacom communications. It had not been necessary for this tacom on *Wildfire* to advise him of Director Gneiss's location. He opened the screen to his personal inbox, selected the general message there – audio-visual – and opened it. The image of a woman, grey-haired and jowly, appeared on one of his screen sections – Rishinda Gleer of Combine Oversight.

'Fleet Captains, officers and men, your unprovoked attack on Orbital Combine has of course provoked the expected response. I see that the missiles you have fired at us will arrive in fifty minutes. Perhaps I should update you on the casualty figures before we cease to be able to count them. Thus far the course you have embarked upon has cost, up in orbit, the lives of approximately 200 Fleet personnel and eighteen Combine personnel. On the surface 715 Fleet and GDS personnel have died, but that figure is still on the rise since there is now riot- ing down there and certain revolutionary groups and belligerent supporters of Fleet or Combine have taken advantage of the chaos, in some cases deliberately creating more disorder by opening asylums. Chairman Duras has declared martial law, and Parliament has voted unanimously to revoke Fleet's wartime preroga- tives. Parliament has also ordered the arrest of Admiral Harald on charges too numerous to count. Any who facilitate his arrest or otherwise removal will *not* be regarded as complicit in Fleet's recent treasonable actions. Consider, all of you, that you are attacking your own home planet, and you could be killing family or friends. You may *already* have killed family or friends, so please stop this madness now.'

Harald grimaced: carrot and stick – again not

unexpected, but not very pleasant to hear. He opened the
message from Director Gneiss:

'Admiral Harald, I am not going to waste words in
trying to dissuade you from your course, since if mere
words could have dissuaded you, they would have done
so by now. Through your sister and your service record,
I know that you are not unintelligent, so will have already
made your calculations.' Gneiss paused for a moment,
and Harald abruptly paused the message. This was the
first time he had ever seen Director Gneiss so closely
imaged and it now struck him that there was something
decidedly odd about the man. Here he was delivering
some vitally important message, yet from his demeanour
it was almost as if he did not care about the content.
Harald set the message playing again.

'Now, I think it pertinent to point out to you that
your sister is aboard one of the Combine defence platforms. That was a tactic of Oversight I was not
completely in agreement with, but perhaps it might stay
your hand a little.'

You're lying, Harald thought. *I know exactly where my
sister is, and her presence there will not stay my hand at all.*

Gneiss continued, 'That consideration aside, it
seems you will carry through your plans with a ruthless
efficiency. But let me appeal to you now: you can still
save many lives without sacrificing your aims, unless
those aims are solely for massive death and destruction.
Order all your groundside base commanders to
surrender at once. All bases that have not been taken over
by the GDS have been targeted by Combine's orbital
weapons. Now, I know you'll at once assume that we
won't hit the . . . sixty per cent of your bases that lie
within urban areas. You would be wrong. The wardens

are currently evacuating all the residents from the areas surrounding those bases, and the weapons we have aimed at them are not linear projectiles or explosive munitions, but high-intensity close-focus masers. We can excise those same bases with an accuracy measured in feet. They will burn, as will everyone inside them. Order their surrender.'

Gneiss paused again, gazing at something out of view. Harald wished the man was in reach for he felt an overpowering urge to prod him.

'Finally, Admiral Harald, your supporters believe you aim to restore Fleet ascendancy within the Sudorian system by slapping down us usurpers in Orbital Combine.' Gneiss returned his gaze directly to the screen. 'All your actions apparently indicate this but, as I said before, I know your sister. And I have researched your other siblings. I know their history, and I know their antecedents. I know *your* antecedents, Harald, for of course I knew your mother.' Gneiss paused yet again, but this time some intense but unidentifiable emotion twisted his features. 'Your goal is apparently one thing, but in reality it is something else. I think, somewhere inside, you realize that your will is not your own. Perhaps, if you can recognize that truth, we can halt this now. I look forward to hearing from you soon, Harald Strone.'

Harald felt a sudden surge of anger. *Stupid games.* Gneiss understood nothing and Harald should concede him nothing, and perhaps, in his last moments as Combine turned to wreckage around him, Gneiss would understand the futility of his petty attempts at manipulation. Then, abruptly as it had come, Harald's anger disappeared and he considered the situation with calm rationality. After a minute of contemplation, he nodded as he came to a decision.

'*Wildfire* tacom.'

'I hear you.'

'Send a message to our groundside base commanders. I am ordering them to stand down and surrender themselves to GDS.'

'You're what?'

'I don't intend to repeat myself. Them dying down there will make little difference to my plans, and would be a foolish waste of future resources.'

'Understood – am sending message now.'

Corisanthe Main was the primary target, and once it was his to control . . . Harald suddenly found himself mentally groping in a blank spot and felt a moment's panic. He drew back. That station was the target because, with the Worm aboard, it was Combine's power base. He must focus solely on that objective. The ground bases were irrelevant: everything ended at Corisanthe Main.

But why hit Combine anyway?

There had been so much going on that he had little time to consider anything beyond immediate objectives – just making cursory preparations as in his dealings with Lambrack and any other rebellious Captains. He felt with all his heart he was doing the best thing possible for Fleet. Fleet needed to be strong to face internal threats and now external ones. Sudorian defence could not continue being divided between it and Combine . . . Harald closed his eyes on an unaccustomed confusion. He realized that this did not entirely account for his own hatred of Combine, and his ultimate aim to board Corisanthe Main and take complete control there.

Doubts, now?

Something seemed to shift inside his head, and suddenly he realized such introspection was foolish. Combine must be brought down, Fleet must be the ultimate power, and Corisanthe Main must be his. That was all he needed to think about now.

Yishna

Ensconced in a study unit overlooking Centre Cross Chamber, Yishna inspected station schematics and cladograms showing energy output from the various reactors. She pulled across her microphone, turned it on and selected, on a touch-screen, the OCT she wanted to contact.

'Dalepan, you'll need to install a heavy-duty cable from junction Oz56v through to Oz78v – I'm transmitting to you that section of the schematics now.'

'And where will I obtain the cable?' Dalepan asked.

Yishna called up another display showing a manifest of recent supplies brought aboard. 'Stock Room Eight, and if you don't find it there you'll find it still awaiting collection on Dock Eight.'

She heard Dalepan issuing instructions and returned her screens to disaster planning. Now supposing a hit on a particular section of Quadrant Two, she checked the resultant protocol the computer threw up: these doors would close; power would be cut to these doors so would have to be rerouted; potential loss of life, fifty souls; potential Ozark containment breach. *In this instance refer to Emergency Ozark Protocols – permissions through Station Director.*

There it was again, and Yishna felt a chill sweat break out on her body. If, or rather when, the station came

under attack, her earlier interference with those protocols would almost certainly be revealed. Yet, knowing
what she had done and being in a position to now easily
correct matters, she found she could not. There seemed
some block in her. Every time she went to access the
Director's 'eyes only' files the task suddenly seemed
insurmountably difficult, and the harder she pushed herself the more frightened she became. Shadows loomed
and nightmares threatened, and something seemed to
shift titanically within her psyche.

'I can't find any heavy-duty cable,' said Dalepan,
interrupting her thoughts.

And there was always something else to do.

'Let me put a tracker on the manifest,' she sighed.

The tracker quickly found the cable at neither location, so logically it must be in transit between them.

'Someone must be moving it right now,' she told
Dalepan.

'Well, I figured – what the hell is that?'

Just as he spoke, an infernal light glared in through
upper ports in the roof of Centre Cross Chamber.

'Attention all personnel!' Director Gneiss's face
appeared on one of her touch-screens, his voice issuing
from the screen speaker and also over the public address
system. 'Our telescope arrays have been monitoring
Fleet manoeuvres between here and *Carmel,* and twenty-
five minutes ago Fleet hilldiggers fired approximately a
thousand inert relatavistic projectiles at Combine stations.
Expected time of impact is thirty-eight minutes from
now. This is an act of war and in response we are neutral-
izing all Fleet satellites in orbit that could pose a danger
to us militarily or be used for intelligence gathering. It is
fortunate Fleet evacuated those satellites first. All per-

sonnel are to don suit helmets and check suit integrity before moving to their stations.' Gneiss paused for a moment, and Yishna thought he looked almost bored. 'Okay, most of you know what to do now – those of you who don't, check with your superiors. Further updates and announcements will be made on Media Channel One. That's all.'

Yishna immediately began searching for exterior views of activity from Main and from other stations. While she did this a rumbling noise dragged her attention up to where armoured shutters were closing across all the Centre Cross ports.

It's really happening. My brother . . .

On her screens she soon observed ships launching from Corisanthe stations II and III. They were big, well armed, but nothing like the scale of the hilldiggers. Defence buoys were also going up: robotic spheres containing a honeycomb of hard ceramocarbide steel whose sum purpose was to detect incoming projectiles and put themselves in their way, the honeycomb being specially designed to break those projectiles apart. Once all these had departed, the energy screens would also go up, and rail-guns and beam weapons would be made ready. Soon a lot of fast-moving metal would be flying about out there.

Yishna dragged her spacesuit helmet a little closer as she continued to flick through these various scenes, then paused the display at something she could not identify: Corisanthe II was rail-gun-launching a stream of large pill-shaped objects through a window that remained in its growing defences. These objects were now speeding away from Sudoria, out towards interplanetary space. She considered asking someone about them, but instead decided to track the information down herself. Keying into current launches from Corisanthe II, she immediately hit a security block, but one she possessed the clearance to get round. A little further work pulled up a schematic of one of the unfamiliar objects on her screen. It seemed they contained new concealment technology that had not been made available to Fleet, and this was wrapped around an old plutonium-based technology. They were atomic stealth mines – all of them in the megaton range – and so a rather unpleasant surprise awaiting Fleet.

Then the schematic abruptly disappeared as Dalepan appeared before her. 'About that cable?'

Prosaic interruption, but on such mundane details might their lives depend.

McCrooger

The food, drink, and gentle exercise seemed to be doing the trick, and I now felt some optimism while striding around the circular corridor. Big mistake: an abrupt change of course threw me stumbling towards a wall, and I put out a hand to steady myself. As my palm hit its slick surface my forearm bones snapped with a gristly crunch, and a spike of bone stabbed out through the muscle. Turning I shouldered into the wall, and, gripping my wrist, stared at the injury with disbelief. It just didn't seem to make any sense. I then reached out to a nearby pillar, tried to grab hold and couldn't, so held one hand in place with the other as I tried to pull the bones straight so they would heal in the correct position. The broken end of the bone disappeared back into muscle with a glutinous sucking sound, and agony washed up my arm, bringing with it a tide of blackness.

After an unknown time, consciousness returned to me. I found myself lying on the floor, my face in something sticky. Blood? Blood all around me in a spreading pool. My arm was bleeding copiously and I knew that even for a normal human this degree of bleeding wasn't right. It seemed, along with ridiculously brittle bones, I had also developed some form of haemophilia.

'Help,' I managed, but it only came out in a whisper. Again, 'Help.' No one around. I knew there was no way of getting to my feet, since I felt like a wet rag, but if no one turned up soon it seemed likely I would bleed to death. Summoning every fragment of will I could muster, I managed to roll over onto my back. I groped down my chest with one hand and closed it over my pendant, which was now just a shapeless lump. Bringing it up near my lips I managed one hoarse, 'Tigger,' before even the energy to speak deserted me.

Normal perception began to break apart then. Nightmare creatures slid out to shake their twisted limbs at me, gape with slobbering mouths and slink away again. A dark figure loomed, studying me analytically, and I could hear the sound of footsteps on a hollow bony floor . . . which slowly changed to a sharp awareness of my own breathing and heartbeat and, somehow, of the autonomous system that kept them going. I felt incredibly weary and it seemed that there, in that deeper knowledge of my own function, lay my answer. I knew instantly that I could, through an act of will, simply stop everything. I guessed this to be something like the perception which must be experienced by those who delivered their famous last words and then promptly died; they knew they could let go their hold on life at any time, and so chose the appropriate moment.

While carrying the original Spatterjay virus, I hadn't really been human and so could not have died like a human. But I didn't know what carrying IF21 inside me meant. The fact that I leaked blood was so unusual for me in itself, but could I actually bleed to death? Would I die if my heart stopped or if I stopped breathing? I don't know whether it was these thoughts that initiated it, but suddenly I found myself at a point of utter stillness, deep in a personal silence. I had just allowed my heart and lungs to grow still, and blood no longer pumped from my arm – yet I remained functional, presumably due to the transference of oxygen and nutrients through the viral fibres of IF21 to where they were needed, as would have been the case with the original virus. With the shutting down of those two crucial organs also went all those involuntary twitches that are the signs of life. Perhaps other autonomous functions had also closed down. Lying there in that silence, I realized my body might not die, yet that I myself could. To complete my death I only needed to shut down my brain, which I now felt I knew how to do. However, I was an Old Captain and 'the long habit of living' was a difficult one to break, so I just lay there *not* dying.

Next, voices impinged upon my silence, and I saw people staring down at me. I realized they believed me to be dead and so were taking no action. By restarting my heart and lungs, I initiated all sorts of activity around me. Soon Flog was carrying me, cradled like an infant, a silver tiger pacing at his side. A tourniquet of woven hide wound above my elbow seemed to have lessened the renewed blood flow, but not stopped it. Or maybe there just wasn't that much of it left inside me. Something had changed, too: my breathing and the beating of my heart no longer seemed entirely autonomous. It was as if by consciously interfering with the living process I had now taken over responsibility for it, so must keep a small hard kernel of willpower constantly focused on the task of making those organs work. To allow myself to die now seemed rather less an act of will, more a case of ceasing that act.

'He's dying,' Tigger confirmed for me to Rhodane as I lay on my organic bed inside the spin section. A Brumallian I did not recognize attached a drip, while another placed metal clamps around shattered bone in my numb open arm. 'He'll not last more than another month,' Tigger added.

'What is doing this to him?'

'I told you about the two viruses inside him, and how one of them needed to be sacrificed – the only one we could kill – to ensure his survival. Well, it now looks like the one left behind is killing him anyway.'

'How so?'

I never heard the rest for I blacked out. Later I woke in a panic, thinking that by slipping from consciousness I might also release the reins I held to my heart and lungs. However, that hard lump of willpower was too stubborn to renege on its duties because of mere uncon-sciousness.

'How is it killing me?' I asked.

Even before opening my eyes I knew only Tigger occupied the room with me.

'IF21 does work like the original Spatterjay virus – transferring nutrients and oxygen around your body and occasionally carrying nerve impulses. Unlike the original, this one isn't replacing muscle and bone with something stronger, but with something weaker. The nerve impulses it carries aren't always the ones you want either, and it's also destroying some parts of your body to feed its own growth.'

'It's destroying my autonomous nervous system,' I suggested, opening my eyes.

Tigger squatted beside my bed, peering down at me with mild but implacable amber eyes. He paused for a long moment before replying. 'You're aware of that?'

'I am.'

'Well, it isn't just that it's screwing. Add to the list your immune system, your body's ability to produce T-cells and clotting cells, and really,' Tigger shrugged, 'all your major organs. By the state of your liver it looks like you've been a bit too partial to the sea-cane rum for far too long.'

'Any *good* news?' I quipped.

'Some. The IF21 may still not kill you.'

'Really.'

'Quite likely the hilldigger on its way out to us will do that instead.'

I can't say that I was a great fan of Tigger's morbid humour.

'Then you must do what we discussed.'

'I intend to – just preparing myself for the AI-upon-AI melding.' Tigger tapped one claw against his metal skull. 'I need to be in full control – can't just give instructions.'

'Right,' I said, staring at the ceiling. Only after a moment did it impinge upon me what Tigger was saying. 'You're saying this ship's computer is AI?'

'Yup, even under the two hundred and seventy-first revision of the Turing Test,' Tigger replied.

It seemed that the ship, after receiving instructions from the Consensus, carried them out in the way it saw best – in the same way that, under the impetus of consensus, Brumallians would go into battle, but it would be up to them to figure out how best to avoid getting themselves killed. It would seem that the Consensus knew how to delegate.

'I'll ask the ship,' Rhodane had told Tigger, shortly after the drone let her know his intentions.

And the ship apparently replied, 'Yes, I *would* like to make these alterations to myself, since a hilldigger is now heading directly towards us.'

After hearing all that news, I closed my eyes again.

'There's something else I can do,' Tigger informed me.

'Hit me with it.'

'Once melded, I can create the means to stick you into hibernation. Then I could get you back to the Polity.'

'I'll think about it,' I said.

14

The Brumallians were an implacable and merciless enemy. They did not negotiate, did not communicate, and they gave and accepted no quarter, so this was a fight that could only end with one contender lying bleeding on the ground. In the latter stages of the War the people of Sudoria knew all this with utter certainty, which was why, when the hilldiggers arrived at Brumal, their final strike against the enemy came close to genocide. Many records were destroyed during the revolt that resulted in our present Parliament, but a sufficient number have survived to tell us the true story. The Brumallians had wanted peace, they wanted a ceasefire, they wanted an ending, but for the first twenty years of conflict they were asking for these things from the plutocrats – people who were making fortunes out of building massive warships and stations in orbit, and out of manufacturing munitions. These approaches were either dismissed or, worse, responded to with treachery. I shall include below a report that details the capture of a small Brumallian ship sent to us with negotiators aboard, and what happened to those captives when they were sent to a bioweapons research establishment. The Brumallians stopped talking after their first big warships took apart a hilldigger. Directly after this the sudden spate of representations to them from the plutocrats were ignored. This occurred only a few months before those same plutocrats were due for their appointment with a bolt gun and a Komarl rock.

– Uskaron

Tigger

Using full-spectrum scanning of the interior of the ship, Tigger studied its cellular structure of compartments linked by intestinal corridors. Within a scattering of compartments inside the spin section he noted Brumallians monitoring and tending to organic machinery with the focus of veterinary surgeons. The crew seemed almost like components in the ship's immune system – little nano-doctors attentively ensuring its health. It was all rather primitive really. Polity ships, though not the product of an organic technology, did not require ministering to with such finesse.

He had always been interested in how a society that ruled by consensus could manage to conduct a war where decisions needed to be made instantly and without consultation. He had supposed that some Brumallians had been selected as commanders and on them the Consensus had delegated authority. This he subsequently discovered to be true, but within certain limitations: to those individuals who proved the best at any task, the authority over that task had been delegated, so the weapons inventors were left to their own devices, literally, and those devices then passed on to those most capable of manufacturing them – and so on. But that had not been enough. The Brumallian Consensus wanted the war won, and the enemy rendered incapable of attacking again. Implementing this was not something that could be efficiently governed by the ebb and flow of public opinion – they realized they needed overall commanders to make hard tactical and logistical decisions. They grew them.

'The hilldigger has us within firing range of its long-range weapons, but I believe the Captain will not order any firing until close enough to be certain of hitting us with a tactical warhead – two hours and thirty-five minutes from now,' concluded the ship AI whom Tigger had named Rosebud.

'I'll be with you in ten minutes, Rosebud,' Tigger replied. 'I gotta reconfigure some of my internal systems anyhow.'

'Why did you give me that name?' asked the AI running this organic vessel.

Tigger transmitted the relevant files concerning an old celluloid film called *Citizen Kane*. After a long delay while he found his way to a corridor that would take him around the spin section, the AI came back with, 'But they burnt the sledge.'

'It was only a film,' replied Tigger, adding, 'and a metaphor.'

Tigger passed below the outer rim of the section, which slid above him like a moving wooden ceiling, then worked in towards the hub along another corridor snaking through the interior without any regard for up or down. At the end of this corridor he found Flog and Slog awaiting him, in evident agitation.

'Now, why're they here?' Tigger sent to the AI.

'They were bred to fight non-Consensus attackers. My command override controls them, but it does not override their inherent distrust of you, especially now you are moving into so sensitive an area.'

'The Polity –' said Slog, reaching out a hand that brushed down Tigger's back.

'– we must permit?' finished Flog, floating backwards before Tigger into the chamber beyond. They were reluctant to allow Tigger into here, perhaps programmed to guard the ship's AI at all costs.

Tigger, only managing to keep himself to the floor by use of his claws, continued pacing forwards.

'We are –'

'– commanded.'

Flog opened his mandibles in threatening protest, then, clutching at a grey branch above his head, pulled himself aside, floated over to one wall and clung there. Tigger halted in the centre of the chamber and observed what lay before him. Rosebud seemed like some giant synapse, ten feet across with branching outgrowths piercing its surroundings. Just visible behind it, the wall of the spin section constantly revolved, as if the AI was turning it manually. Tigger could see the design antecedents here, with the AI acting as an interface between the crew – who were mainly located in the spin section – and the rest of the ship. Further development had resulted in the crew doing less, and the interface doing more, until it finally developed consciousness and the crew became mere adjuncts to it.

Now Tigger was ready, his internal structure primed to come apart and shift to the required connection points, organo-optic plugs ready inside him layered with living nerve tissue grown from samplings he had already taken from the material of the ship. He took one pace forward, and a ripple passed down the length of his body. His cat features began to lose definition and his head began to sink away. Another pace and one leg retracted into his body – only to reappear, stretching and extending as a tentacle from his back. His whole body shortened and spread out sideways. Amoeboid, with outgrowths taking hold of the grey branches around him, he slid forward to fall upon Rosebud and engulf it. He pushed in the plugs like stings, directing them once they were inside Rosebud with cell-form metal muscles, and there began to connect, and there began to lose himself. Fleetingly he observed Flog and Slog being ordered from the chamber after they had surged forward to try and tear him away, misunderstanding his actions as an attack. As the entrance sphincter closed he saw them raging outside.

'This is unexpected,' said Rosebud. 'You will destroy me.'

'I will not,' Tigger replied.

'I am a river, but you are the sea.'

'Though I'll absorb everything that you are, I'll nevertheless keep what you are which is distinct, and return you to yourself once I depart.'

'My consciousness will not be my own.'

'Sleep, then,' Tigger instructed.

Rosebud, though with an organic basis, was an AI many generations removed from Tigger. Primitive, Tigger considered, but not in any derogatory sense. Overall, Rosebud became a rather small adjunct to Tigger's extensive mind. Tigger became the ship, and came to control the ship absolutely.

He studied the fusion drive, which, though controlled by organo-optics, was an additional artefact added to the ship's structure. The ship had been grown with the facility to accept this addition – the ability to grow such an engine being beyond present Brumallian technology.

An analogy would be someone growing a human body without legs, but with the nerves and empty sockets in the pelvis exposed and ready to accept grafts of mechanical legs. Similar gaps in the outer body of the ship contained grafts of a rather more lethal nature. He studied their contents, chose one close to his location – a missile cache – and, using ship's systems, opened a missile and began making alterations to it. Simultaneously he began extruding a cell-form metal limb in that same direction.

The engine was running okay, but Tigger made some adjustments to increase its efficiency by six per cent, and initiated the growth of some additional systems that would raise it higher. Subsequent inspection of other systems on board revealed many other things he could do to increase efficiency, but doing something about them was not his main purpose in this melding . . . or, rather, subsumption.

The drone focused his attention on the ship's outer skin. It lay three feet thick, layer upon layer of polycarbonates and ceramics, with nerve fibres threading convoluted paths through to access sensor heads dotted like hair follicles over the hull. An outer layer consisted of electromechanical refractive cells, and simple projectors also linked into this network: a simple chameleonware skin that could, within limitations, blend the ship with its background, not just visibly, but along a wider band of the EM spectrum. It was non-reactive, which basically meant the ship would not be picked up by passive sensors unless the drive was operating. However, it would be quickly revealed the moment a searcher used any form of active scan.

Tigger now needed to make this chameleonware

wholly reactive, so that if any form of scan intersected with the ship when only vacuum lay behind it, the 'ware could refract it away from the scanning ship. He also needed to link in the sensors, so on the dark side of the ship they could scan any background other than vacuum and project it from the scan side, with a suitable delay, to project a return consistent only with whatever lay behind the ship. This required the individual control of billions of discrete refractors, sensors and projectors.

Tigger applied his extensive intellect to the task, then redoubled his efforts when he *felt* the first terahertz scan from the distant hilldigger.

The Captain of that other ship now knew the precise location of the Brumallian ship. Tigger therefore assigned more and more of his own processing space to the task of hiding. Within what had now become his own body, he observed the dismay of the Brumallian crew as the systems they nurtured fell out of their control. He shut down the drive flame. His cell-form limb reached the missile cache and deposited part of itself inside the casing behind the warhead. Ship's systems closed up the missile and loaded it to a coil-gun barrel extending to breach the hull.

By now the hilldigger was within range to fire a war-head. Tigger detected the flare of a single drive flame departing the massive vessel. He fired his own missile, simultaneously initiating the chameleonware of his ship and the part of himself deposited in the missile. From his own vantage point the missile looked no different, but it contained a Polity antimunitions package that projected a false image of this ship to the distant hilldigger. Those aboard the hilldigger might have detected a brief anomaly – the Brumallian ship repositioning in an eyeblink and abruptly changing course – but the Sudorian missile would not be smart enough to recognize what had happened.

A long drawn-out hour passed while Tigger worked frantically. What he had done would only work once, since those aboard the hilldigger would be sure to analyse debris and find it very lacking. Now he continued to extend himself throughout the ship, using nano-technological methods to absorb material and reform it as part of himself. Slowly he reached the outer hull and began to spread out, rebuilding sensor heads, refractors and projectors into composite and much more efficient instruments. He would have done this first of all, had there been time, but hopefully he had provided time enough to do it now.

The hilldigger missile finally slammed down on the Brumallian ship it detected. Tigger detonated the missile he had fired. The two missiles and the illusion of a Brumallian ship disappeared in a sun-bright explosion. Tigger continued to work. Another hour passed and he observed the hilldigger turning, then firing a massive spread of inert rail- or coil-gun projectiles to cover possible locations of the hidden ship. *They caught on fast.* He tracked the course of every projectile and saw that dumb chance had put one directly on target. It came faster than the original missile, and was only seconds away. One spurt from his main drive would put the ship out of the way, but would also locate it clearly for the beam weapons the hilldigger was now close enough to use. Tigger fired up a steering thruster hidden on the other side, turning the ship to present one particular area at a particular time.

The projectile struck, and punched through, exploding

fire through the ship's internal spaces, jetting fire from its exit on the other side. Still turning, the ship presented new Polity chameleonware which wiped out the same fire to the hilldigger's scanners. Then the feedback from Rosebud screamed through Tigger – the ship's agony.

Didn't these fools know their ships could suffer?

The spread of the chameleonware continued autonomously. It needed to. Tigger crashed into oblivion.

Harald

On his instructions the eight remaining hilldiggers of the Fleet began to put some distance between each other, randomizing their formation since they were now close enough to Sudoria that the possibility of running into hidden defences could not be discounted.

In the Admiral's Haven, Harald gazed at all eight hilldigger Captains displayed on the screens arrayed before him. 'Our plan of attack is not complicated, but then complicated plans have a tendency to go wrong. And this will not.' Not much response from them to that, but he had expected none. 'If you would all turn your attention now to the graphic, I will detail how it should run.' On his own eye-screen he observed the graphic representation, updated realtime, of the disposition of Combine stations and ships surrounding the planet Sudoria. Using his control glove he shifted his selector to frame Defence Platforms One and Twelve.

'Once these two have been destroyed, only Platforms Eleven, Two, Three, Four and the main stations remain relevant for our purpose. The hole in planetary cover we will shortly have made will give us ready ingress to the defences of Orbital Combine. If you will observe the

trajectory of our last fusillade . . .' He panned the view
back to a rapidly approaching icon representing 1,500
projectiles, then slashed a line from them to Sudoria. 'As
you see the missiles will come in low and fast over Platform Eleven, through the gap created by the two
destroyed platforms, and will impact on the side of Platform Two. Eventually it too will fall.' Harald paused,
inspecting their expressions. Most looked satisfied; a few,
notably Orvram Davidson, looked grim.

'Once Platform Two is down, we move into low orbit
then harrow up Platforms Three and Four in a line, until
reaching Corisanthe Main.'

Two Captains began speaking at once: Tlaster Cobe
and Orvram Davidson. Davidson then fell silent and let
Cobe speak. 'But, taking that route, we'll come under fire
from Corisanthe II.'

'Yes,' replied Harald, 'which is why only four ships
will be conducting that attack. When they have dealt with
Platforms Two and Three, those ships will then be in
danger, at which point *Desert Wind*, *Harvester* and *Slate*
will assault Corisanthe II.'

'There are over a hundred thousand people aboard
Corisanthe II,' reminded Davidson.

'I am aware of that fact,' said Harald. 'There is a
similar number on Corisanthe III, which has been growing in recent years since Combine began assembly of its
space liners there. We will also need to attack that
station, to prevent resupply to the other stations from
there. This is why I am relating this plan to you now, so
you have a chance to voice any objections.' He studied
the faces before him. He expected no protest from those
he had already chosen for the assault on Corisanthe II,
but Cobe and Davidson of *Stormfollower* and *Resilience*

respectively, and perhaps Schumack of *Musket,* might begin to show signs of rebellion now.

'I am sorry, but I cannot—' began Davidson.

The screen showing Captain Lorimar of hilldigger *Slate* suddenly blanked out. Almost immediately Harald received a concerted scream from the tacoms aboard all the other ships, 'Minefield!' He stood up and, using his control glove, crowded the images of all the Captains into one screen, noting that Davidson, Cobe and Schumack had now cut their connections. There was no tacom connection from *Slate* – absolutely nothing. Before he even needed to ask for it, the tacom from *Wildfire* – the ship nearest to *Slate*'s location – sent him visual feed which he now projected on one of the empty screens before him. Debris glittered across space, and tumbling through it came the rear section of a hilldigger, exposed girders glowing against darkness and its engine galleries open to vacuum.

Harald just stared, unable to make any sense of what he was seeing, until someone's gasp of '*Slate*'s gone' set his mind in motion again. Thousands had just died, and an entire hilldigger was just a spreading cloud of radio-active detritus. He felt a horrible, bone-deep guilt and, though he was accepting what he was currently seeing and hearing, he just didn't know how to react. Then he detected, amid the chatter, the words, 'Stealthed mines.'

'What do you have for me, *Harvester* tacom?' Harald managed.

'Am relaying now. They are invisible to most forms of scan, but we get a time-discrepancy on laser detection,' replied the tacom officer serving on that ship.

At last feeling some control, Harald called up views fed from other ships on the large screens before him and in his eye-screen. An explosion a hundred miles out from *Desert Wind* blanked instruments for a short while, but it proved that they were now able to detect these near-invisible mines. Slowly, in a representative view, the mine-field began to be revealed.

'They're moving,' came a general tacom report.

The flare of drive flames created brief constellations out in vacuum. However, the same flames immediately located every mine for Fleet's instruments. More explosions – two mines drawing too close to *Harvester*. Harald realized that Combine had expected that, after one or two detonations, the mines would inevitably be detected, so had programmed them to become missiles like this, giving them the remote possibility of causing more damage.

'Remove them,' Harald instructed, and multiple explosions filled space around the hilldiggers. Switching from view to view, he coldly studied the spectacle, but these camera angles also presented him with an unwelcome reality: *Stormfollower*, *Resilience* and *Musket* were turning. It disappointed him that all the Captains he suspected might rebel, had now done so.

'Captains Davidson, Cobe and Schumack,' he broadcast. 'Return to formation, or you will lose command of your ships.'

After a long delay, Davidson reinstated his comlink. 'A hundred thousand people? To be honest with you, Admiral, I have not been in agreement with all your actions since you took command, but my loyalty to Fleet has so far kept me from disobeying. Now I cannot obey you any longer. Captain Ildris once gave me a lecture on the responsibility of command and one particular phrase stands out in my mind: "History has taught us that saying one was only obeying orders can never be an excuse for committing atrocity."'

Even while Davidson spoke, Harald opened com channels he had long ago prepared for this moment. Communications were the key, he had told Yishna, but even she could not have guessed to what extent he meant this. Immediately the tacom officers aboard the three departing ships, though quite possibly still loyal, were frozen out. But routed through their equipment, Harald began to seize control of the hardware of those ships. With a single thought he shut down their engines. With an analytical omniscience he gazed through Bridge cameras at the three Captains and their crews, as they began to realize that the controls were no longer responding to them.

Other views showed emergency lights flashing in various vital sections of each ship. Harald observed a crowd of engineers struggling into survival suits as they abandoned the engine galleries of *Resilience*, once the last of the stragglers got out of there, the heavy blast doors quickly closed off that particular area. As weaponry areas – also equipped with blast doors because of the danger from exploding munitions – were abandoned because of similar false emergencies, Harald closed them off too. Exterior views showed him airlocks opening those areas to vacuum – if anyone remained behind, their life-spans would now be measured by the air supply in their survival suits. Harald next shut off all the internal lifts, and the internal rail system, closed off more selected areas and opened more to vacuum, shut maintenance tunnels, locked spacesuit lockers, disabled EVA units and shuttles. He set recognition programs to work through the camera systems, ready to alert him should

the crew try to return to any vital zones, and there prepared some nasty surprises for them should they try.

'Captain Soderstrom,' he finally broadcast. 'As we
agreed, in this eventuality, I am slaving *Stormfollower* and
Musket to your ship, *Harvester*, and you will take them in
with you when you attack Corisanthe II. *Resilience* I will
slave to *Wildfire* for the attack on Corisanthe III. Meanwhile, myself and Franorl, in *Ironfist* and *Desert Wind*, will
take out the defence platforms and assault Corisanthe
Main.'

'You can't do this,' protested Davidson.

Ignoring him, Harald restarted the engines of the
three ships, and turned them round.

McCrooger

The spin section juddered to a halt and a stink of barbe-
cue immediately filled the air. Luckily someone had
thought to strap me into my bed, so I wasn't thrown
across the room.

'I will get you there . . . that is all I can promise,'
someone informed me, in neither Brumallian nor
Sudorian. Tigger, then.

The ship was shuddering and, now in zero gravity,
I immediately threw up. The vomit departed in a straight
trajectory and splashed on the ceiling, little bile-coloured
globules rolling away from the point of impact. I weakly
pawed at the straps, then looked up to see Rhodane, who
fought her way through the malfunctioning door then
pulled herself across the room and down beside me.

'Are you hurt?' she asked.

'Nothing broken,' I replied. 'But if we are now under
attack I don't particularly want to stay here.'

Rhodane shook her head. 'The drone allowed us to take a hit. The others are now analysing what happened, but it seems that receiving the hit was the only option to keep us safe.'

'What?'

'If Tig-ger' – she stumbled over the name – 'had used the main drive to move us out of the projectile's path, the hilldigger would certainly have spotted us. The conceal-ment technology he employed managed to hide the energy released by the strike.'

'Anyone hurt?'

Rhodane looked shifty. 'Just one casualty . . . but the projectile passed through a mostly unoccupied section of the ship and automatics are now sealing it off. We are still travelling towards Sudoria and, unless it changes course, we should be out of range of the hilldigger within a day or so.'

'Who died?' I asked, though even as I asked I'd already guessed.

'Our prisoner – from decompression.'

Admittedly I could feel no great sympathy for some-one who had tried to shoot me, but that still wasn't a great way to go. They must have moved him out of the spin section, I thought, and wondered if he had again been glued to a chair somewhere, in which case he wouldn't have been able to get to safety. But then my condition here wasn't much better. Feeling a growing frustration with my current feeble state, I again pawed at the straps securing me. Rhodane watched me for a moment, then hauled herself over to the nearby wall beside something that looked like a collection of wasp's nests. 'We have no contact with the Brumallian Con-sensus, but aboard this ship there is general agreement that this might be best,' she announced. She detached one of the oblate containers from the collection of the same, then returned to me. 'Of course, you are not part of any consensus, so we need your approval too.'

'Approval of what?' I eyed the container.

'This contains a biomed mutualite. Things like this were used during the War to sustain life in the critically injured, and to restore to function those with lesser injuries.'

'How, precisely?'

'It grows inside your torso, where it can take over the function of your liver and kidneys, and assist your heart and lungs. It also manufactures its own host-specific drugs, phagocytes, enzymes and much else besides.'

'A parasite?'

'No, a mutualite.'

'But designed for Brumallians? I think you under-stand that internally I am very little like a normal human, let alone a Brumallian.'

'Believe me, I understand. I've also studied the information Tigger made available about your condition and taken a look inside you with one of the med scanners here. If we don't do something for you, you won't be walking from this ship alive. Apparently Tigger offered to put you into stasis, but you didn't say what you wanted before he . . . went out of contact.'

'Out of contact?'

She waved a hand in irritation. 'The drone retains control over this ship, but is no longer responding to us.' She now watched me carefully. 'But a place has already been made ready for you – for putting you into stasis. We would rather you didn't take that option, since that would defeat the whole purpose of your presence aboard.'

'Spell it out for me.'

'You were our insurance to get this ship safely down onto Sudoria, and then to get the evidence of Fleet's crimes to Parliament.' She shrugged. 'Things have changed. Fleet just launched an attack on Orbital Combine, so you might assume that our chest of evidence is as trivial as evidence of common assault brought against someone who graduated to murder. That's not so, and this evidence must be revealed, spread and generally known.'

'I understand.'

'You do?'

'I've been around for a while. The Sudorians are currently trying to kill each other and unscrupulous politicians might find it expedient, at some later date, to blame it all on a common enemy. The Brumallians need to cover themselves, because once the fight between Fleet and Combine is over, then will come the finger pointing, and whoever survives will find it easier to point the finger at the Brumallians rather than at their own kind.'

'You *do* understand.'

'I also understand that Tigger provided this ship with chameleonware.'

Rhodane grimaced and said, 'Tigger's chameleonware may well get us away from this hilldigger, and before this conflict began could have taken us through Orbital Combine's defences and down to the surface . . .'

I weakly held up a hand. 'I apologize, I'm not thinking straight. You'll need me down on the surface the moment you turn off the chameleonware. As I understand it, a Brumallian ship has never yet landed on Sudoria, so they might find it particularly disconcerting?'

Rhodane shook her head. 'We'll have to reveal our ship before then. There'll be a lot of automated weaponry going off, and hurtling chunks of debris. The slightest fault, the slightest error, the slightest bit of bad luck and we end up breathing vacuum. We need to go in under a meteor defence umbrella. So we need to reveal ourselves to Combine.'

I replied, 'But whatever way you cut it, you don't want me in hibernation.' I nodded towards the container she held. 'Okay, give it to me.'

Rhodane broke off the top of the vessel and held it out. Something glubbed wetly inside. 'You just swallow it.'

I did as instructed, though gagging and heaving as something large and slimy filled my mouth and reluctantly slid down my throat. I fought the urge to vomit again and flushed hot, with sweat beading my face. Lying back, I concentrated on just holding things together. I felt bloated as if after eating a huge meal, then that feeling drained away to be replaced by a hollow hunger, so I guessed the mutualite had now moved down from my stomach into my intestines. Then I grew cold, felt dry and papery and somehow insubstantial, but after a moment was able to talk again.

'How long until it's working?' I asked.

'It's usually quick, but in your case that's questionable.'

'Undo these straps for me.'

She complied and, still feeling fragile, I pushed myself upright.

'I'm feeling much better,' I said, then immediately blacked out.

Orduval

The armoured car bucked, the blast slamming the seat up underneath him. As the vehicle crashed down again, now flinging him from his seat, all became a chaos of falling, yelling bodies. Smoke filled the air and somewhere a disc-gun hissed and crackled. He was crawling towards the door, now hanging open and sideways on, when Chief Reyshank grabbed his shoulder.

'No, stay here.'

Reyshank and Trausheim crawled towards the door, following two other wardens outside. Firing continued; the *spang* of metal off metal.

'Launcher!' someone yelled.

'On it,' someone else replied.

There came a *whoosh* then the nearby *crump* of an explosion, followed by a grumbling tumble of rubble and the clanging of something metallic falling. More weapons firing. All of the wardens were outside the vehicle now. Orduval got groggily to his feet and again began moving over to the door. Then Trausheim stepped back inside and caught hold of his arm, 'Come on.'

He stumbled out into dust-filled air, glimpsed a warden uniform on the ground, soaked with blood and raw flesh exposed through rips. 'Move,' Trausheim urged.

In the shelter of nearby buildings, while some of the wardens moved ahead to check sidestreets, Orduval looked back towards the car. It was sprawled on its side with one tread hanging off. Across the street from it lay a caved-in building, which he guessed was either where that launcher had been, or was the source of the sniper fire after a mine had turned over the armoured car.

'What now?' he asked Reyshank.

The chief gestured him to silence as he listened to his earpiece, then after a moment replied, 'We're pulling out. If we stay here, we'll give the Groundstars too many extra targets – the Coplanetaries already pulled out an hour ago. We're all hoping the fight'll go out of the Groundstars once the Fleet base gets hit.' Reyshank paused for a moment, noticing Orduval's puzzlement. 'You know about the Groundstars and the Coplanetaries, don't you?'

'I know the Groundstars support Fleet and the Coplanetaries support Combine, just a couple of groups amidst many. I didn't realize they were so dangerous.'

'Well, the Coplanetaries aren't really much of a threat, but the Groundstars are ever since Base Commander Fregen supplied them with arms.'

'And it's his base that's going to get hit . . . by Orbital Combine?'

Reyshank nodded. 'Most base commanders have surrendered, as per Fleet orders, but Fregen is holding out. His base is in a high population-density area so he's reckoning Combine will hold off.'

They moved on, trying to stay under cover for as long as possible, but breaking into a run across any open ground. At one point a group of youths appeared from a sidestreet, picking up chunks of rubble and throwing them, but soon retreated after the wardens fired over their heads. Orduval noticed that the youngsters all wore armbands bearing the image of a white flower on a purple background. This indicated they were members of the Orchid Party, which now mostly consisted of

student agitators looking for any excuse to throw rocks
and wreck property. He spotted the corpse of a woman
lying in a doorway, but no sign of the injury that caused
her death. Every street seemed to have its own burning
ground car, and the chatter of weapons fire remained
constant, though thankfully distant. As they neared the
outskirts of the city a light glared from behind them,
casting black shadows, followed by a hissing rumbling.

'Combine just stopped holding off,' Reyshank observed.

Orduval glanced over his shoulder to observe a thick
pall of smoke rising from some distant point of the city.
Within that oily blackness a hot bar of light stirred,
reaching down from the sky. He recognized the effect of
a microwave beam heating the smoke rising from the
base, and no doubt from the burning corpses it contained. He felt sick and, as they continued up the street,
wondered just how bad things were getting elsewhere.
Support for either Combine or Fleet was variable among
the planetary political units, but also among revolutionary and protest groups. With the two main Sudorian
factions now in open conflict it struck him that their
society might soon fall apart. Only the GDS wardens
seemed capable of holding things together, yet here they
were retreating.

When they finally reached an area where the damage
seemed somewhat less, Reyshank broke into a ground
car.

'You come with me,' he pointed to Orduval, 'and you
three.' He indicated Trausheim and two other wardens.
'The rest of you head over to Bleak Street and link up
with Jarden.'

The next minute, Orduval was sitting between two

wardens in the rear of the car as it pulled away. To his right he glimpsed the maglev tram track, between suburban houses, then the road drew adjacent to it as they left the city behind. Glancing back, he saw the bloody eye of the setting sun peering at him through columns of smoke, and here and there flickered the muzzle flashes of automatic weapons.

High in the sky burned other fires, and sadly they weren't stars.

McCrooger

After sliding for some time in and out of unconsciousness and the land of nightmares, I woke feeling relatively better; that is, I did not feel myself only a short pace from entering the underworld. Rhodane had resecured the straps across me before she departed, but this time I managed to undo them without any trouble and, pushing myself upright on the bed, felt no urge to vomit.

One additional shove sent me drifting towards the door, which opened easily – obviously some repairs had been made. Pulling myself out into the corridor, I noticed a pronounced drift towards the floor, which told me the spin section must be slowly getting up to speed again. I moved along the corridor in bounds that grew steadily shorter, only halting when the jarring of my feet against the floor reminded me of the fragility of my bones. Meanwhile, the gradually increasing spin seemed to be trying to drag the meat from my skeleton. My injured arm began to ache, as soon did many other parts of me. After a little while, when it seemed the spin had stabilized, I moved on, and finally reached the area best described as the Bridge, and entered it through another one of those fleshy doors.

Inside, Brumallians sat in organic control stations that seemed melded around them. These in turn encircled a concave floor that I knew to be a view screen with facility for semi-holographic projection. Rhodane leant out of her own station to observe me as I entered, then eased herself out and walked over. She wore a headset that looked like a horseshoe crab impacting with the side of her head.

'Would it be foolish to ask how you're feeling?' she enquired.

'I feel like someone has beaten me from head to foot with rocks, but, as you can see, I'm standing, so that's a plus. What's the situation now?'

With one hand clasped against her headset she gestured over to the dish screen. The screen itself darkened and stars resolved, and then from the surface of it a hilldigger rose before me, flickering as waves of interference occasionally erased it. 'They gave up some hours ago. We were worried they were going to head for Brumal next, since the hilldigger's next logical target would be our launch site. However, its course is now away from Brumal, out towards another hilldigger that didn't join the rest of the Fleet.'

'And Sudoria?'

Again a wave of her hand, and now Sudoria rose before us, the dish screen itself cupping the glare of the sun. The planet itself remained constant, but views of the stations surrounding it kept flickering in and out of existence, though I did get one brief glimpse of something disappearing in a ball of flame. 'Fleet jamming is lighter here and we can now open communications with

Combine. I was going to come and get you.' She again waved at the display and Sudoria disappeared, to be replaced this time with a blank grey floating screen. 'Now let's talk to Combine.'

Yishna

Surprisingly, Defence Platform One had remained intact even though severely damaged by the missile hits from *Blatant*. On one of her screens she observed the last of the repair teams and GDS investigators leaving it, to take cover aboard a better-defended satellite. The ruined platform was only partially covered by others located at three compass points, though completely lacking in cover at the fourth point, where Twelve, which was also being evacuated, still lay under construction. It occurred to her that the positioning of Dravenik's hilldigger *Blatant* near Platform One, and the ensuing events, had not just been an excuse for this conflict, but a preparation for it too. For Combine's defences had been weaker there, and *Blatant*'s return strike against Platform One had weakened them further.

'First impacts in twenty seconds,' said Gneiss over general address.

Yishna finally latched down her suit helmet, then sat tense in her chair, tightly gripping the arms. Twenty seconds later, space above Sudoria filled with incandescent explosions and vapour trails as projectiles struck defence buoys or were intercepted by beam weapons. Glittering menisci occasionally flashed into existence as projectiles struck station energy shields. Though projectiles were targeted at stations all around the planet, the main attack was, of course, concentrated almost a quarter of an orbit away, over the cross formation of five defence platforms with the wrecked Platform One at its centre.

Yishna watched the contrails and explosions rapidly draw closer over One and Twelve. The first strike on One cut straight through the massive wrecked disc and punched a column of fire down towards atmosphere, where it began to dissipate in a glowing cloud. Further hits kept tilting and straightening the platform, relative to the planet. Chunks of it came away and trails of debris burnt down towards Sudoria. The platform began to slowly come apart just as Twelve now began to receive its first strikes.

Yishna released her grip on the arms of her chair then pulled up displays fed from Combine Tactical. She could easily discern her brother's initial plan of attack and, of course, Tactical had anticipated it too. A cruiser was already moving into position below Platform Two, ready to move in below the gap Harald was creating and then fill it with defence buoys. She quickly switched back to the display showing her that specific area, then abruptly froze when Corisanthe Main jolted underneath her. She waited anxiously for the howl of breach alarms and then the application of one of the Emergency Ozark Protocols, all of which, because of her meddling, would result in an ejection of the containment cylinders. After a moment she realized she was holding her breath, and let it out slowly as the quadrant guns began grumbling. That had been a close one, obviously slamming into the energy shields, and the station staggering under the blow like a knight taking the impact of a mace on his more rudimentary shield.

She sipped flavoured water from the spigot inside

her helmet to moisten her arid mouth, wondering what Harald's objective could be once he had made a hole in Combine's defences. Tactical had come up with many suggestions, most of them involving the steady destruction of the platforms one by one. To Yishna this seemed quite likely, yet somehow inelegant. She grimaced, returning her attention to her displays, just in time to see Platform Twelve's shield now go down.

Antimunitions from the beleaguered platform filled space above it with explosions, which, like an insect swarm, drew closer to the platform, then three strikes occurred simultaneously all on one side. The platform tipped ninety degrees, and began to drift. A glancing strike on what was its underside set it spinning like a coin. Checking Combine Tactical, Yishna saw that the fusillade was now over. Platform Twelve had not been destroyed, but for the present it was useless. Spying a couple of inter-station shuttles heading over towards it, she wondered if there would be anyone still alive inside to rescue, and a bitter nausea filled her. She then noted the cruiser, a 1,000-foot-long armoured tongue, begin edging out from under the aegis of Platform Two.

Platform One was now just a spreading mass of glowing wreckage sliding slowly towards atmospheric burn-up. Far below this, a disc-shaped cloud extended over the area where one of the projectiles had penetrated down to ground level. Being deep in a desert region, there were hopefully few casualties involved.

The cruiser finally began to fire buoys up at a slant, wave upon wave of golden beads all heading towards one targeted region of space. Cutting the view now to Platform Two, Yishna there observed guns and missile racks swinging over to point in the same direction. Obviously the next strike was already on its way. Abruptly her screen flickered off, then on again, to show her Gneiss on a private channel. The Director looked wired, even slightly unstable. Yishna had never seen him like this before.

'Yishna, how goes it?'

'We're as prepared as we can be. That's all I can say.'

'Then it's time for you to turn your attention to other matters.'

'Those being?'

'You are still Orbital Combine's representative in matters concerning the Polity and the Consul Assessor.'

'Aren't such matters rather irrelevant at the moment?'

'One would have thought so, but we have just been contacted by someone supposedly approaching on a Brumallian ship – which we cannot yet trace – who claims to be the Consul Assessor. You will deal with this as you see fit, Yishna, because right at the moment I've enough problems.' His image winked out, but a holding graphic up in one corner of her screen gave Yishna a link to the exterior com channel. She hesitated before reaching up to touch it. Could this be some new devious plot of Harald's? Abruptly she stabbed the graphic with her finger, and sat back.

The figure appearing on the screen before her she quickly recognized as David McCrooger, but not the same seemingly indestructible individual she had met. In some ways the look of him reminded her of Orduval, for he seemed to be ravaged by some terrible illness. She quickly began to assess what she was seeing. This could easily be a false image, of course, but why make him look so diminished? She answered her own question: because that changed image of him would be the more believable one. So, apparently he was aboard a Brumallian ship? Maybe her brother had laid hands on one and was trying to use it to penetrate Combine defences . . .

'Yishna Strone,' said the image before her.

'And you would have me believe you are the Consul Assessor?'

'Yes, I would – and as a matter of urgency.'

'When responding to urgency it's easy to make mistakes.'

He stared at her, then gave a tired smile. 'I could repeat verbatim all the conversations we had last time we met, and you could then assume they were recorded by Fleet personnel. So what can I say now to convince you?'

'Well, let's start with those same conversations, shall we?'

He looked to one side. 'I recall you asking me what would be our policy on imprisoned sentients, should we intercede here, and the question seemed rather important to you. I explained to you how amnesty is granted in the case of corrupt totalitarian regimes, though those guilty of capital crimes would be checked for socio- or psychopathic tendencies.' Now looking at her directly, he went on, 'I finished by telling you that intercession was unlikely. I wonder if I truly answered your real question, because though humans are sentient, not all sentients are human.'

Was it him? 'Director Gneiss tells me you claim to be now aboard a Brumallian ship, yet we can detect no such vessel within transmission range.'

'We've used Polity technology to conceal the ship.' For a long moment he gazed at her expectantly.

'We?'

'Myself, the Brumallian crew – and your sister.'

The screen view expanded to encompass Rhodane. Yishna felt a tightness in her chest, and suddenly did not know how to react to this.

'Why . . . what are you doing here?' she demanded of her sibling.

Rhodane replied, 'Well, currently we're busy dodging both incoming projectiles from Fleet and defensive fire from Combine. As you can imagine, Yishna, revealing our position now is not something we feel inclined to hazard, since Combine automated defences would zero in on us immediately. What we want is for you to give us a safe corridor down to the surface of Sudoria.'

'Why?'

'Firstly, to deliver me safely to my destination,' said McCrooger, 'and secondly, so I can deliver to your Parliament some crucial evidence of Fleet's recent manipulation of events.'

'I think we're already past the point where such evidence might be considered to have any relevance.'

'Relevance to Sudorians,' he replied.

'So you would like Combine to allow a Brumallian ship safe passage down to the surface of Sudoria – something that never happened throughout the War nor since?'

'The simple answer is yes,' insisted McCrooger.

'We wouldn't be able to do so without consulting Parliament, and I suspect their answer will depend on the quality of the evidence you offer. We need to see it first, and assess it.' Yishna leant forwards to check the tactical readouts. Another fusillade was on its way in, its main focus on Platform Two, but with enough strays elsewhere to take out any undefended ship. 'It should be possible for us to give you a corridor to Corisanthe III – Oversight Committee permitting.'

McCrooger shook his head. 'That's not an option. Your side is the main opponent of Fleet, so allowing you access to the evidence we bring would destroy its veracity.'

'Then I remain reluctant to let you through. This could be merely Brumallian opportunism. That ship of yours could be carrying fusion or biological weapons – just what we built our defence platforms to prevent reaching the planet's surface.'

'Then perhaps someone should board us to check? Perhaps yourself?'

'One individual alone boarding your ship is unlikely to find anything cleverly concealed.'

'True, but we both know that you are capable of probing concealment of the kind that is not merely physical.'

Yishna wasn't so sure she agreed with that, but the idea of just getting away from Corisanthe Main, even to board a Brumallian ship, definitely appealed to her. She put that channel on hold, then put through a call to Director Gneiss. A second holding graphic appeared, and drawn-out minutes passed before Gneiss replied.

'Yes, what is it?' he said, distracted, inward-looking.

Since the Director looked a little impatient, Yishna reported the recent conversation as quickly as she could.

'The decision is yours' – he glanced aside, probably at another screen, then turned back to her – 'since you've now been raised to probationary membership of the Oversight Committee. Your area of expertise is defined as all matters relating to Polity contact.'

'But allowing a Brumallian ship through is surely a security matter?'

'Is it? We all know who's culpable in recent events, and it certainly isn't the Brumallians. Uskaron's book cast the reasons for the War with them into extreme doubt, and that's been reinforced by our own studies of Brumallian society. We're agreed that an attack from them is very unlikely, and it seems clear they're now bringing evidence to show their innocence in current matters. You yourself must decide what to do.' His image blinked out.

Shortly afterwards the details of a safe corridor leading down to Sudoria appeared in its place. Yishna flicked back to the other channel.

'I'm sending you coordinates for a safe corridor. You've one hour to reach its entry point, where I'll join you. Then, when I've ensured you're carrying nothing nasty aboard, you'll enter the corridor and proceed down to the surface.'

McCrooger nodded briefly, and Rhodane smiled, before Yishna cut the link. Then, using the touch-screen, she quickly created a list of items from stores. Next she opened another link. 'Dalepan, are you aware of my new status?'

'I am,' the OCT replied, 'as it's just gone up on all the public message boards.'

'Very well. I'm sending you now a list of items I want placed aboard the shuttle at Dock Three.'

Dalepan studied the list for a long moment. 'Am I allowed to ask why you need these particular items?'

'We've got a Brumallian ship coming in to land on Sudoria – protected by Combine weapons. The Polity Consul Assessor is aboard, but I'm to check it's not carrying anything else we wouldn't want arriving down there.'

'I see then the purpose of the scanners, though you're unlikely to find any concealed biologicals. However, I fail to see the purpose of item six.'

'Insurance,' Yishna replied.

'But not the kind to ensure your safety.'

Perhaps she was being overly paranoid – being aboard Corisanthe Main tended to produce that effect. She eyed the item he referred to: one of the megaton-range stealth mines that had earlier destroyed the hilldigger *Slate* – quite enough to vaporize a Brumallian ship while sitting in its docking bay. After a moment she transferred the mine's detonation code to her baton, which she then detached from its slot in the console before her, and placed in her pocket.

15

The Sand Churches arose almost certainly because of the oppression during the time leading up to the War. However, even then they were regarded as the lunatic fringe by the majority of the population. During most of the War itself, the Churches made few advances, the numbers joining them rising hardly at all. It was only in the last decade of the War that their memberships increased, along with a growth in belief in the supernatural (hence the rise in the irrational belief in this Shadowman). This is puzzling. Why, when it seemed we were on the road to victory, did this swing happen? Religion flourishes under oppression and in ignorance, but in those last ten years Parliament was not oppressive and ignorance was a luxury we could not afford. I freely admit that I have no answers to this.

– Uskaron

Harald

Weapons fire rumbled through *Ironfist* and, on the selected screens before him, the view of Sudoria kept blanking out as ship's defences intercepted some intervening missile or mine, filling surrounding space with blinding EM radiation. He sat with his hands resting on the arms of his chair, enthroned at the centre of a growing storm, and in a small part of his mind wondered if he should really be enjoying this so much. But he dismissed that thought and focused on Platform Two, as a fusillade of coil-gun missiles began to arrive there.

Multiple explosions filled space over to one side as the first projectiles slammed into some buoys, the debris from those impacts knifing towards the platform. Then finally some intact projectiles got through to detonate against the shields, momentarily throwing the curving menisci into view. Harald observed a couple of explosions aboard the platform, doubtless shield generators overloading, but the remaining shields held and not one projectile succeeded in reaching the platform itself. He had not expected otherwise, and once the fusillade ceased he observed a cruiser coming out of cover to launch another cloud of buoys, whilst under the entire defence umbrella other ships began moving in to resupply the defence platform. The fleet would have to move in closer now, so the hilldiggers could effectively employ energy weapons and atomics. When that time arrived, in about another three hours, it was going to get vicious.

'Captain Ashanti, begin your run on Corisanthe III. I am hoping it won't be necessary for you to destroy the station, just keep it nailed down.' On his eye-screen Harald watched *Wildfire* and *Resilience* begin their departure from the main body of the fleet. 'All other Captains, on my lead we concentrate our attack on Platform Two. *Harvester*, *Stormfollower* and *Musket* will strafe from close orbit, until I give the order for them to make their run on Corisanthe II. When ready, myself and Franorl will begin our atmosphere-level attack.'

Another channel blinked for his attention, and he opened it to see a small fleet of Combine cruisers moving out to flank the hilldiggers. This struck him as a brave but rather pathetic response.

'Franorl, deal with that, would you.'

Desert Wind began to turn. There was no visible sign of the ship using its coil-guns but Harald knew, from tacom channels, that Franorl had already opened fire. One of the five cruisers flew apart, strangely without producing even a hint of flame, another tilted and began to drift away. Two of them turned and began heading back for cover while the last one closed in on its drifting fellow cruiser. Harald watched them intermittently over the next half an hour, also switching occasionally to views of other Combine activity, and to monitor *Wildfire*'s run. As the rescuing cruiser docked with the crippled one, both cruisers abruptly disappeared in a massive explosion. Harald just sat there, mystified, until he started checking recorded telemetry. Evidently Franorl had launched a slower-moving nuclear missile which had just arrived. Comparing the timings, Harald realized Franorl must have fired the missile during the rescue attempt, and not in the initial fusillade. He suddenly did not know how to react to this, since he found he did not consider such an action . . . quite honourable. Next he felt a sudden contempt for himself. How could he quibble about matters of honour considering what he himself was doing? He abruptly stood up, checked timings and realized that, unless Orbital Combine came up with something unexpected, he had a few hours yet now to spare. Everything else could be handled by the ship's automatic weapons and by its highly trained crews.

What am I doing?

This question only recurred to him at moments like this, when he was tired and when action of one kind or another ceased for a small while, and as always his reply to it was that he was fighting for the survival of Fleet. Though an inadequate answer on an intellectual level, he felt its truth in his gut and that was enough. Surely he should get some sleep now, but the need for it had left him directly after he killed Carnasus. Perhaps he should do his rounds of the ship, make himself visible, inspire confidence . . . Almost without thinking about it, he called up internal views of *Ironfist* and began checking operations. When he realized what he was doing, he deliberately shut down his tacom helmet and control glove, removed them and dropped them into his chair.

The Bridge was all activity as he stepped down into it. Many of the crew shot glances at him, then returned their attention instantly to their consoles. Though the ship's defensive armament was firing automatically, there was plenty to occupy everyone, particularly damage control since, though nothing major had got through, *Ironfist* was perpetually sustaining damage from debris.

His two guards falling in behind him, he approached the crewman monitoring the ship's manifest. 'Status?'

The man shot out of his chair, not having seen the new Admiral approaching. He was young, probably still a teenager, and stood there with his mouth open, the look on his face of one who expected to be berated.

'What is our present internal supply status?' Harald asked.

The youth took a deep breath. 'We have used only

four warheads.' He glanced at his screen. 'Capacitance is at sixty per cent, and we can keep the reactors running at this rate for eight days . . . Admiral. Though we've been losing shield generators,' he gained confidence, 'we've more than enough at the present rate of breakdown. The greater problem is getting them installed quick enough. And we now have less than a quarter of our stock of coil-gun missiles remaining.' He brightened. 'But supply ships are already on their way from *Carmel* with new stock.'

'Thank you,' said Harald. 'Return to your duties.'

'I think we'll check the engine galleries now,' he told his two escorts.

The lift section behind the Bridge, his means of getting to any of the four rail lines, was obviously very busy. By one of the lifts waited a damage-control crew with a lev-plate loaded with high-pressure sealant guns and a welder, stacked on top of sheets of hull metal, and out of another lift, just arrived, stepped a couple of officers and some crew, most of them immediately hurrying off in different directions. However, one of the officers stopped before Harald, then turned and fist-saluted over his side arm. Only the fist did not remain a fist as it opened, closed again and drew. Harald found himself looking into the barrel of a gun. With a vicious crack that barrel disappeared behind its own flame. Harald felt the bullet strike his temple, felt his own skull breaking open. The force of impact snapped his head aside and spun him round. Then he felt nothing.

McCrooger

The explosions we saw on the screen, around Sudoria and around the hilldiggers now approaching that world, seemed a distant thing that I could not help viewing with some detachment. What brought home the horrible reality was the occasional *thwack*, followed by flashing yellow lights denoting a hull breach, as some piece of debris travelling at thousands of miles per second slammed right through our ship. This being an organic vessel, the holes punched through its hull were closed up rapidly, but that did not dispel the vulnerability I felt. The ship might be able to heal itself easily, but if one of those pieces hit me . . .

'She is due to arrive shortly,' said Rhodane, ducking into the quarters I shared with Slog and Flog, who as usual lately were off lurking around the spin-section hub where Tigger had subsumed our ship's AI. I swung my legs off the bed and stood up a little shakily. It had been another one of those horrible disturbed sleeps, and everything around me still looked slightly distorted. 'How are you?' she added, studying me carefully.

I'd never spoken to Tigger about the distortion and the nightmares, because they seemed too personal, and having to admit that, as well as my body falling apart my mind was too, seemed just a bit too much to bear. But I chose to speak to Rhodane about it now because of some obscure desire to 'clear the decks' before our next 'action'. It is a good thing I did, because her reply was the key that started things sliding into place and interlocking in my mind.

'I'm not great,' I replied. 'I've been having some

twisted nightmares ever since I arrived in this system, and some of them even while I'm awake.'

She gazed at me for a long moment, her expression giving away nothing, then said, 'But you did not experience them on Brumal?'

I thought about it. A lot had happened to me on Brumal, but nothing like that. It struck me now that it had been my only *normal* time here in this system. 'No, not on Brumal.'

'I told you it was an oasis of sanity,' she said. 'That's where I finally found mine – and the change I've since undergone has helped me hold onto it,' she frowned, 'though sometimes my anger at Sudoria returns, and I wish I could raise the rest of the Brumallian ships to attack whatever will remain when Fleet and Combine have finished with each other.' She paused speculatively. 'I think the Consensus blocks the cause of those nightmares. Shared sanity?' She shrugged. 'I don't know.'

I absorbed that information then revealed, 'Sometimes there's a dark figure. It tried to be my father, but that facade did not last. I feel it's trying to say something to me, but just doesn't know how.'

'So the Shadowman is not the Sudorian conscience,' she stated obscurely.

'That went right over my head, Rhodane.'

The ship juddered violently. She tilted her head for a moment, then gestured towards the corridor beyond the door and led the way out.

'What would you say is the average incidence of mental illness among any normal human population?' she asked.

'Define "normal human".'

She gave me an annoyed look. 'On Sudoria, three

out of four people end up having treatment for some kind of mental illness. Most Sudorians are meanwhile on some kind of drugs regimen to control one mental malady or another. There are more asylums on Sudoria now than there are schools.'

This was complete news to me, yet something Geronamid and Tigger had to know about. So why hadn't I been told? Probably because by knowing I would not necessarily respond as Geronamid required me to.

Rhodane went on, 'The Shadowman is a common hallucination of some of those conditions. Since Uskaron's book came along our rate of mental illness has been attributed to societal guilt, and the Shadowman is considered the manifestation of the Sudorian conscience. But quite evidently you're not guilty of involvement in a genocidal war, nor are you even Sudorian, so why then are *you* seeing him?'

We reached the ladder leading up out of the spin section, and Rhodane climbed it ahead of me. I felt a resurgence of nausea as soon as we reached the nil-gee part of the ship. As we propelled ourselves along one of the intestinal corridors corkscrewing into the bowels of the vessel, I asked her, 'What was the explanation for the Shadowman, before Uskaron's book appeared?'

She glanced back at me. 'There were so many of them. To some he was the manifestation of the War dead, to others he was some dark angel who had somehow brought about the War. The explanations given by the Churches varied from complete denial of his existence to the claim that he was evil incarnate and only when all Sudorians bow to their doctrine will he be driven away.'

'Do you see the Shadowman, Rhodane?'

'Only in paintings.'

'Do your three siblings see him?'

'No more than I do.'

'Perhaps he is not required by you?' I suggested.

Her reply was a blank look, no more.

The corridor opened out into an oblate chamber in which the Combine shuttle rested like an ingot inside something's gut. The vessel's airlock was open and Yishna floated beside it gripping one rung of the steps curving round the shuttle's outer skin. She was clad in an insulated suit similar to Rhodane's, gloved and hooded but with no mask across her face. On seeing us, she pushed herself free, drifted over to the chamber wall, then propelled herself from there towards us. She was smiling at first, but the moment she caught hold of a nearby organic protuberance to halt herself, the smile faded and her eyes dulled as their nictitating membranes closed.

'Rhodane,' she studied her sister, 'like Harald you have mutilated yourself.' Her face had suddenly turned ugly with anger.

'Perhaps I am merely expressing my inner self, Yishna.'

'You make no sense,' Yishna snapped. 'Am I to believe the supposed reason for your presence here when you deliberately make no sense?'

Why was she so angry? She had already seen Rhodane on the display when we arranged for her to come here, and she had been smiling at us but a moment ago. Now she turned towards me.

'Consul Assessor,' she said tightly, 'you have been unwell?'

I could see the shape of things now, but there were still some details I needed to slot into place. I said to her,

'The Shadowman doesn't need to reveal himself to you, Yishna.'

With her gloved hands Yishna fumbled a control baton from her belt. The nictitating membranes had lifted from her eyes, and now they glistened with tears. My shoulder slammed into her chest, flinging those tears free to glitter alone. As we tumbled through the air I managed to wrest the baton away from her.

I think she let me take it.

Orduval

With a hand pressed against the comlink in his ear, Reyshank skidded the car to a halt, raising a cloud of dust. 'Damn, madmen,' he growled. Leaning over and searching through the pack at Trausheim's feet, he pulled out a coms helmet, stepped out of the car and walked a little distance away while fitting it on. Following the others from the car, Orduval gazed up and took a shaky breath of the cool night air.

Scarves of glowing gas spread across the firmament and bright explosions lit high up in orbit. Shooting stars cut across almost perpetually, and occasionally something would take longer to burn up in atmosphere as it descended, echoing distant sonic booms through the darkness and leaving a glowing trail. It was a stunning and awesome sight, but Orduval found difficulty connecting it with suffering and death, and he felt ashamed.

They were parked next to an abandoned desert farm, around which an underground network of water pipes supported a small oasis. Reyshank muttered and exclaimed in the background, while Trausheim and the two other wardens took their packs from the car and began delving after flasks of cold tea or bars of biltong and dried fruit. Finally the Chief removed the coms helmet and returned to them, looking pale and ill. He gazed around at his men, focused on Orduval for a moment, then addressed them all.

'We nearly lost the capital,' he said. 'In fact we have effectively lost the city centre and an entire outlying district.'

'My apartment is in Gaskell Street,' said one of the men, almost in a whisper. That street was somewhere in the mid-city, Orduval recollected, though he wasn't exactly sure where. 'What happened?' the shocked man finished.

'They're not sure who did it yet,' said Reyshank, 'but someone tried to detonate a nuclear warhead from a wartime defensive missile. Luckily, being over twenty years old, it didn't go fissile, but the chemical explosive brought down the administration tower and has spread radioactives all across the city. The estimate is of a thousand dead, though we probably won't know the real cost for some time yet.'

'What happened to Parliament?' asked Orduval.

Reyshank held up a hand to silence him, then continued to address the warden whose home was in the stricken capital. 'You've a wife and children back there, haven't you?' The man nodded tightly. 'Take the car,' said Reyshank, 'but stay out of the other cities. It's getting bad.' The warden hesitated and seemed about to say something else, but Reyshank just gestured sharply towards the vehicle. After a moment the man nodded then hurried over and climbed in. When the car had disappeared in its own cloud of dust, Reyshank turned back to Orduval. 'Fifteen parliamentary members were killed,

the rest have been evacuated. Just as most of the population there who are still listening to instructions are
being evacuated.'

Orduval gazed after the departing car. *Why had
Reyshank let it go?*

'Listening?' wondered Trausheim. 'You said those
who're listening are being evacuated.'

'We've got martial law in place but it seems few
people are taking heed of the wardens. We've had to pull
out of twelve major cities because arms caches have been
broken into and the only targets all the rival factions can
agree on are the GDS wardens. Some idiots – we assume
in the Orchid Party – have also decided that a good way
of stirring things up further has been to open the
asylums.'

The remaining warden, whose name Orduval had
yet to learn, gazed after the vehicle, now in the distance.
'What are our chances of getting this back under control?'

'Not the greatest.' Reyshank hauled his pack up off
the ground and gestured to the abandoned farmhouse.
'We'll wait in there.'

Following them, Orduval wondered about the
importance of his own concerns now. 'Why did you let
that car go?' he asked, gazing round at the desolation.

'Have patience,' said Reyshank. 'We're going to be
picked up here.'

Trausheim kicked in the door of the farmhouse,
releasing a cloud of glimmer bugs and the overpowering
smell of decay. They decided instead to wait under some
nearby acacia trees, around a fire fuelled by the farmhouse door and some rotting furniture found inside the
building. The rumbling from the sky continued, but

seemed to descend to a background murmur as Orduval thoughtfully chewed on a piece of biltong. At one point they heard the sound of lunatic bellowing, but when Trausheim grabbed his weapon and stood up, Reyshank ordered him to sit down again. After they had eaten and drunk their fill they sat there in silence, then Reyshank suddenly got up and moved off through the trees towards the desert's edge. After a brief hesitation, Orduval followed him.

'Fleet have destroyed two Defence Platforms,' said the Chief, gazing out across the empty sands. 'The plan of attack seems quite simple, though what their final aim is I don't know. However, I do know that Harald will need to neutralize the Corisanthe stations, no matter what else he's after.'

'There's over a quarter of a million people aboard those stations,' Orduval noted.

'Maybe more . . .'

Having originally noted Reyshank's queue and the scar on his face, Orduval suggested, 'You were in Fleet?'

'I trained during the last years of the War, and went down to Brumal during the occupation.' He turned his face into view, pointing to the scar on it. 'I got this from a quofarl before I managed to blow its head off. But I feel no loyalty to Fleet now, and no agreement with what they're doing. What about you, then? The Admiral is your brother, after all.'

'How did you know that?'

'Harald Strone and Orduval Strone? I had my suspicions, and Duras confirmed them for me.'

'You spoke to Duras?'

'Oh yes, he chose me to pick you up, when we still only knew you as Uskaron, because he and I knew each other from our service days. He became very interested indeed in you when we later learned your real name.'

Out over the desert, Orduval saw a constellation of lights that seemed to make no sense to him. Other stars weren't visible there, and those lights seemed too constant to be the result of explosions. After a moment he realized they were just below the horizon. Buildings maybe? But there was nothing out there, and anyway these lights seemed to be on the move.

'Here comes Parliament,' explained Reyshank.

'What?'

'It's of Combine manufacture.' He smiled wryly at Orduval. 'GDS has three of them: mobile incident stations in the event of planetary disaster. It seemed safest to take Parliament aboard this one, so at least the chance of us losing the rest of the planetary government has been reduced.'

The lights were now revealed as windows in some enormous floating structure: like a tall city building turned on its side and floating a few thousand feet above the dunes.

'They brought this out here for me?' Orduval asked.

'It would be nice to think so,' replied Reyshank, 'but no. We're only a few hundred miles from the landing site.'

'What landing site?'

'For the Brumallian ship that's arriving here with the Consul Assessor and your two sisters aboard.'

Orduval swore, but then he smiled.

Harald

He opened his eyes to the aseptic look of scoured aluminium in *Ironfist*'s medbay, the taste of copper in his mouth and the astringency of antiseptic in his nostrils. With his head throbbing unremittingly, he tried to remember which particular operation this was, which surgical enhancement he had just undergone. Only after a moment did he remember that all those he had planned had been carried out many months ago.

'Try to take it easy,' said Jeon, leaning over him.

Harald tried to sit upright but felt incredibly weak. He kept his face empty of expression, not wanting her to see the panic he felt, for he did not recall why he was in this place. Turning his head so as not to meet her eyes, he gazed steadily across at an instrument trolley, observed the bloody wadding and soiled instruments.

Noting the direction of his gaze, Jeon said, 'I did the best I could after you told them all to get out.' Harald could remember nothing about that. She stepped over to the trolley and picked up a steel dish in which lay a lump of grey metal with shallow flanges spiralling round it. 'You were lucky really. This is an explosive slug but it failed to detonate. It lifted a piece of your skull and lodged next to your brain. Had it gone off there wouldn't be anything left of you above the neck.'

Someone had tried to kill him – that much was clear, if all the details were not. He felt a sudden surge of rage, which he immediately fought, disliking such lack of control.

'You do understand me, don't you?' she asked.

'I unnerstan yo per . . .' He stopped talking, horrified that his mouth was mangling the words, like on the first and last time he had got drunk on going to his first ever party aboard *Ironfist*. He could feel one side of his mouth twisted down and wondered if he looked like someone who had suffered a stroke.

'What – is – happening?' he articulated carefully.

'Franorl took command in your absence and pulled the fleet back. All ships are holding station, safely out of range of beam weapons. We're maintaining a bombardment and we're still taking hits from Combine's rail-guns, but we can sustain that.'

What was she talking about? And what was Admiral Carnasus up to?

'Admiral, what are your orders? Do we continue with this? I can give you something now to keep you on your feet, but I don't know how long it will last.'

Admiral?

'We – must not – withdraw.' The words seemed to come out of him automatically, even though he had no clear idea what she was talking about. Summoning some core of will, he took command of his body and sat upright. Dizziness assailed him, and in the fug that billowed through his mind he recalled feeling the warm grip of a small Combine handgun, and saw the slugs from it smashing into Admiral Carnasus's skull. Sudden grief clutched at his throat, and tears began to run down his cheeks. He reached up to wipe them away, then tried to put that memory into context. He had killed the Admiral and, from what Jeon had just told him, he realized his plans to move against Combine must be well advanced.

But only vague details punctuated by the odd disconnected sharper scene floated up into his consciousness. He recollected the fleet being gathered around *Carmel*, but did not know if that was something recent or went back to a time when Carnasus was in command. He also recollected giving the order to fire on a Brumallian city. Something else of importance had

happened then, but he could not recollect it. He slotted
these events into his initial plan, which he remembered
clearly, and found that they fitted in well. However,
he needed to know if anything had *not* gone to plan, he
needed to know what had happened to him, and most
importantly he needed to feel some genuine commit-
ment to what he had been doing, for it seemed strangely
lacking at that moment.

'My . . . memory of recent events is unclear,' he said.
That was a victory of will for he hardly slurred the words
at all.

'That's totally understandable,' Jeon replied. 'I've
injected drugs into you to limit the concussion and some
powerful anti-inflammatories, but the trauma to your
brain . . .'

He tried something he thought might be safe. 'Was
my assailant captured?'

'Your guards killed him. He was a subaltern from
Engineering,' Jeon supplied. 'He probably bought into
that offer made by Parliament. There will probably be
many others like him in Fleet, so perhaps you were right
to send all the surgeons away and insist on being treated
by only me.'

What offer from Parliament?

Even though possessing no knowledge of what Jeon
referred to, Harald thought it through and concluded:
Parliament must have rejected Fleet's claim on the
Defence Platforms and sided instead with Orbital Combine. Knowing Harald to be the main instigator of the
present crisis, they must have offered some sort of
reward or even just amnesty to anyone in Fleet who
managed to bring him down. Parliament's offer would be

recorded. He looked around the room, vainly trying to locate his com helmet.

'My helmet?' he demanded.

'You weren't wearing it.'

Harald nodded, then wished he hadn't. He reached up and felt the hard line of surgical glue and the stiff blood-crusted hair above. The skin there felt dead to him, probably because of the anaesthetic Jeon had used. He carefully swung his legs to the side of the surgical table and just sat there motionless knowing he wasn't ready to stand yet.

'Earlier you said . . . you can give me something?'

'I've some Vrastim and Tenoxalate,' Jeon replied, picking up a small box plastered over with old-style storage labels. 'Obviously, you are aware of the risks?'

Of the drugs suggested one was a battlefield stimulant and the other a cocktail of enzymes, endorphins, vasoconstrictors and sugar accelerants. The Tenoxalate cut down on pain and could force continued usage out of the most damaged tissues, but could also result in dangerous formations of scar tissue prone to turn gangrenous, and also in extreme weariness. The Vrastim served to counter the last effect, so combined the two drugs could even put someone with multiple gunshot wounds back on their feet. Staying on these drugs for too long would result in dependency, followed shortly afterwards by organ failure. Even coming off them before they got their hooks into you would result in shock, then the probable requirement of further surgery to remove dead tissue, after which recovery would be long and slow.

Harald gazed at Jeon, it suddenly occurring to him that she could give him any drugs she might choose, and he wouldn't know the difference until they were in his veins. Could he really trust her?

Then the illogic of his paranoia struck him. She had just cemented his skull back together. Why would she now bother to do that?

'Okay, give them to me,' he told her.

Jeon opened the box and removed twinned glass vials, one containing a clear fluid and the other something peaty. She clipped them to the access port in a tube trailing from Harald's arm to a nearby pressurized saline feed – pressurized because gravity feeds weren't used in ships where gravity could fail. Harald watched the twin vials slowly emptying, felt a sudden fizzing in his limbs, and a lightness of breathing resulting from an adrenal surge. Suddenly he felt a great urge to get out into the ship's corridors and run. Instead he carefully pushed himself off the surgical table and stood up.

Jeon picked up a sealed injector pack and placed it beside the labelled box, then turned her attention to the two emptying vials. Once they were drained she took a sterile swab and, pulling the tube from his arm, pressed the swab into place. 'Hold that,' she instructed.

Harald obliged, feeling thoroughly alert now, but still there were holes in his memory, fuzzy and disconnected incidents he could not put into context, occasional oddities like the phrase 'Polity Consul Assessor' – itself a collection of words that seemed to make no sense at all. Jeon now handed over both the box and the injector pack.

'The two drugs must always be injected together, but use no more than one dose every two hours. I know you'll be strongly tempted to use them more frequently as the initial effect begins to wear off, but be warned that cutting gangrene out of someone's head is a rather different matter to removing it from elsewhere in the body.'

'I am not so stupid,' Harald protested.

'No, you're not,' Jeon admitted, 'but you'll still over-use the drugs. People like you, and me, always do.' Now she picked up a tube of capsules. 'These are painkillers which you dissolve under your tongue. Use them sparingly.'

Harald pocketed the drugs then, shaking at first but slowly getting it under control, he walked over to the door. Pausing there, he gazed down at himself. Despite some sponging down of his foamite suit, there were still bloodstains at his shoulder and all down one side as far as his knee. Though tempted to change into a new uni-form, he decided that keeping this suit on would remind people of what had happened. He opened the door and stepped through with Jeon behind him. Four guards out-side immediately came to attention. Noting that two of them also wore blood-splashed uniforms, he wondered if it was his own blood or that of his would-be assassin.

'We'll head for the Bridge,' he decided, because that seemed the most likely location of his missing com helmet – and because, at that moment, he did not know in which direction it lay.

The guards turned smartly to face down the corridor, two setting out ahead of them, with the other two falling in beside himself and Jeon. After a couple of turnings they finally arrived at a bank of elevators. There Harald felt himself tensing up as he warily watched two technicians depart one of the lifts. He had no direct memory of it, but strongly sensed he had been shot in a place like this. One of the guards confirmed this for him by training his disc carbine on the departing technicians, while the other three carefully watched the surrounding area. Harald now transferred his paranoia onto them, nervous of their weapons, which could be turned on him at any moment.

Finally their own lift arrived.

'I'll be returning to my station on the Bridge within the hour,' announced Jeon. 'I have to check that recent upgrade to the U-space scanner. We need to keep a watch out for that Polity artefact.'

Harald nodded to her knowingly, and she departed along the corridor. As he stepped into the lift, he tried to put together all she had said to him. The last he could remember, she had worked from her own separate research area, yet now she must have a station on the Bridge. But 'U-space scanner' and 'Polity artefact'? Obviously there was a great deal of information he needed to reintegrate.

Having drawn smoothly to a halt, the lift unit revolved till its exit aligned with the entrance to the Bridge. Harald stepped out and surveyed, seeing many gazes turn towards him. He knew he should say something encouraging, but was terrified of revealing his ignorance. Raising a hand in greeting instead, he hurried towards the stair leading up to the Admiral's Haven. Leaving his escort below he quickly climbed it alone. Once out of everyone's view he allowed himself to slump in exhaustion. But when he spotted his com helmet and control glove, like an addict drawn to his fix, he quickly stepped over and picked them up.

At first there seemed to be something wrong with the resolution of the eye-screen, then he realized the problem was in his eye itself. This defect required him to use the entire screen for just one image at a time. He proceeded to access his private records and Fleet logs, carefully scanned and reintegrated information, then began to relearn the history of all recent manoeuvres in an attempt to bring himself back up to date. Yet when, many hours later and after another shot of the drugs Jeon had provided, he stood up and prepared to go down into the Bridge to issue orders, he felt a hollow detachment from all he had done or intended to do. It almost seemed as if, like some automaton, he was carrying through the schemes and Machiavellian plans of someone else – and someone he did not know too well.

Yishna

She gazed to her left and to her right, eyeing the quofarl on either side of her. She had never thought she would ever get so close to such creatures, having only ever seen them before on a screen. But now here were two of them ready, like asylum orderlies, to restrain her. Quite rightly too.

What had made her take out her control baton? What had so angered her about Rhodane that she had been prepared to take her own life in the process of taking her sister's? Well, it seemed to be the same thing that had driven her to alter the containment breach protocols aboard Corisanthe Main, and whether that was psychosis or some exterior influence almost did not matter. Either way it was not really part of her own conscious mind.

'Feeling better now?' asked McCrooger, who stood before her.

'What did they give me?'

'A powerful sedative and anti-psychotic. I'm guessing they interfere with the signal, or the program, or
whatever it is.'

Signal or program? Yishna felt she should ask more
about that, but felt a huge reluctance, and the opportunity went away as he held up her baton and continued,
'Now, I'm guessing this signals Combine to either drop
the umbrella or fire on us?'

'Near enough,' Yishna replied.

He stared at her for a long moment. 'I see . . . so
neither of those. Something aboard your shuttle then?'

She gave a sharp nod, both chagrined and glad of the
quality of the mind before her.

'Do you still feel the urge to . . . use this item?'

'I was only taking precautions,' said Yishna, then
cringed at her blatant lie. The baton had been in her hand
before she even knew what she was thinking, and her
finger was ready poised over the button to send the
mine's detonation code. Her sister, Rhodane, something
about her, about some lack of *connection*, had caused a
resentment and a twisted terror to arise within Yishna.
True, she had stopped herself from actually operating the
damned thing, but wondered if she could have held out
much longer had not McCrooger tackled her.

'I shan't dignify that statement with a reply, because
we have no more time to spare. Director Gneiss is
demanding to speak to you, and won't cover us down to
the planet's surface until he's done so. Meanwhile, every
moment we stay here we are in danger.'

'Then let me speak to him,' said Yishna.

'But you might tell him this ship presents a danger.'

'I might, but it would take a lot more than any claim
from me to persuade him. What I brought aboard that

shuttle was my own idea. He doesn't believe the Brumallians to be a threat.'

'Very well, stand up.'

Glancing at the quofarl on either side, Yishna pushed herself to her feet. It was only then that she realized she was experiencing gravity, and wondered briefly if the Brumallians had conquered that technology. Once out in the corridor, however, when she saw the curve of the floor, she realized she must be in some part of the ship that had been spun up.

'The drug?' she managed, as she walked between the quofarl.

'Like Rhodane, you find it difficult to talk about what that drug is suppressing,' he said.

'I . . . yes.'

'The Shadowman has you by the throat, Yishna. Though her mind has been shaped by him, he has no hold on Rhodane any more. And your reaction to her, I suspect, was either due to that – the elimination of a faulty tool – or to the possibility, however remote, that the evidence we're bringing here might end this war.' The door opened and he used sign language to the two quofarl, who then chattered something in Brumallian, before stepping back. They entered some kind of control room where Brumallians sat enclosed in organic technology. Rhodane stood over on the other side of a viewing pit, with something clinging to the side of her head. Immediately Yishna felt another surge of resentment towards her, and just could not fathom why. Fortunately it was weaker than before, so one she thought she could control.

Out of the viewing pit rose the holographic image of Director Gneiss.

'Yishna, where've you been?' he asked. On the surface he evinced suspicion, but underneath that display Yishna wondered if there was anything at all. She did not even want to try to analyse that impression, as she was currently having enough problems with her own emotions.

'I've been scanning this ship,' she lied, glancing towards Rhodane, whereupon her emotions ricocheted between resentment, outright hate and strangely a deep sibling love. She tried to push all that emotional clutter aside and operate on intellect alone. 'It seems clear of anything untoward.'

'Whatever.' Gneiss waved a dimissive hand. 'I just wanted to be sure you're all right before clearing the ship to land. I'm sending over your route and destination coordinates right away. You'll be landing on the edge of the Komarl, where Duras will meet you.'

Yishna gazed at Rhodane, who nodded briefly. Gneiss now blinked out, and Yishna felt McCrooger's hand close around her upper arm.

'Well done,' he said. 'I could see that was difficult for you.'

'The Shadowman?' Yishna queried, remembering his earlier words. Somehow, down deep, she knew exactly what he was talking about, yet there seemed something blocking that information from her conscious inspection.

'Certainly not racial conscience . . .' said McCrooger. He turned to Rhodane. 'We're going in now, I take it?'

'We have our route cleared down to the surface, and shields and defence buoys are being deployed to cover us,' said Rhodane. 'It should take us about two hours to reach our landing coordinates.'

Soon came a rumbling sound, as a Brumallian ship entered the atmosphere of Sudoria for the first time ever.

16

One would have thought that economic collapse on Sudoria would have resulted in automatic victory for the Brumallians. What actually happened is a perfect demonstration of how artificial and insubstantial is this human construction called an economy. Why were some people starving when others were growing more than sufficient food? The extent of the madness operating up to the point of the revolt was revealed when entire warehouses packed with hoarded food were broken into. It was all about money and greed. The people were being taxed savagely to pay for the war effort and further enrich the plutocrats, but because of this tax burden they could not afford to buy sufficient food and essential goods. The subsequent introduction of a fair rationing system after the revolt began to settle unrest, and the fate of Cairo-Desit got people back to work, now knowing they were working for their very survival. Had the owners of those warehouses been prepared to reduce their prices, they might not have ended up drive-bolted to rocks out in the Komarl. It was a simple economic mistake with harsh consequences.

– Uskaron

Director Gneiss

'If you had a spare spacesuit to sell here, you would net enough profit to buy yourself a shuttlecraft,' observed Roubert Glass, the Director of Corisanthe III. 'The price for one suit is now about a hundred times what it cost only a few hours ago, but few people are ready to sell since there's only about one spacesuit for every 800 citizens aboard.'

'I see you're wearing yours,' observed Director Gneiss. Indeed, Glass, who was a thin and rather sickly-looking specimen with anaemic blonde hair contrasting starkly with his narrow dark face, appeared to be wearing a spacesuit obviously a few sizes too big for him. Gneiss turned his attention to another screen, showing a view of the station itself from a nearby satellite that had thus far survived the bombardment. Corisanthe III, which had originally started out as a simple cylinder, was now vaguely disc-shaped – after conglomerations of industrial units, private accommodation and the connecting infrastructure had spread out gradually from the cylinder's waist, till eventually subsuming it completely. Spotting an anomaly on the vast structure, Gneiss instructed the satellite to focus in. This revealed, in appalling clarity, a gaping hole in one of the surrounding units. Something had obviously detonated there: either a missile had got through or more likely a shield generator had blown catastrophically. He could now see living quarters standing open to vacuum, and in the surrounding cloud of debris he spotted blankets, furniture, a view screen, and three decompression-bloated bodies, one of them too small to be an adult. A one-man EVA unit was working nearby, equipped with a grab claw

and a vacuum glue gun. The operator was collecting
debris and sticking it together in a conglomerate to be
hauled inside – the quickest way of clearing free-floating
debris that could otherwise become a danger to the station.
This ghoulish mass of detritus contained bodies as well.
After a further moment of close inspection, Gneiss drew
the focus back.

Above the station the menisci of its energy shields
flashed into view intermittently under the impact of
missiles fired by the approaching hilldiggers. Ships
crammed with people were constantly departing from
below the station, while other ships were returning
from the surface of Sudoria. Nevertheless, ensconced in
his office aboard Corisanthe Main, Gneiss could tell by
the numbers he called up that this civilian evacuation
would take months. Hopefully their assessment of Harald's
strategy was correct, and he did not intend the total
destruction of this place but merely to break supply
chains by keeping the station on the defensive.

'*Wildfire* and *Resilience* are bearing down on you
again,' warned Gneiss. 'Clearly, whatever problem caused
Fleet to pull back has now been resolved. We want you
to get as many of your attack craft out as you can, and
while you can. The evacuation will meanwhile have to
cease.'

'"We"?' enquired Glass.

'I am acting commander for the duration of this
emergency, and I require you to get as many of your ships
out of the station as you can. I don't want them trapped
there when they could better serve us out in space.'

In reply Glass merely sent a couple of camera feeds
that now flashed up as icons on Gneiss's screen. As he
connected to them he observed panicked crowds milling

about within the main concourses of Corisanthe III, and a riot breaking out in the storage areas to the rear of the cargo docks.

'We were going to cease the evacuation anyway,' commented Glass. 'As you can see, it's getting out of control down there.'

Gneiss silently eyed the ugly scenes. He could spot station security personnel trying desperately to keep order and medical staff stretchering out the injured. Against the far wall of one storage area rested a stack of bulging body bags. One of them was still open, with a woman kneeling beside it rocking back and forth in grief. There was no sound accompanying these images, and they seemed all the more poignant for that. Gneiss sensed that soon things would be getting even worse: additional shield generators blowing, more areas of the station decompressing, more panic, more body bags.

'Why did they withdraw?' wondered Glass.

'My intelligence is that there was some sort of attack on Admiral Harald,' replied Gneiss. 'My source informed me that he was assassinated, but I rather doubt that since this would all be over now if he had been.'

'Too much to hope for,' Glass said glumly.

'Quite.' After a brief silence between the two men, Gneiss continued coldly, 'Keep me informed of the situation with those ships.' He then moved to put his links to Corisanthe III on hold.

'Wait!' said Glass. 'We're getting something . . . a message laser from the *Resilience*.'

It had to be a surrender demand, Gneiss decided as he observed the image of a young man in a Captain's uniform fill the screen. But this was no Captain he recognized, so perhaps other intelligence received earlier

that told of some sort of reorganization of the command
structure in Fleet was true.

'This is Captain Orvram Davidson calling Corisanthe III. Please respond.'

'Should I respond?' asked Glass.

'Connect him to me, if you would,' Gneiss
instructed.

In the corner of the screen an icon lit to indicate that
the connection had been made. On his own screen, Captain Davidson would now be seeing Gneiss himself.

'This is Director Gneiss, Combine military
command for the duration. What can I do for you,
Captain?'

'I think rather I can do something for you,' said
Davidson hurriedly. 'I have little time over this link, since
it's jury rigged and will soon be detected and shut down.
You need to know that not all of the ships now attacking
Combine are doing so willingly, nor are they still under
the command of their legitimate Captains and crews.
Harald has managed to slave the controls of my own
ship, *Resilience*, to those of the *Wildfire*. *Stormfollower* and
Musket are similarly slaved to *Harvester*. After using false
emergencies to get my people out, he closed the blast
doors on weapons systems and engine galleries and then
opened those areas to vacuum.'

'Do you seriously expect me to believe that you can
do nothing at all?' asked Gneiss.

Davidson winced. 'I sent twenty crew to break through
to the coil-gun breech. Supposedly a flak shell acciden-
tally detonated after they gained access, and I've heard
nothing from them since.'

'You are a soldier, and you must find a solution,' said
Gneiss, without a flicker of emotion.

'Yes, but it is extremely difficult here,' said the Captain. 'Harald has shut down all the lifts and the internal railway, closed spacesuit lockers and shut down EVA vehicles, and strategically opened many intervening areas of the ship to vacuum.'

'What do you expect from us – that we don't fire on you? You must understand that, though I sympathize with your plight, there are over 140,000 non-combatants on board the station you are currently approaching.'

'I understand that perfectly, which is why I am now sending you this.' A package arrived at Gneiss's screen. He opened it and studied the blueprint of a hilldigger, with shield generators and their fields of cover highlighted. All the generators were numbered.

'This is not new information to us,' observed Gneiss.

'It has cost us a further five lives and may yet cost us more,' said Davidson, 'but in two hours' time, as *Resilience* draws close enough to Corisanthe III to employ beam weapons, we will destroy shield generators fourteen, sixteen and twenty. This will allow you to fire on our ship's engines, and on the main reactors feeding the weapons systems – as you can see indicated on the schematic.'

Gneiss could indeed see the targets mentioned. 'We will endeavour not to hit anything else,' he said, knowing that all three targets could result in a chain-reaction detonation.

'And *we* on board will endeavour to survive,' replied Captain Orvram Davidson.

Orduval

The mobile incident station was a massive rectangular vessel half a mile long, bristling with com and scanning gear interspersed with the occasional gun turret or missile launcher. Its flat sides were inset with windows and its partially camouflage-painted hull lay open along the rear corner, with internal joists exposed, for construction had yet to be completed. It came in to land on the Komarl sands, blowing up a storm around it before settling down with a grinding roar. On one of the screens in the control centre, Orduval observed the flat circular feet extending below to crunch down on the sand and adjust the station level. Gazing out of a window he felt sure, even at night, that he recognized this stretch of desert. Wasn't that mount rising over there in the distance his erstwhile home?

'Reyshank has told me you've some important research to conduct. Another book perhaps?' suggested Chairman Duras, ensconced in one of the control chairs, his fingers intertwined over the head of his cane, as it balanced on the floor before him.

Leaning against the window frame, Orduval turned towards him. 'When will that ship with my two sisters arrive?' He nodded towards the sky still lit by the fires from the battle raging above.

'Within the hour, and with the dawn,' Duras replied, with a touch too much poetic drama, Orduval felt.

'You yourself chose the landing site?' he asked.

'Parliament chose it – those of them aboard this vessel. This part of the Komarl lies far enough from the nearest city that any detonation here will have little effect and, should any biologicals be deployed, the prevailing winds blow out into the deep desert. We also have ground installations targeting that ship should it deviate from its predetermined course here. We're probably taking unnecessary precautions.'

'I see.' Orduval paused for a moment, trying to get his thoughts in order. Yes, he needed to talk to Yishna about what had happened aboard Corisanthe Main at the time when he and his siblings had been conceived, but that did not seem quite so important now. 'There will be a better time for me to conduct my . . . research,' he added, in response to Duras's earlier enquiry.

The Chairman nodded. 'Then if you don't want to tell me about that now, perhaps we can fill in our waiting time discussing your previous books.'

'My history of the colonization, you mean?'

'Please don't pretend to be obtuse.'

Orduval grinned. 'I guess you'd like to know about my conclusions on the War?'

Duras studied him intently. 'I would like to know the source of proof that *The Outstretched Hand* went to Brumal with hostile intentions, and how you managed to place that proof on my secure system.'

Orduval gazed out at the night-time desert, and considered the impact of what he must now reveal. No one here knew about Tigger and, by binding agreements, the drone was not supposed to be in the system anyway. However, those who might object most strongly were currently fomenting a civil war, so their protests would seem somewhat irrelevant now.

'Fleet has maintained a strict embargo on Polity technology, but you have to wonder how the Polity found out so much about us in the first place—'

Duras interrupted, 'So the Polity still has something operating here amongst us?'

'Yes, it's a mechanism, an artificial intelligence, which calls itself Tigger. It obtained the proof that our very first physical contact with the Brumallians involved missiles, not handshakes. As Tigger said, "*The Outstretched Hand* held a knife." On the same day as my book was released, Tigger used some stealthy technological means to place that same information on your system.'

'Considering its source, we could question the veracity of such information.'

Orduval turned to him. 'But you won't, because even though you weren't alive at the time, you feel certain that it is true. Those who took us to war profited hugely during those first twenty years, we all know that now, so it is but a small step of logic to surmise that they started the War intentionally.'

'Yes, that's true.' Duras looked tired, and he stared down at the floor, seeming at a loss to add anything else. Really, it did not matter so much now, considering what was going on above. Orduval turned to scan the rest of the control centre. The GDS technicians responsible for bringing the incident unit in to land were now leaving their posts and heading off. A group of delegates from Parliament stood clustered in deep discussion over by the rear doors. As he understood it, Parliament would reconvene in due course, so the Consul Assessor could present the Brumallian's evidence against Fleet. He understood why the residents of Brumal might want this so as to themselves escape the finger of blame, but did not see how it could benefit his own planet, Sudoria, now.

Eventually an officer in the GDS stepped over to join

them. He nodded towards the desert, now growing lighter with the onset of twilight. 'The Brumallian ship is arriving, Chairman.'

'Thank you, Pierce.'

The officer bowed and returned to his controls.

Peering up at the sky, Orduval could see nothing yet. He turned to Duras, who was now struggling to his feet, depending heavily on his cane. 'You'll be going out to meet them now?'

Duras seemed about to reply, then his eyes narrowed as light flared through the windows. Orduval swung round, feeling an immediate frisson of fear. The shape now descending towards the dunes was one he felt must be eternally imprinted on the Sudorian psyche. For this was the shape of the age-old enemy, and here it was descending on their homeworld. Another name for shapes like this was the Tears of Satan in reference to some ancient personification of evil, and indeed the descending ship looked like a giant teardrop, but with landing rockets blazing beneath it. It was the sight of these flames that dispelled any fear in him, because they meant the Brumallians still did not possess gravtech, being obliged to counter gravity so crudely.

'Yes, I'll be going out to meet them,' replied Duras, 'once the area is secure.'

As the rumble of the incoming ship's drives began to reach them, Orduval saw dust clouds being kicked up as balloon-wheeled armoured cars hurtled out towards the ship.

'Along with who else?' he enquired.

'A GDS combat group led by Reyshank, who I trust,' Duras replied. 'Should there be anyone else?'

'Will you board the ship itself?'

'I have requested as much, since I'm curious to see inside one of those things. I never got a chance during the War.'

'I want to go with you.'

'And so you shall.'

Duras gestured with his cane towards the back of the control room, and slowly led the way. Following the Chairman, Orduval checked some of the screens about him and there saw views of launchers swivelling into position, and he picked up snatches of conversation from the crews controlling the weapons: 'Target acquired . . . warhead load prepared . . . Combine link-up confirmed . . . satellite masers . . .'

As they entered the lift and descended, Orduval's stomach churned with a variety of twisted emotions including joy at the prospect of meeting his sisters again. Had they changed much? How would they react to the changes in him? The lift finally shuddered to a halt and revolved to access the opening. They stepped out into the rear of a bay in which some GDS troops were scrambling aboard two balloon-wheeled armoured cars. A door ramp had been lowered onto the desert sand, and distantly the rising sun was etching the horizon distinct from the sky. Reyshank was standing ready by one of the vehicles, and waved them over. Soon the pair were crammed aboard, surrounded by ten heavily armed GDS wardens, and the car lurched out of the bay into the nascent morning. It was far too noisy to speak while travelling, but the journey was thankfully short. Soon the vehicle drew to a halt and the wardens swarmed out onto the sand ahead of them.

Following Duras outside, Orduval gazed around at the perimeter set up by GDS armoured cars, then up at the ship. Perhaps it was the lack of light, but what struck him most about the vessel was not its strange appearance, but the smell. It reminded him of the kind of odours found at the coasts of Sudoria's small briny seas and somewhat of the smell encountered in the cooled underground buildings where Sudorian farmers raised their less heat-tolerant livestock. He knew, at once, that he was in the presence of some immense living creature.

The ship creaked and groaned constantly, but not with the familiar sound of cooling metal. This was more like that heard from a settling woodpile. Orduval could feel heat on his face from the rocket-burned sands, and the occasional waft of smoke blew across. They had advanced to within fifty yards of the ship when, with a liquid crunch, a thirty-foot-wide hemisphere blistered out from the organic hull. A hole appeared at the centre of this extrusion, widening into an entranceway from which spilled out a segmented tongue that after a moment ridged up into steps.

Reyshank and his men reached the steps first, and clambered up inside the ship through a draught of chill air. Without hesitation, Duras entered next, followed closely by Orduval. Within was an oblately spherical chamber, where an interstation shuttle rested bound to one wall with vine-like growths. Here awaited the GDS soldiers, spread out and at their guard, some of them shivering violently. Orduval also felt the extreme cold in here, but noted a breeze against his legs as the cold air from the interior poured out into the desert morning, and glancing up saw a warm fog materializing about the ceiling as the hot desert air slid in.

In the centre of the chamber stood Yishna and

Rhodane. With them were the Polity man McCrooger and two quofarl clad in bulky cooling suits, who stood guard over a prosaic-looking chest. Despite the nervously anticipated presence of his two sisters, Orduval found his attention immediately fixed on McCrooger. The man looked very different indeed from how he had appeared in those early broadcasts from the ship that transported him insystem. Now he was rail-thin, sickly-pale, and hardly able to support his own weight. Obviously he had suffered wounds, judging by the dressings covering his arm and one shoulder. Could the Brumallians have tortured him?

Orduval finally turned his attention to his two siblings. He wanted to go over and greet them, but something about Rhodane checked him and his grin disappeared as suddenly he felt a deep and puzzling distrust of her.

'Would that be the evidence you have brought us?' Duras indicated the chest with a wave of his cane.

'It is,' said McCrooger, stepping forward with an invalid's care.

'Then,' announced Duras, 'after I have taken a look around this ship here, we must take it across to the incident vehicle, where you can present it to Parliament.'

Abruptly the floor juddered, and behind them the hatch shut with a huffing sound. Recovering his balance, Orduval looked up to see that a projection hovered in the air immediately over their heads. It looked familiar, like some kind of animal, though seemed unable to hold its shape for long and kept collapsing formlessly like a blob of mercury floating in zero gravity.

'Orduval, I was wrong,' said a mechanistic voice. Amber eyes blinked within the metallic mass, then faded.

'You caused your own fits . . . to escape . . .' The shape disappeared.

The news hardened something inside Orduval. Into the stunned silence that followed he said, 'That was Tigger telling me . . .' but somehow he could not go on.

Duras turned to gaze at him curiously. 'Telling you what?'

'Telling him how he escaped the grip of the Shadowman,' said David McCrooger. 'And why he is once more in its grip.'

McCrooger

I glanced round at Rhodane and Yishna, and saw that both of them looked slightly ill. Well they might feel so, since their superb intellects were in conflict with something they registered unconsciously but could not allow themselves to *know*. Of course they probably did not feel quite as bad as I did. It seemed to take all my will to prevent my legs from shaking and I felt ready to vomit. I even wondered if I was about to bring up that mutualite I'd swallowed earlier. Also the temperature inside the ship was rising, and though the Sudorians here seemed to be enjoying this and the two quofarl were protected from it, I was sweating heavily. And if that wasn't enough discomfort, there was that continuous weird distortion of my perception, and hints of dark figures lurking at the periphery of my vision.

'Once more in the grip of the Shadowman?' Duras repeated. 'An interesting conjecture.'

'Do *you* dream of the Shadowman?' I asked him. 'Do all of you?' I turned to the soldiers in the room. They all looked slightly unnerved by my question.

'I have nightmares,' admitted Duras, 'which get worse if I don't take my medication. It is a common complaint.'

'Yes, very common, I gather. So many of you are now on medication, aren't you? Or in asylums? You're all drowning so deep in this that you cannot see the surface.' I then wondered if the distortion I was aware of all the time was what they had come to view as normality, the younger of them having grown up with it and the older having lived with it for thirty years.

'What do you mean by that?' Duras huffed.

I held up a hand, but snatched it back down when I noticed it shaking. 'Please, bear with me,' I said, and turned to Yishna. 'Yishna, what exactly is an information fumarole breach?'

'I beg your pardon?'

I didn't reply, since she'd heard me plain enough. As I awaited her reply, she smoothed her hands down her body – something she usually did when aiming to be seductive, but now just a nervous reaction. Realizing this unconscious gesture, she snapped her hands down by her sides. They too were shaking.

'I cannot discuss such critical Combine research so publicly,' she reproached me.

'A fumarole breach is more than just a power surge,' Orduval intervened blandly. 'I know that now. Why else did Fleet ships take the equipment damaged by fumarole breaches and drop it into the sun?'

I glanced at him, saw his thoughtful and pained look. He nodded to me as if he knew where I was going but found it difficult to help me. Turning back to Yishna, I began, 'Let me guess. An information fumarole breach is when, somehow, equipment is infected by informational viruses or by nanotechnology. And you and your three siblings were apparently conceived *during* such a breach.'

There had to be more to it than the coincidental timing – something I didn't know.

Orduval came to my rescue with, 'We were actually conceived inside the Ozark Cylinder in which the breach took place.' So, that was how the Worm's nanotech got to Elsever's womb. I watched Orduval for a moment, hoping he would add something more, but it seemed as if just saying that had required a huge amount of effort, and he now looked utterly weary.

Yishna looked pained, but remained silent.

I went on, 'Perhaps then you can tell me about bleed-over? That's much more in the public domain, and there seems less secrecy about it.'

'Bleed-over is a U-space effect generated by the Worm,' she finally replied.

'And those experiencing bleed-over, what do they feel?'

Almost with gratitude, since it took them away from the other subject, Yishna explained about the feelings of anger and other emotions that had quite possibly resulted in the Exhibitionists and other strange cults developing aboard Corisanthe Main. I waited for her to understand the most obvious implication of what she was telling me, but it seemed to have completely passed her by.

I tried again: 'There's things you need to understand about U-space, Yishna,' I began. 'It requires a huge amount of energy to actually penetrate that continuum but, once there, small amounts of energy to cover huge distances relative to realspace. If bleed-over is a U-space effect generated by the Worm, it could just as easily also be present anywhere within a few light years of here as on

Corisanthe Main itself.' I spread my hands to encompass the group. 'You are *all* suffering from bleed-over. *I* am suffering from bleed-over.'

'I had thought something . . .' Yishna began, then trailed off.

She still wasn't getting it. She, and it seemed all the scientists on Corisanthe Main, had been assiduously measuring and cataloguing bleed-over and fumarole breaches, yet utterly failing to understand what they were. As far as I gathered from the research I had managed to conduct while here in the Sudorian system – mostly through the console Yishna had given me – only the cultish elements of the major station had come close to understanding, with their concept of telepathic inductance.

'What does this all mean?' Duras interrupted.

'It means that you are feeling what the Worm feels, it having been broken into four and held confined for decades. It means that an alien entity utterly incomprehensible to you is attempting to influence you, maybe even manipulate you, and the Shadowman is just one aspect of that influence. Is it any surprise your asylums are so packed?'

Yishna made a sound that seemed to begin as a denial then just trailed away.

'Why is this so important now?' asked Duras, getting right to the point.

I replied, 'Because quite evidently it has increased its influence. Somehow, through an information fumarole breach, it has fashioned four instruments to do its bidding. They are called Yishna, Rhodane, Orduval and Harald.'

'This is preposterous.'

Orduval and Yishna were now each watching me

with the intensity of a cat observing a caged hamster. Rhodane's gaze was less unnerving, just.

'Really?' I said. 'All four of them, as you know, have been functioning well beyond human norms to push themselves into positions of power. Rhodane came near to raising the Brumallians against Sudoria, but for the Consensus interfering with the signal or with her programming.' Duras stood straighter on hearing that, his gaze sliding to Rhodane then to the two quofarl. 'Yishna is now second only to Director Gneiss on Corisanthe Main. Orduval . . .' I paused, having no idea what he had been up to, though he had obviously been in communication with Tigger and he was *here*.

'I tried,' he himself supplied, 'but I could not do very much.'

Duras gave him an irritated look. 'The writer Uskaron did enough,' he said, then turned to me. 'Yes, perhaps you have something, though I've yet to see it clearly.'

Orduval was Uskaron – I wasn't sure how that fit the theory that was even then developing in my mind. For I did not see the Worm's intentions as peaceful, and only by following a twisted logic could his books be contrived as anything like as destructive as what Rhodane had intended to do and what Harald was already doing.

'So Orduval wrote books that changed the whole attitude of a planet,' I said.

Orduval held his hands out to either side. 'Perhaps.'

Yishna and Rhodane stood gazing at their brother with new-found respect.

'There was always something familiar—' began Yishna.

'And then there's Harald,' I interrupted.

'It seems a very convoluted way for the Worm to gain its freedom,' challenged Duras.

I paused before replying, as I wasn't entirely sure that freedom was the motive here. With whatever it had already done to Elsever Strone and her unborn children, I felt it had ably demonstrated how it could break out of containment at will.

I continued, 'You must understand how its influence on all of you is huge, especially on the four children of Elsever Strone. They alone don't dream of the Shadowman – the Worm's attempt to create a human face for itself – and they don't need to, since its control over them is so much more direct.'

'This is all conjecture,' argued Duras, but I could see the fear in his expression.

I turned back to Orduval, looking for more information, some way to convince them. 'What did Tigger tell you originally, about your fits?'

He looked somewhat bitter as he replied. 'He decided that I am sensitive to U-space, and that it was disruptions in the U-space continuum that caused my fits.'

'Yet Tigger changed that argument just now, told you that you caused your own fits to escape.'

'Yes, he did.'

It occurred to me then that his books might also have been a way to escape that pervasive influence – they might have been the antithesis to the Worm's manipulation of him.

'To escape what, though? To escape the influence of the Worm, the control it held over you through U-space, control that it is reasserting now, as is evident from your current reaction to Rhodane who is mostly free of it. It's a similar reaction I observed in Yishna once she boarded this ship. You see, it made you, and it made you all more able to receive its signal.'

At this point Yishna muttered some curse, and we all turned towards her. Her eyes were closed tight and her hands trembling.

'He's right,' she said, then paused with her mouth still moving but nothing coming out. Then she shook herself, perhaps trying to break the words free. 'The . . . Ozark Protocols.'

'Tell me, Yishna,' I said.

'I altered them. In some cases they originally called for the destruction of the Worm, so I changed that to . . . survival. It wants to survive.' She gasped, and now subsided to her knees. Rhodane immediately squatted down beside her and placed a comforting hand on her shoulder. Orduval moved over too and stood staring down at them, his hands clenching and unclenching spasmodically.

'You have all, for a long time, carried that worm in your heads,' I told them. 'You need to be rid of it.' I focused now on Duras. 'It is not the Worm that needs its freedom, but all of you need to be liberated from it.'

'You may well be correct there,' said Duras, 'but you may have noticed that we are in the middle of a war.'

'Let me put it another way,' I said. 'If you can remove the Worm from Harald's head, there will be no more war.'

Harald

Carnasus had ordered his old Admiral's chair moved up into his Haven just after the end of the War – an action then filled with significance. Harald's guards were even now bringing the chair back down to place it in its former central position on the Bridge. He wondered how many around him understood the significance of that move, since most of them, like himself, had been children when the chair was originally moved. Around the spot where the chair would be relocated, technicians were connecting up the new screens Harald had ordered. Waiting until the chair was finally in position and the legs bolted down, he walked over, placed his hand on the old cracked hide of the seat back, then opened his com helmet to general address.

'If I could have your attention please, this is Admiral Harald,' he began.

Everyone on the Bridge turned towards him. On the single image showing in his eye-screen he observed the crew down in Engineering also pausing in their tasks to glance up at the public address screen. Testing a link to one of the larger screens arrayed before him, he called up an image from one of the ship's refectories, and saw the crew gazing up from their hurried meals. He felt a moment's trepidation, but before his head injury he had worked out the wording of the short speech, so it had to be right, didn't it?

'Those of you who know any history will perhaps understand that fifty years ago Corisanthe was merely the name of a small desert town, until one of the residents built the core station that eventually developed into the ones we know today.'

Probably everyone did know that fact, as it had been regularly covered in the main history curriculum in most schools since the War.

'Back then,' he continued, 'just about everything in orbit around Sudoria came under Fleet jurisdiction – a security requirement necessary during our war against Brumal. Then thirty years ago Fleet encountered the Worm and, believing it to be some new weapon controlled by the Brumallians, they attacked it and managed to break it into four segments which in turn contracted down to those items currently held aboard the station we are now approaching. Fleet used a converted troop transport to get these four pieces to the original Corisanthe Station, where they were secured in four containment canisters, then the outer enclosing cylinders were swiftly constructed around them.'

He gazed about him, checking that he still had everyone's attention.

'While this process was ongoing, over two thousand *civilian*' – he placed a sneering emphasis on the word – 'scientists were brought up to study the Worm, and significant technological advances resulted from their research. These advances enabled us to win the war against the Frazerworldlers, so we can never begrudge them that. However, in the later stages of the war, this scientific population of the Corisanthe Station frequently came into conflict with Fleet, raising petty objections to our security protocols, when not squabbling amongst themselves. So immersed were they in the importance of their research, they seemed to forget about those fighting and dying at the front.'

Harald slowly paced in a circle round the chair, called up some more screen views, and continued.

'As the scientific community grew, the demand for extra space resulted in the division of the original station into three. Shortly after the War, many of the discoveries they had made were allowed into the public domain, and this resulted in a sudden growth in high-tech industries, whose management in turn began to finance that ongoing research. Fleet authority was thus gradually being displaced until Parliament, in its wisdom, decided to take away what remained of such authority and hand it over to a consortium of industrial companies who in themselves had by then become a political force and whose representatives made up a substantial portion of Parliament. These companies went on to build ever more satellites and stations, then in time amalgamated to become the entity we now know as Orbital Combine.'

He paused again to consider the emphasis of his next words.

'This division of our strength was foolish in itself, but even more so when it seemed evident we might face threats from beyond the Sudorian system. It had to be tolerated, however, since it arose by democratic means. But those who acquire power tend to scrabble for more, and so we have seen Combine building its Defence Platforms and ships as it prepared to usurp Fleet's former position as sole protector of Sudoria. And now Combine has moved directly against us and, for the good of the Sudorian people, we must bring that organization's power to an end.'

Many impassive expressions from those keeping their own counsel, and rather less nodding in agreement. Harald felt sweat trickling down from his forehead. Would they obey him? Could he trust them to obey him?

'We have the means to do so,' he confirmed. 'It must

always be remembered that it is the Worm that raised Combine to power, and the Worm still remains the central basis of that power. Remove control of the Worm from that amalgamation of companies known as Orbital Combine, and you remove what binds them together. Then Combine will assuredly fall apart.'

Harald slipped on the control glove that had been hanging at his belt.

'I require only one thing of all of you: that you do your duty, as you have always done and always will, on behalf of the Sudorian people.'

Stepping back he seated himself in the former Admiral's old chair. Within the Bridge itself, hands drummed on consoles, and there arose a murmur of approval. This same busy but muted applause occurred throughout the ship. Harald felt that their reaction was nowhere near enough, and decided then that he must consolidate his power further – but not right now.

The speech had sapped his strength and a nugget of pain was growing inside his skull. He quickly shut down general address, then double-checked to be sure his image no longer appeared on any screens throughout the ship. Quickly he slipped a painkilling capsule into his mouth and, as it dissolved, he removed the paired syringes from a belt pouch and carefully injected the combined drugs that Jeon had provided earlier. His weariness began to disperse, but the pain in his head increased – probably exacerbated by the stimulant. A bewildering surge of anger hit him, and he sat for a while with his eyes closed, his fingers digging into the chair arms. Slowly, the pain began to subside, dragging the strange anger away with it. Opening his eyes, he realized he could not afford too many more lapses like this over the coming hours.

Calling up new images on the screens before him, Harald confirmed that the ships were ready to move in closer to Sudoria. Defence Platform Two still hung tilted in vacuum, a gaping hole in its side with what looked like an oxygen fire raging inside it. Its shields were failing and below it he could see an inter-station shuttle departing. They were now evacuating. Before speaking, Harald worked some saliva into his dry mouth.

'Soderstrom, ignore the support ships now,' Harald instructed. 'Concentrate all fire from your own ship and from *Stormfollower* and *Musket* on the platform itself. I want it completely out of commission within the next half-hour.'

Those three ships, holding a V formation above the stricken Defence Platform, with Soderstrom's *Harvester* at point, showed no sign that their firing pattern had changed, but now only the shields directly above Platform Two flashed in and out of visibility, and the attendant supply ships were left unharried to make their escape towards Platform Three. Harald then switched to a more distant view, transmitted from one of the many camera satellites Fleet had deployed. Now that he had acquired more data, on that original view he overlaid a schematic of the projected reach of the shields and weapons on the remaining platforms. As he had supposed, knocking out three platforms gave him a nearly clear run down to atmosphere below the platforms, where few weapons and shields were directed. Of course taking a hilldigger down into atmosphere was fraught with its own problems. As far as he recollected it had only been done twice, and then only into the thin upper reaches of Brumal's exosphere, whereas here it would be necessary for them to go down nearly as far as Sudoria's thermosphere – almost fifty miles deeper.

Beside *Ironfist*, the hilldigger *Desert Wind* held station as before.

'Are you ready, Franorl?'

'I'm ready, and I'm bored with waiting if you really want to know. How are you feeling, by the way?'

How am I? Harald was functioning quite ably but could no longer feel any lasting emotional engagement with what he was doing. In fact the only emotions he seemed to be experiencing were those sudden strange surges of anger. Also, the pain in his skull seemed to be just waiting to expand with joyous abandon.

'I am still alive, which certainly wasn't someone's intention,' he replied.

'I was advised that your injuries were severe, else I would not have pulled the fleet back,' Franorl explained.

Harald expected the Captain to have received an eyewitness account of the attack on him, and his injuries, since he maintained spies amidst Harald's staff. The man was a climber and warranted close scrutiny. Harald was beginning to feel that he had trusted Franorl, and some others, too readily. Only Jeon herself truly knew how serious Harald's injury had been and how close he had come to death, and he did not intend to make that knowledge available to any of those he distrusted.

'Merely a concussion, from which I have recovered well,' he replied. 'Now, observe Platform Two.'

The shields above the platform were now constantly lit up and in motion. A shimmer in space above them, almost like a heat haze shot through with flashes of green-ish light, showed that *Harvester* and the two ships slaved to it were currently using their beam weapons. On the platform itself pinpoints of fire flared brightly wherever shield generators began burning out. Then small, relatively cool explosions began to ignite outwards from the shields. The attackers were now launching atomics which the Defence Platform's beam weapons were intercepting and vaporizing. The constant shifting of shields was an attempt by those in the station to cover lost ones, but the bombardment was becoming too much, and eventually projectiles began to get through. And only one was ultimately required.

A sun-bright explosion blanked all the instruments for a couple of seconds. When they finally came back online, the platform was flying apart on the periphery of a fireball. The ball deformed, elongated as gravity dragged it down, began to disperse higher up so it took on the shape almost of a flowering cactus. Debris streaked down into the atmosphere, burning up. A chunk of something looking like a burning tram carriage tumbled past Harald's immediate viewpoint.

'*Now*, Franorl, we begin our run,' said Harald. Then he spoke, over general address to his Bridge crew. 'Begin descent into atmosphere. Main engines at half power until we hit the exosphere, then one-eighth drive and steering thrusters only. Firing Control, I want you to use defensive fire only until we are below the level of the platforms.' It was not necessary for him to issue that order out loud, since the crew had already received the attack plans, but he felt this crucial moment demanded his vocal reinforcement. Now contacting the Captain of *Harvester*, while observing that ship and its two slaves on-screen, he ordered, 'Soderstrom, move into position over Corisanthe II, and remind them there just what hilldiggers can do. I don't want to see a single supply ship leaving that station intact.'

Around him, *Ironfist* rumbled as its main drive ignited. After a moment he observed flares of light from the formation of the three other ships as their drives started up too. Then followed a detonation in the engine section of one of the rear two vessels, tipping it up and spewing debris out into vacuum.

'Soderstrom, what was that?' he enquired coolly.

After a short delay Soderstrom appeared in Harald's eye-screen. 'An explosion in *Stormfollower*'s engine galleries. Understandably, Tlaster Cobe isn't speaking to me.'

Harald opened some connections to *Stormfollower*, and his view into the stricken ship's Bridge showed it to be partially abandoned, though the Captain still stood there surveying the Firing Control screens. Then, attempting to link to cameras in the engine galleries, Harald found they were all blanked out, which could be due to either the explosion or to sabotage. He began running checks through the entire vessel and soon found what had happened. From a camera forward of the galleries, he observed a party of three crewmen in spacesuits moving through a section he had opened to vacuum on seizing control of this same ship.

'Soderstrom,' he snapped, an ugly suspicion rooting itself in his mind, 'that ship was slaved to yours. So you knew precisely what to watch out for.'

'With the greatest respect, Admiral Harald, running one hilldigger during a battle is enough of a chore. Attempting to also control two others whose crews are out to thwart you is no easy task.'

Harald made a comlink through to the Bridge of

Stormfollower. 'Captain Cobe, I see that you have managed to cripple your own ship.'

The Captain looked up directly into the Bridge camera. In a timeless gesture he held up his fist and extended his mid finger, then returned his attention to his screens. Gazing at his own screens Harald observed that *Harvester* and *Musket* were parting company with *Stormfollower.* He also observed that Soderstrom was running a security check on *Musket,* and as yet had found no attempts at sabotage. The sudden violent surge of anger he felt caught him off guard. Desperately trying to control it, he found himself panting and tightly gripping his chair arms. But the feeling would not go away, and in the end there seemed only one way to assuage it: he must sacrifice something to his rage. On making that decision he felt some degree of control return, so he linked in again to the systems of *Stormfollower,* then struggled with a quartered eye-screen as he programmed in the alterations he had to make. After a moment he observed the blue-red flames of the steering thrusters igniting down one side of the crippled hilldigger. Finally he spoke to the Bridge of that ship again – and to *Musket* too, so the Captain there might know the cost of rebellion.

'Captain Cobe,' he began, with gritted teeth. When the Captain did not look up, Harald continued. 'If you check your navigation control, you will see that I have input a program to your steering thrusters. They will sufficiently change your trajectory to take you down towards Sudoria. If Combine does not destroy you first, you will enter atmosphere in eight hours' time and begin to burn up. What remains of you and your ship should impact the Brak sea only a little while after that.' Cobe looked up at last. 'Harald, out.'

17

The downsizing of Fleet after the War and the almost explosive growth of Orbital Combine has caused a power shift in Sudorian politics. But a hundred years of dominance and tradition is not something easy to put aside. For all this time the social and economic system of Sudoria had been a support industry for Fleet, and at the end of the War almost one-third of Sudorians were either serving in Fleet itself or working in the orbital war industries. Fleet began to lose its grip on power when Corisanthe Main was essentially removed from its control by Parliament and new high-tech industries began to burgeon from there. Fleet's grip was further loosened by the simple fact that people were tired of war, and rather liked the idea of making some money and better lives for themselves. Conscription continued, but since the Brumallians had been bombed into near oblivion, few saw any further point in it, and meanwhile GDS became disinclined to hunt down draft dodgers. Fleet power has therefore been on the wane for some time, but the people of Sudoria must remain forever vigilant. Like some big beast in its death throes, Fleet might strike out again and, with the hilldiggers still under its control, its last bite might kill us all. Though the very idea of civil war

*was unthinkable twenty years ago, now it is a very real
possibility.*

– Uskaron

Director Gneiss

He observed *Stormfollower* first hanging crippled in
space, then being sent on a new trajectory by its steering
thrusters. The injured ship would pass close to Defence
Platform Seven, which he felt would only need to keep
its shields up as a precaution, since it struck him as
unlikely that it was a target. However, Harald might still
have control of *Stormfollower*'s weapons, so should Combine send rescue craft to intercept it? It seemed obvious
that Tlaster Cobe had taken a similar route to the one
Orvram Davidson intended to take. Gneiss wondered if
the latter Captain might have changed his mind now.
Perhaps not, for the nature of his sabotage was subtle and
might not even be found out.

The other two hilldiggers, *Harvester* and *Musket*,
were now pounding away at Corisanthe II, whilst *Wildfire*
and *Resilience* were together hitting Corisanthe III.
Gneiss had warned Glass to keep sufficient weapons free
for the moment those three shield generators on
Resilience went down. Taking one ship out of play there
would give some relief to Glass's station, though it still
remained in danger of being destroyed.

The Director now turned his attention to *Ironfist* and
Desert Wind. Both ships were rapidly heading down into
the gap Fleet had created, and Gneiss contemplated the
loose thread that could completely unravel Combine's
defences, for putting those two vessels below the level
of the platforms would take them out of the firing arc of

Combine's big guns. From there Harald would be able to steadily work his way around the planet, obliterating every Defence Platform and perhaps much of Combine's industrial base and infrastructure as well. Of course it would not come to that, because at some point wavering members of the Oversight Committee would be contemplating the destruction of everything they had helped build and authorize the deployment of gravtech weapons, despite collateral damage caused to the planet below. Gneiss naturally would then vote against the committee majority.

When hungry I deny it, when thirsty I don't drink. All the pressure forcing me to do what I must do, I counter, and so at last manage to remain me.

He closed his eyes for a moment and rubbed at his temples. Did he want Fleet to wipe out all the Defence Platforms and knock Orbital Combine from its place in the sky? Did he so abhor that stagnation to which Dalepan had referred while drugged out of his mind that he was prepared to countenance the destruction of Combine to end it? With robotic precision he had always carried out his duties as they were considered appropriate by Oversight. He did not stint in that respect, yet at his core he felt almost despair at the prospect of his own organization repelling Fleet – and as a consequence his own situation here remaining unchanged. It was a dilemma he could not resolve – one that had held him in stasis ever since that time in Ozark One when he had first felt that other *will*. He gazed at his screens, trying to find some way out without losing himself. A contact icon lit, and he automatically opened it.

'I've received a rather strange message from one of Chairman Duras's staff,' said Dalepan, who was gazing out at him with an expression twisted by some strange emotion.

'And the message is?'

'Apparently Parliament has reviewed the evidence from Brumal and found it sufficient to implicate Fleet in abuse of power. In the eyes of Parliament, we are now the innocent parties in this dispute.'

'That is so gratifying to know. I'll try to remember it when I find myself attempting to breathe vacuum.' He paused, assessing. 'But I have yet to hear any *strange* message.'

'Apparently the Chairman now wishes this Brumallian evidence to be presented to the Oversight Committee. He wants that Brumallian ship to come up here and deliver it to us. His tone was all rather low-key, as if he hoped the whole business would be approved without much notice.'

Curious. Gneiss leaned back in his chair. In the midst of a struggle where such evidence now mattered not one wit, the Chairman wanted it brought *here*.

'Inform them that if the Brumallian ship approaches this station without permission – and it does not have my permission – it will be destroyed. Then I want you to contact the Chairman for me. Inform me at once when you have arranged that.'

His response was precisely what it should be, yet he knew that even in the midst of the distractions of battle he *wanted* the Chairman to give him sufficient reason to allow that ship to come here.

Something to stir the waters?

The Chairman must have been ready waiting, for after only a moment Dalepan looked up. 'I have him for you.' The screen blanked for a second, then Chairman Duras appeared.

'What can I do for you, Director Gneiss?' he enquired.

'You could explain why, right in the midst of a battle, you feel it so necessary to get evidence to us of Fleet's complicity in recent events.'

'As Chairman, I need only make my explanations to Parliament,' Duras replied primly. 'You previously assured me that Orbital Combine bows to the will of Parliament.'

Almost automatically, Gneiss shot back, 'Is it genuinely the will of Parliament for a Brumallian ship to bring this evidence here?'

'Parliament agrees that this evidence should be presented to you as soon as conveniently possible.'

'Sending such a ship here now would be most inconvenient. I am not inclined, whilst we fight for our lives here, to have any Brumallians aboard this station.' Gneiss felt a sinking sensation as he realized he did indeed possess the power to deny the Chairman's request

'But no Brumallians as such will be joining you there.' Duras smiled tightly. 'Those who will take the evidence aboard Corisanthe Main are your own employee Yishna, her siblings Orduval and Rhodane, and the Polity Consul Assessor. I believe that Combine Oversight has shown itself anxious to discuss some matters with David McCrooger?'

'Yes, you're quite right.' Only one valid objection remained. 'However, there are many security matters to consider, the foremost being that in our present situation we cannot safely allow a Brumallian ship to dock here.'

'It will not be necessary for it to dock. Yishna's inter-station shuttle is aboard it.'

Gneiss paused, a feeling of excitement, almost joy, suffusing him. 'Then in that case I must accede to the will of Parliament. Send us your evidence. Send us the ship.'

'Always a pleasure,' said Duras, giving a token bow before he signed off.

'Dalepan, tell me immediately that ship launches.'

'It has already launched,' the OCT replied. 'Yishna will be here within the hour.'

Gneiss sat back and absorbed that news. Within the hour three of the four children of Elsever Strone would be here aboard this station.

I knew your mother, you know.

Gneiss remembered gazing across at the brilliant child Yishna Strone and wondering just how he could have uttered those words so casually. Elsever herself had been brilliant, beautiful, and Oberon Gneiss had loved her from the first moment he saw her, while she had reciprocated with a tolerant affection and often outrageous flirting. At that time occupying the position of Military Director of the civilian contingent, under the oversight of Fleet Command, Gneiss knew he had to be very careful how he related to other station staff. But when it seemed Elsever was getting bored with their never-quite-consummated liaison, he knew he had to do something.

He put down his next actions to a kind of madness that seemed to be growing throughout the station at that time, and which now expressed itself in the strange cults and factions that had evolved up here. Here aboard Corisanthe Main they had seemed disconnected from the War, a separate enclave where the rules just did not apply. So he had responded to her flirting, dined with her in one of the military refectories, then invited her back to his cabin. They had talked about their precious charge and about the studies that were being conducted on it. Taking a risk for the first time since his childhood, Gneiss accepted drinks from the bottle of station-distilled alcohol she had brought along with her. They had ended up in bed.

The sex had been . . . difficult at first, and his gratitude to Elsever – for never pointing out her undoubted knowledge of his virginity before their encounter – only increased his love of her. As their relationship progressed, a deeper madness seemed to infect him, and he revealed to her things he had never revealed to anyone else. They spent hours in his cabin talking, drinking, making love. Then one day he took her to his office and showed her his biggest secret of all. Before being made Director of the civilian contingent, he had been Military Director during that period when the Ozark Cylinders were being built. It being within his power, he had ordered private access to one cylinder to be built for him. He showed her, took her down in his lift to Ozark One where, in zero gravity, they stripped naked but for their breathing masks and had sex. As if the Worm had been waiting for the opportunity, it caused a fumarole breach precisely at that time.

'It touched me!' she had screamed.

He felt the horror, for it had touched him too. Yet, the ensuing physical examinations showed nothing, and subsequent tests revealed but one change: Elsever Strone was pregnant. Something changed utterly then: Elsever drifted away from him, and seemed to fold herself around the process of gestation. Whenever he saw her, she always looked frightened but seemed as unable to communicate the reasons behind this, just as he seemed unable to communicate his disturbing feelings to her. Then, after the birth, came her suicide. With relentless exactitude, Gneiss relocated all the personnel who had been involved in the tests and the investigation. Then, over a period of years, he changed the records: lost those bits about him and her being naked in Ozark One without escort, also lost most references to himself.

It had touched her.

She had known what it had done, and somehow that had been too much to bear. That she used the explosive to destroy her body might be due to shame – perhaps she didn't want anyone to know what it had done to her. He sometimes wondered if maybe *it* had not wanted anyone knowing what had been done to her.

Yes, Yishna, I knew your mother, because I am your father – at least in part.

Gneiss returned to his consoles, and to his duty.

McCrooger

Acceleration placed a heavy boot on my chest and crushed me down into the living mattress of the couch. I felt something pop in my lungs and coughed salty fluid into my mouth, but didn't bother to check if it was blood. I lay there labouring for each breath and wondering if I should just stop breathing and let IF21 and the mutualite take over and do all the work. I didn't, however, because that seemed just too much like giving up. Finally the foot came off my chest and I became weightless. Quickly pushing myself across the room, I forced open a container – something like a clam extruded from the wall – and removed items from inside it. The gun Duras had given me went underneath my foamite shirt, and spare ammunition clips went into various pockets. Hopefully I would have no use for the weapon. I then turned and pushed off towards the exit from the room. While in mid-air I heard a vicious *smack*, then a sound like hail hitting a tin roof, and knew we were once again approaching the orbital battle lines.

Reaching the sphincter door I heaved my way through it. In the corridor beyond I saw Rhodane and Yishna, obviously having come from their acceleration couches, circling each other like wary hounds. Though Rhodane claimed to be just about clear of the Worm's influence, I wondered if she was being entirely candid. If that could be true of any of us.

'How long until we reach Corisanthe Main?' I asked, just to try and break their focus upon each other, and not because I particularly wanted to know. I could already feel the damned place looming, and the perception-distorting effects within the ship had not so much intensified as taken on a weird symbolic meaning.

Rhodane turned towards me. 'We'll be in low orbit within an hour, then we must take Yishna's vessel to shuttle us across – though Director Gneiss has agreed for us to come, he will not allow a Brumallian ship to dock with the station.'

'You think he bought it, completely?' I wondered.

It was Yishna's turn to reply. 'He would be a fool to believe our only purpose is to bring along that evidence. I think he let us come because he is curious about *you*.' She paused for a moment, her gaze twitching back towards Rhodane. 'Director Gneiss follows the rules, but for his very own reasons.'

Rhodane grimaced, shook herself, then began propelling herself along the corridor. Orduval joined us on the way, and soon we reached the large chamber where Yishna's craft awaited. Slog and Flog were waiting there too, the evidence chest hanging in the air between them. They looked agitated, knowing what we were going to do next, but unable to come with us. At least they weren't suited up for Sudorian temperatures, so it looked like they had grudgingly accepted the Director's order.

I considered what we were about to embark upon. Yishna's alteration of the Emergency Ozark Protocols would result in all the cylinders being ejected even if there was a breach in only one of them. The fact that all four would be ejected simultaneously demonstrated even more how powerfully she had been manipulated than just the fact of her altering the protocols at all. To me this indicated that the Worm realized that once any single one of those protocols was used, it would be in danger, so that was then time for it to leave, all four parts of it together.

While Yishna opened the shuttle's hatch I gripped hold of a glassy handle protruding from one wall and pulled the pendant from my shirt. It had changed now, taking on again the form of a tiger, but one made of wax that had been placed too close to a fire.

'Tigger,' I said, 'are you able to reply?'

Momentarily something shimmered in the air, then blinked out.

'Tigger, if we succeed, the cylinders will be beyond the station shields within twenty minutes. It should then be evident which canister has been breached. You need to hit that one first, and the rest of them after. Only total destruction of that creature will break its grip on these people.'

'I . . .' again that flickering in mid-air, followed by the brief appearance of two amber eyes '. . . can do this.'

It wasn't really enough. I pushed myself away from the wall and down to where Rhodane and Orduval were conversing in subdued tones. At my approach, Rhodane smilingly reached out to briefly rest her hand against the side of Orduval's face, before she turned to face me.

'Still not enough of a response from Tigger,' I stated flatly.

She nodded agreement. 'Enabling a ship to feel pain was considered, by consensus, to be an incentive, since it prevented the ships making decisions without first considering all the repercussions. I would have thought Polity AIs able to handle pain.'

I shook my head. After my few recent intermittent communications with Tigger, I'd learnt exactly what had happened. 'It's not the pain, but the repetition of it Tigger is having trouble breaking out of. The two AIs are interlinked, and that's causing a feedback loop.'

'I will have to remain behind,' Rhodane glanced at Yishna, 'though I would rather have come with you, just to make sure. Yishna understands what needs to be done, but I wonder if the Worm may understand what she is doing and somehow intervene?'

It would have been nice if, after having things carefully explained to them, the Brumallian crew could be relied upon to do what needed to be done from this end, but they weren't in full consensus – being understandably reluctant to fire upon Combine – so it wouldn't get done without one wilful half-Brumallian to remain behind and push them towards the consensus we required. It had only been her input into the small consensus aboard the ship that had enabled us to bring it up here in the first place.

'Can you be sure you'll be able to fire those weapons when the time comes?' I asked. 'The crew seems to be still having trouble with the ship's controls.'

'Your drone's melding with this ship's AI caused that. I'll be able to get round it so long as neither AI chooses to interfere.'

'They won't,' I said, with more certainty than I felt.

Orduval and Yishna – after a rather silly tug-of-war, followed by Rhodane's intervention – managed to take the chest away from Flog and Slog and convey it over to the hatch. They climbed inside with it, and I followed. The two of them took the main seats, while I strapped myself into one of the two fold-down passenger seats right behind them. A scraping and rattling ensued and beyond the front screen I observed the vine-like growths that held the vessel in place parting and sliding away. Within the shuttle the temperature, already higher than in the Brumallian ship, began to rise. My two companions shed their jackets, but I was wearing little I could remove. I soon began sweating and wondered if I could stand yet another temperature change, since down there on the planet I'd come close to fainting, and once back on the Brumallian ship again had begun shivering and even noticed my hands turning a nice shade of frosty white.

'The bay is now clear,' came Rhodane's voice, from the console immediately in front of Yishna, whereupon she and Orduval strapped themselves in. After a moment there came a roaring, and I could see bits of organic detritus blowing past the screen. Then the craft tilted and was soon tumbling out into vacuum. Thrusters corrected attitude; a steady increase in acceleration pushed me back against the bulkhead. Were we all just being used as puppets, seemingly unable to comprehend our minimal chances of success? IF21 shifted violently inside me. I coughed, spat blood, and held on tight.

Some time later Yishna said, 'Here comes our escort.' I glimpsed the flare of steering thrusters, their light bursting over the screen, followed by some kind of globular craft swinging past, then descending out of sight. Shortly afterwards the immense station Cori-santhe Main ascended into view and grew ever larger. Now I had seen ships in the Polity that were larger than that station, but this thing hung in my perception with a mass that seemed to extend beyond the skin of reality. I knew that, like the mass of a planet distorting spacetime about it to extend its influence well beyond, this huge station sat at the heart of those perceptual distortions that influenced the minds of all Sudorians. Eventually we flew past one of the Ozark Cylinders, and I felt a shiver of apprehension while gazing at that featureless tube.

'We'll have to move fast once we're in,' said Yishna. 'I'll lead the way up to Centre Cross. The automatics should register the presence of three of us here aboard, as required, but after that there'll still be more security to get through.'

'You are sure you can do this?' asked Orduval, turning to inspect her closely.

She returned his gaze, her expression bland, her emotions rigidly under control. 'There are only two people in the Sudorian system who could penetrate that security.'

Ah, you yourself – and Harald.

'That's not what I asked,' said Orduval.

'I can do it,' Yishna replied, her expression now

twisted into an amalgam of pain and anger. 'I've been a puppet all my life, and today that ends.' She returned her attention to the screen.

We slid into a narrow bay, where I could see machined parts moving like the internal components of some engine, and hear automatic clamping systems crashing all around us. The sickening lurch of artificial gravity dragged me down, and it felt as if something might be tearing loose below my breastbone. Something else clonked to one side and I heard the explosive roar of air entering an evacuated space – an airlock had attached. I unstrapped and moved back into the small rear cargo space, where the evidence chest lay secured beside some other large object underneath a concealing tarpaulin. Where one corner of this covering had been pushed aside I observed whorled metal studded with crystalline dots like sensor heads, and guessed this was the same object Yishna had so nearly detonated aboard the Brumallian ship.

Stepping out behind me Yishna and Orduval picked up the chest, while I opened the craft's hatch and heaved myself out into a segmented airlock tube that expanded in girth to meet a door larger than the hatch I'd just departed. The controls were simple enough – I'd seen the same on the Fleet ship that originally brought me into this system. I opened it and stepped through.

'Welcome, Consul Assessor,' said the individual standing before me.

I gave him a short bow and said, 'Thank you for allowing me to come.'

He was wearing a spacesuit, though with the helmet off and fixed to his belt. So were the two guards standing behind him, but with disc carbines slung in front of them. The primitive utile area we were in smelt of machine oil and hot electronics, and seemed to be used generally as a store for boxes of spare parts – some of them with the lids hinged back to reveal their foamite-wrapped contents. The area was missing a wall on one side and it was possible to see into part of the station's structure, and from there emerged a constant whining and thumping of hydraulics, the metronomic booming of weapons fire, a cacophony of voices, and the familiar grumbling of engines and generators. I scanned up, looking for cameras, but spotted none. I had to wait on Yishna, for she would decide where exactly we must make our first move. I privately wondered if she could manage even that.

'Dalepan,' Yishna acknowledged the man.

'Yishna,' he responded, then to us all, 'I hope you will understand that, under present circumstances, there are certain security procedures I must strictly adhere to?'

'Why, is there a problem?' Yishna quipped.

'Consul Assessor, please excuse this.' Dalepan waved one of the guards forward.

I extended my arms sideways. 'I have a weapon here.' I nodded down. 'No security breach was intended – it was a gift from Chairman Duras.'

The guard halted for a moment, and eyed me, then turned back to Dalepan for guidance. Dalepan nodded once and the guard came forward to search me, relieving me of the weapon I had mentioned. Next he searched Yishna and Orduval, but found nothing at all on them.

'Now the chest,' said Dalepan.

Yishna frowned, then after a moment's hesitation she squatted down beside our ostensible reason for being here. 'You'll understand that this chest contains sensitive information.'

Here, then.

From her control baton she sent the code to the lock, while one guard stood watchfully over her. As the lid popped she immediately reached inside. It was smoothly done. The stun-bead shotgun she pulled out had a wide matt-black barrel, and it made a sound like a hammer hitting a lead sheet. The first guard flew up off his feet and hit the rear airlock door. Standing up, she fired twice more, flinging down the other guard, and then Dalepan. She gazed at him for a long moment as impact anaesthetic beads rattled and rolled about the floor, then she shook herself as if the sight had momentarily hypnotized her.

'Okay.' She stooped and removed from the chest a small knapsack that she slung over one shoulder, then shoved the shotgun back into the chest and closed the lid. 'Let's get moving.'

Orduval went over to check the three downed men.

'They're fine,' he said. 'In the asylum I saw some of the more violent patients being knocked unconscious by these. They'll be out for an hour or so, and if they're lucky they won't suffer concussion.'

Yishna dragged the first guard away from blocking the door, opened it and stepped through. I retrieved my automatic – put it down to a sentimental attachment – and followed her, with Orduval at my heel. We moved on along a wide corridor, encountered a group of personnel moving a lev-pad loaded with munitions, passed open doors through which we could see other staff working on some kind of generator.

'Where are your suits?' someone shouted after us.

'We've only just got here,' Yishna replied, turning.

'Yishna Strone,' said another, then peered at me curiously. 'Would you like me to fetch you some suits?'

'No need,' replied Yishna, hurrying on.

We entered another of those curious revolving lifts the Sudorians seemed so fond of and, copying Yishna, I strapped myself down in one of the four seats of the buggy. When we were all in place, it ascended at what to me felt to be about two gravities. I was slick with sweat once the buggy halted and, even though our arrival point was nil gee, I experienced problems propelling myself after the other two.

Centre Cross was impressive, pretty similar to the interior construction of one of our larger Polity ships. I could see people at work in large cabin-like structures poised at the end of multiple jointed cranes. Cables snaked everywhere and equipment was scattered all about. Yishna pointed out one of four caged shafts leading up from the lift nexus to one of the four quadrants of the station, where presumably lay the entrance to one of the cylinders.

'Let me go first.' Orduval led the way into this caged tube.

Yishna eyed me. 'Can you manage this?'

'I'd best go ahead of you.'

She waved me on distractedly while opening her knapsack and checking its contents. Inside I knew there was some computer hardware, a selection of cables and the Sudorian equivalent of a limpet mine. As I began pulling myself up after Orduval, I found it increasingly difficult to breathe, as if I was pulling myself through a hundred-per-cent-humidity jungle. Luckily, once moving, I needed to make only a few corrections to my course.

I decided then I would slow myself very carefully near the end, since my brittle bones might not withstand an abrupt impact.

'Faster!' Yishna suddenly shouted from behind me.

Orduval accelerated, but then came a vicious smacking and clattering sound from ahead of him, pieces of metal spanging off the cage tube, sparks scattering through the air and fizzing out like welding spatters. He grabbed a nearby bar and jerked himself to a halt. I clipped him in passing and myself entered the impact zone, somehow passing through it unscathed. The firing ceased and Orduval then Yishna quickly propelled themselves after me. Glancing up I saw armed figures in spacesuits descending towards us. We had reached the airlock door leading into the cylinder, where Yishna first input a code using her baton, then abruptly used some other tool to lever up the panel over the electrical locking mechanism.

'Move back from the door!' bellowed an amplified voice.

From her knapsack Yishna removed a box and a coil of cable, plugged one end of the cable into the box and the other end into something behind the panel. After a moment she cursed, then scrabbled in her knapsack for something else. A fusillade of disc-gun missiles crackled against the bulkhead to our right and left, scarring metal and hitting us with splinters that hurt like the grit flung from a shattered grindstone.

'This is your last warning!' the voice bellowed again. 'Move back from the door!'

'I've got it!' said Yishna, in triumph.

As the door began opening, it seemed the marksmen could hold off no longer. The racket was horrible, vicious.

Sparks and coils of metal zinged through the air all around us. I saw Yishna spin to one side, clutching her shoulder. Orduval jerked forward as if someone had just placed ice against his back. I felt a violent tugging at my clothing. Glancing down I saw a great splash of blood across my middle, spatters of blood elsewhere, some of them spreading.

'Oh,' said Orduval, sounding both surprised and somehow disappointed. He made a glutinous coughing sound. Then, turning slowly, he released his hold and drifted, head bowing and breath exhaling in a long sigh. There was a hole in his back nearly the size of someone's head, and blood pumping from severed arteries was beading in the air.

'Orduval!' Yishna's cry was anguished.

I guess the cage cut down on the number of pro-jectiles that got through, but not enough. In one brief moment Uskaron had become just a legend that would live on here. I felt sickened and unutterably sad. Yishna's grief echoed all around me, as the suited figures descended around us. The door was fully open now, but I knew that other security precautions lay within, and that without her expertise I would be going no further. I didn't even know how much of the blood spattered on me was my own, but in any case I shut down my heart and lungs and allowed myself to go limp. I lapsed imme-diately into the apparent death that only Rhodane knew to be illusory, I don't know why.

Harald

Ironfist shuddered under multiple impacts delivered by the weapons on Platform Three, but its shields were still holding well and those impacts grew less intense as, with a roar reaching a crescendo, the great vessel entered upper atmosphere. On one of his screens Harald observed some detonations in the mid-section of *Desert Wind*, which then slewed aside from a growing debris cloud. He waited for a few minutes, to watch the same ship straighten up. Then, checking a tactical feed, he swung his view to one side to see a Combine assault vessel bucking under the multiple impacts of coil-gun missiles, before spinning down out of sight, burning as it went.

'Franorl, status?' he barked.

The other Captain did not answer immediately so Harald pulled up a view of *Desert Wind*'s Bridge.

Franorl looked harried as he stood, arms akimbo, over one of his crew.

'The fire suppressant isn't working,' said the subordinate. 'And I can't shut down the line.'

'Then close the section down and vent it.'

'But, Captain, we're in atmosphere.'

'Very *thin* atmosphere,' Franorl observed.

Switching to another camera, Harald felt his gut tighten as he observed, from inside the ship, a hole ripped through the hull, glowing wreckage and two charred corpses stuck to the deck. Almost in sympathy with this horrible image, his head began to throb violently, and he automatically reached into his pocket for his painkilling capsules, taking two of them at a time now.

Pulling his view back behind closed bulkhead doors, Harald saw crew clad in survival suits battling an oxygen fire, which was fed by a broken line and maintained by the partially molten remains of a white-hot shield generator. Metal was burning. He heard the order given to evacuate that entire section and watched them run for safety, some not making it in time through the rapidly closing bulkhead doors. Another set of doors near the impact site then opened, and the air pressure inside exploded into the meagre atmosphere outside, sucking with it both fire and remaining people. Some crew members managed to hold on, others became fuel to the flames and burned a greasy yellow as they screamed out into the gulf. The inferno diminished but, still fed by the line, did not go out until a brave engineer in a heat-resistant suit finally tracked down the line's source and closed it manually.

'Franorl, status?' Harald demanded tightly when this was all over.

Captain Franorl appeared on Harald's eye-screen. 'We took a hit, sir, but we have it under control now. Minimal casualties.'

About thirty, by Harald's count.

The roar reached a climax, as if *Ironfist* had now entered the peak winds of some hurricane – which in essence it had. The firing upon them had become intermittent, but it seemed Combine personnel were now using steering thrusters, trying to tilt Platform Three so as to bring its big guns back on target.

'Increase to one-quarter drive,' Harald ordered. 'We need to get—'

Tactical alert.

Harald tracked down the source and called up the relevant views. *Resilience*, poised out from Corisanthe III, had taken a major pounding. There were three definite hits upon the hilldigger which had rather neatly taken it out of action. He felt a surge of uncharacteristic panic upon seeing this so soon after the enemy's successful strike against Franorl's *Desert Wind*. Were Combine forces employing some new type of weapon? His panic slowly receded as he carefully analysed the three strikes made upon the ship, and realized how conveniently placed they were. A now familiar anger flooded in to replace the panic and he found himself up on his feet, pacing back and forth before his array of screens.

'Orvram Davidson,' he said, addressing the mutinous Captain of *Resilience*. 'Perhaps you did not learn anything from Tlaster Cobe?' He would now put Davidson's hilldigger on a course to ram Corisanthe III. Those aboard the station would then have to destroy the approaching ship or themselves be destroyed. However, even as he opened up the channels to seize control, there were further explosions aboard *Resilience*: fuel lines, generators, a whole network of systems. The sabotage put the steering controls of that hilldigger beyond Harald's reach.

Orvram Davidson now appeared on one of Harald's large screens. 'Oh I did learn, Admiral Harald,' replied the Captain. 'I think we've all now learned that our over-all commander is quite insane, and was so even before some sensible soul managed to put a bullet in his head.'

This reply was delivered on uncoded general address, so could be picked up by anyone, even though Harald had supposedly shut down the young Captain's ability to broadcast. The voice coming from the screen speaker also seemed excessively loud. Harald paused in his pacing and glanced about the Bridge, noting how crew were turning to look over towards him, though hurriedly returning attention to their tasks upon catching his glance. The ache in his head still growing, despite the painkillers, Harald began tracking *Resilience*'s systems, trying to find out how Davidson had managed this communication. Abruptly, vividly, he remembered Cheanil, wounded aboard Defence Platform One, and then apologizing for her stupidity in getting herself shot because she could not resist grandstanding. Harald cursed himself for his idiocy in contacting Davidson to indulge in similar grandstanding, before trying to seize control. Yet he also felt a gratitude to Davidson as other memories began to surface clearly in his mind's sea.

'You know, Harald,' continued Davidson, 'I almost made the mistake of respecting you, and I really wish you could have been my Admiral. I would have followed you readily into battle, confident in the soundness of your tactics and knowing we had every chance of winning. But not into battle against my own kind, Harald. Never against my own kind.'

There it is. Somehow Davidson had managed to do a bit of reprogramming of his own – the ship's computers were telling Harald's programs that there was one less broadcasting array than there actually was, so they were ignoring it, ignoring the one Davidson was using. Harald began to cut and paste some of his control programs to get around this problem, meanwhile wondering how much help Davidson might have received from other supposedly loyal officers.

The Captain continued, 'We see it revealed in Uskaron's history, when he asks why it is that some of the worst monsters seem to be the most capable of men, when the—'

With tired contempt Harald shut down Davidson's

ability to communicate. What a puerile question, and
certainly not the one Uskaron – who had Harald's utmost
respect – actually did ask. As Harald recollected, the
question was rhetorical: Why do people follow
capable monsters into war? And the answer to this provided a whole chapter on fear, manipulation and the
powerlessness of the individual.

Abruptly weary, Harald slumped back in the Admiral's chair.

It didn't seem so comfortable now.

Director Gneiss

Upon observing Harald's failure with *Resilience*, Gneiss
allowed himself a tight little smile, which faded as soon
as he brought his attention back to the other rebel
hilldigger, *Stormfollower*. Within a few hours it would hit
atmosphere like *Ironfist* and *Desert Wind*, but without the
benefit of engines to keep its million-ton weight in the sky.
Making some calculations, Gneiss assessed that the ship
would remain pretty much intact on its way down,
though by the time it hit the Brak sea it would be burning inside, and any of the 4,000 or so aboard who
survived the descent would probably be glad to finally
die. Perhaps because of a strange kind of excitement he
felt at the prospect of finally meeting the Consul
Assessor, Gneiss also felt impelled to take an action
that was rather out of character. He abruptly opened
communications with the Station Director of Corisanthe
III.

'Roubert, how are you holding up there?' he asked.

Glass gazed at him suspiciously. 'That depends
almost entirely on what you are going to request of

me, and how much it is going to cost this station in wealth and lives.'

'Do I seem so transparent to you?' enquired Gneiss.

'On the few occasions when you want your intentions to be read, you are utterly transparent; the rest of the time you are as opaque as the Worm itself.'

Gneiss just stared at him, not quite sure what to make of that.

'What is it you want, Gneiss?' Roubert Glass asked impatiently.

The question seemed to knock Gneiss's mind back into motion, as if for a while it had simply stalled. 'You have now only to defend your station against the attacks from hilldigger *Wildfire*, and I see that you've been able to launch some supply ships to service Defence Platforms Three and Four.'

'Yes, we sent eight ships, and lost one of them. What's your point?'

'My point is that there, within Corisanthe III, you have two space liners near to completion – ships capable of taking thousands of passengers . . . tourists . . . on cruises beyond Sudoria.'

'Those lumbering giants won't be able to help us.'

'I don't intend for them to help us. I am thinking about 4,000 or so Fleet personnel.'

'Why would I want to risk my own people to save them? In fact, it's distinctly possible that if I order my men to do so, they'll mutiny.'

'I'm talking about *Stormfollower*,' said Gneiss.

'I know precisely what you're talking about, Gneiss, and I think this is one for the Oversight Committee. You've been given powers to conduct our defence, but I'm not entirely sure this is a defence matter.'

Gneiss sat back, thinking how easy it was to forget the limitations of his powers. After a moment he put out a call on the conferencing channel reserved for Oversight. His screen immediately divided into six. One of the frames remained blank, his own; Glass occupied another frame, then over the next few minutes other members of the committee began to appear. Only one frame did not fill, that of the Director of Corisanthe II, who probably had enough problems already to deal with. However, a number in the corner of that frame showed that Rishinda Gleer had been made his proxy. Once assembled, Gneiss explained his plan to them all.

'It all seems very altruistic,' said Rishinda, 'and I am wondering if at present we can actually afford altruism.'

'Then try to look at it from a completely selfish perspective,' said Gneiss. 'Very shortly we'll be receiving evidence that exonerates us in the current crisis and confirms Fleet's aggression as the cause. Once this fight is over, such evidence will put us in a very good position, as far as planetary politics is concerned. However, many in Fleet and many supporters of Fleet will still be strongly against us. A life-saving rescue such as this will likely put over 4,000 Fleet personnel in our debt, and may go a long way to change the attitude of the rest.'

'Gratitude is very much overrated,' observed Glass, 'and can quickly sour.'

'That is all a matter of degree,' said another committee member, 'and something that can be debated endlessly.'

'We do not have time for debate,' added Rishinda.

'Then let's consider the possible cost,' said Glass. 'Our liners are unarmed, so if we send one out it will have to remain, where possible, under our shields, and where that is not possible would have to be defended by war-craft. This could not only cost us lives, it could well cost us the liner itself.'

'Why would Harald want to attack an unarmed liner heading away from where he is conducting his attack?' asked Gneiss.

'It would be nice to think the man is operating with utter logic,' said Glass. 'But remember it was he who sent *Stormfollower* on its way down anyway. What purpose does that serve?'

'Maybe an object lesson to the crews of the other ships whose control he has usurped?'

'We have no time for all this,' interjected Rishinda, peering at something off-screen. 'I suggest we put it to the vote now.'

'Seconded,' said Gneiss. 'Those against sending the liner?' Two vote icons clicked up. 'Those for sending it?' Four, including Gneiss's own, now clicked up. Assuming that Glass voted against the rescue mission, that meant Rishinda and her proxy vote must have voted for it, since if she had not there would have been three votes against. The frames then began to wink out until only Glass remained, his image brought forward to fill the entire screen.

'How long will it take you to prepare a liner for launch?' asked Gneiss.

Glass peered at him carefully, his expression amused. 'Very little time at all. Guessing that this idea might be mooted, I started fuelling the liner and warming up its reactors some while ago.' He checked something to one side. 'In fact a small command crew is boarding right now.'

Gneiss found himself annoyed at his own assumptions.

Of course there was no way he could tell if Glass really had voted against rescue. Maybe Rishinda's votes had been the two opposing ones. He shut down the connection with Glass and leaned back. Then, observing that Dalepan was trying to contact him, he opened that connection next.

'We've had a problem with our visitors,' announced the OCT.

'Problem?'

Dalepan was looking decidedly uncomfortable. 'Internal security has been very tight. We could not afford any attempts at sabotage.'

'What are you trying to tell me, Dalepan?'

In a flat monotone, Dalepan imparted the bad news.

18

After Fleet's hilldiggers had finished pounding Brumal,
ground forces were landed and hand-to-hand fighting ensued.
Fleet marines and GDS troops had already fought their
enemy in this way aboard ships and stations, often when the
objective had been to obtain intelligence, capturing prisoners
to interrogate or technology to study. Initially the groundside
fighting was savage, especially against the surviving units of
the quofarl, but the Brumallians had been demoralized by the
blows struck against them, and that firm consensus that
had maintained them for a century was breaking down.
Gradually they just abandoned their effort, and the Sudorian
forces, still fiercely keen to exact vengeance for a century of
war, ceased to be units of soldiers and instead became exter-
mination squads. I have no doubt that the intention of many
serving in Fleet was genocide, but luckily the Admiral and a
majority of his Captains became appalled by the atrocities
committed on the planet below them, and were also sensitive
to the growing revulsion felt by those back at home to what
the media managed to broadcast of their 'Sudorian Victory'.
The killing then ceased, fortunately before the discovery of
three surviving Brumallian cities. We won the War, it was
finally over, but few felt the inclination to celebrate victory,

seeing it rather as a timely ending to something sordid and demeaning.

— Uskaron

Harald

Wildfire's bombardment was not sufficient to keep Corisanthe III nailed down, but then his original plan had been for more than just one hilldigger to deal with that major station. He rubbed at the line of hardened glue on his head. The ache seemed to have now travelled down to seat itself in his eye-socket, which was making him increasingly irritable, so those abrupt surges of anger were occurring more often. He guessed this was as much due to the pressure he was under as his injuries. How much easier it would have been if he could depend totally on those around him.

As his own ship *Ironfist*, accompanied by *Desert Wind*, now approached the next Defence Platform, Harald studied Corisanthe III on one of his screens. He instantly noted a deal of activity to one side of the point where the resupply ships had been departing. Combine assault ships were now gathering there, and he wondered if this was the beginning of some attack planned on *Wildfire*. Then he observed a line cutting down the surface of the nearest section of station. This line grew wider and wider and after a moment he realized he was watching a massive set of space doors opening. They finally slid back to their limit, then something huge began to nose out. In shape it was like the bow of an ocean-going ship, the glint of wide inset windows along its sides.

Some new weapon, perhaps?

His eye-socket throbbed as if in response to this

thought and, folding aside his eye-screen, he ground the heel of his hand into his eye. It seemed this discomfort was the price he must pay, since to remain alert he must continue with the stimulants, and they tended to negate part of the analgesic's effect. Nevertheless, he took another of the pills and, while it dissolved in his mouth, returned his attention to the screens.

While it was always possible that this was some new weapon, Fleet intelligence had long ago identified Corisanthe III as the final assembly point for Orbital Combine's newly constructed space liners. So it now seemed rather likely that one of these passenger vessels was being brought into the fray. What they hoped to achieve with a civilian-format vessel, he had no idea, since it would possess no more than anti-meteor defences and certainly could be no match for a hill-digger.

Just then, *Ironfist* juddered in the shock wave of a nearby nuclear detonation, and this returned Harald's attention to his ship's present surroundings. At this moment, both hilldiggers were using defensive fire only, and that was mainly directed against Combine assault craft, since the platform itself could not bring much weaponry to bear on them. Though he felt no affinity with such emotions at that moment, it was both sad and amusing that these giant Defence Platforms were so vulnerable to attack from their underside. He recollected that the reason for this was that Parliament did not like the idea of Combine being able to point massive weapons down towards Sudoria, so political wrangling had resulted in certain alterations to the original plans. However, Harald could not allow himself to feel too complacent about that, since Combine had already deployed weapons sufficient to destroy Fleet bases down there.

'Engines to one-sixteenth,' he instructed. 'Franorl, go to a sixteenth at 200 miles' separation. No changes to current plan.' The other Captain gave a sloppy salute over his side arm, while keeping his attention focused on his tactical screens.

Desert Wind now quickly pulled away from *Ironfist*. Ahead, and above them, the Defence Platform hung in a purple-blue firmament in which the stars were just visible. Unlike the other versions of these platforms, like the ones he had already destroyed, this one was not disc-shaped, but a flat square pierced through with a central spindle, its armaments spread over the upper surface and the docking facilities on the surface below. Four ships were currently docked there, two of them obviously some kind of assault craft, the other two being large inter-station shuttles regularly used to transport both person-nel and cargo. Even as he watched, one of the latter began to depart. Maybe they were evacuating; Harald decided to let the shuttle go.

'Firing Control, prepare loads for Silos One to Four, then fire on positional confirmation,' said Harald, irked that he still felt the need to speak when already his orders had been given. Checking through the ship's control systems, he found the missiles already loaded and prepped to fire once *Ironfist* reached a predetermined location. In reality, his presence here on the Bridge was superfluous, or at least until something did not go quite to plan.

Desert Wind passed far below the platform, detona-tions from intercepted missiles lighting the air above the ship and spreading a laminated haze, the occasional

Combine assault craft blazing and going out like a meteor.

Then *Ironfist* reached its firing point and Harald felt the ship shudder.

Balanced on blades of flame, the four missiles launched and wrote smoky curves in the sky as they accelerated up towards the platform. Outside views then became intermittent and hazy, as beam weapons fired down from the platform at the approaching missiles also impacted on the ship's shields and filled surrounding atmosphere with ionization. However, there was enough reception for him to see the four missiles throw out a red glow and begin fragmenting, then turn painfully bright and just burn away, their four smoke trails expanding and abruptly petering out.

'Do you have them located, Franorl?' Harald enquired once com came back online.

'I'm sending you the coordinates now,' replied the other Captain.

Harald sat back, clamping down on the urge to take yet another painkiller, for now he most definitely must remain alert.

The first four missiles had actually been duds, but those on the Defence Platform weren't to know that. They most certainly would have employed every weapon they had available, believing that if just one missile got through they were dead. Franorl, with his uninterrupted view, had now located the exact positions of those weapons aboard the platform.

'Let's take out those firing positions and send them the real thing now,' said Harald.

Ironfist seemed to heave under the recoil of multiple launches, coupled with the increased vibration from generators taking load. Coil-accelerated projectiles began impacting on the platform, not as effectively as those that could be fired from *Ironfist*'s main coil-cannon, but hard enough to rattle any shields that could be deployed or otherwise tear off chunks of armour or punch holes through the platform. The two assault ships that had been nested below the platform – raptor-bodied and with short elbowed-back wings – abruptly dropped, fusion engines igniting, and accelerated away. Harald did not for a moment suppose they were running. As expected, their courses began to curve round to bring them back towards *Ironfist*. They did in fact reach the hilldigger, for Harald heard fragments of them impacting on the hull.

Beam weapons turned metal glowing, sometimes molten. Fired upon from both the widely spaced hill-diggers, the platform ultimately could not sustain the attack. Finally, its defence collapsed, and the attackers could rake the platform's underbelly without hindrance.

'Firing Control, prepare loads for Silos Five to Eight, and fire at your convenience,' Harald ordered. Meanwhile, on one of his larger screens, he called up a closer view of the Defence Platform. Hearing the low sound of these latest missiles launching, he glanced to a side screen and watched them accelerating up from *Ironfist*. Halfway to the platform he observed one of them impact against a shield and spew glowing debris in every direction. It did not detonate, however, as the missiles were set for positional detonation, since the premature explosion of one missile might throw all the others off course. As he watched, the last interstation shuttle dropped away, accelerating hard. He rather suspected the last of the platform crew was aboard it, and had most recently been operating the platform weapons via remote consoles. The three missiles passed close by the departing shuttle and punched right into the platform's underside. A heartbeat, and then the platform seemed to expand as if the very fabric of space was being stretched. Next came a brief glimpse of its structure parting over an expanding ball of fire, then all was consumed by an inferno that grew painfully bright, before filters cut out the glare.

The shuttle by now lay well clear of the fireball, but even so it could not outrun the shock wave. Abruptly it jerked sideways, then began to fall, rolling along its axis with fragments tearing away from it. It fell for five miles, attitude jets firing to try and straighten its course. Yet, even though they achieved this, it now seemed they were all it possessed to keep it in the air. Harald watched a deliberate hard change of course, and was unsurprised to note the vessel being set to collide with *Ironfist*. As it hammered down towards the hilldigger, it spat out a sequence of spheres – one-man re-entry pods.

'Firing Control, is someone going to do something about that shuttle?' he enquired tightly.

'Yes, Admiral, I was waiting until the pods were clear,' came the harried and somewhat off-hand reply.

'Well, whoever put it on a collision course with this ship should have thought of that!' he shouted. 'Destroy it now!'

'Yes, Admiral! At once, Admiral!'

Harald seethed as he watched a short-range interceptor missile streak up and pierce the shuttle's belly. Thermal load: the shuttle flew apart in another fireball, most of it vaporized or turned molten. Beyond it the pattern of re-entry pods disrupted. The technology of such pods was tough, so Harald reckoned that most of them would be able to deploy their parachutes. Their contents were not so rugged, however, and he estimated that about half of the parachutes would be dangling corpses to the ground.

As abruptly as it came, his anger receded. He could easily have waited a little longer – those had been totally unnecessary deaths. Just like those of the crew aboard *Stormfollower* . . .

'Platform Four has somehow managed to tilt itself to enable the deployment of its main weapons,' Franorl warned him, his image taking over one of Harald's screens, and his words banishing that brief moment of introspection.

'Something like that was not unexpected,' replied Harald. 'Anyway, our tactics against this platform would only work once.'

'So you are going to use . . . the weapon?' enquired Franorl.

Harald felt his suspicions confirmed by Franorl's reserve. From what he could recollect and from what he had scanned in his own records, Franorl was less averse to causing mayhem than Harald himself, yet now this sudden reluctance? He gazed at the Captain and, while giving his orders, carefully gauged the man's reactions.

'Firing Control, bring main weapon capacitance up to full,' Harald ordered. Then on general com he announced, 'Shipwide alert, condition Aleph. This is Admiral Harald speaking. Prepare for gravity wave recoil. You know the drill since you have performed it many times. But this time it is for real.'

As he came off general com, one of the officers in charge of internal ship's logistics immediately came on instead. 'All back-up reactors to standby mode. Suit for possible breach and run airlock integrity tests. Seal and crash-foam damaged areas. All rail transport and internal lifts will be locking down in twenty-four minutes from now. Engineering, prepare for main engine shutdown . . .' and so it continued.

Franorl bowed in acquiescence, and his image winked out.

Firing the main weapon of a hilldigger, its gravity disruptor, was no simple task. Hugely destructive, it was also excessively dangerous for the one wielding it. There were other likely consequences as well. Once Fleet resorted to such weapons, it could well mean that Combine would deploy them too. Franorl's recent reaction was probably indicative of how the other supposedly loyal Captains also felt. Harald now called up access to numerous programs on his screen. He had prepared the means for seizing control of those hilldiggers whose Captains seemed likely to rebel, and as necessary he had already done so. What his remaining 'loyal' Captains did not know was that he possessed similar access to the controls of their ships too.

McCrooger

While keeping their weapons trained on her, they injected Yishna with a sedative, using some type of gunlike syringe. Watching her carefully, I wondered if at the door the Worm had divined her intentions, and had slowed her down just enough. The sedative knocked her out within seconds, whereupon a female medic sealed her shoulder wound with a large gummy dressing, before she was loaded onto a floating gurney and towed away. The medic then moved on to Orduval, gazed frowning at the huge hole in his back, then gestured over one of his companions.

'The morgue,' she said, as she next propelled herself over to me.

Without much ado Orduval went into a body bag, the basic design of which had not changed in a thousand years. The medic took rather more time over me since, as far as I knew, I had no catastrophic wounds. After a visual inspection – just turning me round in mid-air – she took out a hand-held scanner to check me over.

'Quite strange-looking . . . almost deformed,' commented one of the armed security personnel.

'Actually, *we* are the deformed ones,' replied the medic. 'Apparently this is what our ancestors looked like.' She peered at the readout from her scanner, grimaced and shook her head. 'Though I'm guessing our ancestors weren't composed like him internally. He's got a Brumallian mutualite in there, and that's the least strange thing about him.'

Yeah, I certainly knew about the mutualite. Shutting down my heart and lungs had introduced a deathly quiet the last time I tried it. This time the reduction in the noise level allowed me to hear the glubbing and squelching of the beast inside me. I could also feel it moving, which was not a particularly pleasant sensation.

'But he's dead?' suggested the man.

'Well if he isn't, he's doing a very fine impersonation of a corpse,' she quipped.

'The morgue?'

'No, he goes up to Bio-containment. There's a casket there with his name on it.'

While two others opened up a body bag for me, I observed, just past them, another suited figure clamping something that looked like a portable heater, with attached gas bottle, to nearby cagework. I couldn't figure out what this thing was for until it made some stuttering gobbling sounds, as it sucked down free-floating droplets of blood and and stray gobbets of flesh. Clearing the air, no less. Then the body bag closed out any further view of my surroundings.

'How come there's already a casket for him?' asked someone.

'That was all worked out before he even arrived,' replied the medic. 'The intention was to keep a bio-containment casket on standby close to him at all times.'

'Seems rather ghoulish.'

'No, just good sense. No one wanted him to die, but if he did, we didn't want to lose vital information. And his body *is* vital information.'

Such a comforting thought, but at least it dispelled the slight worry I had that corpses might normally be expelled straight into vacuum.

I guess they subsequently dragged me along through the cagework tube, since the bars would account for the jolts I kept receiving. They then sat me in one of the seats of the lift buggy, which began to ascend at half its previous acceleration. Next I was carried out into a grav section, loaded onto a gurney with squeaky wheels – a strangely primitive mode of transporting a body when you had access to anti-gravity, and perhaps indicative of how they had yet to fully understand the science behind that technology. Numerous crashings and bumpings later, I heard something like a vacuum-sealed door opening, then my gurney came to a halt.

'Do you want him in there?' someone asked.

'No, out of the bag and on the slab,' the medic replied.

'Are you going to . . . you know?' said the first speaker, suffixing his question with a slurping sound. I got a horrible vision of the gesture that had accompanied that sound: one representing the double-handed scooping of offal. Was she now preparing to do an autopsy? I hoped her heart was in good order, since it would need to be sound when I finally sat up and told her to put her scalpels away.

The body bag parted right above me, giving me a view of a white ceiling with pairs of light bars inset – one bar producing white light and the other bacteria-killing ultraviolet. Cold air fingered my face and I felt my eyes starting to water in response. The medic woman leant over to peer down at me, and I very nearly shifted my eyes to look into hers. Until then there had been no twitches or ticks to give me away, but now I felt as if I was rising from a pool, and floating poised just at the surface. I sorely wanted to start my body running again. Perhaps some survival impetus was taking over, for maybe being too long in this state would render me unable to recover from it.

'No, I'll not start cutting him up just yet,' said the woman. 'Director Gneiss wants to take a look at him first.'

'Hardly surprising that,' said the other, 'Gneiss taking an interest in alien corpses.'

Laughter ensued and I listened to footsteps retreating, followed by the thump of a heavy door closing. For a moment I considered allowing my heart to beat normally and allowing my lungs to inhale. However, if this was a bio-containment area there might be sensors operating. I decided to bide my time and considered the fortuitousness of Director Gneiss coming to see me here, and meanwhile puzzled out how best to take advantage of the situation.

We had failed to cause the containment breach that would have instigated the ejection protocol. Alone I would never be able to gain admittance to any of the Ozark Cylinders, and I doubted that Yishna, having just seen her brother die and herself taken a hit in the shoulder, would be of any help right now, even if I could track her down aboard this huge station. Should I give it all up? No. What other routes could I try? I could try to convince Director Gneiss that the Worm was ultimately responsible for the present conflict, and ejecting it to awaiting destruction would bring an end to that conflict. Despite the fact that I was dead, my face twisted in a sneer, for I wasn't entirely sure I believed my own reasoning. The offspring of Elsever Strone had believed, because they could feel the Worm inside their heads. I'm certain that Duras only partially believed, and that his reasoning, in allowing us to come up here on this half-baked mission, was that if the Polity Consul Assessor did something outrageous, that would raise the bargaining position of Sudoria when it came to future negotiations with the Polity. There was also the chance that I might be right, of course – a secondary consideration. From everything I understood about the man, Director Gneiss would believe absolutely nothing unless it was backed up by cold empirical fact. It was an admirable trait, but one I could do without him possessing now.

Time passed, though I don't know how much. I wondered if the human body clock was some kind of biological mechanism that counted the beats of the heart, and therefore in me had ceased to work properly because it had nothing to count, for my sense of time passing now seemed quite hazy. Eventually I heard the thump of the vacuum-sealed door opening.

'You may return to your duties,' said an implacably stern voice.

The door closed and I thought I was alone again, until I heard a sigh followed by the slow approach of footsteps.

Cold empirical fact?

I sat bolt upright, my hand snaking under my foamite top, then emerging to offer Gneiss a cold empirical fact in the form of the handgun Duras had given me. I didn't suppose anyone would get in trouble over my having retained it, since checking to see if a corpse is still armed might be considered rather anal.

'You are now going to apply one of your Emergency Ozark Protocols,' I informed the Director.

He gazed at me with his weird eyes, then smiled a disconcertingly crazy smile.

Harald

He ran the display a couple of times, and felt a deep disquiet. The Brumallian ship must be the same one he had sent Captain Lambrack to destroy. Harald had received brief reports of contact and weapons fire, but nothing subsequently from Lambrack, who had disobeyed the order to destroy the launch site on Brumal and continued out into the system. Lambrack must have missed this ship, or more likely simply allowed it to go past unharmed. Somehow it then managed to reach the surface of Sudoria, where some Fleet spies reported

Chairman Duras going aboard with security personnel, then departing a few hours later. Whereupon this ship launched from the planet's surface, and approached Corisanthe Main, where an interstation shuttle left it to dock with the station itself. The ship had since disappeared, and Harald could only suppose it now lay within one of the blind spots of Fleet coverage. Why was it here and, most importantly, would it have any effect on his plans?

Harald shut off the display and sat back for a moment. The appearance of this Brumallian ship should not have any effect on his original plans, since what happened next was all about firepower. He decided to dismiss the intruder from his consideration, and returned his attention to their present situation.

Because the technology was so risky to use, Fleet did not run many tests of its gravity disruptors. The last such test Harald remembered was when he had been a mere apprentice in the Engine Galleries. But, then, maybe there had been other tests the memory of which the bullet had scoured from his mind.

Readying the gravity disruptor for firing also created all sorts of strange effects throughout the ship. Infrasound and ultrasound spikes directly affected mood, so mock tests were conducted, producing similar sounds, and crew were instructed to practise interacting with each other without any emotional input. What these mock tests could not duplicate, however, was the sounds the ship made as huge forces began to distort the very fabric of space around it, and as the gravitic effects of that distortion began to twist and stretch the ship itself like a piece of bread dough.

Numerous alarms began sounding, until an officer

managed to shut them down, thereafter tracking the breaches and breaks on an electronic flow chart, and delivering instructions on what to do about them to the maintenance crews via his com helmet. Internal lights dimmed and in some places went out completely to be replaced by low-energy emergency lighting.

'Begin your run to the cover point,' Harald instructed Franorl, then watched *Desert Wind* accelerating away, its belly thruster stabbing down into atmosphere as the great ship laboured back up into vacuum.

Defence Platform Four now lay just a few hundred miles ahead and above them and, rising over the curve of Sudoria, Corisanthe Main became just visible beyond it, picked out by the sun which now lay behind *Ironfist* itself. Some thousands of miles over to Harald's left, still in planetary twilight, lay Corisanthe II, and when he turned a camera in that direction he could see flashes, as of an approaching thunderstorm, from the battle being fought between that station and the hilldiggers *Harvester* and *Musket*.

'I will be reaching cover point in thirty minutes,' Franorl informed him, by voice only. 'The troops are ready for station insertion.'

Harald nodded to himself, but carefully since his headache seemed to hang like a lead weight in the jelly of his brain. Via his eye-screen he accessed cameras located on railway platforms within *Desert Wind,* and there observed the first of 1,500 Fleet marines disembarking from the trains and heading for the lifts to take them down to the insertion craft crammed waiting in the docking bays. The men wore armoured spacesuits, carried disc carbines, grenade launchers and portable impact shields, and they were the reason *Desert Wind* had only played a minor role in the present orbital firefight. Harald had wanted to keep them safe and ready for the takeover of Corisanthe Main.

He now tried dividing his eye-screen so as to view simultaneously the docking bay and the platform, but found, despite managing to divide his perception on one occasion since his injury, that he could not manage it now, as his eye just performed like an unenhanced one. Sudorian medical science had enabled him to get up and function again after such a serious injury, but he suspected his present problem might be due to damage to the enhancements rather than to himself. In irritation he flipped the eye-screen aside and abruptly stood up. Too abruptly, for dizziness assailed him and he needed to lean over and prop himself against a chair arm. After a moment the fit passed and, on shaky legs, he crossed the Bridge to climb the stairs.

Once safely up in the Admiral's Haven, Harald removed his com helmet and control glove, then headed for the ensuite facilities. After using the toilet he started to splash some water on his face, then realized that he had not washed properly for some time. Twenty-five minutes remained before the other ship was in position and it seemed unlikely anything unexpected could happen within that time. Deciding to take advantage of the interval, he quickly closed down the computer units within his foamite suit then reached inside to disconnect the interface plugs from the sockets grafted along his collar bone. He then quickly stripped off the suit and undersuit, and stepped into the shower. He cleaned carefully around the collar-bone sockets, soaped himself down, scrubbed the blood from his hair and, finally feeling refreshed, stepped from the shower booth and went to find a replacement suit. Once dressed again he felt so much better that he even began thinking he could tolerate his headache enough to forgo taking further drugs for a while. With his com helmet in place and control glove back on, he headed for the stair while flipping the eye-screen back across. The image he summoned first was to be an exterior view of Defence Platform Four as seen from *Ironfist*. But nothing appeared. He began to run a diagnostic program to give him an audio report, then noticed from his left eye that the eye-screen was showing something after all. Puzzled, he removed the helmet, carefully keeping a finger on the automatic cut-off switch so that the helmet remained functional. Now he could see clearly that the screen was showing precisely the scene he had requested.

Blind?

Placing a hand over his left eye, he could still see everything from his right eye, including the screen image, but as he moved that screen closer, things started to get a bit strange at about a foot and a half from his face. Much of the helmet was simply no longer visible. Moving it closer, more and more of it disappeared from view, including the screen itself, and even the hand holding the helmet. The enhanced vision of his right eye was no longer registering anything that came within a certain range of it, which he recognized as both a hardware and an organic failure. This sudden knowledge jerked him to a halt, his mouth suddenly dry. Then came that uncontrolled surge of anger and he hurled the helmet away from him. Gasping, he staggered to a nearby seat where, seemingly without his conscious intervention, his hands sought out the containers on his utility belt. Two painkillers went into his mouth, after a hesitation followed by a third. He loaded syringes with the other drugs, and injected them into an arm that was now quite tender. He then sat and just stared, his mind seemingly on hold.

'Admiral?' asked a nervous-looking subaltern from the top of the stairs leading up from the Bridge. 'I'm sorry to disturb you, sir, but Captain Franorl has reported that he is now in position.'

Harald abruptly pushed himself to his feet. Where had the time gone? Another mental organic failure?

He waved the subaltern away and strode over to pick up his com helmet. He removed the earpiece and microphone, discarding the helmet itself as he headed for the stair, but snatching up his control glove on the way. Down on the Bridge, he moved with apparent decisiveness over to the Admiral's chair and sat down.

'Disruptor status?' he demanded, using the control glove to transfer his visual com helmet functions to one of the screens ranged before him.

'Gravity disruptor ready to fire,' came the reply from Firing Control.

Harald called up a series of views showing him the Defence Platform, above and ahead of them, and another view along the entire length of *Ironfist*. 'Are non-grav sections now prepared for inversion?'

'All are prepared.'

Harald now opened communication with hilldiggers *Wildfire* and *Harvester*. 'Captains, are you within close range of or else within your specified cover points?'

The Captains of those two ships quickly replied to confirm. *Wildfire* lay only a few minutes away. *Harvester* – and the ship slaved to it, *Musket* – was at that moment moving into its designated cover point.

'Very well, you know what to do now.' Shutting off

that link, Harald opened his microphone to general address. 'Invert the ship,' he ordered. 'Engineering, stand by for fast engine restart.'

Ironfist's steering thrusters came on all along one side, and the great ship began to roll. On the Bridge, of course, with a fully functional gravity floor, everyone maintained their positions easily. However, because of the effect of the planet below, they could all feel the ship itself turning over. Within a few minutes *Ironfist* was lying on its back relative to the planet, its underside facing up towards the platform. Most importantly nothing stood between the head of the disruptor, mounted below the ship's nose, and that Combine Defence Platform.

'Fire disruptor.'

The ship then seemed to heave like some animal about to vomit. All around the Bridge could be heard the creaking and cracking of internal structures. Around the disruptor itself, which resembled two projecting fins curving forward, a shimmering haze appeared. With a thump that Harald could feel in his bones, that same shimmer sped away, became a wavefront propagating through the thin air, and then through the vacuum beyond. To either side the wavefront feathered: it was directional, but only in the way that a tsunami is. Harald quickly magnified his view of the Defence Platform just in time to see the wave strike it. At the forefront of the impact the platform seemed to stretch, almost like an oil spill riding over a wave in water. But, as the wave passed through it, the platform just ruptured and came completely unstitched. There followed some explosions, from munitions detonating, but surprisingly few. Platform Four just came apart.

'Get us to the cover point, *now*!' Harald ordered. 'Engines to full power!'

Ironfist's main drive threw out a bright fusion flame, a mile long, from four fusion-chamber mouths each 600 feet in diameter. The flame was so bright because of the secondary burn of atmosphere. Even protected by the automatic adjustment of the gravity floor, some crew staggered and others toppled over as the massive acceleration threw the million-ton hilldigger forward, as steering thrusters then turned it over, and as the belly thrusters went to maximum power to throw it up out of atmosphere. Now, Harald knew, was the most dangerous time. It would take them less than twenty minutes to reach the cover point, since they had already been heading towards it at half speed behind Franorl's *Desert Wind*, and if the Combine Oversight Committee could manage to get its act together within that time and order the use of their own disruptors, *Ironfist* would be going the way of Defence Platform Four. Harald, however, had bet on them not being able to come to a decision that quickly. He sat clutching the arms of his chair, the screens before him running a chaotic series of views and code streams because he had not meanwhile offlined his control glove.

Engine shutdown was followed by the sideways pull of steering thrusters at turnover, as the massive ship flipped over from nose to tail, the decelerating blast of the main engines now bringing them into their cover point. He glanced over at the seemingly panicked activity evident at Damage Control. It was a risky option to put the ship under this sort of strain right after using the disruptor. The recommended strategy was for a full maintenance check to be carried out, from engines to nose. Doubtless there would be hull breaches, cracks or breaks in the ship's skeleton. They would either make it or not.

'We are now in the cover point,' a voice announced.

Harald unclenched his fists and smiled, more for the reassurance of those around him than because he felt any desire to. Their cover point lay close to Corisanthe Main, on a line running directly between that station and Corisanthe II. *Harvester* and *Musket* rested midway between Corisanthe II and III, whilst *Wildfire*'s position was close to Main, on a line drawn between Main and Corisanthe III.

Here then was another weakness in Orbital Combine's defences – one they seemed not to have recognized. He surmised that Combine's gravity weapons – the ones he wasn't supposed to know about – would be sited on the main three stations. The problem with such weapons was that the gravity wave, which propagated from a spacial distortion, had substantially more range than any conventional weapon. Even using such weapons in interplanetary space, during the War itself, had been a risky option. Here, in the vicinity of Sudoria, where everything was so *close*, it became riskier still. Because the stations rested at the points of a narrow triangle with Main at the apex, the firing of such a weapon at the Fleet ships where they were presently positioned by any of the two Corisanthe stations closest to them risked the destruction of the station that lay closest to the weapon's target. That risk was substantially less if such a weapon was fired from Corisanthe Main aiming at *Wildfire*, *Desert Wind* or Harald's own ship, *Ironfist*. However, if Combine did attack, they could not fire three weapons at once since the ensuing disruption would be sure to destroy their own stations. Yet if Combine limited itself to firing at just one ship, it risked immediate retaliation from the other two.

Harald was betting the members of the Oversight Committee were too cowardly to take such a risk. However, he was not betting on his own Captains being prepared to use their gravity disruptors. He would control that option.

McCrooger

First came a rush of dizziness, then I felt the kind of high you get from sucking on pure oxygen. The sound of my heart was loud, intrusive, and my lungs ached and bubbled as I breathed. Here I was holding the station Director at gunpoint and making demands, and I wondered if I would even be able to stand upright once I was off this slab.

'Why would you, an envoy from the Polity, want me to do that?' enquired Gneiss.

'Because the Worm instigated this present conflict.'

'I thought you had brought us evidence proving Fleet the guilty party?'

'Fleet is just the tool that Harald is using, and Harald himself is one of the tools the Worm is using.'

'Ah,' he said, taking a pace forward, 'the children of Elsever Strone.' He paused, a brief look of pain crossing his features. 'I would like to have known Orduval, but sadly that was not to be.'

My hands were sweaty, and the gun was beginning to feel rather heavy; I brought my left hand up to support the butt and concentrated on keeping the barrel on target.

'The protocols,' I reminded him.

Gneiss focused back on me. 'I am presuming that since you know that the protocols exist, you also know what they entail?'

I didn't know the full consequences of all the protocols, only that, after Yishna's interference with them, they would now eject all four Ozark Cylinders from the station, and that at some point those cylinders would pass beyond Corisanthe Main's shields, to where they could be destroyed.

He continued, 'Do you want me to use the protocol that results in the thermal and EM sterilization of the cylinders?'

I shook my head, mainly trying to shake off the sweat running into my eyes.

'Which, then?' Gneiss asked, mistaking my gesture.

Thinking muggily, I said, 'The one that results in the ejection of a cylinder.'

'But what will that achieve?'

Damn, I definitely wasn't thinking straight. 'Perhaps you've forgotten, but I'm holding the gun. What will be achieved, you can leave me to worry about.'

'Very well, there is one other small problem.'

'Enlighten me.'

'Without some sort of containment breach, I can only accede to your demand by using the system access in my office,' said Gneiss.

I swung my legs off the slab while eyeing him closely, trying to read him. Sometimes he showed strong emotion but at seemingly inappropriate moments, while the rest of the time he was disconcertingly blank, perhaps because, facing him, my point of focus immediately became those odd-looking eyes. I guessed he probably had some way of alerting station security from his office, or hoped he could engineer some sort of intervention on the way there. I stood up, shakily, then stepped to one side.

'I guess you'll have to take me to your office, then,' I conceded, just to see how he would respond.

'You will be seen by others,' he pointed out, which threw me completely.

'Then it's up to you to find a way to get me there without being seen.'

He gave a mild nod of agreement, almost as if I had posed a little puzzle for him the resolution of which he deemed of no consequence.

'Over there,' he pointed, 'is a locker storing bio-containment suits. They look little different from emergency survival suits, which many of the crew are now wearing since they enable greater freedom of move-ment than spacesuits.' Peering at my gun, he added, 'You will be able to conceal your weapon in the belly pocket.'

I just could not make this guy out. He showed no emotional involvement in what was happening to him – in what I was forcing upon him – yet surely that could not be right, for this man was station Director of Corisanthe Main. I was also getting an impression from him of complete disregard for his own safety. Almost as if he would be prepared to take a bullet, just as an intellectual exercise.

I lowered the gun, since my arm was aching, and moved back towards the lockers he had indicated. I took hold of the handle of one and pulled and, still watching him, groped about inside. After a moment I pulled out a package, and quickly recognized a suit similar to the one I had worn on the escape-pod taking me down to Brumal.

'You're bleeding,' he observed.

Glancing down I noted fresh blood staining my dungarees, and a trail of droplets leading back to the slab. I could survive without my heart beating or my lungs breathing, by dint of IF21 distributing oxygen about my body, but I wondered if my body could survive without any blood inside it.

'Kneel down,' I instructed Gneiss, 'and place your hands on the floor under your knees.'

With a slightly puzzled look he obliged. I quickly placed my gun on the floor, opened the packet and pulled on the containment suit. It came with its own integral overboots, so would at least prevent me from dribbling more blood all over the place. I pulled up the hood but did not bother to close the mask since I had no idea how long the small oxygen supply attached to the belt would last me.

'Okay, you can stand up now,' I said, the gun once again in my hand.

Gneiss straightened up, shaking some feeling back into his hands. 'Shall we go now?'

I nodded, and he turned and strode over to the door. Quickly moving up behind him I pressed the barrel of the gun into his side. 'I think you should understand something, Director Gneiss.'

'That being?' he asked, as he pushed down the big lever of the door handle.

'I'm dying,' I replied. 'I probably won't leave this station alive. I truly believe that what I'm now forcing you to do will solve a lot of your problems, and I'm prepared to do anything towards that end. If you cross me, I promise I'll kill you.'

With an unreadable look, he opened the door and

we stepped out into the corridor. I thrust the gun into my suit's belly pocket, but retained a firm hold on the butt.

We got about twenty feet along the corridor when a worried-looking woman immediately zeroed in on Gneiss.

'Sir, we've been trying to raise you on your personal com . . . ' she said.

'I switched it off.'

'The situation has become very serious. Oversight has been trying to contact you. Fleet has just destroyed Platform Four with a gravity disruptor. The Fleet ships are now—'

Gneiss held up his hand. 'I'll deal with this when I reach my office, where I won't get very quickly if you feel the need to tell me the whole story here.'

'I'm sorry . . .'

Gneiss quickly moved on and I followed him closely. The woman gave me a puzzled look and turned away. Thereafter no one ventured to approach us, and I got the impression that their Director was someone the other station personnel liked to avoid. We entered a lift that took us up only a little way, then entered a series of corridors where everyone we encountered seemed in a great hurry. Gneiss paused by a long narrow window with a view out across the station and into open space, where distantly could be seen Fleet's firework display.

'Almost certainly Harald will have placed his ships where the use of gravity weapons by Combine will result in huge collateral damage to Combine itself,' he said.

'So presumably Combine has prepared for that,' I suggested.

'The Oversight Committee lacks foresight.'

'But you are on the Oversight Committee and, as far as I can gather, you are also in charge of running Combine's defence.'

'Yes, so it would seem.'

His strange nonchalance covered up something else I was only just beginning to perceive, some need in him.

'Harald is responding to the Worm's will in the only way he knows,' I said, studying him carefully. 'But I see I am not telling you anything you don't already know.'

His reaction to that was odd. He noticeably jerked as if coming out of a reverie, and for a brief moment looked actually scared.

I prodded him in the back with my gun. 'Your office.'

The office itself was spartan and lacking in much to personalize it. A picture on one wall displayed a desert scene, while some mostly empty shelves held partially dismantled bits of hardware. A full-length oval mirror in an ornate frame stood opposite a desk loaded with consoles and a framework for opening the soft scroll screens they used here. There was a couch with a low table nearby. Nothing on the table but a film of dust.

'Now you must initiate that emergency protocol,' I said. 'I'll be looking over your shoulder and, believe me, I know more about your computer systems than you might suppose.'

He looked at me as if offended by such an inference, then his gaze strayed over my shoulder, towards the mirror behind me. Vanity? I just could not see the possibility of that vice within him, so even the presence of that mirror struck an incongruous note. Just to remind him, I pulled out the gun, and gestured with it to the desk.

'Unfortunately I misled you,' he said, and the weirdly

crazy expression that momentarily passed over his face made me step back a pace.

'If you could elaborate,' I prompted.

Again that glance towards the mirror, then he focused on me and leant forward a little. 'I cannot initiate any of the emergency protocols. No director should possess the power to destroy all or part of the Worm, or even eject it from this station, without good reason. So the protocols only become viable once automatic systems have picked up a definite breach in one of the canisters.'

'Then why let me come here at all?'

'Because, as you so rightly pointed out, you are holding a gun.' He peered at the weapon. 'Finely made, too. It looks like the kind manufactured for ship or station assault. Is the ammunition armour-piercing? Such weapons often use such bullets for the penetration of armoured spacesuits.'

What was he wittering on about?

'Yes, the bullets are armour-piercing.'

He continued, 'I believe the reasoning behind such weapons is that, when you're assaulting a ship or station, the possibility of your bullets causing an atmosphere *breach* is rather irrelevant, since you'll be wearing a spacesuit.'

'Do you think that would stop me from firing in here?' I asked. 'Please don't make that mistake.'

Almost as if to challenge me, he took a pace forward. I wasn't intending to kill him, but I doubted I could subdue him in any other way. Rewind a few months and I wouldn't even have needed the gun, but now I felt drained in more senses than one, since every time I took a step now, I could feel the blood squelching in my boots.

If he went for me, I would probably end up with broken bones, and that might hasten my end.

His gaze wavered, sliding past my shoulder again to the mirror. What was it about that damned mirror? I quickly stepped to one side and took a proper look at it. Its frame, I noticed, had an even patina all round except in one particular place, for the snake's head incorporated in the design was highly polished as if by the frequent touch of a hand. I now recognized the design of the frame was an Ouroboros – a snake swallowing its own tail forever – and I thought that entirely appropriate. I quickly brought my gaze back to him.

'We use optical diamond so the Worm can be viewed,' he told me. 'It's a foolish conceit, since there is no need for us to actually see it, and diamond, though incredibly hard is also incredibly brittle.' He paused for a moment, his gaze cast down, introspective. 'When we were lovers I took Elsever down there to see my charge. I was foolishly proud as well as in love. I think *it* was just awaiting the opportunity . . . or perhaps it had even manufactured that opportunity.' He looked up again. 'That was when it touched her, of course.' Then he drew his lips back from his teeth, almost as if he were in pain – and threw himself at me.

I had him in my sights all the while. He seemed to make no attempt to avoid getting shot, but I couldn't do it. I flicked my finger away from the trigger as with both hands he grabbed me by the loose material across my chest, hoisted me off the floor then propelled me backwards and slammed me against the mirror. I felt ribs crack and something again began bubbling in my lungs. The gun barrel was pressed right up against his guts, and

I knew that in a second I could blow them and part of his spine out of his back.

'It touched her! It touched her!' he shrieked in my face. Then his expression changed, looking lost. 'I have to stop you.'

He let me slide down until my feet rested on the floor, then drew his fist back to deliver a blow I knew would cave in my face. With my former Old Captain strength I could have pulled his head off; as weak as I was now, only a few options remained to me. Despite the Sudorian differences, he was still human, so possessed a human physiology. I brought my knee up *hard*.

Gneiss made a sound like loose cloth getting sucked through a small hole into vacuum. He released me, staggered back, and cupped his testicles protectively. I brought the gun butt down on the back of his head, and he collapsed. I just stood there gasping for breath. Then I started coughing up bloody phlegm. I really just wanted to slide down to the floor, and wait for everything to go away. *No, not yet.* I understood his dilemma, understood what he had been telling me. I reached down and took hold of his wrist in both hands and with a struggle that almost had me crying in frustration, dragged him closer to the mirror, and propped him up next to it. Then I pulled his right hand up high enough to place it against that polished snake's head in the mirror frame.

The mirror instantly revolved into the wall, revealing a small lift beyond. I stepped inside and it immediately revolved closed again. Then it took me down.

19

Those we left behind have rediscovered us. Our ancestors left the Solar System, in the midst of savage corporate wars, in the hope of starting something new, something worthy. Looking back upon our history here, can we honestly say we have since transcended our bloody past on Earth and within the Solar System? Humans can now change themselves physically in ways that utterly outpace the slow meander of evolution, and it seems, from what we have heard about this Polity, that human science has produced powerful artificial intelligences that put the organic fat in our skulls to shame. Yet what about morality? Does that, too, evolve or does it remain a construct relevant only to our hunter-gatherer past? Does it now have any relevance in the modern human universe at all? I wonder if our distant kin from the Polity know. I wonder if they are 'better' than us.

– Uskaron

Harald

Firing from the Defence Platforms and from the Corisanthe stations was becoming intermittent as the hill-diggers held their positions, themselves using defensive

fire only. Harald guessed that the members of the Oversight Committee were beginning to realize that they now
might not win this, but any satisfaction he might otherwise have felt was muted by the ache in his head. He
began checking logistics and tactical assessments. If they
continued to engage in a straight shooting war with conventional weapons, Fleet would likely run out of supplies
and need to withdraw. Harald, of course, had no intention of withdrawing.

Turning his attention to another view provided by a
couple of Fleet spy cameras, Harald observed the Combine passenger liner was now well out from Corisanthe
II and apparently moving to intercept Tlaster Cobe's
Stormfollower, which at present appeared not to be
moving despite the glow from its steering thrusters, but
would eventually enter atmosphere. The liner, though a
civilian vessel, was accelerating much faster than could
Fleet vessels of comparable size. Harald decided there
and then that once he had seized control of all of Combine's resources, he would have Fleet engineers take a
close look at those engines. But what to do now, for the
liner would reach *Stormfollower* within the next half-hour.
He considered having *Harvester* and *Musket* launch a
missile strike against the liner, then suddenly felt
bewildered.

Why do that? Why destroy that liner; why send
Tlaster Cobe and his entire crew to their deaths; why
waste a hilldigger by smashing it into Sudoria? Nausea
assailed him. He bit down on it and in that moment
experienced a sudden reversal. He decided his previous
decision about Cobe was a mistake he needed to correct,
for the lives of *Stormfollower*'s crew and maybe for his

own sanity. And anyway he could afford to be magnanimous.

Now decided on what to do, Harald accessed *Stormfollower*'s systems, but soon realized that stopping its descent would be no easy task. The necessary code seemed almost slippery and sometimes there were bits of it he just did not understand now. Eventually, however, he found what he wanted and sent his instructions. Views from a distance showed him a hundred or more steering thrusters on *Stormfollower* shutting down, then another hundred or more coming on. Using orbital mechanics programs, Harald made his calculations. Not enough. Despite the steering thrusters now fighting against it, *Stormfollower* was still on course to slam into Sudoria. No technology aboard the hilldigger itself could prevent that.

'Get me Director Gneiss,' Harald ordered. 'I think it's time for us to talk.'

While he waited for the connection, he again assessed *Stormfollower*'s chances. Combine's solution would be to dock with the huge vessel, offload its crew, and then run to the nearest available station. That strategy, rather than trying to pull the hilldigger out of its current descent, would get the passenger liner out of danger the quickest. But perhaps there was another option. Harald began to make further calculations factoring in the evident power of that liner's engines.

'Is Gneiss refusing com?' Harald enquired after a couple of minutes' silence.

'Admiral,' replied the tacom, 'it seems that Director Gneiss is currently unavailable, but there are other members of the Combine Oversight Committee who are prepared to talk with you.'

'Who do you have?'

'Rishinda Gleer.'

Harald grimaced, remembering the message she had sent to Fleet, which had resulted in him receiving a bullet in his head.

'I'll speak to her,' he conceded.

After a moment, looking grave and tired she appeared on the screen before him. He smiled at her without much sincerity. 'I will not bother to waste time with any of the civilities, since we have moved well beyond that now.'

'Civilities are for the civilized,' Gleer noted acidly.

'Whatever,' said Harald. 'You must order your forces to cease fire at once.'

'And on what basis do you make this demand?'

'I suspect you already know, but I'll spell it out for you anyway. Fleet hilldiggers are currently occupying positions where you will be unable to use your gravity disruptors against them without causing serious damage, if not the complete destruction, to one or all of the Corisanthe stations. However, those same hilldiggers are now with impunity able to fire gravity disruptors at your stations.'

'That, Harald, is not entirely true. We can still quite easily destroy *Wildfire*, *Desert Wind* and your own ship without substantial risk to Corisanthe stations II and III.'

'Perhaps so,' Harald admitted, 'but none of your stations can fire on *Harvester* and *Musket* without risking such destruction, and should you open fire on us, they will proceed to destroy your two most highly populated stations.'

'I do not believe that either Captain would be so bloody-minded, especially after losing their Admiral and knowing they would be going against the direct orders of Parliament.' But even as she spoke the words, Harald noticed that firing upon the Fleet vessels had reduced abruptly.

'I have to wonder if you are prepared to bet the lives of hundreds of thousands of Combine citizens on what you believe,' said Harald. 'Though you should be aware that the Captains of those ships will shortly be losing the ability to refuse such an action.'

'You are a cold bastard,' said Gleer, her face turning as grey as her hair. Harald felt that he had correctly guessed her current location as being on one of the two threatened stations.

'Sentiment tends to cost more lives than it saves.' Harald gave her another false smile. 'But I see that Combine stations are already ceasing to fire upon us.' He nodded. 'That being the case, I will restrain my vessels from firing on the passenger liner you have sent to intercept *Stormfollower*.'

'So generous of you,' Gleer sneered bitterly.

Sudden anger surged in Harald. 'Though I am always prepared to change my mind,' he spat. 'I'm speaking to you like this because I want to prevent unnecessary killing. Should I decide to close down this link right now, then, at my convenience, one of your stations will cease to exist. Please let me know if you are unclear about any of this?'

Rishinda Gleer glared back at him. 'I am not in the least unclear. We have reached a predictable impasse. If either side makes use of gravity disruptor weapons, the results will light Sudoria's sky with falling debris for some time to come. Now, you were saying about *Stormfollower* . . .'

Harald stared at her irritably as he fought against the impulse to simply shut down communication. Finally, he managed to get himself under control.

'Yes, my calculations indicate it would be possible for your liner to hard-dock with *Stormfollower* and divert it back out into space. That should take approximately five hours. I will meanwhile not fire upon either ship, since I have nothing to gain from doing so.'

'So, simply on a whim you set that ship on a course to destruction, and now equally on a whim you wish to save it. How am I supposed to trust you?'

'I must leave that to you.'

'Very well, I will now relay instructions to the Captain of the *Freesky*. So what else, Admiral Harald?'

Harald grimaced on learning the name of the civilian liner.

'What else, indeed,' he replied. 'Why clearly Orbital Combine must now publicly declare its surrender to Fleet.'

'That is not going to happen,' she snapped.

'Then, for now, this conversation is at an end.'

Harald shut down the link, then after a moment opened a link to *Desert Wind*.

'Franorl, close on Corisanthe Main and begin your assault.'

Next he opened communications with *Wildfire* and *Harvester*, and shortly Captains Soderstrom and Ashanti were gazing at him from a divided screen. On another screen he eyed the progress of the programs he had initiated earlier. With satisfaction he saw that they had penetrated the two ships and were functioning precisely as intended: seizing control of their systems and putting online the hardware concealed aboard both vessels some months previously.

'It seems my Captains are showing a degree of reserve about employing gravity-disruptor weapons,' he challenged them.

The two Captains managed to display a reasonable facsimile of puzzlement, but Harald was not convinced. He saw Ashanti glance to one side, as if someone nearby had addressed him, but the screen microphone aboard *Wildfire* did not pick up what was said. However, the man's sudden reaction of quickly suppressed rage told Harald all he needed to know.

'With our assault on Combine reaching such a critical juncture,' Harald continued, 'I cannot countenance any hesitation, and I certainly cannot risk either of you disobeying my orders.'

'I would never disobey you, sir,' Soderstrom protested.

'We have given you our total trust,' said Ashanti, 'and you cannot give us yours?'

His head throbbing severely, Harald wanted to shout at them, but he continued, 'As you will by now realize, I have taken control of some of your ships' systems. They will hold their current positions, with their gravity disruptors directed towards the main targets. Should you attempt to move them out of position without my express permission, your main drives and steering thrusters will shut down.'

'This is madness!' Soderstrom snarled. 'You mean we'll need to get your permission to move our own ships if we come under attack?'

'There will be no attacks you cannot deal with from

your current location, and I've allowed you to retain control of all your conventional weapons and defences.'

'Allowed?' said Ashanti.

'Yes, allowed – though I now control the firing of your gravity disruptors.' Both Captains seemed to have nothing to say about that, so Harald went on. 'Look at it this way: should we fail in our objective, should we lose this battle, you as individuals cannot be held to account for any destruction those weapons may meanwhile cause.'

'We became culpable the moment we ignored Parliament,' said Ashanti.

'Whatever.' Harald waved that away. 'I cannot afford to gamble Fleet's future on the whims of individual Captains.'

'Just the whim of one Admiral, then,' Ashanti replied.

Harald shut down the communication.

McCrooger

The lift's direction of acceleration changed abruptly, and had me staggering to one side, where I braced myself during another abrupt change. Then it decelerated and grav disappeared. Becoming weightless, I grabbed a nearby handle. The lift opened onto a chamber in which the glints of light, here and there, were certainly not provided for illumination. Nevertheless a swirling metallic glow gave me enough light to see by. After a moment I started having trouble breathing and my lungs felt leaden. At first I thought this was just one of my own problems, then I remembered how the Ozark Cylinders were filled with inert gas surrounding the canister in which the

Worm fragment was held. I closed up my mask, and the discomfort slowly faded as the suit automatically oxygenated. Pushing myself out of the lift, I peered into the shadows and eventually spied what must surely be my destination – the source of that weird glow – and I launched myself down towards it.

What exactly is 'alien'? There are so many living worlds in the Polity that burgeon with alien life, but once you begin to familiarize yourself with that life, how much the word applies becomes only a matter of degree. After a while it ceases to be alien and becomes just a matter of taxonomy. You can understand it, how it functions, how it came to be, where it fits in its local ecology.

But this was *alien*. This was gazing at something unfathomable while your mind struggled to fit it into a mould, to define it, categorize it, to remove it from that part of the consciousness that is still a primate screaming at the dark. I clung to the worn knurling of the framework positioned before the diamond pane and gazed at something I just could not encompass – and never really wished to. Then I raised my gun to point it at the damned thing and, bracing myself for the recoil, pulled the trigger back and held it there. So I would die in the process – I felt near enough to that state already for it not to matter to me.

The gun fired with oiled precision, considering all it had been through, and emptied a clip of about ten bullets into the diamond. I then opened up my containment suit and pulled out another ammunition clip. Were those hair-fine cracks appearing before me? It was difficult to tell with that swirling *otherness* behind. I discarded the first clip, watched it float away from me, and found my mind drifting similarly. I loaded the second clip and fired again, trying to hit exactly the same point at the centre of the circular diamond window. Definitely some damage evident now: sparkling diamond fragments gyring away, angel dust glittering in the air – and a crack. I had begun to empty the third clip when my world turned inside out. I could see one of the bullets travelling balletically slow. Chunks of diamond folded out, and a stream of something like mercury, in which it seemed segmented worms and insectile skeletons were sub-merged, licked out into the inert atmosphere. Then I was hurtling backwards, tumbling through the air as madness flowed out and around me. I could hear klaxons screech-ing, but their noise seemed so prosaic and worldly that they meant almost nothing to me. Then the floor slammed up against me, the canister came crashing down nearby, and other equipment rained down in a deadly tangle. Snakes of cables submerged me, and I think it was those that saved me as some massive device crashed down on top. I belatedly realized that the Ozark Cylinder had been ejected from the station; the initial acceleration bringing me and all the rest of this paraphernalia tumbling down. The other thing, now coiling and swirling above me, had seemingly been affected not at all.

I realized I'd stopped breathing, that my heart had stopped too, and I felt no inclination at all to force the seizing clockwork of my body back into motion. Zero gravity returned, shifting the debris and cables about me, removing their weight but not their mass. Underneath them I felt almost safe, comfortable, enclosed as if under the downy covers of a bed. I considered succumbing to the kind of sleep you don't wake up from, but a fasci-nation with the thing now cruising about above me kept me conscious.

It now had a wormish shape, but one seemingly formed out of a compacted mass of steel and silver skeletons, like thorny baroque sculptures. It was now elongating, with a simultaneous narrowing of its girth. During this transformation it started to look insubstantial, its elements gradually parting and a pearly glow issuing from between them, then the elements becoming translucent, fading. Then abruptly it turned blindingly bright and stabbed towards the cylinder wall, impacted hard and simply began boring through the metal.

A shock wave skidded me along the floor still buried under the wreckage, like a bug being smeared under a foot. Incandescent vaporized metal and plastic and chunks of wreckage exploded into the chamber as the Worm tore its way through. Nothing hit me directly, but then nothing needed to, since I was already pretty well broken up by then. Then the Worm was through, and the debris cloud went into abrupt reverse as the inert atmosphere all around me roared its way out through the massive hole punched in the cylinder wall.

I lay there wondering why I felt no pain, concluding that my body was now so nearly a corpse that I was beyond feeling. I could see that my right leg was missing below the knee and that a rip down one side of my suit had exposed my intestines and one shattered rib to vacuum. I was actually steaming – the fluids rapidly boiling away from my body – and wondered if I could remain conscious even while my present environment turned me into something with the consistency of dry leather and kindling.

However, two huge bulky figures suddenly loomed over me, one pulling away the wreckage while the other heaved me free. The one holding me then launched himself away, and it seemed but a moment before we were out in open space, Sudoria turning below us, stars above, and a pillar of rainbows over to one side. Some leviathan mouth then closed over us, and Slog and Flog dragged me deeper into intestinal spaces. I glimpsed Rhodane's worried expression, and felt something pressing against my neck.

'We've got you,' said Tigger, and that was the last I heard.

For a while.

Harald

For a few seconds after their ejection the cylinders rising from Corisanthe Main maintained their cross-shaped formation, then they rose beyond the station's shields. Suddenly the Brumallian ship was there, firing missiles, but none of them reached their target. Simultaneously, each cylinder tore open and bright eels of fire looped out to connect to each other, the empty wreckage of the cylinders tumbling away as something toroidal, and seemingly composed of bones and light, rose and expanded. Fiery tendrils stabbed out and touched the approaching missiles, which glowed briefly and were gone. Harald had watched the grainy recordings of that occasion before the end of the War when Fleet first encountered the Worm, but could remember nothing from then looking like this. But this must definitely be that . . . object. What else could those Ozark Cylinders have contained?

'Franorl, cease firing!'

The other Captain had been taking heavy fire from Corisanthe Main, and returning it with devastating effect now his ship had managed to knock out numerous shield generators aboard the station. He had redirected some weapons fire towards the Brumallian ship which had closed on one of the cylinders but also lay dangerously close to that expanding luminous ring. Perhaps he feared some attack from the enemy vessel against the assault craft currently departing his hilldigger.

'They're with the Brumallians!' Franorl shrieked.

Harald gazed at the image of this man who found plotting and murder so easy, but was now failing under the exigencies of such vicious warfare. He was clearly panicking.

'Do *not* fire on—'

The ring abruptly distorted, a loop of it flashing out over hundreds of miles and travelling along the entire length of *Desert Wind*. Franorl's image winked out. All contact with *Desert Wind* shut down, then Harald's screens blanked and the lighting on *Ironfist*'s Bridge flickered out, to be replaced by the muted glow of the emergency lights. He looked up, noting instruments gone dark and crew frantically trying to operate dead consoles. A huge electromagnetic pulse? If it had been enough to affect *Ironfist* like this, then *Desert Wind* and those assault craft were certainly out of play.

'Verbal report!' Harald stood up. 'All stations report status.'

As the crewmen around him gave their assessments, the lights reignited, consoles began to respond, and Harald's own screens came back online. He sat down again, tried out his control glove and wondered if its inaccuracy was due to the EM pulse or because his hands were shaking so much. He swore viciously. Orbital Combine had done the unexpected: their power base was

Corisanthe Main, and it was their power base precisely because the Worm had been aboard. By releasing it like this they had removed his prime target. Corisanthe Main was now of even less importance than the other stations.

But was that all?

Could they now somehow control the Worm, use it as a weapon? Harald thought not, but some change had certainly occurred, for the Worm had seemed unable to defend itself when Fleet had first attacked it all those years ago. It then occurred to him that being able to use such levels of power as it had just used, the Worm had not been 'contained' at all. It could have broken out at any time, so he wondered when it had ceased to be a *prisoner*.

With some difficulty, as his systems rerouted, Harald managed to take a close look at the other hilldigger. *Desert Wind*'s drive and steering thrusters were now out, and numerous explosions had blown debris into space all along its length. Though the assault craft were still moving under their initial impetus, Harald suspected all their systems were dead. Upon reaching the station they would simply crash into it. This would be the case for Franorl's ship too, though some hours later since it was moving much slower. But without defences or weapons, none of them would even reach the station. Even as Harald watched, two of the assault craft exploded, then something big detonated midway along the hilldigger, jarring it sideways. The Combine gunners were not hesitating to capitalize on their advantage.

'Get me Gneiss, get me Gleer, get me any of those Oversight fuckers,' Harald demanded.

Nothing for a while, so all he could do was stare at the carnage, and at that expanding loop of . . . whatever it was. He felt a terrible hollowness as his doubts about his present course returned to haunt him. Angrily he dismissed them, but felt his anger still growing at this wrecking of his plans. He now realized how the taking of Corisanthe Main, the closing of his fist around Orbital Combine's heart, had somehow grown more important to him than ultimately defeating it. Yes, other ways to that end still remained viable, but his original plan seemed to have a richness he could almost taste. To win in any other way seemed scrappy, untidy, the resolution of a sordid human struggle.

'Gneiss here.'

The station Director smiled at him – something Harald had never witnessed before. He felt his anger rise to a new pitch. Gneiss must have realized how much releasing the Worm would hurt him. This was *personal*.

'I cannot even begin to fathom how you decided to commit such a crime against the Sudorian people,' Harald hissed.

'What crime, precisely?' Gneiss enquired.

'The Worm was one of our greatest assets and now you have flung it away.'

'I have done no such thing,' Gneiss replied. 'For reasons that presently escape me, the Polity Consul Assessor managed to gain entry to one of the cylinders and there caused a breach. Subsequent events remain a puzzle to me.'

Harald jerked back as if the man had slapped him. The screen view now expanded to include a figure standing at the Director's side.

'But not a puzzle to me,' confessed Yishna. 'A breach should have resulted in the ejection of only one cylinder, but it was my own alteration of the breach protocols, some time ago, that resulted in the ejection of all four cylinders. And it was Rhodane, aboard that Brumallian ship, who fired those missiles in an attempt to destroy the Worm.' She paused, and Harald was sure he read both fear and puzzlement in her expression. 'We made an earlier attempt to cause a breach, but station security forestalled us. Orduval was killed.'

'Are you all insane?' Harald demanded. He just could not see the purpose of his sibling's actions.

Rhodane? Orduval dead?

'Not any more,' Yishna replied. 'Despite the failure of our plan, I think everything's going to be all right now. Can't you feel it going away?'

Harald's gaze strayed to another screen where he observed how the Worm ring had broken at one point and one end of it was spearing away into infinity. Returning his gaze to his sister, he noted the dressing on her shoulder, the intensity of her gaze. Her words still made absolutely no sense to him.

'I asked you if you're insane,' he stated. 'You have yet to provide me with an answer.'

'We've both been working for the same master, Harald,' Yishna told him, 'but now it's leaving us. This is now over. There's no need for any further loss of life. Surely you *know* this? You must be able to feel it too.'

All Harald could feel was his headache growing in direct proportion to the ball of rage inside his guts. He studied his sister and noted her speculative observation of him. 'You still make no sense, sister. I am here to reinstate Fleet power and remove the threat that Orbital Combine poses to us all. I had hoped that by seizing Corisanthe Main and taking control of the source of

Combine's power I could bring this present conflict swiftly and neatly to an end.'

'Brother, there are no swift and neat endings to civil war.'

Harald allowed her his false smile. 'In that you are incorrect. Because of a certain reluctance I've observed on the part of their Captains, I have now assumed control of the gravity weapons on board both *Wildfire* and *Harvester*.' He held up his hand, enclosed in the control glove. 'I can now end this conflict merely by inputting some simple commands.'

Her expression became at first puzzled then changed to one of growing horror.

'Your head injury,' she said. 'We know about that.'

'My head is perfectly fine, thank you.'

The horror in her expression turned rapidly to calculation.

'I begin to understand.' She studied him closely. 'With its prime instrument still operating, it does not need to endanger *itself* by being here.'

'Ah, so apparently you *are* insane,' said Harald.

Abruptly Yishna leant forwards. 'Let me come to you. Let me explain it all.'

Harald nodded. It seemed somehow appropriate to him to have his sister at his side here, aboard *Ironfist*, as he proceeded to destroy the three Corisanthe stations.

McCrooger

The salvo fired by *Desert Wind* had come dangerously close to erasing our Brumallian ship from existence, and if the Worm had not acted when it did, we would have been dead. Even though *I* wasn't dead, I wondered if the state I was in could really be described as life.

'It acted simply to defend itself,' Tigger informed me. 'Be thankful *Desert Wind* distracted it from us.'

'I figured that,' I replied, while gazing through the ship's sensors at the departing alien entity. After a moment I returned my gaze to my physical self, floating in some womb-like bladder, my body dead, spinal blocks in place, while some oxygenated fluid was being routed from an independent supply to circulate in my brain. Organic cables and tubes had been connected directly into my optic nerves, and elsewhere into my brain through holes carved in my skull.

I'd looked better.

The chameleonware was in operation now so we enjoyed a grandstand view without the danger of being attacked directly. Tigger had keyed into all and any uncoded communications, and we were listening intently as the drama continued to unfold.

'What's happening down on the planet?' I asked.

Tigger summoned up for me pictures of riot-damaged cities, burning buildings, pockets of civil disorder scattered here and there. GDS wardens were now back in control of three of the eight cities they had earlier been forced to abandon. Chairman Duras and what survived of Parliament had now returned to the capital in the mobile incident station, but no one was concerned with debating anything until the present emergency was over. Everyone kept looking to the skies.

'They're showing less inclination to kill each other down there,' Tigger observed, 'but that might be as much due to physical exhaustion as to the removal of the Worm's influence. These are humans, and as such are prone to after-the-fact justification of their actions, so that justification might include insisting that they were right, and that those actions should therefore continue.'

'Quit the moralizing, why don't you?'

'Sorry – moving up from drone to ship AI has given me preachy tendencies.'

'I preferred the old Tigger.'

'All right, the Worm has been driving these people bat shit for decades. Its departure doesn't necessarily mean they'll suddenly become less crazy. In some cases the exact opposite might occur.'

'Are you thinking of Harald?'

'Not really,' Tigger replied. 'He, like his siblings, is a different matter entirely. Its influence on them has been extreme, and he has perhaps found himself a convincing justification for what he's doing.'

This was pretty much what I had figured. The Worm had set him in motion, and kept prodding him in the direction it wanted him to go. He thought all along he was fighting for Fleet when in reality the Worm had been using him to exact its own vengeance, or simply to cause misery and destruction, for whatever motive. I knew this for certain now. I'd witnessed one Worm segment tear out through the wall of Ozark One, and I'd later seen Tigger's analysis of the energy levels involved in the damage it had done to *Desert Wind*. The Worm had not really been a prisoner for some time – maybe even twenty or so years. Now it was gone and Harald was still running on autopilot – a tool set in motion and no longer requiring its close influence.

'Can you do anything about him now?' I asked.

'We could try a direct attack on the *Ironfist*, but I don't see that ending well for us.'

'No, I mean can you somehow break his control over those other ships?'

'I would first need to get in close to *Ironfist* and then it would take me an hour or more to actually break into his systems. There's a good chance he would detect my interference and, as we know, his finger is on the firing button. Also, as shown during my attempt to stop the bombing of Vertical Vienna, he clearly has some means of detecting me.'

'So you're not even going to try?'

'Of course I am, but I rather suspect this will be all over before then, one way or another.'

Tigger then showed me a conversation recorded on camera aboard Corisanthe Main. I felt a tightness in a throat that was probably no longer connected to my brain. Perhaps I would have cried without those things plugged into my eye-sockets.

Oh, Yishna . . .

Yishna

Despite the drugs, her shoulder ached, and controlling the interstation shuttle was no easy task with just one arm that felt quite numb. In truth, she felt numb inside too.

Orduval . . .

She felt personally responsible for his death and for everything else now happening. Knowing she had been striving to end this madness and herself had not fired a single shot did not lessen that feeling of guilt. She and her siblings were a unit, co-responsible. Perhaps if they could have properly understood what the Worm had wanted, all this mayhem could have been avoided. Perhaps if she had understood bleed-over, and realized how everyone was being affected . . . Yet the problem with attaining such understanding was that there had been no real basis for comparison. The only other records of asylum statistics dated from the period of the War and that was not exactly a normal time . . . But, damn it, she *should* have understood.

Her escort abruptly veered, and she simultaneously received instructions through her console for a course change. A brief scan of her surroundings showed her the reason why. Two miles ahead and to the left of her she observed one of the drifting assault craft from the hill-digger *Desert Wind* being tracked in by a Combine warcraft. While she watched, the warcraft hard-docked and began to slow down both vessels. This was due to more negotiation with Harald's underlings. The assault troops from *Desert Wind* had been given permission to surrender, and Combine craft were now diverting their crippled assault vessels away from the station. The hilldigger itself might be more of a problem, but not hers. Harald was her problem, and he had said nothing more since his recent communication with her.

As her craft approached the rear of Corisanthe Main's shields, her escort abruptly dropped away to the left and decelerated in readiness to return to the station. Checking a graphic display of the shields, she saw two of them parting ahead of her. Now would be a good opportunity for one of Harald's ships to fire something big at the station, but she did not expect this response from him. Despite his head injury he must surely now be feeling something of what she herself felt: that removal of impetus, that lack of a previously intense driving force, something missing in her skull. Yishna wondered if she

could live with the lack of it – if any of them could. She
felt just as capable as before, but seemed to have lost any
need for that capability.

She passed between the two shields and watched
them close behind her. Laying in a course to *Ironfist*
entailed taking into account the larger chunks of debris
floating about out here. But there was also a lot of
smaller stuff – difficult to detect because it was moving
so fast. Only a few seconds after departing Corisanthe
Main's aegis, one of the five miniguns aboard her shuttle
began chuntering to itself, and something had flared to
one side of her main screen, before objects started
pattering against the hull. There was always the chance
that she would not make it to *Ironfist*. That would simplify
matters for her considerably.

With its new course set the shuttle accelerated, and
chuntering from the miniguns became almost constant.
Though she had no time for sleep, Yishna closed her eyes
momentarily just to rest them. For a second she felt herself begin to drift, then a sudden surge of panic jerked
her upright and fully awake. She realized the reaction
stemmed from the absence of that something in her
skull, and with wry distaste decided that this must be
how so many Sudorians felt as they slid into mental
collapse.

Now over to her right lay the enormous hilldigger
Desert Wind, dead in space, in a pall of smoke. Some
Combine craft were nosing about it, but there could be
nothing aboard Corisanthe Main with engines powerful
enough to overcome a million tons of inertia in time.
Instead they would have to send for a civilian liner like
the one presently towing *Stormfollower* to safety.

Not my problem.

Yishna focused ahead and eventually *Ironfist* resolved out of the darkness. The graphic display showed its shields parting before her, and a tacom aboard contacted her a moment later.

'Proceed to Docking Bay Eight,' he instructed her.

'It would be helpful to know where Docking Bay Eight is located,' she observed.

He grimaced officiously, but shortly afterward she received a ship schematic and a radio beacon to follow in. First her shuttle drew alongside the nose of *Ironfist*, then headed on along the length of the massive ship, as if travelling beside an iron cliff, finally to slow, thrusters bringing her to a halt before an open bay door lit with the infernal red of emergency lights. She cruised in between two huge pillars, which revolved to present docking clamps to catch the craft like a tossed ball. The impact threw her forward and she yelped at the stab of pain from her shoulder. There was nothing gentle about this procedure, which confirmed she was entering Fleet's realm. The clamps dragged the shuttle down to the floor of the bay. Then, sliding in floor slots, the pillars themselves dragged it to the rear, where a docking tunnel connected. Yishna unstrapped herself, pushed up from the seat, and in nil gravity made her way unsteadily back into the cargo section. Pointing her control baton at the airlock, she opened the inner door, pulled herself inside, then closed it behind her. When she finally entered the docking tunnel, she closed the outer door and, again using her baton, firmly locked it. The shuttle was Combine property and she did not want Fleet personnel poking about inside it.

As she reached the end of the tunnel Yishna began to feel the effects of gravity. A door opened ahead of her, and she spied a Fleet marine peering towards her down the sight of a disc carbine. He kept her on target as she approached, then finally withdrew to let her pass through. Yishna stepped out into a semi-circular steel lobby before a bank of lifts. Three marines awaited her there, along with one Fleet officer – a grey-haired woman with razor eyes.

'Yishna Strone,' said the old woman.

'Yes, that would be me,' Yishna replied, tired and irritable. 'And you are?'

'Com-res Jeon.'

Com-res? Harald had sent a research officer to collect her?

'I am afraid it will be necessary for you to be thoroughly searched,' Jeon added.

'Really? I've been searched once before by Fleet personnel and I cannot say I enjoyed the experience. Will this search also include an exploration of my more intimate cavities, followed by a beating?'

The older woman looked genuinely insulted at this. 'Fleet personnel would never—'

'Spare me the platitudes.' Yishna began trying to remove her spacesuit, and when, because of her damaged shoulder, it became evident she was having difficulties, one of the marines stepped forward to assist. He was young and good-looking, so she gave him a special smile and watched him blush. Once down to her usual clothing, she quickly retrieved her baton from the spacesuit's belt cache, then turned to Jeon. 'Do I need to take off any more?'

'That will be enough,' the woman replied. She nodded to the same young marine, who did a quick touch search of Yishna, then stepped back.

'Now can I see my brother?' Yishna asked.

Two marines remained behind to guard the access to her shuttle – why, she had no idea, since the small craft would have been intensively scanned on its way in, and they would have discovered there was no one else aboard. Accompanying Jeon and the young marine, she entered a lift that shortly deposited them on a platform right beside one of the hilldigger's internal trains. As they entered the vehicle Yishna gazed about at the vast internal space and the massive machinery surrounding her. She briefly speculated on the psychological effect on Fleet personnel of being enclosed in so massive a war machine. Then she dismissed such idle speculation. She was tired, her shoulder hurt, and she urgently needed to acquaint her brother with some unpalatable truths.

A short, high-acceleration train ride brought them to another platform, then another lift, then more corridors. Hard metal all around and the taste of steel in her mouth. As she entered through the rear doors of *Ironfist*'s Bridge the marine remained behind in the lift while, without a word, Jeon walked away from her and sat down before a console. Two waiting security personnel eyed her carefully, then one of them stepped forward.

'I've already been searched,' she said tiredly.

The man, a scar-faced individual with two fingers missing from his right hand, ignored her comment and searched her anyway, and with notably more robustness than the young marine. He extracted the baton from her pocket, studied the personal device for a moment, then ran a small hand scanner over it.

'If I was going to hit him, I'd use my fist, not that bloody thing,' she said.

He grinned and tossed the baton back to her, then

led the way across the Bridge, his companion falling in neatly behind her. Shortly they reached the stairs leading up into the Admiral's Haven, whereupon the scar-faced guard waved her ahead. As she climbed, she felt a sudden nervousness at meeting Harald again. But once she reached the top of the stairs, shock displaced that feeling.

For a moment she thought a ghost had appeared to haunt her, for Harald looked as cadaverous as Orduval had done during his later years in the asylum. Yet this was certainly Harald: the hard uncompromising expression, the long blonde hair tied back, that blank re-engineered eye. She noted the sealed wound on his head, but there was no way of knowing how serious that injury had been.

'Come in, sister.' Harald gestured to a low chair directly facing the sofa he had risen from.

Rather than sit as instructed, Yishna walked over to the narrow window giving her a view across the hill-digger's exterior. She felt no connection with him, none of that sliding into a strange fugue state that usually happened between the Strone siblings when they met after being apart for a while. Was that because the Worm had now gone, or was it a side-effect of his head injury?

'How are you, Harald?' she asked, then winced at such a commonplace.

'I've been better,' he replied drily. 'I see we both bear our war wounds, so how did you receive yours?'

'I was shot by Combine security officers while trying to break into that Ozark Cylinder.'

'Then we both have the distinction of having been shot at by our own side. But now is not the time for civilities; those are only for the civilized, I'm told. You have something to say to me?'

Gazing out across the hilldigger, Yishna felt a sudden

panic. Out there lay the three Corisanthe stations, containing hundreds of thousands of Sudorians. All Harald needed to do was pick up his control glove and send some codes, and all of them would be gone. She took a shaky breath.

'The Worm,' she began, 'started affecting the Sudorian people from the moment we captured it, then some little while after that, it began to manipulate them.' She turned towards him. 'Indirect evidence of this is the distorted society to be found on Corisanthe Main, and the levels of mental illness on Sudoria itself. Bleed-over was direct evidence of its reach extending beyond the supposed containment canisters. I have my suspicions that Director Gneiss is himself evidence of that same reach.'

'Really,' he said.

'Really,' she replied. 'You know that Sudorian mental-illness rates are ridiculously high. And the Shadowman? If we had been thinking straight we would soon have recognized that for what it was. It was simply the Worm trying to present a human face, perhaps the more easily to twist us to its will.'

'But I have never seen a Shadowman in my life.'

'No, because the Worm's communication with us is so much more direct, for we too are direct evidence of its reach.'

'And at some point you'll explain your obscure assertions.'

'Our mother,' she continued doggedly, 'had her womb standard-monitored for conception. She conceived us during a fumarole breach on Corisanthe Main.' She turned towards him. 'Now that you are the Admiral you have access to all Fleet's secrets, so you will know precisely what is meant by a fumarole breach?'

Harald nodded carefully. 'I do know.'

'Then add to that the knowledge that she conceived us actually within the Ozark Cylinder where the breach occurred.'

'Really?'

'Yes, really. And after giving birth to us she didn't die in an accident. Combine covered up the true details. She stepped out of an airlock without wearing a spacesuit, and then detonated a home-made explosive strapped against her body. They never managed to recover even bits of her.'

Harald did not look as shocked as she had hoped – just slightly puzzled.

'And the relevance of this?' he suggested.

'Who was our father?' she countered.

'Does it matter?'

'It matters because I don't think our *real* father was human at all.'

Harald smiled in that superior manner of his and crossed his arms. She noticed he wasn't now wearing his control glove, and momentarily speculated on the possibility of killing him hand to hand. But no, Harald had always beaten her and he always would. He was the best of the four of them – the most perfect example of what they were all meant to be.

'I feel I should point out the absolute requirement for sperm in such matters,' he said.

I'm not going to get through to him. He's playing with me.

'Maybe there was sperm involved, but something alien had much more of an influence on our conception, and on our subsequent development, than any merely human father.'

'Evidently,' said Harald.

Yishna was momentarily stunned. There was no sarcasm in his voice; he wasn't ridiculing her. He just seemed to be agreeing with an established fact.

Evidently.

He continued, 'I've thought more about this since our last conversation. I've thought about it a lot. The connections I've worked out take that fact beyond mere coincidence. You've now confirmed some of them for me, and given me others to ponder. It strikes me as highly likely that the Worm was sentient and that, after healing sufficiently to break away from its prison, it instead chose to remain there and toy with us – to wreak vengeance upon us.' He paused for a moment, unfolded his arms and began reaching for something at his belt; then abruptly snapped his hand away in irritation. 'In fact we've been manipulated by it.'

'Precisely,' said Yishna, feeling a loosening in her chest.

'So *precisely* what relevance does this have to our situation now?' Harald asked.

Her sense of relief was short-lived. 'Don't you see yet? This whole conflict was caused by the Worm!'

'I do *not* see that. Yes, I see the Worm's manipulation of us, but that was just an aggravating factor. This conflict has really been about Combine scrabbling for power, and thus weakening the effectiveness of Fleet at a time – with this Polity now barging its way in – when we need to remain strong.'

She had failed. He was obstinately holding to his beliefs, no matter their source.

'You don't really believe that,' she protested. 'I think

you're just afraid of what will happen to you if you stop now.'

Anger twisted his face – that last shot that had gone home. He turned away, then lowered his gaze. She saw he was now looking at his control glove, which rested on a table nearby.

'To face this new threat from outside, the Sudorian people need to be united under a single force,' he said.

'The Polity is not a threat to us, Harald.' Her hands down at her sides, she walked over towards him. 'I've spoken with their Consul Assessor, and I know that for sure. Do you doubt my judgement?'

He glanced at her. 'Did you know that their machines are already lurking here among us?'

And so he slid into his paranoia. What a mess must have been churning around in his mind while ensconced up here in this disconnected Haven. Maybe he *had* felt the Worm's departure. Or maybe it did not matter either way. It was so difficult to abandon faith for hard reality. He stepped nearer to the table, stooping to reach for the glove.

Yishna took a long step forward, then brought her foot up in a hard arc, the toe of her boot directed towards his face. He dropped into a squat, as if only ducking, but his leg swept out just above floor level at her other foot. She managed to avoid it, but retreated slightly off balance, bringing her one usable arm up defensively, anticipating his attack. He snapped himself upright, one fist shooting out. He wasn't close enough to hit her, yet something slammed into her guts, sending her stagger-ing backwards. Suddenly she could no longer breathe and her legs felt weak. There came a cracking sound as something hit her leg, and it gave way. Collapsed on the floor, she gazed in bewilderment at her knee: broken open, bone and blood. She peered down at the blood soaking into her clothing from a wound low down on the right of her belly.

'Did you really think you could bring me down?' Harald enquired.

She looked up into the barrel of the small Combine handgun he held – the one she had seen in his cabin what seemed an age ago.

He continued, 'Jeon will patch you up – I don't want to lose a sister as well as a brother.' He slid the handgun back into his belt, then stepped over and picked up the control glove.

'You . . . don't want me to die. Yet you are prepared to kill . . . all those people?'

'It's necessary,' he said, 'and anyway I don't know them.'

'Then I'm sorry.'

'You're sorry?'

'Yes . . . for the crew of this ship.'

Yishna held up her control baton, turned one of the twist rings round by one click, then pressed the transmit button.

'What have you done?' he bellowed.

Yishna closed her eyes, as the floor slammed up at her and everything turned to fire.

McCrooger

I felt the sudden acceleration, which meant my inner ear was still functional at least, but it took me another second to understand what was happening. Tigger had reacted to the electromagnetic pulse with a speed that only artificial intelligences are capable of, so we were already beginning to move away just as that eye into Hell opened in the mid-section of *Ironfist*. A blast front sped either way along the length of the hilldigger, and fire illuminated it from the inside, as if it were an iron bar fresh from the forge, then began exploding from ports, bays and breaks developing in the structure. The megaton range explosion of that mine in the cargo area of Yishna's shuttle swamped all in a fireball. As the first blastfront hit us, it tumbled our Brumallian ship through vacuum, knocking out all the sensors.

I was grateful for the blindness.

Epilogue

McCrooger

The planetoid hung in the bloody glare of a red giant, the ring around it far too even and too close to the surface to be mistaken for any natural formation.

'I'm astounded,' admitted Rhodane, gesturing about at the Polity vessel we were aboard.

I guessed Polity technology *was* astounding. Feeling an itch on my nose, I scratched it quickly, satisfied at dispelling this minor irritation. I too was astounded: should synthetic skin itch or was my other nose itching? I glanced past her as Slog, and one of the other Brumallian crewmen from the organic ship, entered the viewing pod to join us, then returned my attention to that glowing ring. While I watched it, I considered the update relayed to me here from the AI Geronamid.

After the surrender of the remaining hilldiggers, Orbital Combine had mooted the idea of its taking control of them but, at the instigation of Chairman Duras, this had been quickly slapped down by Parliament. Those surviving vessels would remain under the control of the Sudorian Parliament, and apparently Combine must hand over control of its Defence Platforms too. I considered this an astute move on the Chairman's part. For, without the Worm at its core, that amalgamation called Orbital Combine might easily come apart with the result of further conflict. Parliament needed to assert its authority, and become the only organization in full control of such hefty weapons.

'What's it doing?' Rhodane asked.

'Feeding, as far as we can gather,' I replied. 'It's definitely sopping up solar energy, and there's also some piezo-electric effect within it, generated by the tidal forces of the planetoid.'

While political moves continued in Parliament, there was still a great deal of work to be done. On the surface of Sudoria itself there was the wreckage to clear, fires to put out, but this was balanced out by a sudden freeing of human resources as it was discovered how many mental patients were abruptly recovering. In space the two crippled hilldiggers were being moved to a safe orbit, meteor guns were kept firing perpetually to vaporize chunks of debris, and the night skies of Sudoria glittered with falling stars. A day ago Geronamid had chosen to offer Polity assistance, but Duras had politely replied that though Parliament would like a Consulate established on Sudoria, and would also like to begin trade negotiations with the Polity, no assistance or intervention would be required. I think that was precisely the answer Geronamid wanted, anyway.

Rhodane stepped up beside me.

'How are you feeling?' I asked.

'Lost,' she replied, 'and somehow cheated. I should be grieving now but for what the artificial intelligence here has done to my mind.'

'On request, it will return you to your previous state.' I paused, studying her. 'Do you think that experiencing the grief would make you a better person, that the pain is somehow advantageous?'

'I don't know.'

'Neither do I, really, but I trust that the AIs do. They repair us when they can, and never stand in the way of us improving ourselves. I've never known them to be overanxious about our suffering if it might be of benefit to us.'

As for Brumal, Duras allowed the parliamentary meeting, assessing the evidence the Brumallians had presented, to be broadcast. The inhabitants of that planet were innocent, they had always been innocent. This added impetus to everything Orduval had inspired with his books, and already there were those in Parliament suggesting that the Polity should establish a Consulate on Brumal too. Surely it was only fair?

Slog and the other Brumallian crewman moved off to continue their exploration of the ship, just as Flog and the others from the organic vessel were doing while their ship sat in a repair bay. AI-controlled telefactors were busily swarming inside it and all over its hull, repairing, adjusting, and also extracting Polity technology from amongst organic Brumallian technology.

'And you?' Rhodane asked me.

And me?

By the time those same telefactors had extracted me from the ship, my body below the neck was unrecoverable. Above the neck my brain still functioned, but even that was wadded with IF21 fibres, and consequently suffered a disease similar to the ancient malady called Alzheimer's. The AI here had offered me a number of choices. There was flash-freezing and bio-gridding, memcording, and the one that I chose – DTM or destructive transfer mapping. This entailed the electro-chemical destruction of my brain, whereby those structures being destroyed would be simultaneously mapped into the brain of a clone created from my body. Of course, it would take time for that clone to be force-grown in an amniotic tank, but my old self wasn't dead yet. The Golem body I stood in, with its ceramal skeleton and syntheflesh covering, was merely a radio-controlled remote, while the real me still bubbled in another tank somewhere aboard this same ship.

'I'm well enough,' I admitted.

She nodded, studying me closely. She knew the body standing before her was a machine, but it looked no different to the original healthy version of myself.

'And that?' she asked, pointing at the distant ring around the planetoid.

'What about it?'

'What is it?'

I shrugged, but before I could reply a voice grated from behind us, 'It's an alien machine, or it's a living alien, or it's both.' We turned to see a silver tiger sitting there, then Tigger continued, 'There's no real way of making a distinction, and anyway we're probably not going to be given a chance.'

'Why not?' asked Rhodane.

Tigger paced up to stand beside us, nodding his muzzle towards the ring. 'It's already powered up now, and there are definite ripples in the U-continuum, which means it's about to jump.'

Even as we returned our attention to the ring, it broke at one point and began to contract and emit kaleidoscope light. We watched in silence as icy dust blew up from the planetoid while the Worm nosed out towards interstellar space.

'It could be heading back to Sudoria, to finish what it started,' I suggested.

'If it does, it'll find a Polity dreadnought awaiting it,' Tigger replied. 'But it won't do that – it's intelligent enough to know when to run.'

'Are we going to follow?' I enquired.

'No.'

Star-bright, the Worm extended as straight as a laser, then suddenly snapped out of existence.

'So it will remain a mystery?' I suggested.

'Yes,' Tigger replied.

I smiled, and kept my thoughts to myself.

Brumal and Sudoria had been involved in a century-long war which, without that worm turning up, could have continued for centuries more. So great was the bitter investment in the conflict that for it to end at all – without outside intervention – it needed to end decisively with one very definite winner and one very definite loser. The Worm had turned up shortly before Tigger was sent there to survey the system.

I continued gazing at the same view, my patience that of a machine because my consciousness now resided in one. Eventually Rhodane, being merely human and still recovering from an emotional beating, despite what the AI here had done to her mind, made her excuses and returned to her cabin. Tigger, who until then had remained utterly motionless, got up on all fours, arched his back lazily, then came over to take Rhodane's place beside me.

'If Polity AIs find something they don't understand,'

I said, 'they study it, and they throw huge resources at it until they do understand it.'

'There's not much they don't understand,' Tigger replied noncommittally.

'I'm not going to dance around this,' I continued. 'Was that thing something we constructed?'

'No.'

'But we knew about it?'

'Well, I didn't bloody know.' Tigger turned to glare at me. 'Geronamid only just gave me the full story.'

I nodded to myself. 'In Orduval's book he mentions the Ouroboros – the worm that eats its own tail forever. That was like the original war between the Sudorians and the Brumallians. He admitted to a feeling of superstitious awe that a space-borne worm essentially broke that ring, brought the war to an end. Tell me about non-intervention.'

'They discovered it about fifty years ago, and watched it as it wound along the edge of the Polity,' said the drone. 'It seems it's an alien nanotech device programmed to survey any civilization it encounters – something like me in a way, though not so bright. The AIs studied it as it studied the Polity. They understood it; they know it.'

'Then?'

'They manipulated it. They changed its course to bring it straight into the midst of a fight that had been going on for too long and, before any other ships reached it, knocked it out of U-space and kept it out.'

'So they *did* intervene.'

'Yup, they knew that whichever side reached it first would attack it, and, from whatever was left of it, would gain either the technology for U-space travel, gravtech or some other overpowering advantage that could bring the war to an end. And then, after the Worm regenerated, as it was quite capable of doing even from the smallest remnants, it was supposed to simply free itself and depart.'

'What happened?'

'Well, even machines can get pissed off. It wanted vengeance, so it began manipulating from its ostensible prison, and when Gneiss put an opportunity in its way in the form of Elsever Strone right in the process of getting impregnated, it grabbed that opportunity, interfered, and made her four apocalyptic children.'

'So it could have escaped at any time?'

'Yes, but instead it just used its tools to foment a civil war.'

'So why did it go when it did?'

Tigger shrugged. 'I guess it expected Harald to finish the job for it.'

I considered that answer. By remaining it could have caused more harm, while making certain Harald achieved its aims for it. But then, thinking like that, I was giving human motivations to something utterly alien – and maybe Tigger was too. It was a probe of some kind, so perhaps it had merely been studying the Sudorians, and perhaps fomenting a civil war was a way of providing itself with more information about them. I rather suspected that certain AIs of a higher level than Tigger probably knew the precise answer to that.

'Funny that, about worms – and the war being like an Ouroboros . . .'

'AIs read books too, and I guess they thought it an elegantly poetic solution. It was also so easy: a little manipulation of an alien device to put the technology it contained right where it was needed, rather than a massive Polity intervention with warships and troops, and then subsequent long-term policing here that needed to last until the two sides stopped hating each other and hating us.'

I thought about the recent deaths in Verticle Vienna, and aboard the Combine stations, aboard Fleet ships, and in the civil rioting down on Sudoria's surface. I considered the mass graves on Brumal, and how an earlier Polity intervention could have stopped all that.

'Yes, elegant and poetic,' I said.

I turned away from the view, my artificial body feeling suddenly cold and tired.

Visit **www.panmacmillan.com** to read more about all our books and to buy them. You will also find features, author interviews and news of any author events, and you can sign up for e-newsletters so that you're always first to hear about our new releases.

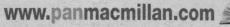

www.**pan**macmillan.com

GIFT SELECTOR
YOUR ACCOUNT
WISH LIST
WAITING LIST

HOME | ABOUT US | IMPRINTS | TRADE/MEDIA | CONTACT US | ADVANCED SEARCH | SEARCH [ ] GO

BOOK CATEGORIES | WHAT'S NEW | AUTHORS/ILLUSTRATORS | BESTSELLERS | READING GROUPS

Coming Soon...

Reading Groups

Competitions
Feeling Lucky?

Extracts
Sneak Previews

Interviews

Events
Meet Our Stars

Reviews
What The Critics Say

News & Awards

Editor's Choice
What We're Reading